Paul Doherty was born [...]
ied History at Liverpool [...]
obtained a doctorate at Oxford for his thesis on Edward
II and Queen Isabella. He is now headmaster of a school
in north-east London and lives with his wife and family
near Epping Forest.

Paul Doherty is also the author of the Hugh Corbett
medieval mysteries, The Sorrowful Mysteries of Brother Athelstan, the Canterbury Tales of mystery and
murder, THE SOUL SLAYER, THE ROSE DEMON
and THE HAUNTING, all of which have been highly
praised.

'Vitality in the cityscape . . . angst in the mystery; it's
Peters minus the herbs but plus a few crates of sack'
Oxford Times

'The book is a pleasure to read and written in an uncom-
promising prose, the plot developed with intriguing
twists and turns. Doherty's deep understanding of the
period and the nitty-gritty of historical detail are to
the fore without intruding on the rhythm of the plot.
Superb entertainment' *Historical Novels Review*

'The maestro of medieval mystery . . . packed with salty
dialogue, the smells and superstitions of the fourteenth
century, not to mention the political intrigues' *Books*
magazine

'Paul Doherty has a lively sense of history . . . evocative
and lyrical descriptions' *New Statesman*

'As always the author invokes the medieval period in
all its muck as well as glory, filling the pages with
pungent smells and description. The author brings
years of research to his writing; his mastery of the
period as well as a disciplined writing schedule have
led to a rapidly increasing body of work and a growing
reputation' *Mystery News*

Other Mysteries of Ancient Egypt

The Mask of Ra
The Horus Killings
The Anubis Slayings

Also by Paul Doherty and available from Headline

The Rose Demon
The Soul Slayer
The Haunting

An Ancient Evil
Being the Knight's Tale
A Tapestry of Murders
Being the Man of Law's Tale
A Tournament of Murders
Being the Franklin's Tale
Ghostly Murders
Being the Priest's Tale
The Hangman's Hymn
Being the Carpenter's Tale

Hugh Corbett medieval mysteries
Satan in St Mary's
Crown in Darkness
Spy in Chancery
The Angel of Death
The Prince of Darkness
Murder Wears a Cowl
The Assassin in the Greenwood
The Song of a Dark Angel
Satan's Fire
The Devil's Hunt
The Demon Archer
The Treason of the Ghosts
Corpse Candle

The Sorrowful Mysteries of Brother Athelstan
The Nightingale Gallery
The House of the Red Slayer
Murder Most Holy
The Anger of God
By Murder's Bright Light
The House of Crows
The Assassin's Riddle
The Devil's Domain
The Field of Blood

The Slayers of Seth

Paul Doherty

headline

Copyright © 2001 Paul Doherty

The right of Paul Doherty to be identified as the Author of
the Work has been asserted by him in accordance with the
Copyright, Designs and Patents Act 1988.

First published in 2001 by
HEADLINE BOOK PUBLISHING

First published in paperback in 2002
by HEADLINE BOOK PUBLISHING

A HEADLINE paperback

10 9 8 7 6 5

All rights reserved. No part of this publication may be
reproduced, stored in a retrieval system, or transmitted,
in any form or by any means without the prior written
permission of the publisher, nor be otherwise circulated
in any form of binding or cover other than that in which
it is published and without a similar condition being
imposed on the subsequent purchaser.

All characters in this publication are fictitious
and any resemblance to real persons, living or dead,
is purely coincidental.

ISBN 0 7472 6469 4

Typeset by Palimpsest Book Production Limited,
Polmont, Stirlingshire

Printed and bound in Great Britain by
Clays Ltd, St Ives plc

HEADLINE BOOK PUBLISHING
A division of Hodder Headline
338 Euston Road
London NW1 3BH

www.headline.co.uk
www.hodderheadline.com

Dedicated to the memory of three beloved babies,
Jacob, Louis Stephen and Rosa May, the children of
Corinna and Stephen Black of Woodford Green and
their cousin, Anthony Peter Carl Hayes of Dagenham

List of Characters

THE HOUSE OF PHARAOH

Hatusu:	Pharaoh-Queen of the XVIII dynasty
Senenmut:	lover of Hatusu: Grand Vizier or First Minister, a former stonemason and architect
Valu:	the 'Eyes and Ears' of Pharaoh: royal prosecutor

THE HALL OF TWO TRUTHS

Amerotke:	Chief Judge of Egypt
Prenhoe:	Amerotke's kinsman, a scribe in the Hall of Two Truths
Asural:	captain of the temple guard of the Temple of Ma'at in which the Hall of Two Truths stands
Shufoy:	a dwarf, Amerotke's manservant and confidant
Norfret:	Amerotke's wife
Ahmase and Curfay:	Amerotke's sons

THE PANTHERS OF THE SOUTH: THE SLAYERS OF SETH

Karnac:	commander

Nebamum: Karnac's manservant
Balet: Peshedu: Heti: Thuro: Ruah: Kamun

HOUSEHOLD OF GENERAL PESHEDU
Vemsit: Peshedu's wife
Neshratta: Peshedu's daughter
Kheay: Peshedu's daughter
Sato: maidservant
Meretel: advocate

OTHER CHARACTERS
Chula: Keeper of the Dead: priest of Anubis
Shishnak: chapel priest in the Temple of Seth
Lady Aneta: General Kamun's widow
Intef: physician
Felima: widow woman
Lamna: widow woman: perfume-maker
Ipumer: scribe in the House of War
Hepel: scribe in the House of War

HISTORICAL NOTE

The first dynasty of ancient Egypt was established about 3100 BC. Between that date and the rise of the New Kingdom (1550 BC) Egypt went through a number of radical transformations which witnessed the building of the pyramids, the creation of cities along the Nile, the union of Upper and Lower Egypt and the development of the Egyptians' religion around Ra, the Sun God, and the cult of Osiris and Isis. Egypt had to resist foreign invasion, particularly by the Hyksos, Asiatic raiders, who cruelly devastated the kingdom.

By 1479 BC, Egypt, pacified and united under Pharaoh Tuthmosis II, was on the verge of a new and glorious ascendancy. The Pharaohs had moved their capital to Thebes; burial in the pyramids was replaced by the development of the Necropolis on the west bank of the Nile as well as the exploitation of the Valley of the Kings as a royal mausoleum.

I have, to clarify matters, used Greek names for cities,

etc., e.g. Thebes and Memphis, rather than their archaic Egyptian names. The place name Sakkara has been used to describe the entire pyramid complex around Memphis and Giza. I have also employed the shorter version for the Pharaoh-Queen: i.e. Hatusu rather than Hatshepsut. Tuthmosis II died in 1479 BC and, after a period of confusion, Hatusu held power for the next twenty-two years. During this period Egypt became an imperial power and the richest state in the world.

Egyptian religion was also being developed, principally the cult of Osiris, killed by his brother, Seth, but resurrected by his loving wife, Isis, who gave birth to their son, Horus. These rites must be placed against the background of the Egyptians' worship of the Sun God and their desire to create a unity in their religious practices. The Egyptians had a deep sense of awe for all living things: animals and plants, streams and rivers were all regarded as holy, while Pharaoh, their ruler, was worshipped as the incarnation of the divine will.

By 1479 BC the Egyptian civilisation expressed its richness in religion, ritual, architecture, dress, education and the pursuit of the good life. Soldiers, priests and scribes dominated this civilisation and their sophistication is expressed in the terms they used to describe both themselves and their culture. For example, Pharaoh was the 'Golden Hawk'; the treasury was the 'House of Silver'; a time of war was the 'Season of the Hyaena'; a royal palace was the 'House of a Million Years'. Despite the country's breathtaking, dazzling civilisation, however, Egyptian politics, both at home and abroad, could be violent and bloody. The royal throne was always the centre of intrigue, jealousy and bitter rivalry. It was on to this political platform, in 1479 BC, that the young Hatusu emerged.

By 1478 BC Hatusu had confounded her critics and opponents, both at home and abroad. She had won a great victory in the north against the Mitanni and purged the royal circle of any opposition led by the Grand Vizier Rahimere. A remarkable young woman, Hatusu was supported by her wily and cunning lover, Senenmut, also her First Minister. Hatusu was determined that all sections of Egyptian society accept her as Pharaoh-Queen of Egypt.

In all revolutions in Ancient Egypt, Pharaohs needed the army. The cruelty of the Hyksos tribes, which swept in and occupied the northern kingdom, was deeply entrenched in Egyptian culture and folklore. 'Hyksos' is a general name given to the Asiatic raiders who plundered the great cities of the Nile and cowed Southern Egypt into submission. They depended for their support on well-armed chariot squadrons. The Hyksos chariot was much heavier than the Egyptian model and had the same impact on lightly armed infantry as a tank would on First World War soldiers. However, Egypt produced its own saviour, Pharaoh Ahmose, Hatusu's grandfather. He reorganised the Egyptian army, developed a faster, more versatile form of chariot and divided both infantry and chariot squadrons into organised regiments, giving them names of Egyptian Gods, animals or birds. Ahmose broke the power of the Hyksos and they quickly became nothing more than a memory but the power of his new army remained.

Hatusu would depend upon the support of the regiments which protected the Nile and garrisoned the forts and castles from the Delta, south to the Third Cataract. No Pharaoh could afford to alienate the army. Ambitious officers were ever ready to exploit this dependency, even during the glorious heyday of the opening years of Hatusu's reign.

Paul Doherty

EGYPT c.1478 BC

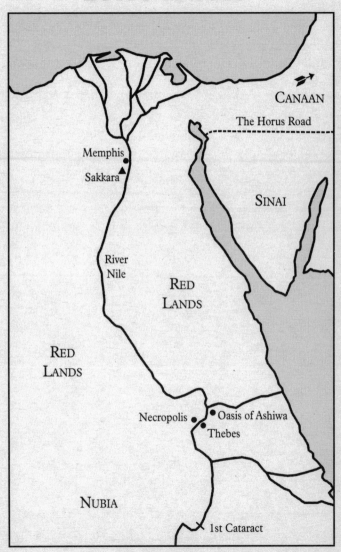

CANAAN

The Horus Road

Memphis

Sakkara

SINAI

River
Nile

RED
LANDS

RED
LANDS

Necropolis • • Oasis of Ashiwa
Thebes

NUBIA

1st Cataract

SETH: one of the most dangerous and
oldest of Egyptian deities.

PROLOGUE

A hostile day for the power of Egypt, the third of the second month of Perit, the Season of Going Out, when red-haired, mischievous, malevolent Seth had opposed the sailing of the Sky God Shu in his barque. Most people in the city of Thebes had spent a quiet day. The great temple forecourts lay silent; the markets did little trade. Householders tended to stay at home, offer prayers and make signs and incantations against ill luck. When the sun began to sink, turning to brilliant hues the rocky outcrop which overlooked the Necropolis on the west side of the Nile, a collective sigh of relief went up. Libations were made to the Gods. Some people even came out to watch the sun's dying rays glint on the electrum sheeting of the obelisks, tall shafts of huge granite soaring up to the sky in front of the Great Houses of the Divine: the sun transformed these sheets in shimmering flashes of light. The day was ending and, with it, the menacing hostility of red-haired Seth, the God of War. He would

3

now leave the Black Lands, the place watered by the great Nile. He would flee Kemet, the earth richly nourished by the river, to live with his warlike demon cortège in the searing heat of the Des-hert, the Red Lands to the east and west of Thebes. The Red Lands were a place of chaos: dry rocky outcrops, searing heat, the dwelling place of the lion, the panther, the high-crested hyaena and the slayer of souls.

On a day such as this, the malevolent influence of the Red Lands made itself felt. The Thebans were highly relieved when darkness fell and Ra began his nightly journey through the underworld. Nevertheless, the day was not complete: ill fortune, evil acts, even murder might still take place. The God Seth, who had murdered his half-brother and was in constant conflict with Horus, his nephew, might, like the assassin he was, come creeping back along the narrow alleyways or broad basalt-paved avenues of Pharaoh's great city. He'd slink in like a hunting fox or foraging rat, ready to cast his evil shadow and prompt the souls of men to raise dagger or club against their own kind.

In the Temple of Seth, in the holy place reserved for the priests, stood a red-bricked chapel. This was the private chantry or worshipping place for the Nakhtu-aa, the Strong-Arm warriors of Pharaoh, the heroes of the great war against the Hyksos, those cruel invaders who had rejoiced in their title 'the Blast of God'. From their city of Avaris to the north, the Hyksos had brought the Season of the Hyaena to the two kingdoms of Egypt. The Hyksos had eventually been defeated by Ahmose, the grandfather of the present Pharaoh, Hatusu. He had led his chariot squadrons north and, with the help of the Gods, had driven these cruel invaders from the Black Lands out across the desert. Some had perished in the wilderness of Sinai. Others had taken ship across the Great Green. The rest had fled west into the Land of Oblivion or south beyond the Third Cataract.

The Hyksos had gone but the marvellous deeds of Pharaoh's army had not been forgotten. The regiment of Seth had played a prominent part in this victory. Seth may be hostile to man but he was still regarded with dreadful awe by Pharaoh and her subjects. Accordingly, it was only apt and fitting that the regiment of Seth had played such a crucial role in the expulsion of the foreign invaders. The Nakhtu-aa of that regiment, a group of young officers, no more than ten in number, had displayed such ferocity and courage it had won them the nickname of 'Panthers of the South' or 'The Slayers of Seth'. Now the years had rolled on. Ahmose, Hatusu's grandfather, had been followed over the Far Horizon by her own father and then her half-brother. Hatusu, not yet past her twentieth year but displaying the wisdom and courage of an experienced warrior queen, now wore the Double Crown of Egypt and the sacred coat, or nenes, whilst her soft, manicured hands gripped the flail and rod, symbols of Empire.

Times may change but the courageous exploits of the Panthers of the South, The Slayers of Seth, had not been forgotten. In the temple, Balet, one of the Panthers of the South, a former commander in the regiment of Seth, knelt on a cushion and gazed at the naos, or tabernacle, bearing the statue of his dreaded regimental God. Balet was now past his fiftieth year and coming here, worshipping before his patron, always evoked memories. The past was all around him. The chantry was quite large, lit by clerestory windows high in the wall. The Red Chapel had been fashioned out of brick specially imported to reflect the colour of Seth's hair. The columns down the transepts were of red porphyry; at base and top the carvings were of juicy pomegranates with scarlet leaves, interspersed by small nuggets of gold. The floor was sandstone, whilst the roof had been painted a brilliant blue with a red sun and scarlet stars. Balet knew every inch of this chantry. At the far end, behind the naos, hung the trophies – the shields and swords of his companions, their leather cuirasses, helmets and greaves. The armour had not been cleaned but taken direct from battle and dedicated to the God of War. Balet narrowed his eyes. He always looked for his . . . Ah yes, that's where it was: the shield, the broad dagger and, above it, his own helmet. How many years had it been? Twenty-five at least. Yet, he would always remember that night when fame and fortune had come to him and the Gods had stooped to bless him.

Balet lifted his fingers to his face, a gesture of prayer and obeisance. He caught the faint smell of natron with which he had washed his hands before entering the chapel, as well as the faint cloying perfume he had dabbed on each wrist. Balet was rich, and rather fat for he did like soft meat and drank deep of the wines he specially imported. However, on that memorable night, the Night of the Panthers, he had been slim, hard-bodied, resolute, eager to bring glory to Egypt's name and receive Pharaoh's smile.

He and his eight companions, together with their leader, Karnac, and his manservant, Nebamum, had gathered in Pharaoh's tent. Ahmose, the present Pharaoh's grandfather, had been lounging in his leather camp chair, his armour piled high on the floor, the favourite chariot horses hobbled and grazing outside. Pharaoh had stared beseechingly at them.

'To the north,' he'd begun, 'sprawls the camp of the Hyksos. At its centre, in a specially built pavilion, the Hyksos have placed their great sorceress, Meretseger, the incarnation of the Scorpion God. According to my spies,' Pharaoh's fear had been obvious, 'Meretseger makes the blood sacrifices and calls on all the demons in the city of Avaris to oppose our march.'

Balet, only twenty-five years old, had listened carefully. He was already a skilled fighter. He had been given medals – the golden bee and the silver eagle as rewards for courageously slaying Egypt's enemies in hand-to-hand combat. But sorcerers, witches and warlocks were another matter. As Pharaoh spoke, Balet had realised what horrors this she-devil of the Hyksos might summon up.

'When our armies meet,' Pharaoh had explained, 'Meretseger will go out in a great chariot drawn by horses, caparisoned with blankets soaked in the blood of Egyptians. Behind this chariot will be dragged prisoners of war whom she will sacrifice on a makeshift altar.'

Balet had looked quickly at their leader, Karnac, a

tough, thickset officer, a man born for war. Karnac too had been concerned – not because of spells, amulets or blood sacrifices but the effect Meretseger might have on Egypt's army.

'So, your Majesty,' Karnac had lifted his hands, head slightly bowed, 'the Hyksos intend to frighten our souls before attacking our bodies?'

'Yes.'

Pharaoh had turned and gently tapped his war crown, resting on its stand. 'Our troops will not expect this. May the Gods help us. If I slip or stumble or make a mistake, once Meretseger has played her role—'

'Or worse still,' Karnac had interrupted, forgetting court protocol. 'The Hyksos are sly and cunning. Our scouts talk of sandstorms blowing in. If one of these occurs on the day of battle, if the sun should slip from the heavens or be blocked by some cloud . . .'

'They will cry Meretseger.' Pharaoh had finished the sentence for him. 'But my warriors,' he'd smiled, 'my Panthers, my Nakhtu-aa, whom I always,' he'd tapped his chest, 'keep close to my heart – you have the opportunity to remove this evil and bring great glory to Pharaoh.'

He'd looked around his tent, guarded by his Maryannou, braves of the King. No one could approach whilst Pharaoh imparted his wisdom to this crack unit from his regiment of Seth, the pride and glory of Egypt.

'You carry Seth's banner.' Pharaoh had pointed to where it lay on the floor, bearing its device, the cruel head of Seth, his red hair peeping out from behind a doglike mask. 'Seth will be with you. His shadow, like the Angel

8

of Death, shall go before you and, with black feathery wings, confound and confuse the hearts and minds of the Hyksos.'

Balet had knelt, hardly daring to breathe, wondering where this great Pharaoh would lead them.

'Tomorrow night,' he'd declared, 'the moon will be shrouded: a mere silver disc in a dark sky. You are to enter the Hyksos camp, slay Meretseger, and bring back her head and the ten Scorpion Cups which she has filled with the blood of her victims.'

Balet had gaped.

'Slay Meretseger!' Karnac had exclaimed. 'Bring back her head! The Scorpion Cups!'

Balet had been fascinated. He'd heard of these ten gold cups, each with a pure silver scorpion carved on the side with rubies for eyes; they supposedly stood on a gold tray.

Balet broke from his reverie of the past and glanced at the ledge to the side of the naos. He got up, bowed towards the tabernacle and walked over.

'It's no sacrilege,' he whispered.

He stared at the treasure, which winked and glowed in the soft light of the alabaster oil lamps placed in niches round the walls. He touched the pure gold tray; it already bore three of the cups. He picked one up. It had no handle, more like a beaker than a cup: about nine inches high, slightly narrowed at the base and about five inches across. The cup weighed heavy in his hands, the silver Scorpion emblazoned there, with its cruel tail ready to strike. The red rubies glowed, giving the dreaded arachnid a macabre, lifelike appearance. Balet put the cup down. When he died, his cup too would be placed on this tray.

Balet returned to the cushions and, grumbling and muttering at the pain in his right knee, knelt down. He stared at the baskets of fruit, the platters bearing food, the wine jugs placed before the tabernacle of the Gods. There had been no flowers, no fresh fruit nor strong wine that fateful night . . .

After Pharaoh had opened his heart to them, Karnac had been most insistent. They were to fast, grease their bodies in oil, and coat their weapons with dust so no reflection could be picked up.

The following night, Karnac led his nine companions out of Pharaoh's camp. Like hunting panthers, they slipped through the darkness towards the Hyksos camp. Along the way they met and killed enemy guards and scouts. Karnac was, in all things, a brilliant soldier, a man who seemed to sense danger before it ever emerged – a man his followers believed had been divinely touched by Seth himself, a true killer, born and bred: the only man Balet had ever been frightened of.

At last they reached the rocky outcrop overlooking the Hyksos camp. Crouching like a hunting pack, they stared down at the campfires of their enemies. Karnac squatted like a marauding animal, searching for weaknesses, gaps in their quarry's defences. The noise of revelry carried on the cold night wind, now and again interspersed by hideous screams.

'The Hyksos,' Karnac whispered, 'are enjoying them-selves with their prisoners.' He turned, his face blackened with fire dust. 'Do not be taken alive. Men from the Seth regiment must not be nailed to poles and carried before the Hyksos army as trophies. If one of us becomes wounded and is unable to move, as an act of mercy, you must cut his throat. If we fail, fight to the death! The Hyksos show no mercy. Meretseger will soon discover why we have come here. She is hideous and heinous. The Hyksos know how to kill a man. They'll bury you alive in the hot sands or smear you with honey and peg you out in the Red Lands.' He glared round. 'Do not be taken prisoner!'

They were agreed on that. Hyksos atrocities were notorious throughout Southern Egypt: men sacrificed on altars; children slain without mercy; women raped, beaten, their hands and feet tied with red twine before they were thrown into the Nile as bait for the crocodiles. Karnac said no more. Now and again he'd turn his head slightly, as if listening for the sounds of revelry to die. Egyptian scouts and spies had agreed on one matter: the Hyksos had marched south from their city of Avaris, phalanx after phalanx of infantry, the earth shaking with the rumble of great-wheeled chariots and the drumming hoofs of war horses. They were confident of victory. Hadn't they smashed one Egyptian army after another? So brazen were they that they'd sent impudent messages to Pharaoh ordering him to keep the hippopotami quiet amongst the thick papyrus groves along the river banks outside Thebes! The Hyksos prince claimed their roaring disturbed his sleep and, as Pharaoh couldn't control it, he was marching south to take care of all such nuisances. Ahmose had no choice but to fight but he was a strong and wily Pharaoh. He believed the Hyksos were overconfident. They depended on mercenaries, desert wanderers, the flotsam and jetsam from the sea coasts. Ahmose, meanwhile, had been secretly training his own army, organising them into regiments, building new chariots swifter, more manoeuvrable than those heavy, lurching carriages of the Hyksos. But the enemy had two advantages: their reputation for ferocious ruthlessness and the power of the witch Meretseger.

'They'll eat and dine well,' Karnac whispered, 'and sleep like heavy-bellied hogs.'

Oh, how the Panthers waited. Those hours seemed to stretch like eternity. The sweat-soaked bodies of the Nakhtu-aa were whipped by the cold desert wind. Arms had grown stiff, throats dry, mouths dust-filled. Below them, the campfires began to ebb, the sound of revelry faded. Karnac gave the sign. Like some wild animal he had detected a path through the Hyksos defences. He opened the sack he carried and began to issue small pots of paint and gaudy rags. At first his companions were confused until Karnac's plan was explained.

'We are going to walk in.' He took a piece of twine from the sack and told his manservant, Nebamum, to turn.

'We shall pretend to be Hyksos?' Balet asked Karnac.

'Yes, my sharp-eyed falcon of Egypt. I have been watching that camp; their sentries are lax. We shall be a group of swaggering mercenaries returning with a prisoner.'

'But they'll ask for passes? Demand proof?'

'We've got that.' Karnac patted Nebamum's shoulder. 'Are you ready?'

Nebamum, thin and sinewy, the youngest of the group, grinned and nodded. Before they'd left Pharaoh's camp, his master had told him what was about to happen. Karnac brought his hand back and slapped his servant on the cheeks and mouth. Even in the poor light Balet saw Nebamum's lower lip break, the blood spill out.

'I am sorry,' Karnac whispered. He nicked Nebamum's shoulder with a dagger to draw more blood. Nebamum winced but did not protest. 'From now on we act the part,' Karnac ordered. 'Nobody talks. I know some Hittite. The guards are tired, half-drunk on beer and wine.'

They left their hiding place. Karnac placed a rope round Nebamum's neck and led him like a dog. The rest clustered about. Balet felt as if he were walking between heaven and earth. All he was aware of was the hard pebbly ground, the grunts of his companions and the ever-approaching lights and stench of the Hyksos camp. The Nakhtu-aa took one of the paths leading in. They passed prisoners nailed to posts. On the palm trees, a little distance away, they glimpsed corpses swinging by their necks, turning slowly in the night air, black bundles against the night sky.

Balet grasped his weapons. The Hyksos had set up a defensive line – carts and chariots. Between gaps in these, soldiers clustered in the torchlight. As they drew closer, they saw a Hyksos forcing a woman to kneel in the dust, knife to her throat, to commit an obscene act to the merriment and catcalls of his companions. They hardly stopped as Karnac and his companions, dragging Nebamum behind, passed by. Balet would never forget that sight. The Hyksos, with their hair down to their shoulders, cruel faces smeared with war paint, their armour a motley collection seized from the dead or pillaged from the ports and towns they had ransacked. The young Egyptian girl, no more than fifteen summers, knelt naked, the Hittite officer, kilt pulled up, his erect penis thrust towards her face. One of the guards called out. Karnac shouted back in a guttural tongue. The man laughed.

The Egyptians entered deeper into the camp. The stench from the latrines mixed with the scent of heavy perfume and odours from cooking pots. Hyksos soldiers lay everywhere – some in orderly units, others sprawled on the ground, wineskins and goblets beside them. The Egyptians stood aside as a chariot thundered by them: two helpless prisoners lashed to its carriage were being dragged and shaken through the dirt, too weak and bruised even to cry out. They passed more Hyksos brutality: a cooking pot, filled to the brim with decapitated heads, the blood trickling down the side. A prisoner lashed to a pole, the rope round his neck slowly choking him to the macabre music of gasps and grunts. The rope would shrink and the prisoner would slowly strangle to death. Here and there stood the pavilions and tents of the officers and the Hyksos nobles. Balet could not believe their luck in proceeding unchallenged.

Deeper and deeper they went into the camp. Karnac had been correct. They were accepted for what they looked:

Hyksos mercenaries bringing in a prisoner. They reached a makeshift perimeter fence. The officer here was more collected and composed, though his eyes were heavy with sleep. He stepped in front of them, hand raised. Karnac answered in Hittite. The officer, satisfied, stood aside. Balet caught the word 'Meretseger'. Karnac was pretending they were taking a prisoner direct to the sorceress.

At last they reached the centre of the Hyksos camp which Karnac had glimpsed from their rocky outcrop. This was the royal circle, ringed by torches lashed to poles; their flames, fed by pitch and tar, fluttered bravely against the wind. More guards, some dressed in ceremonial armour. To the right lay the Hyksos prince's pavilion, to the left a strange-looking tent, its cloths draped over the poles to give the impression of a temple. Outside stood a huge cart bearing an altar. In the torchlight Balet could see the blood marks down the side. This was where Meretseger made sacrifice. Karnac stopped. Balet looked down. The ground was soft and wet with blood flowing from the cart.

Soldiers were milling about; officers in their costly cloaks, their scabbards and war belts decorated with jewels which sparkled in the torchlight. Balet believed the Gods walked with them that night. No one accosted them.

Karnac, pulling Nebamum, strode across to the temple pavilion and pulled back the flap. Balet and the others followed. A soldier inside, possibly a bodyguard, sprang to his feet. Karnac, swift as a striking cobra, plunged his sword straight into the man's throat. He caught him by the shoulder and lowered him gently to the ground. Another member of their group placed his hand over his mouth to silence the death rattle.

The sorceress Meretseger squatted on a pile of cushions on the far side of the tent. Balet was aware of a sunburnt face, creases round the eyes and mouth, iron-grey hair cascading down to her shoulders. The sorceress's eyes were hideous, dark pools of hate and malice yet a faint smile played on the bloodless lips.

'I was right.' She lifted her head. 'I thought my death would be tonight. It was prophesied, but I'll die in good company. You, scum of the desert, shall die as I do.'

She lifted a war horn to give a warning blast. Karnac was faster. He pushed Nebamum away and leapt towards the sorceress. She threw the hunting horn at him. Karnac knocked it aside. Standing back, gripping his sword with two hands, he dealt one well-aimed blow. The sorceress's head leapt like a snipped flower, the blood gushing up like water from a fountain. The trunk stayed still as the head rolled into the far corner. Karnac seemed oblivious to any danger, not stopping to think, even issue orders. He kicked the blood-spouting body to one side and, grasping the head by the hair, pushed it into a leather sack.

In the shadows behind the cushions stood a table bearing the tray with the ten Scorpion Cups. Like a servant clearing the room after a banquet, Karnac simply scooped these up with their tray and threw them into the blood-filled sack.

Noises came from outside. Karnac gestured to the others to move either side of the entrance. Two soldiers came in.

Balet and the rest closed about them. A short, vicious fight, sword and dagger falling, then the corpses were dragged aside. Karnac, grasping the dripping sack, strode to the entrance of the pavilion. His blood-spattered face broke into a smile.

'If we leave as quickly and as quietly as we came, then we are truly blessed.'

They left, sliding through the circle of light, back on to the path leading out of the camp. Karnac strode ahead purposefully, that hideous sack grasped in one hand, the other resting on the hilt of his sword. On one occasion they were stopped by a sentry who noticed something was wrong with the sack. Karnac joked and the man drew back. They had almost reached the horse lines and chariot park when the night air was riven by the sound of war horns and shriek of trumpets. The alarm had been raised. Ahead of them the Egyptians glimpsed thorn barriers being pulled across the entrances to the camp. All around, soldiers were being roused. A runner sped by them, bearing messages to the picket lines.

'We have no choice!' Karnac shouted. 'We must run!'

Clustered together, the Egyptians broke into a wild frenetic scramble to the entrance Karnac had chosen. Here the soldiers, sluggish or drunk, failed to act fast enough. The gate leading out of the camp still stood open. At first Karnac's group were taken for Hyksos, roused by the alarm. However, an officer, sharper than the rest, became suspicious and, shouting at his men, tried to push them against some sort of barrier before the gate. Swords and daggers were drawn. Karnac, Balet and the others hit the enemy line. A ferocious, bloody struggle ensued.

Balet would never forget it: knife and sword glinting in the poor light; men grunting and swearing; fingers clawing at him. A dagger scored his right shoulder. Nebamum received a numbing blow to his left leg and went down. The halter round his neck saved him; Karnac pulled him away.

At last they were through, and apart from Nebamum, their unit had received no major injuries, just a few cuts to others. Karnac screamed at them to move as fast as they could. They were soon away from the camp, the darkness cloaking them. The Hyksos, now fully roused, followed in hot pursuit. Karnac, however, knew the terrain: the gulleys and paths. Even so, occasionally the Hyksos would catch up and a bloody mêlée would ensue. The broken, night-shrouded terrain prevented the Hyksos sending squadrons of war chariots in pursuit.

Balet believed he was journeying through the Under-world – the desert darkness; the awful screech of the night marauders as they scented blood and drew closer. Now and again a group of Hyksos scouts would close. Karnac would order them to stand and turn. Blood was spilt. More Hyksos corpses left for the hyaenas. They fled on, desperately seeking the Egyptian outposts, praying that the dawn would not find them exposed and vulnerable. They had been so fortunate. Only Nebamum, as he became more conscious of his injury, began to moan, stifling screams.

Karnac took a piece of cloth and thrust it between his servant's lips.

'Silence!' he hissed.

On they hastened, sounds of pursuit echoing behind them. Deliverance, however, was at hand. Pharaoh had sent out scouts and these covered their retreat. They reached the Egyptian camp. Pharaoh welcomed them as if they were the messengers of Ra. They were fed and feasted, Pharaoh's own physicians tending to their cuts and Nebamum's leg. The news spread like fire and, by the time the sun rose, they were being hailed as heroes.

Pharaoh had the entire Egyptian army paraded, and manifested his face to them. Seated on his throne, the air around him wafted sweet by perfumed, ostrich-plumed fans, Ahmose ordered the names of the Nakhtu-aa to be inscribed in the *Book of Life*. He also proclaimed their titles would be carved on the pylons and gateways of his palace, the House of a Million Years.

Medals were awarded. Each of the heroes received the title of 'Friend of Pharaoh'. Meretseger's head, together with the tray of Scorpion Cups, was paraded through the camp to the sound of trumpets.

Three days later the Egyptian and Hyksos armies met in bloody battle. Pharaoh won a decisive victory. The Hyksos war squadrons were shattered once and for all. Prisoners, in their thousands, were dispatched to the mines of Sinai. Two years later the Hyksos princes sued for unconditional peace and were banished for ever beyond Egypt's borders . . .

Balet started from his dreams of the past at a knock on the door. It swung open. He relaxed. It was only the priest,

Shishnak, and his handmaiden, Neferta. Shishnak was tall, about Balet's age, a former soldier. He still walked and stood like one; his shoulders were slightly hunched though his clean-shaven face was youthful. Beside him, Neferta looked more like his daughter than his wife. She was dressed in an elegant gauffered robe, a perfume-drenched wig on her head, her sweet face heavily painted with dark rings of ochre beneath sloe-like eyes.

'You've been here long,' Shishnak murmured. He gestured behind him. A servant came in bearing a platter of bread, strips of roast goose and a small jug of ale.

'I've been reminiscing.' Balet got to his feet.

'The night of your great triumph?' Shishnak asked, hitching his robe around his shoulders. 'A great victory, my lord!'

Balet nodded. He watched the servant put the platter of food on a small table just inside the door and quietly retreat.

'I was there too, you know,' Shishnak gabbled on. 'I was a foot soldier.'

'Yes, yes, of course.'

Balet just wished the priest would leave and take his doll-like wife with him. Every old soldier now claimed to have been present at that great battle. Balet had grown tired of listening to the reminiscences of others. The priest pointed to the tray of Scorpion Cups.

'I like touching them. The possessions of heroes,' he added.

'Yes,' Balet absent-mindedly agreed: Pharaoh had decreed that each of his heroes would receive a Scorpion Cup, whilst he would keep the tray. Ahmose had built this chapel especially and placed the tray here. When one of the Panthers died, his cup was left as a bequest.

'Such wonders,' Shishnak breathed, staring round.

He wanted to leave Neferta by herself with this veteran officer. She stood demurely, glancing at Balet from under long eyelashes. Balet coughed nervously and stepped away. He had heard rumours. Shishnak was an ambitious priest. It was customary for officers of the Seth regiment to come here and pray, make their own private devotions, like he was doing now. There had been talk of how Shishnak would bring his wife down and, if certain officers wished, she would kneel beside them and, with her hand, bring them relaxation and ease. Balet certainly didn't want any of that! He didn't want to be indebted to Shishnak. If he needed relaxation and ease, there were temple girls enough. Shishnak was staring down at the Scorpion Cups. Balet deliberately returned to kneeling on his cushion as if eager to pray.

'Shall we leave you?' Neferta's voice was soft, enticing.

'Yes, yes, if you would.'

The priest and priestess left in a gust of fragrant perfume, closing the door quietly behind them. Balet ignored the food. He would have words with Karnac over this. He came here to pray and to give thanks, not to be entertained by the likes of those two! He got up and rearranged the cushions to squat more carefully, listening closely. The temple had now fallen silent. Why had he come here? Yes, to give thanks. Balet's father had been a farmer but, since the raid on the Hyksos camp, Balet had known nothing but honour, splendour and riches. The story was now part of the folklore of Thebes. Everywhere he and his companions went they were treated as if they were sacred to Pharaoh. Even that cunning little minx Hatusu, who had out-manoeuvred her enemies to be hailed as Pharaoh, always treated them with the utmost courtesy and respect. At every important military festival, banquet or celebration, those surviving Panthers of the South were always present and always fêted.

Balet and his companions had grown rich and prosperous. They owned farms; ships, which plied along the Nile to the Great Green. They had treasure deposited in the House of Silver, fertile estates and great mansions beyond the city walls. Balet had married, begot two sons and three daughters. He had been called 'Pharaoh's right arm'. A splendid tomb was being prepared for him and the rest in the Necropolis across the river. On the night of their great victory against Meretseger, Balet had truly believed he had reached the climax of his life. Never again would he face such danger. Never again would he win such glory. It was as if he had been taken to the Far Horizon and allowed to wander amongst the Fields of the Blessed. Everything which had followed seemed second best. In the extirpation of the Hyksòs, the Panthers had performed many great deeds but Balet would never forget the night of their outstanding triumph. Yet, what was wrong? Balet always came here to find out.

He got up and walked to the wall where an artist, a skilled painter at Pharaoh's court, had depicted the Panthers' great achievement in dramatic, vivid scenes. Balet smiled to himself. Of course, like the poets, the painters took as much licence as they could. According to the artist, Karnac and his companions were dressed in gold and silver chased armour, elegant war boots on their feet. They even had chariots accompanying them. Balet followed the painting as he had so many times before. Each scene told part of the story: the slaying of Meretseger, now depicted as a true monster, a demon or blood-sucker from the Dark Halls of the Underworld. Here their retreat: not scurrying through the dark but advancing slowly backwards, shields locked together, lances out.

Balet heard the chapel door open and close but didn't look round. He closed his eyes and quietly prayed that Shishnak or his wife hadn't returned. In fact they hadn't. If Balet had turned he would have glimpsed a truly hideous sight: a hooded, masked figure, all in red, the colour of the dreaded God Seth; in one hand a dagger, in the other a war club, feet shod in soft cushioned sandals. So quietly did he walk that he was very close to Balet before the old officer decided to turn . . .

The death of the scribe Ipumer, who worked in the House of War, was well witnessed. The woman he lodged with, in her fine bricked house near the Market of Perfumes, was roused from sleep long before dawn by a loud hammering on the downstairs door. Lamna, widow of a soldier, a maker of cosmetics and perfumes, opened her eyes and groaned. She rolled on her back, her head leaning against the headrest, and stared up at the cedar-beamed ceiling. She was quite a wealthy woman but she had taken Ipumer in because he was recommended and she felt sorry for him. No, no, that wasn't strictly true. Lamna's fat face creased into a smile and her hands slipped down between her naked legs. Ipumer was quite a handsome, personable young man and she hoped one day, well, perhaps, a little dalliance in the garden? A shared cup of Charou wine in her flower-garlanded pavilion?

Again the knocking. Lamna closed her eyes and groaned. Her apprentices and maids slept in their own quarters at the far end of the house, whilst the old doorkeeper was as deaf as a post. She pulled back the linen gauze sheets, and the thin curtain hung round the bed to protect her against flies and mosquitoes. She pushed her feet into the simple reed sandals and, from a peg on the wall, took down the thick robe. She pulled this across her and tied the girdle carefully. She hastened to the bedside table, dabbed her neck with perfume and put on her best oil-drenched wig. She hadn't time for face-paint or jewellery but, if she stayed in the shadows, Ipumer might not notice the lines and creases.

Again the hammering on the door. Lamna hastily lit the oil lamp and glanced very quickly in a sheet of burnished bronze, which served as a mirror. She looked fetching enough and, after all, this was her quarter of the city. She must remember she had a reputation to consider and, appearing at the door at such a lonely hour, must not be taken amiss.

She grasped the oil lamp, took a bunch of keys from the chest, walked out of her bedchamber and down two flights of stairs. In the small hallway below, oil lamps glowed in their alabaster jars, little bronze caps placed over them to keep the flame safe. Lamna concealed her irritation at the continued hammering. She breathed in deeply.

'Who's there?' she called, knowing full well who it was.

'Mistress, it's me!'

Lamna went to the door and peered through the wooden crack.

'What is the matter?' she insisted.

'Mistress, please open the door. I am not well.'

Lamna put the oil lamp down on a small table and unlocked the door. All thoughts of dalliance disappeared. Ipumer was leaning against the porch wall, one hand grasping his stomach, the other wiping the saliva and vomit from the corner of his mouth. A handsome young man, Ipumer was now pallid, dark rings under his eyes; both his head and sleek, tanned face were matted with sweat.

'Mistress, I am unwell.'

He staggered forward. Lamna grasped him by the arm. He smelt strange, sickly. Lamna would always remember that when discussing the matter with her neighbours.

'Oh, yes,' she would confide. 'I knew immediately something was wrong, not just his appearance. I have seen young men who have drunk too much before. My own husband could be careless in his cups but Ipumer had an offensive odour about him.'

'Like what?' The question was always the same.

'Bitter-sweet, like that of the embalming room.'

Lamna helped the young scribe up the stairs. He had a chamber not far from hers.

'May the Gods help me!' the scribe muttered. 'I feel very bad. I think I will vomit.'

Lamna hurried him on. This had happened before. She remembered that vomiting – bad bile, a dark green liquid which stank and demanded the most industrious application of water and ash.

'You must see a physician,' she insisted as she helped him into his chamber. She tried to ease him on to the narrow cot bed but he refused.

'I will sit in my chair.'

Lamna helped him across to the chair, which had pride of place in the room. It had a quilted leather seat and backing; her husband had once owned it. Ipumer slumped down. Lamna hastened round, lighting oil lamps. The scribe was in a dreadful state. He had lost one sandal and his robe, which had been so crisp and white when he had left, was now stained with vomit and mud. She hastened out, brought back a bowl and placed it at his feet.

'Do you want anything to eat or drink?' she asked.

Ipumer shook his head, mouth opening and closing. He lurched forward, vomiting noisily into the bowl before throwing back his head and staring wild-eyed at the ceiling. Lamna stood near the doorway and tried to ignore the odious smell.

'Ipumer,' she pleaded, 'where have you been? This is not the first time this has happened. Shall I call Intef, the physician?'

The young man shook his head.

'I . . . I will be better soon.'

He lurched forward to vomit. Lamna filled him a cup

from the water jug and put it near him. She stood and watched anxiously. In this last month she had twice come in here, between the eighth and ninth hour in the morning, to find this young scribe writhing in pain on the floor. On both occasions he had told her how, on his way home, he had been taken by violent pains in his stomach. The attacks always passed. Ipumer visited the physician Intef, bought some medicine and the vomiting ceased. Now he brought his head forward, staring owlishly at Lamna.

'Mistress, I am sorry for the inconvenience caused. If I could only take a little sleep, I shall be better.'

'Are you sure? Shall I call for your friend?' Lamna insisted.

'No, no.' Ipumer shook his head. 'I do not wish her to see me like this. Perhaps later?'

No, no, of course you wouldn't, Lamna reflected bitterly. Ipumer, when he was well, was most handsome, of medium height, sharp-featured, always clean and presentable; smelling fragrantly, his robes and sandals always the best quality. Lamna had often reflected on his relationship with another widow who lived close by. She had been left wealthy enough, with a small house and garden, but she was nothing to look at: Felima was rather small and thin. Only the sly God Bes knew what Ipumer saw in the likes of her. Lamna stood in the doorway. What a pity! What a waste! It was Felima who had begged Lamna to give Ipumer lodgings.

A chilling thought occurred. Ipumer ate in the best cookshops, whilst the meals she provided were always tasty and fresh. What happened if Ipumer's illness was from something else? Thebes was full of poisoners. Down by the waterfront, the Scorpion Men and other tricksters sold potions and powders which could choke the life out of a man and send his Ka clean out of his body.

Surely the poisoner wouldn't be the Widow Felima, more of a mouse than a woman? She has even come here and shared a jug of beer with Ipumer out in the small courtyard beneath the grove of palm trees of which Lamna was so proud. Had the young scribe promised marriage to the widow and then rejected her?

And what about myself? Lamna's agitation deepened. After all, she concocted cosmetics, face paints and powders for the ladies of Thebes. Her small workshop below contained potions and mixtures which would kill a man. Would the finger of suspicion be pointed at her?

'Please leave me,' Ipumer called out weakly, gesturing with his hand. 'A little sleep and I will be better.'

Lamna obeyed, closing the door behind her. She returned to her own spacious, and what she considered elegant bedchamber, with its goose-feather mattress on top of reed-hardened slats, the scarlet headrest with the heads of ducks carved at each end, the leather-backed chairs, acacia tables and those costly looking coffers and chests which contained her robes. Lamna ignored all this as she lit more oil lamps.

A young scribe like Ipumer shouldn't be falling so violently ill with such mysterious ailments. She went across to the water clock on its little stand beneath the stone-slatted window. She took an oil lamp, stared in and reckoned it must be somewhere between the second or third hour after midnight. Lamna sat on the edge of her bed and tried to curb her agitation.

Neighbours described her as homely and comely: that's the way she liked to appear because that was the way she was! Ever since her querulous, fat husband had quietly passed to the Far Horizon, Lamna had lived, at least in the public eye, a respectable life. She gossiped with neighbours, visited the temples, prayed and made offerings. She sold her perfumes in the marketplace and, every week, took a skiff across the Nile to visit the small tomb she and her husband had bought in the Necropolis. Sometimes she took food and drink and invited friends along so they could picnic in the coolness of the tomb's entrance. Afterwards they would go in to admire the sarcophagus which contained her husband's mummified corpse and their other possessions: statues, coffers and clothing for when she died and made her journey into the neverending west.

Lamna acted the pious one. She made offerings to the Gods in the Necropolis and always stood, head bowed, hands raised before the great statue of Osiris, Foremost of the Westerners, which dominated the road into the City of the Dead. For the rest, she tried to run her business, letting her chamber to a procession of young men, though she told her neighbours she mothered them in a friendly way. Lamna would listen to their news, rejoice in their triumphs and give them the benefit of her homespun wisdom. Ipumer was no different from the rest. True, he was from the Northern city of Avaris, and had more than his fair share of charm and silver speech. He had soon gained a job as a scribe in the House of War and had won a reputation for popularity amongst the temple hesets, but he was respectful enough. He certainly liked to embroider his past. Lamna had listened, hiding her suspicions about how he had served with Pharaoh's regiments when Hatusu had swept north against the Mitanni.

The widow woman tried not to concentrate on the doubts nagging at the back of her mind. She chattered volubly with everyone, including herself but, now she was alone, she had to reflect. In one way young Ipumer was different from the other young men. Lamna had to face this even though it caused a chill of apprehension. The night was rather warm but Lamna pulled her robe closer around her plump shoulders. She had kept this secret, or tried to. Ipumer, in his cups, hot breath against her face, had confided so many months ago the real reason for his departure late at night and return in the early hours of the morning. Lamna, a true busybody, would have loved to have buzzed like a bee and spread the news but even she had to be careful. She had the sense to know her place in the city of Thebes. The Great Ones ruled here: Hatusu, the reincarnation of a God; Senenmut, her First Minister and, some whispered, her lover; the chief priests of the temple; the judges and, above all, the generals. The House of War was growing in importance. Hatusu had brought her enemies to book but she depended for support on the crack regiments outside Thebes who garrisoned the forts and castles from the Delta to the Third Cataract. Hatusu, the Divine One, also extolled Egypt's glorious military past. Everyone knew about the stories of the regiment of Seth and its band of heroes, the Panthers of the South, veteran officers who, by their courage, ferocity and audacity, had brought great glory to Pharaoh's grandfather. When she'd first heard Ipumer's news Lamna couldn't believe it. Ipumer had fallen in love with the doe-eyed daughter of one of these heroes. Who was it? Ah yes, Neshratta, the elder daughter of General Peshedu.

'May Thoth in his wisdom guide her.'

Lamna raised her hands and eyes to the ceiling. Peshedu! One of Pharaoh's darlings, rich and powerful, owning a great stately mansion outside the walls of Thebes, with luxurious gardens, pavilions, its doors of Lebanon cedar guarded by retainers. Yet it had happened. Secret assignations between Ipumer and Neshratta had lasted for many months: shadowy meetings at night, letters being passed backwards and forwards.

Lamna sucked on her teeth. If the truth be known, curiosity had got the better of her. Quite recently she had stolen into Ipumer's chamber. He had been careless and left his metal coffer unlocked. Neshratta had written fulsomely passionate love letters. Lamna had been shocked and surprised at the intensity of the young woman: she even composed love poems. How did one verse go? Lamna had memorised the opening lines:

> My love causes mischief.
> His voice eats my heart.
> His touch plays riot with my body.

His kisses torture my soul.
In my secret places I harbour and hold him.

Lamna breathed out. Even a heset girl, a temple hand-maiden or a city courtesan would blush at such words. A few months ago, just after the Inundation, Neshratta, together with her father, mother and younger sister, had travelled north to Memphis. Neshratta had written to Ipumer, excusing her absence and begging him not to follow her. Lamna had intercepted the note.

'Oh, for the love of pleasure,' it read, 'please don't join me. Father would say it was I who brought you. I am exceedingly sorry, my lotus love, that where I go, my eyes cannot glimpse you. I promise, the first thing I will do on my return, will be to see you and to share pleasures not even experienced in the Houses of Eternity.'

Lamna had paled when she had read the words. So Peshedu mistrusted his daughter, entertained suspicions about this amorous young scribe? Lamna had become frightened. She'd pushed all this to the back of her mind, deciding not to think about it. Peshedu was powerful. He could whistle up bullyboys. Thebes was full of former soldiers, and death could follow quickly. Is that what had happened to Ipumer? Was he being punished for his arrogance? Would she too fall under the shadow of such retribution?

'"You are richer than the finest wine, sweeter than the freshest honey,"' Lamna murmured.

Yes, that was also a line from a poem Neshratta had

written. Her relationship with Ipumer had not been mere dalliance. They must have lain together under starlit skies and become one.

Lamna had made her own discreet enquiries around the temple forecourts and in the marketplace. Of course, perfume-sellers and cosmetic-makers found it easy to collect the gossip of the Great Ones, who lived in the shadow of the House of a Million Years. The wives of generals, priests and chief scribes were always looking for fresh ways to beautify themselves. Young Hatusu had set the trend for elegant beauty; the women of her court did their best to imitate. At first Lamna had been unsuccessful but, at last, she'd heard that Neshratta was involved in some scandal: a dalliance which had provoked tittle-tattle, hushed gossip about some delicious sexual misdemeanour.

Lamna heard a sound and whirled round. Even though her bed was on the second floor of her house she had to take precautions against snakes and rats. She had rubbed cat fat against the lintel and had fumigated her room, as she had the young scribe's, with gazelle meat mixed with terebinth and incense.

'I'll have to do it again,' she murmured.

She made herself more comfortable on the bed. Her mind returned to the young man who so concerned her. Ipumer often disappeared late at night. This was the third occasion he had returned feeling ill, complaining of violent cramps in his stomach and bowels. It could not be an accident or a coincidence. Lamna lowered herself further down. She moved her fat legs and pressed her cheek against the headrest. She thought of going back to see if all was well but drifted into a vexed sleep.

She was woken three hours later by her maid with a cup of watered beer mixed with juniper juice and soft bread fresh from the oven. She drank and ate hurriedly, washed in the bowl of perfumed water the maid brought, put her third-rate vesting robe on, slipped on her stout market sandals and left the chamber. Ipumer's door was not locked. When she pushed it open, Lamna was relieved to see him lying on the bed, knees up, one hand across his stomach. The chamber stank vilely but at least he had the presence of mind to bring the bowl near the bed. Lamna went across. Ipumer's face was covered in a film of sweat, eyes half-open.

'Ipumer, how are you? Shall I send for the physician?'

'No, no,' the scribe groaned. 'It's too early yet.'

Lamna tiptoed out of the chamber, along the passageway and up the stairs to the roof of the house. Her agitation only increased. She stared around. The sun was rising, a fiery gold disc, its rays now shimmering on the gold- and silver-capped obelisks of the different temples and palaces. Below her in the street a donkey brayed. A camel driver screeched abuse at the cart which blocked his path. The murmur of voices rose. Lamna knelt on the prayer mat and, closing her eyes, prayed for the protection of all the Gods. Was this an auspicious day? Yes, it was, the festival of Bes the ugly dwarf God! Yesterday Lamna had forgotten her prayers. She nervously put fingers to lips: wasn't that a day cursed by Seth? Lamna realised she needed all the help she could get and, turning north, tried to feel the cool morning breeze, the breath of Amun, but she couldn't concentrate.

She went back down and looked at the sick man. If anything, he looked worse. Lamna decided enough was enough. She donned the wig she wore on work days, picked up her small parasol, a reed mesh basket and went out into the streets. They were already busy with pedlars and merchants; young boys and girls were hurrying down to one of the squares where a wandering scribe might teach them. On the corner two barbers were fighting over the best place for their stall. Lamna went down an alleyway, through a gate, up past a tired-looking garden and knocked at a door.

Intef the physician opened it. His wizened, monkey-like face glared at Lamna. She could see he had been drinking: his robe was purple-stained and his cheeks and chin were unshaven. He forced a smile. Lamna sold him powders below the market price and sometimes they shared a bowl of wine. Lamna could be so dexterous at helping him relax.

'What can I do? What is the matter?'

Lamna quickly described Ipumer's symptoms. The physician closed the door, came back and, a short while later, she returned to her own house with drops of poppy and a herbal plaster. Ipumer, however, refused both. Lamna was reduced to witnessing the scribe's continued groans.

'Go fetch the physician Intef!' Lamna ordered her maid eventually.

A short while later the doctor, a little cleaner than earlier, was ushered into the house. He bustled into the scribe's bedroom, took one look at the patient and muttered under his breath. Intef rolled back the sleeves of his gown and opened the covered basket he had brought. He placed the small statue of the God Thoth, carved as an ibis bird, on the table. He mumbled a few incantations and told Lamna and her maid to help him prepare a concoction of poppy seed, fly dung, resin as well as honey mixed with beeswax. He added a few drops of oil to the concoction and ground these together with his pestle in his mortar bowl. Lamna's pet goose wandered in. The physician shooed it out.

'No animals here,' he grumbled. 'My medicine requires that.'

Ipumer faded in and out of consciousness. His face looked hideous – pale, with faint blue marks on his cheeks. Now and again he would gasp for breath. The more Intef worked, trying to force different concoctions down the scribe's throat, the worse the illness grew. Intef lost his temper.

'I don't believe this!'

As Intef pulled aside the young scribe's robes, Lamna glimpsed the blotches on the chest and stomach. She also noticed the sheets where Ipumer had soiled himself. Intef pulled the coverlet back over. He stood and watched. Ipumer's body was beginning to shake. Lamna knew enough to recognise the death noise rattling in his throat.

'There is nothing I can do!' Intef wailed.

'He has been poisoned,' Lamna declared.

'What potion?' Intef demanded.

'I don't know,' Lamna whispered hoarsely. 'But this is no malady of the marshes, infected food or putrid water. He has been poisoned and he will die.'

Ipumer was now convulsing on the bed, chest rising and falling, eyeballs rolling. He was trying to form a word.

'Neshratta!'

His body shook again, then lay still as his head lolled sideways, eyes open, mouth gaping. Intef pulled over the coverlet as Lamna began to cry, though she did not know if it was for herself or the young man whose hideous death she had just witnessed. Intef grasped her by the shoulder.

'What will happen now?' he demanded.

'We must send for the Keeper of Corpses,' Lamna replied. 'Ipumer will be taken to the embalming chambers, the House of Death beneath the Temple of Seth.'

Intef reluctantly agreed. The law was quite clear: any victim of suspected poisoning had to be examined by the temple physicians in the House of Death at the Temple of Seth.

'I'm frightened,' she muttered.

Intef patted her gently on the shoulder. 'We have nothing to fear.'

Lamna could tell from his eyes he wasn't telling the truth.

'You heard what Ipumer said,' she protested. 'He mentioned Neshratta.'

'Who's she?' Intef asked off-handedly.

Lamna thought that he did know but she explained in hushed, hurried whispers. Now and again she stared fearfully at the corpse stiffening under its stained linen sheet. Intef heard her out, trying to hide his own agitation.

'Someone will die for this!' Lamna concluded darkly. 'And you know the sentence for a poisoner? Buried alive out in the Red Lands!'

THE SETH ANIMAL: a strange creature
with the body of a greyhound. It had
a curved snout, pricked-up ears and
almond-shaped eyes.

bowels were a constant concern both to him and his
family, sometimes an embarrassment, always a delight
to talk about. Nevertheless, his preoccupation with his
minor ailments did not blunt Valu's razor-like wit and
a tongue as bitter and as sharp as any cobra. A man
in his early thirties, Valu did not think much of the
advocate kneeling to his far right beside the accused.
Meretel was a clever scribe; he might know the law, be
praised as a great scholar in the House of Life, but it was
here in court, on the field of combat, he had to show his
prowess.

Valu studied his real opponent: Amerotke, Pharaoh's
chief justice in the Hall of Two Truths. Amerotke was a
worthy adversary. He sat carved like a statue. A man of
the same age as Valu, Amerotke had a rather harsh face,
deep-set, brooding eyes, thin nose above lips which could
be generous and laughing but which could also quickly
compress into a look of disapproval. Self-contained, Valu
thought, yes that was the best description of my Lord
Amerotke, friend of Pharaoh, confidant of Senenmut, the
Great Vizier and First Minister of Egypt.

The judge was dressed in a snow-white linen robe
fringed with gold tassels. His head was shaven, apart
from the dark lock of hair which hung down past his
right ear. A gold jacket bearing the insignia of Ma'at, the
Goddess of Truth, the personal gift of Pharaoh, draped
his shoulders. An exquisite chain of office hung round
his neck; its gold-filigreed medallion, shaped in a sun
disc, showed Ma'at holding the feather of truth, kneeling
before her father, Ra. A gold bracelet above Amerotke's

left wrist bore similar insignia, on his fingers the rings of office displaying the images of Thoth, God of scribes, Ma'at of truth and Anubis of judgment. Valu studied these trinkets with barely concealed envy. One day he would be a judge – perhaps even sit here and dispense the words from Pharaoh's mouth. He just wished Amerotke would intervene: Valu needed some indication of what the judge thought about this scandalous case of poisoning which had provided so much delicious gossip in the temples, mansions and marketplaces of Thebes.

'She deserves death,' Valu repeated, leaning forward, bowing slightly.

'We all deserve death, Valu: that is the end of us all. We are here to dispense Pharaoh's justice.'

Amerotke had begun the ritual, that slow dance which would lead to a wild frenzy of argument, counterargument, proof and counterproof. Valu nodded. Amerotke wasn't going to give anything away.

'My lord judge,' Valu pulled back the sleeves of his gown, 'the case is quite simple. Our arguments are lucid, the proof compelling. On the third day of the fourth month of this season, Ipumer, a military clerk in the House of War, left his lodgings and returned in the early hours complaining of severe cramps in his stomach and bowels. Despite the care and attention of his housekeeper and the ministrations of a physician, Ipumer died in hideous agony.' Valu paused for effect. 'His body was taken to the House of Death beneath the Temple of Seth, where, in accordance with the law, physicians from the School of Life examined the corpse. They concluded that Ipumer had been killed by an infusion, a venom rare in this city, extracted from a puff fish.'

Valu paused and glanced to his right. Amerotke's Director of Cabinet, Keeper of the Petitions and their scribes, including Amerotke's kinsman Prenhoe, squatted on cushions, writing-trays on their thighs. They were all busy taking down every word, keeping a faithful record of what was said and done.

'We can also prove,' Valu continued, his voice rising, turning fully and pointing to Neshratta, kneeling on a cushion beside the advocate Meretel, 'how the accused bought the same venom on a number of occasions from a Scorpion Man in the Market of Herbs near the Great Mooring Place on the Nile.' Valu turned back and spread his hands. 'My Lord Amerotke, cause and effect are simple.' Valu used his hands to emphasise his case further. 'Ipumer was killed by the venom. He was in the practice of going out late at night. We know he had a relationship with this young woman. We know that this young woman had tired of his solicitations. We know she bought the venom which killed Ipumer. My lord judge, our case is clear. The accused, Neshratta, is guilty of murder by poisoning. She maliciously plotted that young scribe's death. She deserves to feel the full rigour of the law, execution! To be buried alive in the Red Lands!'

Valu's dramatic words provoked cries and groans, not only from the guards and retainers clustered in the doorway behind him, but those spectators who sat in the transept to Amerotke's left beyond the fluted, decorated pillars of this Hall of Truth. Valu glanced across at the worried face of Peshedu, Neshratta's father. Valu preened. He was a farmer's son and had risen in the courts because the Gods had touched his heart, made him so skilled in law and argument, he had won the patronage of Senenmut. Valu, as chief prosecutor, could present a case against anyone in Thebes. He was the rod of Pharaoh's justice, but, as a man, he quietly relished this opportunity to attack the great, the powerful and rich.

'I hear what you say, my Lord Valu.'

The prosecutor recalled himself. Amerotke, hands on his knees, was leaning slightly forward.

'We are here to dispense Pharaoh's justice so the court will remain quiet. What we need, my Lord Valu, is proof.'

'Proof?' Valu tried to keep the sneer from his reply.

'Yes, my Lord Valu, proof. Is that not so, Meretel?' Amerotke glanced at the young advocate, who had been nodding vigorously.

'My lord, we do not contest,' Meretel retorted, 'that the Lady Neshratta, er, did have dalliance –' he paused at the murmur of laughter – 'a relationship of sorts with the dead scribe. We do not dispute that Ipumer died of a certain poison. Nor do we challenge my Lord Valu's assertion that the Lady Neshratta bought the poison from a Scorpion Man.' Meretel paused. 'However, what we will say, and have gone on sacred oath to declare, is that at no time did Lady Neshratta, either directly or indirectly, administer such a venom to the scribe known as Ipumer.'

Amerotke looked directly at Neshratta. She knelt on the cushion, dressed in a beautiful white robe, a necklace of cornelian round her throat, other jewellery at wrists and fingers. She wore a thick black wig, framing her beautiful face in oil-soaked ringlets which fell just above her shoulders. Lovely, delicate features, dark expressive sloe-eyes and a mouth any man would want to kiss, she did not look like a poisoner. The judge smiled at her. He felt sorry for her. She had the same cool elegance of his own wife, Norfret, a poise, a serenity which probably hid a strong character and a stubborn will. Amerotke had made careful research before this case began. He had discussed it with Norfret, as all Thebes was taken up by the scandal. He felt sorry for the accused; by the time this case was finished, guilty or not, her reputation would be in tatters and the honour of her noble family besmirched.

'My lord?' Neshratta asked, her voice just above a whisper.

'On the night Ipumer died,' Amerotke said, 'did he visit you? Did you meet him?'

'No, my lord.'

'You have taken an oath,' Amerotke reminded her, 'above these sacred scrolls, witnessed by the Goddess. The penalty for perjury is hideous, woman or not, noble or commoner.'

'I did not meet Ipumer.' Neshratta's voice grew stronger. 'I had not met him for at least five weeks before his death.'

'Do you know why he went out that night and other nights?'

'No, my lord.'

'But he did write to you?'

'Constantly, my lord, beseeching a meeting, protesting his love.' Neshratta's voice remained calm. 'Sometimes I replied, sometimes I did not.'

'And this venom?' Amerotke asked. 'Why should a young noblewoman need such a noxious substance?'

'It has many uses, my lord, as any Scorpion Man will tell you. It can be used in beauty preparations as well as for cleaning precious cloths.'

'There will be silence!'

Amerotke raised his hand at the laughter which greeted Neshratta's words. He also used the opportunity to stare at the back of the hall where his manservant, Shufoy, stood, grasping Amerotke's parasol, his bright eyes eager to catch his master's attention. In fact, he was jumping about so much Asural, captain of the temple guard, a distant kinsman of Amerotke, had to place a hand on the little man's shoulder to keep him still. Shufoy was nodding vigorously. Amerotke had dispatched him around the potions and herb-sellers of Thebes to find out what uses the venom might have. Apparently Neshratta was speaking the truth.

'My lord,' Valu spoke up, 'we do not contest that. Many poisons have varied uses, apart from killing a man, but isn't it strange that the Lady Neshratta, who wished to be rid of the scribe Ipumer, bought that very substance on a number of occasions and, on a number of occasions, Ipumer returned from his nightly visits retching and vomiting?'

Amerotke gestured for silence. He was now satisfied

that the bare outline of the case had been made. Every-thing rested on proof. If Valu could prove that, on the night Ipumer had fallen ill, he had met the Lady Neshratta, judgment might be given against her. But, if not . . . ?

Amerotke now permitted the list of witnesses on either side to come forward and speak: physicians from the House of Death; the Scorpion Man who had sold the venom; Lamna, with whom Ipumer had lodged; Felima, the young scribe's confidante. Meretel produced a long list of witnesses, including maids from the Lady Neshratta's household, but the case didn't change. There was no doubt of a long-standing affair between the accused and the dead man but nothing to link her directly to his murder.

Amerotke let both Valu and Meretel interrogate and question. Sometimes he called for order, other times he intervened himself. In the end, he sensed the court was like a dog chasing its own tail round and round, two lines of argument, advancing like armies on parallel roads but never really meeting or clashing. Amerotke scruti-nised Valu. The chief prosecutor was wily and slippery as a mongoose. Amerotke suspected Valu was reinforcing, time and again, how Ipumer and Neshratta had been lovers and that she'd bought poison from which he died. Amerotke glanced to his left, through the pillared portico, at the temple gardens, their lush green grass watered by canals from the Nile. He glimpsed a bubbling fountain, a gentle doe grazing under the outstretched branches of a sycamore tree. Such coolness calmed him.

'My Lord Amerotke.'

The judge didn't like the smile on the chief prosecutor's face.

'I have another witness.'

'I am sure you have,' Amerotke replied drily. 'Then you'd best call him, or her!'

The temple ushers led forward a rather dirty, dishevelled man. His robe was stained and tied by a simple cord but the sandals on his feet were of good quality. The way he carried himself, swinging an ash cane, showed that he was a walker of the roads, probably a pedlar or huckster who bartered and sold in the villages outside Thebes. He was tall, thin-faced, burnt by the sun but bright-eyed and vigorous. The Director of the Cabinet administered the oath and the pedlar knelt on the cushions provided. Valu made the introductions.

'Tell my lord judge,' the prosecutor concluded, 'where you were and what you saw on the night Ipumer died.'

'I had been working late.' The pedlar's voice echoed through the court. 'And because of that I failed to reach the city before the gates were closed. I had no warrant or licence so, my lord, I decided to wait outside.'

Amerotke nodded. Such arrangements were common. Once the curfew was sounded, the conch horn brayed, the city gates were closed. Travellers such as the pedlar had to fend for themselves.

'I went back along the road,' the pedlar declared. 'The night was beautiful, a full moon. The stars—'

'Thank you,' Amerotke interrupted.

'I was looking for some grove,' the pedlar continued oblivious to Amerotke's sarcasm, 'where I could sleep. My pack had grown heavy. I know the mansions beyond the walls: their gates are always locked but, in the shadows, a traveller like myself can find a soft bed under some tree, safe from any brigands or thieves. I found such a place.'

'Where?' Amerotke asked.

'Near General Peshedu's house.'

'How do you know it was his?'

'I know the house very well, my lord, like the palm of my hand. I call his mansion, as do many, "the House of the Golden Gazelle" because of the emblems painted on the gate.'

'I too know it,' Amerotke agreed. He had often passed this opulent mansion in his walks to and from the city.

'Well, my lord, you know the gates front the road. I followed the curtain wall round, down a small trackway. A canal runs there; it feeds water from the river into the house. Small clumps of date and palm trees provide shade. The grass is soft, not sun-parched. Travellers always nestle there but that night it was empty. I took off my pack and made myself comfortable. I heard footsteps on the trackway and looked up.'

'What hour was this?'

'My lord, the city gates had just closed, so it must have been just after midnight.'

'And whom did you see?'

'A young man, the scribe Ipumer. I have been shown his corpse. He was walking very quickly. He held a staff in one hand and was carrying a wineskin and a leather satchel over his shoulder. Oh, I thought, there goes a lover. I glimpsed his face in the moonlight. He looked happy and healthy enough; he was singing softly under his breath. Curious, I watched him go down the trackway. Now, in the wall is a small postern gate. The servants call it "the eye of the needle", it's so narrow. This door opened and a figure came out.'

'Did you see who it was?'

'My lord, I did not. Ipumer greeted this person. I heard the murmur of voices.'

'Male or female?'

'I don't know, my lord, but they kissed.'

Amerotke silenced the court.

'But it could have been a male?'

'Why yes, my lord.'

'Look on the accused,' Amerotke ordered. 'Can you say it was definitely her? Remember your oath! This young woman's life could depend on it.'

Amerotke stared at Valu. He didn't trust the prosecutor when it came to tricks and devices but Valu had integrity. He wouldn't put words into a witness's mouth.

'I can't say.' The pedlar glanced beseechingly at Amerotke. 'My lord, I truly can't. It looked like a woman, and they walked off hand in hand.'

'Then what?'

'My lord, I returned to my possessions and the make-shift bed I had made. I couldn't sleep. It had been a long time,' the pedlar stammered, 'since I had lain with a woman. My throat was dry, my belly empty. I envied the scribe's good fortune.'

'So you lay awake?'

'Yes, my lord.'

'And the lovers came back?'

'About an hour later. I heard the murmur of voices. The gate opened and Ipumer came along the trackway.'

'And how was he then?'

'He looked hearty and satisfied.'

Amerotke leant his head against the high back of his chair.

'My lord,' Valu's voice was silky, yet full of menace, 'on the night Ipumer died he definitely visited the accused's house. She joined him as she had before.'

'My lord, that is not true!' Neshratta declared hotly. 'You've heard the testimony of my maid as well as the porter at our main door.'

'Yes, yes, I have,' Amerotke agreed. He glanced at the witness. 'The accused maintains, and she has been supported by her maid and porter, that she never left her bedchamber or, indeed, the house.'

The pedlar grimaced and spread his hands. Neshratta was whispering with Meretel.

'My lord, we can produce a witness as well.'

'I have not finished!' the pedlar protested.

'Continue!'

'Ipumer passed by me. A short while later the postern gate opened again. A figure came out and went in the same direction as the other two but then returned.'

Amerotke leant his elbows on his throne-like chair and scratched his cheek.

'Did you see this person?'

'No, my lord, but it was certainly a woman. I smelt a heady perfume on the night air. I also glimpsed an oil-drenched wig.'

'And you hadn't seen this before? With the previous figure?'

'No, my lord, but the darkness was thinning; a breeze had sprung up.'

'Tell me,' Amerotke leant forward, 'Ipumer died of a poison. Therefore he must have been given something to eat or drink. Do you think he was carrying food?'

'I glimpsed a wineskin.'

'And the first figure?' Amerotke insisted. 'Was he or she carrying cups, food or a tray?'

'My lord, he or she couldn't have been. They immediately embraced and kissed.'

'But this is strange,' Amerotke insisted. 'Ipumer went down to the House of the Golden Gazelle and met someone. I concede that mysterious person might have poisoned him but, to do so, there would have to be food, cup, platter?'

Silence greeted his question.

'It is a mystery,' Amerotke continued. 'Two figures left the House of the Golden Gazelle: one to meet Ipumer, one after him.' He pointed at Neshratta. 'Remember, you are on oath. Tell me again what you did that night.'

'I stayed in my bedchamber on the second storey. My maid slept outside on a pallet bed. You've heard her testimony and that of the porter who guards the main door to that part of the house—'

'There is a window,' Valu interrupted.

'I am not a snake,' Neshratta countered. 'My lord, there are windows enough but they are latticed.'

'So,' the judge replied, 'to leave your bedchamber you have to pass your maid?'

'Who is a light sleeper.'

'Go downstairs and not be seen by the porter?'

Amerotke steepled his fingers. Both the maid and porter had been called and taken the oath. Like any ordinary citizens summoned here, they had been terrified. Amerotke was certain they were speaking the truth.

'So, who were these two mysterious figures who met Ipumer?'

Amerotke glanced to his right. Peshedu was sitting on a stool just beyond the columns, beside him his fat-faced wife, and Neshratta's younger sister, a tall, comely girl of no more than fourteen summers.

'My Lord Valu, I have a question to ask you,' the judge continued. 'You made careful enquiries before this case was brought to court. Was Ipumer friendly or known to anyone else in General Peshedu's house?'

Valu shook his head. 'They knew of him but he was hated.'

A low murmur of agreement rose from General Peshedu and those around him.

'So, it's doubtful,' Amerotke continued, 'that someone else would leave that house and greet him so affectionately?'

'I agree, my lord. Moreover, Lady Neshratta has not been honest in one thing. I too have been to the House of the Golden Gazelle. Her opulent bedchamber faces north.

True, the windows are latticed but one has a wooden wicker framework which can be taken in or out.'

Valu ignored Neshratta's protest.

'The Lady Neshratta is,' he chose his words carefully, 'young, athletic. A rope ladder is kept in her bedroom in case of fire.'

Neshratta was agitated. Valu had this information all along but kept it hidden. Amerotke had seen him do the same before: Valu would tease an adversary, lull him into a false sense of safety, then strike.

'My lord,' Meretel the lawyer lifted his hand, 'Lady Neshratta had forgotten about the wooden lattice. However, we have heard the witnesses. Lady Neshratta's maid was a light sleeper. The removal of a wooden lattice and the lowering of a rope ladder would have been heard. The garden soil is soft. Lady Neshratta's sandals and feet would have been dirt-stained. Moreover, she may have been glimpsed—'

'Nonsense!' Valu interrupted. 'Lady Neshratta can wash her feet and sandals, can't she? And, as for the testimony of family retainers . . .' Valu pulled a face.

The scribes were busily writing; Prenhoe in particular. Amerotke would go through all this testimony again and study it carefully. Prenhoe lifted his head, a woebegone expression on his face. Amerotke glanced away. Prenhoe and his dreams! When they had all gathered earlier in the small chapel behind the court, Amerotke's personal quarters, Prenhoe had been full of the previous night's dreams.

'My lord, I was gliding over the Red Lands, riding on

the back of a great vulture, its wings thick and feathery. Below me thundered a war squadron of chariots, the electrum a deep purple, the four horses as black as night. Their driver was dressed in armour I had never seen before. The vulture screeched and the driver lifted his head. A skeleton, Master! Death was driving his chariot towards Thebes. The time of Seth, of great killing is upon us!'

Amerotke, washing his hands in the mixture of natron and myrrh, had nodded absent-mindedly.

'I had a dream too,' Shufoy had spoken up. 'I was in a willow grove beside the Nile, two gorgeous girls beside me wearing nothing except beautiful collars of sapphires, rubies and gems—'

'That's dangerous,' Prenhoe had interrupted.

Amerotke smiled to himself. Shufoy's dreams were always about young women. The judge didn't believe in dreams but, this morning, as he walked up the Avenue of Sphinxes into the concourse before the Temple of Ma'at, a messenger from Lord Senenmut had told him about the hideous slaying in the Temple of Seth. One of Thebes' great heroes, General Balet, had been found hideously murdered, his head smashed with a war club, his eyes gouged out. And hadn't a heset girl been found half-eaten by crocodiles? Was Prenhoe's dream correct?

'My Lord Amerotke?'

The judge broke from his reverie.

'If my lord judge is tired . . . ?' Valu soothed.

'My lord judge is not tired!' Amerotke retorted.

'I have other witnesses . . .' Valu offered.

'Oh, I am sure you have! Let us hear their testimonies.'

The pedlar got to his feet, bowed and walked to the back of the hall. His place was taken by a young scribe. He nervously took the oath, purifying his lips from the bowl of natron held by one of the hall ushers.

'My name is Hepel,' he began. 'I am a scribe in the House of War. I was Ipumer's friend, or rather colleague.'

The young scribe was very agitated. Amerotke gestured; a bowl of water was offered from which Hepel quickly sipped.

'Tell me,' Amerotke said, 'this friend, this colleague Ipumer, what was he like?' Amerotke waved his hand round the court. 'I see no relatives, no family, no kin.'

'He was from Avaris, my lord. He trained in its schools and came to Thebes with letters of recommendation. They are kept in the archives.'

'What was he like?'

'Ipumer was a lonely man; he kept to himself.' The scribe measured his words carefully. 'He never talked of any family. No one from Avaris ever visited him.'

'And his work?'

'It was good, my lord. Ipumer was assiduous in his duties. He also enjoyed the company of ladies.'

'Any lady?' Amerotke asked.

Hepel looked at Valu, who nodded and gestured at him to continue.

'He was a regular visitor to the quayside, my lord. To the ale shops and . . .'

'And the courtesans?' Amerotke asked.

'Yes, my lord.'

'And the Lady Neshratta?'

'At first he didn't tell me, but eventually he confessed that he was deeply in love with her and hoped to become betrothed. He entertained great ambitions, did Ipumer. He thought kinship with a powerful family such as General Peshedu's would lead to further advancement. Sometimes I caught him writing letters to her. Now and again he would go down to the marketplace to buy a present. I asked him how he could choose such a high-born lady? Apparently he first saw her at a regimental banquet: one thing led to another.'

'And these assignations?' Amerotke insisted.

'Near the House of the Golden Gazelle at night.'

Amerotke stilled the murmur of astonishment.

'Precisely where?'

'A small trackway which runs along the side of the house, parallel to an irrigation canal from the Nile. There's a small postern door. Ipumer boasted how the Lady Neshratta would meet him outside. He would take a wineskin and she would bring cups. They'd eat, drink and . . .' Hepel licked his lips nervously.

Valu had a smile of contentment on his face. 'Tell the lord judge,' he murmured, 'how the Lady Neshratta was able to meet your friend.'

Hepel took a deep breath. 'Ipumer explained how one of the windows to her bedroom was of the wooden latticed type. She had oiled its edges carefully so it could be taken in and out without much difficulty or creating any disturbance. She had also oiled the rope ladder, which could be lowered. She kept a special pair of sandals hidden beneath a bush at the bottom, as well as a cloak.'

'And this dalliance?' Amerotke insisted.

'Ipumer was a boaster.' Hepel coloured, looking nervously across at General Peshedu.

'Did he claim to have lain with her?' Amerotke insisted.

'Yes, my lord, he did.'

Neshratta bowed her head, shoulders slightly shaking but, when she looked up, Amerotke caught a look of sheer defiance in her eyes. Amerotke shouted for silence in the court, Asural moved threateningly out of the shadows at the back. Neshratta whispered quickly to Meretel, who lifted his hands as a sign to speak.

'My lord, we can counter this witness. Moreover, we only have his word. This is market gossip. There is no proof.'

'Your turn will come,' Amerotke retorted. 'Hepel, listen.' Amerotke was determined to make full use of this witness. 'You were Ipumer's friend – did he ever complain to you of pains in his stomach and bowels?'

Valu's smile widened.

'Yes, my lord.'

'And when did these occur?'

'After his meetings with the Lady Neshratta.'

The court held its breath.

'Are you sure of this? Why didn't he visit the physician?'

'But, my lord, he did. The one who lived near his house: who tried to treat him before he died.'

Amerotke tightened his lips in annoyance. Intef had been questioned; he had not told the court this.

'And what did our noble physician say?'

'That it was colic, something he had eaten.'

'But surely,' Amerotke asked, 'Ipumer was an intelligent man. He would know cause and effect?'

'Yes, my lord. Sometimes he suspected the Lady Neshratta was trying to poison him.'

'And why should she do that?'

'Because she was tired of him!'

The clamour in the court grew. Asural walked around, demanding silence for Pharaoh's judge.

'Yet he still went back! I mean,' Amerotke played with the pectoral round his neck, 'Hepel, if you came to my house and, after the two occasions you dined with me, you experienced deep pain in the bowels, wouldn't you become suspicious?'

'Not of you, my lord.'

Amerotke joined in the laughter. Hepel relaxed.

'Why should he think Neshratta was poisoning him? Did Ipumer know she had bought this venom?'

'Oh yes, my lord, she told him everything. And he . . .' Hepel bit his lip.

'He what?'

'He bought some himself.'

The smile had disappeared from Valu's face. Amerotke raised himself in his chair.

Hepel gabbled on, 'He told me how Neshratta had bought this venom because it was useful in her beauty preparations as well as for other purposes. Ipumer teased her about trying to poison him. According to him, she just laughed.'

'Why did Ipumer buy this venom?'

'He became excitable. He said that if Neshratta did not marry him he would take his own life and answer for it in the Underworld. His blood would be upon her hands.'

Amerotke nodded at Meretel, who was eager to question this witness.

'Do you think Ipumer could have taken his own life?' the advocate asked.

'It's possible,' Hepel agreed. 'He was usually composed but, on the subject of Lady Neshratta, he could become very excitable.'

Amerotke stared down at the court. Shufoy was listening to this tale of love and murder, his mouth slightly open, his disfigured face turned slightly so he could hear better.

'Let me put this question to you.' Meretel followed up his advantage. 'Would you say it was possible that Ipumer, having learnt that the love of his life had bought some poison, also purchased the same substance from a Scorpion Man? That, out of spite, he poisoned himself so as to ruin Neshratta's chances of marrying anyone else? Ipumer hoped totally to disgrace her by having to face the heinous accusation of being a poisoner, a murderer?'

Hepel glanced anxiously at the prosecutor, who gazed stonily in front of him.

'Answer the question!' Amerotke insisted.

'It is possible and . . .'

Amerotke beckoned him to continue.

'Ipumer did have a weak stomach. He often complained of cramps.'

'Meretel,' Amerotke demanded, deciding to shift the balance a little, 'it would seem that Lady Neshratta could leave her bedchamber unnoticed?' The young woman was now sitting composed, a slight smile on her lips.

'Impossible!' Meretel pointed towards Lord Peshedu. 'According to the lord prosecutor's own witness, Ipumer was seen going down the side of the house shortly after midnight. Certainly before the first hour.'

Amerotke looked at Prenhoe, who nodded in agreement.

'My lord may wish to question her but, just before midnight, the Lady Neshratta's sister was disturbed by a nightmare. She came to her sister's bedchamber.'

'Why didn't we hear this before?' Amerotke glowered at him.

'My lord, I apologise. I thought such testimony should be held in reserve.'

'And the maid was never questioned on this?' Amerotke retorted.

'No, no, she wasn't. She was never asked if anyone ever approached the bedchamber door.'

In Peshedu's household group, the younger sister sat close to her father, who placed an arm round her shoulders. Amerotke noticed how she flinched at this.

'She will go on oath,' Meretel added, 'and the maid can be brought back.'

Amerotke agreed. The younger sister was dealt with gently. She spoke in a half-whisper but her story and that of the maid agreed. She had come to her sister's bed-chamber because of a nightmare about a great red-winged bat hovering over the House of the Golden Gazelle.

Amerotke lowered his head. Prenhoe would love such a tale. He dealt with the maid more sharply but her story rang true. The young girl had come and had stayed the rest of the night in her sister's bed, during the very time Neshratta was supposed to be meeting Ipumer out on that lonely, moon-washed trackway.

Valu, of course, objected. Amerotke quietly acknowledged that both the maid and the younger sister could have been well rehearsed in such a story. Yet, unless there was specific proof to the contrary . . . ? Amerotke decided to return to the matter in hand.

'So,' he smiled at Hepel, 'you were a friend of Ipumer, he confessed his love for the Lady Neshratta, so infatuated that if he couldn't have her, he would choose death. Did he have any other great love of his life?'

'I couldn't say, my lord. There were evenings when he didn't go to the House of the Golden Gazelle and he'd meet someone else.'

'Someone else?' Amerotke queried.

'He lived with the widow Lamna. Ipumer was also friendly with another, Felima.'

'My lord,' the prosecutor spoke up, 'if we could return to the events of the night Ipumer died . . . ?'

'Yes, continue.'

'On that evening,' Hepel continued, 'I met Ipumer in the Avenue of Rams. We visited a cookshop.'

'What hour was this?'

'About the seventh after midday.'

'Had Ipumer been home to his lodgings?'

'Yes, my lord, he had come straight from there. He told me that.'

'And what else did he say?'

'How he intended to visit the House of the Golden Gazelle. I asked if the Lady Neshratta would see him. "Oh, I think she will," he replied. "She had better!" Ipumer was very agitated. He ate and drank very little.'

'Had he eaten before?'

'Yes, my lord, his housekeeper had provided him with food, some of which he still carried in a linen cloth; I think he threw this away.'

'And was your meeting long?'

'No, my lord, he left shortly afterwards.'

Amerotke held a hand up. 'So, what happened in the four hours between Ipumur leaving you and being seen by the pedlar approaching General Peshedu's house?'

Hepel just shrugged. Amerotke called for extra cushions: both the widow women had returned. They took their places nervously. Lamna was plump in a pretty sort of way, the sort of woman who would give herself airs and graces. Felima was different, rather small, narrow-faced; she enjoyed a faded beauty, slightly elegant in her mannerisms.

'If a young man goes out to visit the love of his life,' Amerotke declared, 'he would wash, shave his face, change his robe, rub unguents and oils into his skin. But he didn't do that at your house, did he, mistress?'

Lamna shook her head.

'So, did he visit you?'

Felima just stared back.

'He did, didn't he?' Amerotke continued kindly. 'He visited you the night he died. What preparations did he make for meeting his loved one? You are on oath,' Amerotke reminded her. 'You have not been asked these questions before. Now you must answer. He bathed at your house, didn't he? You gave him food, drink and fresh robes.'

The widow woman was nervous but she held Amerotke's gaze. 'Yes, yes, I did that.' Her voice was surprisingly strong. 'I knew the truth would come out. I bathed him myself. It was I who helped him shave his cheeks and brought the oil for his skin.'

'Were you his lover?' Amerotke asked.

'Er, I was not his lover, not in that sense. I was his handmaid.'

Amerotke glowered round the court at the giggling which broke out.

'So, you bathed, soothed and fed him?'

Felima nodded, gnawing nervously at her lip. Amerotke stared to his left. The sun must now be at its height and he could imagine the heat in the concourse and marketplace beyond. He also noticed one of the clerks was beginning to nod sleepily. This case was not, he ruefully reflected, as easy or straightforward as the lord prosecutor had described it. Amerotke raised his hands, imitating Pharaoh, the sign to bring this session to an end. He then picked up the flail and rod, the symbols of his office, which had been lying on top of the books on the table before him. The court fell silent.

'This court will be adjourned!' Amerotke declared.

Valu made to protest. Amerotke glared at him.

'It is Pharaoh's will,' the judge insisted. 'I am the word which comes from Pharaoh's mouth.'

Valu decided to shut up and stay still. Amerotke rose. He turned and bowed to the statue, just behind him, depicting Ma'at, Goddess of Truth.

'My lord judge.'

He whirled round. Valu had his head bent.

'What is it?'

'I crave the court's indulgence,' the prosecutor lifted his head, 'but the Lady Neshratta should be confined. You have dungeons in the House of Death below?'

'Aye, and this is the House of Life,' Amerotke replied. 'The Lady Neshratta will be confined, but to her father's house. Her guilt has not been proved.' He smiled thinly. 'At least not yet. Pharaoh's business is adjourned!'

SETH: the Earth God, Geb, gave
Southern Egypt to Seth.

CHAPTER 2

'My lord judge, I must protest!'

'Then protest.'

Amerotke, seated on a chair in the small chapel, tried to look distracted by gazing round the golden-stoned chamber. On all the walls beautiful paintings of blue, red, gold and ochre emblazoned the deeds and the justice of Ma'at. At the far end stood the naos, its open doors revealing the sacred statue: Ma'at, as a young maiden, the feather of truth in a circlet round her head. The sculptor had finely depicted her exquisite face and form, now covered in a white linen robe. The baskets at the statue's feet were full of bread, fruit and other offerings which Amerotke would distribute amongst the scribes in the Hall of Two Truths. Small tables of precious sandalwood, inlaid with gold and silver, stood against the walls. On either side were Amerotke's personal cabinets where his rings, pectoral, flail and rod were stored by his Director.

Valu and Meretel squatted on cushions before the judge.

To Amerotke's left sat Shufoy, breathing noisily, a gesture of contempt for this prosecutor who dared to pursue his master into his own private sanctuary. Dark-faced Prenhoe was also present, carefully examining a callous on his finger caused by the stylus. Asural, chief of the temple police, leant against the chapel door, arms crossed. Dressed in his bronze greaves, leather war kilt, marching boots and cuirass, Asural looked the reincarnation of Montu, the God of War.

'I must protest,' Valu repeated. 'The court could have continued. The Lady Neshratta should be confined. You showed favour . . .'

Amerotke picked up the damp linen cloth coated with faint perfume, and dabbed at the sweat on his neck.

'I showed no favour,' he retorted. 'This case is not simple. I accept that Ipumer and Neshratta were probably lovers. I accept that she tired of him, that she bought the venom from a Scorpion Man. I accept that Ipumer visited the House of the Golden Gazelle the night he was poisoned. But, what you have to prove, sir, is that she poisoned Ipumer – is guilty of his murder. I know nothing of this scribe but I will be questioning witnesses again when the court reconvenes. Look,' Amerotke reasoned, 'Ipumer met his friend.' He ticked the points off on his fingers. 'He was given food by Lamna. He visited Felima. Any one of those three could have poisoned him that night. I don't know when he left Felima's house: that is a matter we have to examine. Ipumer may have gone elsewhere. Most importantly, I have seen no evidence which proves that the Lady Neshratta gave Ipumer poison. Now, lies may have been told.' Amerotke pointed to the statue of Ma'at. 'But I am the Goddess's winnower. I will separate the wheat from the chaff and judgment will be given. As for the Lady Neshratta's confinement,' Amerotke pointed at Meretel, 'she is not to leave her father's house without my written permission. If she does, she will be confined in the House of Death.'

Valu recognised he had provoked this judge far enough. He sighed and, stomach rumbling, got to his feet, winked at Amerotke, bowed and left, followed by Meretel.

Asural closed the door behind them.

'Do you think she's a murderer?' Shufoy asked.

He stood close to his master. Amerotke kissed his finger and pressed it against Shufoy's little forehead. His man-servant was a dwarf. Years earlier he had had his nose removed because of a crime he hadn't committed. Every time Shufoy stared fully at him, Amerotke felt a pang of compassion. A little man with a great heart and a big soul was how he described his manservant to Norfret. Shufoy was in love with life. Now his bright eyes gleamed with excitement.

'She's very beautiful, Master. Oh, think of those breasts, those legs, that luscious body buried beneath the sand!'

'You are like a goat on heat!' Asural snarled.

'Aye, and as quick as one!' Shufoy exclaimed.

'You smell like one,' Prenhoe added, sucking the callous.

Shufoy hitched the grey robe closer round his shoulders. Amerotke stretched out his hand and grasped a tendril of grey hair, which fell down to Shufoy's shoulders.

'Why don't you have this cut? And, if you are my herald, at least dress the part.'

Shufoy grinned, showing a fine display of white teeth.

'Why must you depict yourself as poor?' Amerotke demanded.

'People show pity, especially the ladies. Master, do you think she's guilty?'

'Here, amongst my friends and kinsmen –' Amerotke paused – 'I have no doubt that Ipumer was poisoned that night. But he could have done it himself. Anyway . . .' Amerotke got to his feet.

Shufoy took the judge's sandals from beneath a table. Amerotke slipped them on, picked up his white outer robe and placed this round his shoulders.

'Asural, see to the clearance of the Hall of Two Truths. Prenhoe, I want your records taken to my house. Shufoy, you are to come with me.'

Amerotke moved quickly so no one could ask further questions. He was soon through the door, going down the passageway which led to a side entrance. The temple was now preparing for its hour of sacrifice. White-garbed priests, heads shaven, black kohl round their eyes, processed amidst great gusts of incense dispersed to purify the air as well as themselves. Cymbals clashed. Temple handmaidens, in their heavy black wigs, garbed in pleated robes of fine linen, silver sandals on their feet, followed behind. Their beringed, painted fingers clutched the sistra, loops of metal attached to a wooden handle; when shaken together, these instruments gave off an eerie, jangling sound. Amerotke and Shufoy sheltered in a small portico as these servants of the temple swept down towards the Hall of Columns and the Holy of Holies.

'Where are we going?' Shufoy asked.

'The Temple of Seth, to see the Keeper of the Dead,' Amerotke replied. 'My Lord Senenmut has demanded my presence.'

Shufoy groaned and rolled his eyes beseechingly. They left the temple and walked down a basalt-paved alley-way on to the main concourse where the marketeers were doing a busy trade. Barbers, armed with curved razors, clustered round their makeshift stalls under the date and palm trees. They were specially busy, helping people to purify themselves by shaving their heads as smooth as washed pebbles before they entered the temple or presented their petitions to the lower courts. A group of soldiers, slightly drunk on cheap beer, staggered about, seeking a house of pleasure, eager to avoid the thick cudgels of the market police who shadowed their every step.

Some stalls were empty, being washed down with pots of water. The fleshers and the sellers of meat had to stop trading by midday. By then the heat had turned their pro-duce putrid. The remaining traders still hoped for custom before the people left to shelter in the cool shadows away from the searing heat. The crowd was cheerful and noisy now the ill-fated day of Seth had passed. Children ran round screaming and playing, vexing a powerful merchant squatting in his makeshift litter slung across two donkeys; he raised his fly whisks and shouted at the children to stand aside. Minstrels, singers, tellers-of-tales stood on plinths trying to catch the attention of passers-by with enthralling stories about what may lie beyond the Great Green, or the horrid demons which prowled the Red Lands. Foreigners from Kush and Nubia, in their strange feathered headdresses and panther-skin robes, rubbed shoulders with Semites in their gaily decorated tunics, and Libyans, with their high-pitched voices, naked torsos gleaming with sweat and oil, dark flounced kilts hanging low beneath the knee. These had taken off their sandals, which they carried on rods slung over their shoulders.

Amerotke grasped Shufoy's shoulder as the little man was distracted by a female contortionist, little silver bells attached to her wrists. She twisted and turned, posing lasciviously to music provided by two young men, one beating a drum, the other piping a reedy flute. Amerotke did not know what Shufoy's main interest was for the day. The little man had many roles: soothsayer, fortune-teller, love poet, amulet-seller, even a Scorpion Man or a physician, possessing a range of remedies which, Amerotke claimed, would kill rather than cure. Shufoy would have loved to have wandered off but Amerotke was insistent. The little man sighed and opened the parasol. It was supposed to provide shade for his master but Shufoy was so small Amerotke had given up reminding him: the judge drew some comfort that his manservant would never die of sunstroke. The crowd swirled around. Shufoy decided to make his presence known. He had a deep, carrying voice.

'Make way,' he bawled, 'for the Lord Amerotke! Pharaoh's Chief Judge in the Hall of Two Truths! Keeper of the Law!

Holder of the Divine Feather! Friend of Pharaoh! Beloved of the Gods!'

Amerotke winced. The more he tried to stop Shufoy the louder the little man bellowed but at least he had an effect. The crowd parted. They crossed the marketplace along the basalt-paved avenue leading to the Temple of Seth. The great square in front of this was also busy but Shufoy forced his way through. They passed the gold-capped obelisks, through the huge pylons which guarded the great gateway, their turrets emblazoned with red, white and green banners.

Amerotke paused to look at the stelae – boastful proclamations extolling the might and power of the dreaded God Seth; beneath these the exploits of the regiment of Seth, particularly the Panthers of the South, in their great war against the Hyksos during the Season of the Hyaena. Amerotke's fingers brushed the inscriptions as he recalled Lord Senenmut's whispered message. One of these heroes had been brutally murdered and Pharaoh Hatusu herself had decided to intervene.

Shufoy was jumping from foot to foot, gazing wistfully across the temple courtyard at a Scorpion Man selling cures for snake bite. The crowd pushed and jostled. Amerotke walked on, up the steep steps and into the shadowy portico before the temple's main gateway. It was cooler here though the light dazzled the vivid paintings carved on the walls so that the scenes caught the eye with their bright hues: Seth in conflict with Horus; Isis searching for Osiris' body.

A temple guard recognised Amerotke and approached.

The visitors were led into the temple along a colonnaded passageway reserved for the priests, and away from the pilgrims surging towards the Hall of Columns. The deeper they went into the temple the darker it became; the windows, high in the wall, provided little light.

Shufoy shivered. He very rarely visited the Temple of Seth, the God of Killing. Everything was so different here from the other temples. The walls did not proclaim Pharaoh's great deeds but Seth's red-handed work. Death and the dark creatures of the Underworld prowled along every wall. The gaudy colours of other temples were missing: no gold-leafed columns or silver-edged mosaics. The main colour was a dark ochre, broken here and there by splashes of bright red. The priests they passed wore strange red wigs with stolae of the same colour draped over their shoulders.

They reached the door at the end of a shadowy passageway. The temple guard opened the door and waved the visitors forwards. They went down steps. Amerotke felt he was entering the nether regions. This was not his world of sunshine, fluted columns, splashing fountains. It was a far cry from the Hall of Two Truths, with its exquisite furniture, spacious columns – the world of Thoth, the God of Writing, with papyrus, palates of red and black ink, styli, water pots. Here, torches of pitch depicted the God of Darkness around whom those grotesque creatures, the Devourers, danced to macabre music. The air was pungent with the smell of natron and other embalming fluids.

At the bottom of the steps Amerotke and Shufoy found

themselves in an underground cavern, its ceiling of blackened timber. Amerotke narrowed his eyes against the murky gloom. Sentries wearing the ram-masks, their loins protected by black leather kilts, stood guard, holding shield and spear. A figure stepped through the swirling steam. He was an officer with a black leather belt studded with bronze clasps, helmet shaped in the form of a ram's head. In a sharp, guttural voice he asked Amerotke his business and hastily stepped back when Shufoy shouted who his master was. The officer waved them forward. Amerotke walked slowly; the ground underfoot was wet and sloppy. At the far end of the cavern a huge statue of the jackal-headed God Anubis peered through the murk, across slabs of stone on each of which lay a corpse covered with a linen sheet. In the centre of the room a huge cauldron bubbled on a bed of burning ash – around it, wooden stands with trays bearing jars and jugs, pots of unguent, paste and dishes of liquid natron.

'Can I help you?'

A figure seemed to emerge from nowhere. His upper torso was uncovered, a white kilt draped the lower half of his body, he carried a ram's mask held on a stick to cover his face.

'Is that to frighten visitors?' Amerotke asked.

The man lowered the mask. His face was thin, young-looking, with deep-set eyes and high cheekbones. He turned the mask and offered it to Amerotke. The judge took it and sniffed at the small pomander of perfume.

'My name is Chula,' the man declared, 'priest in the service of Seth.'

'Also known as the Keeper of the Dead,' Amerotke added.

'A sombre title,' Chula observed, 'but it has a certain ring.'

Amerotke gazed round: this was a hideous place. Now his eyes were accustomed to the gloom, Amerotke could see the walls were decorated with scenes from the *Book of the Dead*, depicting the Amduat, the Underworld through which each soul must pass and answer the questions posed by the forty-two assessor deities. Each soul would have to confess if he had not lied, killed, robbed or been involved in sexual deviancy.

'You recognise your Goddess?' Chula asked pointing to one scene where the deceased's heart was placed on one scale, the feather of truth on the other. The artist had caught the look of terrified anticipation of the man being judged. If he was found righteous he would be allowed to continue onwards into the Field of Dreams and the welcoming warmth of Osiris. If not, his heart would be tossed to the Monster Goddess, Awewet, part-lion, crocodile and hippopotamus. She would devour the heart and so send the soul to oblivion, the second eternal death.

'It has a certain atmosphere,' Amerotke agreed. He stretched out his hand and Chula clasped it. 'This place always terrifies me!'

Hearing a movement Amerotke whirled round. 'My Lord Senenmut!'

Hatusu's First Minister, Grand Vizier and lover stepped through the swirling smoke. He was dressed simply in a white linen gown. He must have been here for some time; his strong, blunt features were laced with sweat. He had also taken off his rings and bracelets and placed them in a small bag which swung from the sash round his middle. Amerotke bowed as Senenmut patted him on the shoulder.

'I expected you sooner, but I know . . .' He smiled bleakly. 'The case of the Lady Neshratta. All of Thebes is watching it. Come! I want to show you something.'

Escorted by Chula they made their way across this cavernous chamber of death. Shufoy racked his brains: he now recalled how this was the place where the corpses of possible murder victims were brought, not just for mummification but a scholarly diagnosis of how their death had been caused. Shufoy had often visited the shops of embalmers and coffin-makers in the Necropolis but this place curdled his stomach. Here and there a sheet slipped, displaying a man, head to one side, his throat slashed from ear to ear. Another had the upper part of his body crushed as if by the wheels of some great cart or chariot; a young woman, whose face was simply a mass of bloody pulp; a negro, both arms sliced off above the elbow, his eyes staring sightlessly. All around clustered physicians, embalmers, scribes, the priests of this place. Each corpse was examined, a faithful record kept before the embalmers moved in with their sharp-pointed instruments to prepare both body and soul for the final journey. Most of these would be buried in the place especially set aside for paupers or the unknown. At one moment Shufoy became so distracted he lost his way. A gust of steam billowed and he had to shout for his master, who came striding back and caught him by the hand.

Chula and Senenmut were waiting in a far corner near three of the mortuary slabs, each covered by a sheet bearing hieroglyphics. Senenmut snapped his fingers. Chula pulled back the sheet covering the nearest corpse. Amerotke instinctively covered his mouth.

'This is Ipumer,' Chula declared.

Despite the work of the embalmers and the physicians, the scribe's body had begun to rot, not due simply to the passage of time but the hideous venom he must have consumed.

'The poison continued its work amongst the vital organs, even after death!' Chula exclaimed. 'The end of the blood flow only heightened the noxious effect.'

Amerotke gazed at Ipumer's bloated face: the dark-green tinge to his pallor, one eye opened. The skin of his torso was marred by the deep red slash which had opened him from neck to crotch so the organs could be removed and placed in Canopic jars.

'Can poison have such an effect?' Shufoy asked, swallowing hard.

'Oh yes. Each poison is unique,' Chula explained. 'This venom rots the corpse. Others, ground from minerals, preserve it. Ipumer was definitely poisoned. No one can deny that.'

The second corpse was just as hideous. General Balet's body sprawled on the slabs. Again the embalmers had done their best. The sightless eye sockets were now bound by a white cloth, and a tight-fitting leather cap hid most of the damage to the left side of his skull.

'I've seen enough,' Amerotke declared. 'How did it happen?'

'Balet was one of the Panthers of the South,' Senenmut explained. 'They have their own private chantry chapel in this temple dedicated to their splendid achievements. You and I, Amerotke, when we were boys, marvelled at such heroism.'

The judge nodded.

'Now, the day he was murdered,' the Grand Vizier continued, 'was one of those cursed by Seth, regarded as unlucky. Naturally,' he continued drily, 'few pilgrims came to the temple. Balet decided to visit the Red Chapel, as it is called, ostensibly to pray, more to reflect on his companions' great exploits. It was a common enough purpose.'

'Did he have enemies in Thebes?' Amerotke asked.

'No, Balet was a widower with two children fully grown. He was wealthy, though a man who continually lived in the past. Taciturn, he kept to himself. According to Shishnak and his wife, Neferta, Balet was alone in the chapel; no one else was around. When they came back, about the hour of sacrifice, they found the door slightly ajar and went inside. I'll show you the place myself. The chapel was like a battlefield. Balet's corpse lay sprawled in a pool of blood, a terrible blow to his head.' He pointed to the cuts and bruises now filled with wax and covered by paste. 'Balet didn't give up his life lightly. He defended himself.' He grasped the dead man's wrist and held it up.

Amerotke could see the cuts on the palms of the hand where Balet had tried to grasp the assailant's blade.

'Was anything stolen?'

'No. Shishnak the priest thought the famous Scorpion Cups, part of the legend, may have gone but all three were still there. Each contained some of Balet's blood, as if the assassin was making an offering to red-haired Seth.'

'A ritual murder?' Amerotke murmured.

Amerotke glimpsed a painting on the near wall from the *Book of the Day and Night*: the Devourers of the Under-world spewing flames into the graves of sinners whilst Horus, leaning on his staff, supervised them. Beneath ran the title 'HE WHO BURNS MILLIONS!'

'What are you thinking, my Lord Amerotke?'

'Ritual murder is as common as thievery in Thebes,' the judge observed. 'I am sure, my Lord Senenmut, that the Keeper of the Dead would agree with me.'

'True,' Chula declared. 'Some murders are acts of passion: a fight in a beer shop or a husband who discovers his wife has been unfaithful.' His narrow face broke into a smile. 'Or vice versa. Yet, it is common enough to have corpses brought here, emblazoned with strange signs: certain parts of their bodies cut off or a curse, scrawled on a piece of papyrus, forced between the dead person's lips.'

'And the removal of the eyes?' Senenmut asked.

'That is rare,' Chula declared. He saw the puzzlement in Amerotke's face. 'I could take off the bandage around Balet's eyes?'

The judge shook his head.

'Well,' Chula continued as if they were discussing how

to prepare a meal, 'the removal of the dead person's eyes is very difficult. You have to cut precisely. This is what happened to Balet. Whoever removed those eyes knew something of medicine. What is strange,' he added, 'is that during the Season of the Hyaena, the Blast of God, when the Hyksos ruled Egypt from their city of Avaris, they often practised human sacrifice on prisoners of war or slaves.'

'And they always removed the eyes?'

'Yes,' Chula confirmed. 'They believed that when the victim's Ka left his body, it would also be sightless and find it nigh impossible to travel through the Underworld.'

'But the Hyksos have been out of Egypt for more than thirty years.'

'Some still survive,' Senenmut replied.

'Yes, but in General Balet's case,' Amerotke insisted, 'it is a chilling coincidence. Here is a soldier whose exploits led to the downfall of the Hyksos. If I remember my history correctly, he and other of Pharaoh's officers invaded the Hyksos camp and killed their great sorceress, Meretseger.'

'Is this some form of revenge?' Chula asked.

'It's possible.'

Senenmut had now moved to the third corpse and pulled back the sheet. Shufoy groaned and turned away. Amerotke felt his own stomach pitch. The corpse of the young woman who sprawled there had not yet been tended by the embalmers; it was still covered in the green slime of the River Nile. The terrible wounds, the raw exposed flesh, showed her body had been attacked by crocodiles.

'Found amongst the reeds,' Chula explained. 'When

crocodiles find a corpse, their frenzy always draws the attention of fishermen. This is what happened here.'

The woman was lying with her back towards them. Amerotke peered over, took one glimpse and quietly prayed. Most of the young woman's face was missing, nothing more than a congealed bloody mess. Death always surprised him with its subtle cruelties. A little chain of bells still hung round the young woman's throat and, from her henna-painted nails, he could tell she must have been a temple heset, a dancer or a singer. Such girls often hired themselves out to customers, bestowing their favours for quite a considerable sum. Then Amerotke noticed the thin red twine which bound the wrists, the same on the ankles, though this had been cut.

'I've examined the corpse carefully,' Chula replied. 'My Lord Amerotke, this was a hideous murder. The young woman was still alive when her hands and feet were bound. Her eyes also were removed and she was thrown conscious or semiconscious into the river. She was found in a papyrus thicket where she probably died. She may have lain two or three hours there before the crocodiles found her. As you know, they are sluggish at night but as the sun's heat increases . . .'

Amerotke understood. In some parts of Egypt crocodiles were sacred animals. However, he found it difficult to believe in such gods, and he suspected Lord Senenmut felt the same. Ma'at, the symbol of her father's truth, was divine, yes, but not those treacherous, long-snouted dragons of the river, with their gaping jaws and razor-sharp teeth. Amerotke had crossed the Nile hundreds of times in his life, and never once had he lost his fear of them. Indeed, only two seasons ago, he and Shufoy had been in a boat which, due to the work of a secret assassin, had dripped blood and provoked the crocodiles to a frenzied attack. Memories of the incident still evoked sweat-soaked nightmares.

'I forgot to tell you,' Senenmut declared, 'Balet's hands and ankles were also bound with a piece of red cord. He was probably killed, his wrists and ankles tied and then his eyes removed.'

'So, it's the same killer?' Amerotke demanded.

'Possibly.'

'I can understand,' Amerotke gestured at the still uncovered corpse, 'General Balet being killed for some grudge or grievance, a bitter memory of the Hyksos war – even that is fanciful enough. But why a young woman? A dancing girl?'

'The Hyksos made such sacrifices.'

'I don't know.' Amerotke shook his head. 'Balet, I suspect, was killed for a reason, a deep resentment, grudge or grievance. His death was made to look like the work of a Hyksos warrior who probably doesn't exist. But this young dancing girl . . . ? Which temple was she from?'

'Anubis,' Senenmut explained. 'She was a handmaid, a dancer, a member of the temple choir, reportedly quite beautiful, with a number of admirers, though rather secretive. The evening before her murder, she disappeared from the temple precincts.'

Amerotke shivered. He was tired of this chamber so full of death. He felt as if the sad ghosts of the corpses, sprawled beneath their sheets, pressed all around. On the far side of the room a priest softly chanted the hymn of the dead; another, close by, prayed loudly as he reached the part of the embalming process known as 'The Opening of the Mouth'. The steam swirled backwards and forwards. The paintings on the wall caught the glow of torches and these dreadful scenes took on a life of their own.

'My Lord Senenmut, I have seen enough!'

They thanked Chula. The Grand Vizier led them out of the Hall of Death, up the flights of stairs. Amerotke was relieved: this part of the temple was gloomy enough but, at least, he was free of the billowing steam, the strange stench and those grisly corpses with their mysterious attendants. Senenmut had brought a robe with him, the type used by a desert wanderer. He put this on and brought the hood up so it covered his head and shadowed his face.

'I am here on Pharaoh's orders,' he remarked quietly. 'I do not want to be mobbed by petitioners.'

They walked back to the Hall of Columns. They crossed this and went down sun-filled passageways. Here the windows were broader and placed so as to catch the sun, which poured through in glorious shafts. The temple was busy: scribes and priests quietly padding through; traders bringing in produce; the occasional pilgrim petitioner who had become lost and stopped, staring about, round-eyed.

Amerotke had little to do with the cult of Seth. Nevertheless, he marvelled at the cunning of its priests. The front of the temple was no different from any other but, like the Underworld, the deeper you travelled, the darker and more sombre the temple became, manifesting the true nature of this killer God. Shufoy was remarkably silent. Amerotke thought he must feel ill or uneasy after their visit. He was surprised because Shufoy's nerve was usually untouched by such scenes. He glanced down: the little man's face was screwed up in concentration.

'What's the matter?' Amerotke asked.

'Nothing, Master, just an idea.'

Amerotke groaned quietly.

At last they reached the Red Chapel, cleverly built on to the side of the temple. The outside hall had large square windows which made the passageway below sun-filled, and the red rock, specially imported, glowed as if it contained some secret fire. The chapel wall on the other side of the passageway was of the same sheer, red stone, specially polished. It depicted, in black and green, the glorious exploits of the Seth regiment.

A priest squatted, dozing, his back against the chapel door. He jumped to his feet as Senenmut approached.

'This is Shishnak,' Senenmut explained. 'My Lord Amerotke, Chief Judge in the Hall of Two Truths.'

The priest bowed, sly eyes watchful, lips twisted into an ingratiating smile.

'My lords, the chapel has been cleaned and purified.'

He opened the door and they walked in.

'The pride and joy of the Seth regiment,' Senenmut explained.

Amerotke could see why. The walls, floor and ceiling were of that same red glowing stone, the favourite colour of Seth. He glimpsed the Scorpion Cups and gold tray on a specially built ledge. Paintings and stelae covered the wall, otherwise there was very little difference to his own chamber in the Temple of Ma'at: the naos, its doors now closed; baskets of flowers; tasselled cushions; and glowing oil lamps, which gave the chapel its own special light.

Amerotke walked round the walls. He understood why an old warrior like Balet had returned here. The scenes and paintings graphically described the exploits of Hatusu's grandfather against the Hyksos, especially the triumph of the Seth regiment, herding prisoners before them, hands tied above their heads, to kneel in abasement before Pharaoh on his glorious throne. Finally, the many exploits of the Panthers of the South, including their invasion of the Hyksos camp, the grisly execution of Meretseger and their safe return to Pharaoh.

'Where was Balet's corpse found?' he asked.

Shishnak pointed to the far wall near the Scorpion Cups. Amerotke walked across and inspected these.

'May I?'

The priest nodded. Amerotke examined the tray. It was of sheer gold, as were the cups. Each bore a silver scorpion; there were now four.

'Balet's son returned his father's,' Shishnak explained. 'That is the ritual, Pharaoh's decree.'

Amerotke held the cup up. This chapel and its cups, were part of Egypt's history and folklore. Every young boy was taught about the glorious war against the Hyksos and the marvellous triumphs of these warriors. Years ago his own father had brought him here to pray. Amerotke felt a pang of sadness and put the cup down.

'General Balet was killed here. You found his corpse. Describe the scene,' he demanded of Shishnak.

'About the hour of sacrifice,' the priest replied, 'I wondered if General Balet needed more wine or food. I had offered it before but he was taciturn, rather moody.

'Was he usually?'

'Oh yes. He often came to pray by himself. The rest, including General Karnac – well, they always drank well and deeply. Balet was ever the silent, lonely one.'

'You'd met him earlier in the day?'

'Yes, both my wife and I came in here. We could see he did not want to be disturbed, so we left.'

'And he didn't seem different?'

'No. An old soldier glorying in the past.' The priest shrugged. 'Nothing unusual.'

'And did you return?'

'My wife and I, we have a small chamber at the end of the corridor. We stayed there. However, before you ask, my Lord Amerotke, we saw or heard nothing untoward. When we came back the door was slightly open. The scene inside was hideous. Cushions, pots, even the oil lamps had been smashed. General Balet lay in a pool of blood. I could see he was dead, killed by a blow to the head. I ran across and turned his corpse over. My wife began screaming . . . those awful black holes.' Shishnak put a hand to his face. 'I thought I was having a nightmare, being visited by the Devourers. Theft, I thought, but the tray of Scorpion Cups was safe, though splattered with blood.'

'This is a mystery,' Amerotke declared. 'General Balet was not in his prime but still a vigorous man, a warrior heavily decorated by Pharaoh for killing his enemies in hand-to-hand combat. Yet he is slain, his hands and feet bound.'

'Oh yes!'

'And his eyes gouged out. The chapel here is in disarray but no one heard a cry, any sound?'

The priest gazed fearfully back.

'My lord, I agree, it is suspicious but I will take any oath my wife and I had nothing to do with this blasphemy. We saw or heard nothing.'

'You may leave.' Senenmut, who had been listening whilst gazing at one of the wall paintings, now joined them. He patted Shishnak on the shoulder. 'You and your wife have nothing to fear. Close the door and guard it.'

The priest scuttled off. Senenmut pulled back the cowl of his cloak and squatted down on the floor, his back to the wall. Amerotke knelt on one of the cushions. Shufoy, his fingers positively itching, went across to peer at the precious cups.

'Hatusu is concerned,' Senenmut declared. 'The Seth regiment was held in high regard by her grandfather, father, half-brother and now herself. The Panthers of the South are cherished heroes. She does not like what happened here.'

He paused and stared at Amerotke. The judge knew what Senenmut was implying: Hatusu had not yet been two years in power. Due to her great victories against the Mitanni, she owed most of the success for her ruthless seizure of power to the loyalty of Egypt's crack regiments, particularly that of Seth.

'Ahmose drove out the Hyksos,' Senenmut continued, 'and driven out they remain. This murder – or should I say bloody sacrifice – of one of our heroes seems to imply that the Hyksos have returned.'

'Fanciful nonsense!' Amerotke retorted.

'No, it isn't.' Senenmut got to his feet. 'Anyway, the day grows on and Pharaoh Hatusu awaits us.'

Amerotke also rose.

'What does she suspect?'

'She regards this murder as only the beginning,' Senenmut declared. 'Others amongst Egypt's heroes might be marked down for death.'

SETH: God of the Deserts, the Red
God, associated with every frightening
phenomenon.

this. The hieroglyphics underneath declared: 'HATUSU, BELOVED OF RA, SHATTERS THE ENEMIES WITH THE POWER OF HER ARM.' Hatusu was depicted as helmeted and armoured, one hand grasping the reins of her furiously charging chariot, the other holding a spear, about to transfix a Mitanni chieftain. All around her thronged generals and soldiers though, of course, not as large or as impressive as their Pharaoh-Queen.

Amerotke looked down the table. Hatusu had convened this meeting. She sat in a throne-like chair at the end of the table. She wore an elaborate wig drenched in oiled perfume, and a flowing robe of fine snow-white linen edged with scarlet ribbon. On her head sat an ornamental crown consisting of a disc, two horns, plumes and writhing serpents, all wrought in silver and gold. A necklace of cornelian encircled her beautiful throat, whilst her face was elaborately painted. On her left sat her chief scribe; on her right Senenmut, who, since his return from the Temple of Seth, had changed and now wore round his throat, wrists and fingers the gorgeous insignia of office.

Hatusu caught Amerotke's gaze. She smiled almost imperceptibly and winked. Her cup-bearer approached. He tasted the wine and handed it to her. Hatusu sipped. She reminded Amerotke of a beautiful cat lapping milk, her eyes watching the powerful men she had summoned here. Amerotke sat fascinated. Hatusu was not yet twenty years of age but she could act and take on a bewildering array of roles. Amerotke had seen her swim naked in the pool at the other end of the room. He had met her in the gardens outside with her robe tucked up, a straw hat on her head, busy with a small trowel amongst the garden beds. He had seen her in armour driving a chariot, cursing and shouting to the great admiration of her household troops. She was born to act, Amerotke concluded. Tonight, with these heroes of Thebes, she'd to play the caring yet mysterious queen.

Amerotke had returned to the Temple of Ma'at, washed, ate and changed. Accompanied by Shufoy, he'd walked to the royal palace. Shufoy was now waiting in the ante-chamber. Amerotke closed his eyes and prayed his little manservant would not get up to any mischief. Senenmut coughed.

'The Divine One will speak!'

The murmured conversation amongst Amerotke's companions immediately ceased. Amerotke stared round. The Panthers of the South looked like brothers: tough, thickset men, heads completely shaven, faces carefully oiled, eyes ringed with black kohl. Some of them sported bracelets, gorgets and necklaces. They smelt sweetly of perfume. Yet these were not soft-skinned courtiers. Their harsh faces, sinewy arms and wrists, a tendency not to keep still and a bluntness of speech marked them as veteran soldiers. They were not overawed by Hatusu, as were men who constantly lived in Pharaoh's shadow and enjoyed her smile and favour.

Karnac, their commander, sat nearest to Hatusu. He had the face of a hawk, jutting nose above thin lips, eyes narrowed as if forced that way by the years of campaigning out in the Red Lands. Like the rest, he wore a ring emblazoned with the insignia of the Seth regiment: a personal gift from Hatusu's father. Next to him sat Peshedu. He had seemed embarrassed when he'd first met Amerotke. A short, rather plump man, Peshedu looked as if he had lived well over the years. His three companions, Heti, Thuro and Ruah, were tough-looking individuals. Since Amerotke had entered the room they'd hardly deigned to glanced at him.

The man sitting next to Amerotke was different. He had risen to greet the Chief Judge. This was Nebamum, Karnac's manservant. He was dressed in a samite robe, a lustrous pearl on a silver chain round his neck. He had smiling eyes, a rather effeminate face, and moved rather clumsily. Amerotke, who had briefed himself on the history of the regiment, realised this was due to an inflammation of the wound Nebamum had suffered when these Panthers had attacked Meretseger.

Hatusu cleared her throat noisily. She was about to speak.

'I have invited you here,' she began, her voice soft but carrying, 'because of General Balet's hideous murder at the Red Chapel in the Temple of Seth. My Lord Amerotke has been summoned because he will investigate his death. I believe,' she added with a wry smile, 'that General Peshedu has already made his acquaintance.'

Hatusu moved the papyrus sheet before her and turned slightly to address Peshedu, a gesture of courtesy. Hatusu always talked as if, at the other end of the table, some God, invisible to the rest, sat and watched her.

'I am sorry about your daughter,' she declared. 'I say

this now. Justice must have its way. Lord Amerotke's reputation for fairness is well known.'

Peshedu opened his mouth to reply. Hatusu raised her hands, fingers splayed.

'If mercy is to be shown,' she added, almost in a whisper, 'then let us at least wait until mercy is needed.'

Peshedu nodded and bowed in agreement.

'General Balet's murder,' Hatusu's voice grew stronger, 'has shocked all Thebes, and, despite our strictures, rumour and gossip abound.' She stared at Amerotke, inviting questions.

'What is this rumour and gossip, my lady?'

The question was a ritual one. Hatusu disliked giving speeches: she presented herself as Commander-in-Chief, prepared to debate and discuss matters. She had been carefully groomed in this ploy by Senenmut, who had advised her on how to treat these great war heroes of Thebes.

'My lady, if I can answer that . . . ?' Karnac broke in.

Hatusu agreed. The general turned in his leather-backed chair.

'I am not here to boast,' Karnac began. 'You know, my Lord Amerotke, the details of our attack on the Hyksos camp. We seized the sorceress Meretseger in her pavilion and took her head. No one knows the witch's true name. Meretseger was not a Hyksos but an Egyptian turncoat favoured by the invaders. I will never forget that night. The sorceress expected her death and screamed obscenities and threats. Her last words were that each of us would die violently.' He paused. 'A few days later the Hyksos army was utterly annihilated. Many captives were taken, including Meretseger's bodyguards. Under question they confessed that Meretseger had expected her death; she'd actually prophesied it and warned the Hyksos prince. She informed these bodyguards that her death would mean the defeat of the Hyksos but that her killers' final years would be shadowed by the "Devourers of the Underworld".' Karnac's severe face broke into a smile. 'We did not care about that. We were the young braves of the Pharaoh, his warriors, Panthers of the South, the Slayers of Seth. The years passed. Pharaoh continued to smile on us. Three of our companions died, now General Balet. According to Pharaoh's decree, their Scorpion Cups have been handed back to be placed on the golden tray in the Red Chapel.'

'Tell me,' Amerotke broke in, 'is Balet the first murder victim?'

Karnac clasped his hands. 'The other three,' he told the judge, 'died of infection. Sickness of the head, heart or stomach.'

'Are you saying they were poisoned?'

'It's possible,' Karnac replied, 'though no foul play was suspected or traced. They have gone to the Far Horizon; their remains lie in our tomb at the Necropolis. We have one tomb for all of us,' Karnac explained. 'United in life, united in death – it was all our wish.'

'But there's no proof that they were murdered?' Amerotke insisted. 'There was no violence, no removal of the eyes?'

Karnac agreed.

'How do we know,' Amerotke asked, 'that this attack was not just a private grudge against General Balet?'

'First,' Karnac replied, 'Balet had no enemies. In the weeks preceding his death he reported nothing untoward, no threats, no animosity. Secondly, if someone wanted to kill Balet, why do it in the Red Chapel? Why remove his eyes? Sprinkle the cups with his blood? Thirdly . . .' Karnac opened the small leather pouch on the table before him. He took out what looked like a coin and threw it down the table.

Amerotke caught it: a silver disc about an inch across, on one side a scorpion very similar to those he'd glimpsed on the sacred cups. He turned it over. The reverse bore a strange hieroglyphic. He weighed the disc in his hand.

'This is not a coin. I don't recognise the sign.'

'It's Hyksos,' Nebamum explained. 'In the past month – I believe it was about the second day, yes, Master? – we each received one.'

Amerotke examined the disc again.

'They are not Hyksos coins,' Senenmut explained, 'but medallions – charms given by Meretseger to her body-guard. They were found in the Hyksos camp after the battle, but then disappeared.'

'We always believed,' Karnac added, 'that the Divine One's grandfather took them as part of the plunder and had them melted down. As my servant said, no trace of them remained in Egypt, until the beginning of this month, when all of us, including Nebamum, received one.'

'And you view this as a threat?'

'Of course we do!' Karnac replied. 'We often met in each

other's houses or at the Red Chapel. At first we thought it was a joke, an idea by one of our group to surprise us. Only when Balet was murdered did we realise their deadly significance.'

'Have there been other attacks?' Amerotke asked.

'Yes.' Nebamum spoke up. 'Three days ago. My master sent me out to order wine at the quayside. It was well past the hour of sacrifice. Darkness was falling. I came back down an alleyway. I wanted to be on the highway out of Thebes before the conch horn blew. A shadowy figure stepped out of the doorway, a war club in one hand, a knife in the other. It was dark, but he seemed like a priest from the Temple of Seth, wearing what I thought was a red wig. He came at me so suddenly I dropped my staff and slipped. The club whistled through the air above me. I scrambled away. The figure turned. He had lost his balance, then made as if to come back. I screamed for help.' Nebamum smiled self-consciously. 'I didn't act the great war hero! A door opened. A woman came out, followed by her husband and children. My assailant fled. They helped me to my feet. The man then offered to walk back with me.'

'Nebamum arrived back in a poor state,' Karnac intervened. 'I rewarded the man who had protected him.'

Karnac's smile widened. Amerotke could see the same relationship existed between master and servant as did between himself and Shufoy.

'So,' the judge summarised, 'each of you, including Balet, received a silver disc.' He tossed it back down the table. 'And you thought nothing of it until Nebamum was attacked and Balet murdered? It would seem,' he chose his words carefully, 'that an old grudge or grievance, like a war wound, has been opened. Someone has come to Thebes to settle accounts.'

Hatusu shook her head as if she didn't understand.

'We have a number of possibilities,' Amerotke continued. 'First, Meretseger was a powerful sorceress. She had her own retinue, perhaps even a cult. For all we know she may even have had her own children. My Lord Karnac, was Meretseger an old woman?'

'I inspected both her head and corpse after the Hyksos defeat. She looked older than she was. In the pavilion that night I thought her hair was grey but this was due to ash from the sacrificial fire. I would say she was . . .' he narrowed his eyes, '. . . no older than her thirtieth summer.'

'When Avaris, the Hyksos capital, was taken,' Amerotke asked, 'were her family and household arrested? Our assailant could be waging a blood feud.'

'We couldn't find anyone,' Karnac replied. 'I recall the Divine One's grandfather demanded a special search. By then, the Hyksos, as well as those who collaborated with them, had either fled or were in hiding.'

'You mentioned other possibilities?' Hatusu enquired.

'Yes, my lady. The second is that someone in Thebes has a grudge, based on envy or jealousy, against these heroes. For reasons best known to himself or herself, the murderer has decided to settle matters, though why now, and for what particular reason, I can't say.'

'And the third possibility?' Hatusu smiled. 'There is another, isn't there?'

Amerotke lowered his eyes and played with the ring

on his finger. The Divine One was always flattering. He glanced up. Hatusu's face remained impassive; she fluttered her eyelids, a girlish gesture.

'Speak, my lord!'

'The assassin could be a member of this group.'

Amerotke sat silently as Karnac and the others loudly protested. They banged the table and stared in disbelief.

'We are a band of brothers!' Peshedu shouted. 'The Gods know that I, for one, have enough problems in my life. Why should anyone here have a grudge against another? If I follow your reasoning, my lord, this assassin means to kill each and every one of us.'

'It may be one of you,' Amerotke replied, 'or someone associated with you.'

'Give your reasons,' Senenmut demanded.

'I have no evidence,' Amerotke declared. 'But listen carefully.' He used his fingers to emphasise the points. 'First, how many people know about Meretseger's curses against you? Secondly, how many people know what her bodyguard confessed? Thirdly –' he gestured at Heti, who had raised his hand to protest – 'thirdly, these medallions. It must be someone who was present at Pharaoh's great victory and seized some of them for his own use. Fourthly, whoever it is is strong, a warrior. Nebamum, despite his fall and his wound, is a veteran, as was General Balet: neither would meekly give up his life. Finally, we come to the general's murder. This is no footpad, an arrow loosed through the dark, but an assassin who could easily get into the Temple of Seth and steal into that chapel. Moreover, how many people knew Balet was going there to worship?'

'But he often did,' Heti declared. 'Balet was well known for his lonely ways. He was a constant visitor. Perhaps the assassin just waited and watched. And as for your other points, my lord, the stories about Meretseger's curses and the confessions of the bodyguard are well known throughout Thebes.'

The other soldiers now joined in, arguing heatedly with Amerotke until the judge, at least openly, confessed he might be wrong.

'It was just a possibility,' he explained, 'but I urge each of you to be careful. If those medallions are a token of death, the assassin will strike again.'

'He must be stopped! He must be caught!' Hatusu declared flatly. She extended her hands as if she wished to embrace these grizzled war veterans. 'Their regiment, the army demands justice and retribution. General Balet's killer—' Hatusu stopped, her eyes blazing with anger. 'I have sworn an oath: I will see him crucified on the walls of Thebes or buried alive in the desert!' She drew in her breath. 'I must be blunt, my Lord Amerotke. I am not only concerned about the lives of these soldiers, precious as they are. I began our discussion by referring to gossip and rumour. Those empty heads who like to wag their tongues and fan the flames of superstition are now saying Seth is angry with Thebes and has stolen in to wreak vengeance.' She waved her hand languidly. 'I am not here to repeat tittle-tattle but, Lord Amerotke, you have the gist of what I say.'

The Pharaoh-Queen glared down the table. Amerotke did: the temple priests, particularly, were not as fulsome in their support of their young Pharaoh-Queen as they should be. Such dabblers liked nothing better than to stir the dirty pool of politics, looking for signs and auguries as to who was not blessed by the Gods. The hideous sacrilege committed in the Temple of Seth, with its echoes of Hyksos cruelty and vengeance, would soon catch the public imagination.

'Meretseger is dead,' Amerotke replied evenly. 'General Karnac took her head. Where does she lie buried?'

'Out beyond the Oasis of Ashiwa,' Karnac replied. 'It's about—'

Amerotke nodded. 'I know where it is, my lord. Ten miles to the north-east of Thebes, out in the Red Lands, near the very place where the Hyksos were defeated.'

'After the battle,' Karnac explained, 'the Divine One's grandfather had Meretseger's corpse and severed head cursed by the priests and buried secretly. Tomorrow morning at dawn all of us, escorted by a chariot squadron, intend to go out there.'

'Why?' Amerotke demanded.

'Something else her bodyguard confessed.' Karnac smiled grimly. 'Meretseger vowed vengeance on her killers. She declared that even if she had to come back from the Underworld to achieve it, she would.'

'Superstitious nonsense!' Amerotke snapped.

'Perhaps, my lord,' Hatusu answered silkily. 'But General Karnac will go and you shall accompany him!'

Shufoy could tell his master was in a terrible rage by the way the judge walked slightly ahead of him, the set of his shoulders and the grim expression on his face. Shufoy was certain he had heard his master utter the words 'Minx, cunning as a vixen'. Something disturbing had happened at that meeting of the Royal Circle. Amerotke had come storming through the antechamber. Senenmut, striding behind, had pulled a face and shrugged in Shufoy's direction. The judge had said nothing but beckoned at Shufoy to follow and was now making his way across the moon-washed palace gardens.

Braziers, fanned by servants, blazed against the cold night air. Tar and pitch torches flared at the ends of poles thrust into the ground, making the shadows of statues, carvings and fountains dance and flutter. Shufoy didn't know where they were going. He knew they were still in the imperial gardens, with its shimmering fishponds, decorated kiosks and pavilions. Fruit trees, date, palm and sycamore trees shaded the water. In the papyrus thickets, the ducks quacked and fought. Birds, dark patches against the night sky, fluttered over the vines to nest in the trees or perch on the statues and gold-topped arbours built in every grove.

Servants passed them carrying baskets or water jars on their shoulders. Soldiers, Hatusu's crack bodyguard, stood armed and silent, holding spear and javelin under trees and in porchways. A trail of lights at the far end indicated the captain of the guard was carrying out his night patrol. Shufoy started as a pet monkey came scuttling by, the collar round its neck jingling, chased by a greyhound pup which, in turn, was pursued by one of the palace pages.

'Where are we going?'

Shufoy ran up and slipped his hand through his master's, using the other to grasp the parasol. He noticed Amerotke had taken his fan out of the small wallet on his girdle and was briskly using it, as if unaware of the evening coolness.

'You are hot and flustered,' Shufoy observed.

He was surprised at his master's reaction. Amerotke was usually so taciturn and calm. The judge stopped and smiled down at Shufoy.

'I am sorry.'

He led Shufoy over to a stone garden bench. They both sat down. Amerotke stretched out his legs and looked up at the stars.

'Tomorrow morning at dawn, Shufoy, we are for the Red Lands: the Oasis of Ashiwa.'

Shufoy closed his eyes and his mutilated face broke into a grimace. Amerotke was a skilled charioteer, a soldier who had fought in the war squadrons. Such a journey would be tedious enough but Ashiwa held harsh memories for Amerotke. Many years earlier – and Shufoy had only pieced together the details – when Amerotke was a boy, his elder brother had been ambushed and killed by Sand Wanderers on what was supposed to be a routine night patrol by young officers. In his cups once, on the day he honoured his brother's memory, Amerotke had confided how the news had reached Thebes. His parents had been almost hysterical when the battered corpse of their son was brought home.

'I am sorry, Master.' Shufoy patted Amerotke on the leg. 'But we will go and then we will be gone.'

'Oh, it's not just that.' Amerotke ran his finger up and down his cheek. 'Hatusu, she can be so imperious.' He snapped his fingers as if imitating her. '"Go here! Go there!" I have pressing business in Thebes!'

'The Lady Neshratta?' Shufoy queried.

'Yes, the Lady Neshratta and that's why we are here!'

Amerotke got to his feet. He put his fan away and walked on more calmly. On one occasion he stopped and savoured the lovely fragrance from the orchard of pomegranate trees. They continued down some steps and across a lawn where chained gazelle and ibex quietly grazed.

Master and servant entered a courtyard, fronted by a three-storeyed, black-roofed building, and crossed to an open door. The guard at the entrance stopped, questioned and let them through. They paused in the spacious hallway, its decorated roof supported by columns of cedar wood, decorated at top and bottom with opening lotus flowers. Scribes and priests milled about, some carrying manuscripts, others writing-trays or satchels. A porter came up and asked their business. Once Amerotke announced himself, he bowed and led them deeper along the passageway.

Shufoy recognised the mansion of the Eyes and Ears of Pharaoh, the Lord Prosecutor Valu, who not only regulated police matters but also controlled a network of informants and spies in Thebes and beyond. Valu's office was stark in its simplicity: white-washed walls with no decoration. Against these stood cupboards, chests and coffers. Valu sat cross-legged on cushions on a raised dais, a sheet of vellum across his knees. He was dictating to a scribe sitting likewise just below the dais. The shutters on the window had been opened. The room was rather cold but well lit by oil lamps placed on wooden stands. The porter announced Amerotke. Valu looked up, dismissing the scribe with a flick of his fingers.

'My Lord Amerotke, you are most welcome.'

He gestured at a far table where a jug of wine was cooling. Amerotke shook his head.

'My Lord, this is not a social visit.'

Valu sighed and got to his feet. 'I thought it wasn't. You are fortunate to catch me here. My physician tells me the poor light will destroy my eyes. I usually work in the gardens.' Valu smiled, though his eyes remained watchful. 'I find the scent of flowers soothing when the brain teems and turns.'

'Ipumer,' Amerotke demanded, 'when he died, you confiscated all his possessions?'

'Yes, they are now under my seal in the storeroom. Do you wish to inspect them?'

'You know I have every right,' Amerotke replied.

'What are you looking for?'

Amerotke paused. Somewhere on the floor above, a singer strummed at his lyre and sang a lilting, soothing love ballad.

'My idea,' Valu explained. 'After a hard day, my Lord Amerotke, to lie on cushions, to eat and drink whilst the mind and soul are given up to divine music, eh? But my question . . . ?'

'I'll tell you when I find it,' Amerotke retorted.

Valu pulled a face, went to the doorway, called back the scribe and muttered instructions. He mockingly gestured to Amerotke to follow his messenger.

'You'll find all there is.'

Amerotke thanked him coldly and followed the scribe out and down some steps into what looked like a small cellar. Torches and oil lamps were lit and, picking up a knife for cutting papyrus, the scribe went across to one of the great baskets, slit the seal and threw back the lid.

'The possessions of Ipumer,' he declared, 'scribe in the House of War. My lord, I shall wait for you outside.'

Amerotke, helped by Shufoy, emptied the possessions out. They amounted to very little: a purse, wallet, belt, rings, a brocaded sash, items of clothing. A writing-satchel containing styli, ink pots, a roll of blank papyrus, bracelets and other jewellery. Amerotke sifted through these.

'Here is a scribe,' the judge declared, 'with a very good job, who holds high office. You'd expect more.'

A silver disc caught his eye and he picked it up.

'By Ma'at's life!' he exclaimed, and handed it to Shufoy. 'It's a silver medallion of Hyksos origin. One of these was sent to General Balet just before he died. So, why should Ipumer be carrying one?'

He described what had happened in Hatusu's council chamber.

Shufoy whistled softly. 'But this doesn't . . . ?'

'This doesn't what?' Amerotke demanded.

'This doesn't make sense, Master. Ipumer came from Avaris, once the Hyksos capital. He carried this medallion. If he was still alive, you could arrest Ipumer as a possible

111

assassin but, from what I learnt in court, Ipumer was more concerned about the beautiful daughter of Peshedu than he was about revenge. However, possession of this medallion forges a link between the dead man and, if I understand you correctly, the mysterious assassin who has sworn vengeance against the Panthers of the South.'

Amerotke agreed and kept on looking, but found nothing else suspicious. Ipumer emerged as almost a nobody, a man with no past, no real friends. He had made none of the wealthy purchases any scribe would make: statues, vases, even items of furniture. It was as if he had arrived in Thebes, taken lodgings with the widow Lamna and lived a hand-to-mouth existence whilst in hot pursuit of the Lady Neshratta.

There was a knock on the door. Valu stepped into the chamber.

'You've found something, haven't you?'

Amerotke explained about the medallion. Valu looked surprised.

'I wondered what was happening.' He smiled thinly. 'The Divine One sent me a message: I was not to investigate Balet's murder. Apparently she has reserved it for you.' He took the medallion from Amerotke's hand.

'What else do you know about Ipumer, my lord Prosecutor? You are the Eyes and Ears of Pharaoh.'

Valu went and sat on a stool on one side of the doorway. He hitched back his robe, scratched a knobbly knee and winced at a spasm in his stomach.

'I am beginning to wish,' he began slowly, 'I had not taken this case. I thought it was as clear as a piece of crystal. Ipumer was the besotted lover and Neshratta the conniving, treacherous woman who grew tired of him and decided to end his life.'

'And now?'

'And now, my lord judge, I am not too sure. Ipumer came from Avaris. He must have arrived with references, credentials, letters of recommendation. He must have been interviewed and his application to be a scribe approved. Yet, when I went to the House of War and asked the keeper . . .'

'Ipumer's records had disappeared?'

Valu nodded. 'I made careful search but the keeper of the records couldn't find them. Someone had deliberately removed them. The more the keeper of the records reflected, the more he believed it may have been Ipumer himself.' Valu paused. 'Nothing else. Despite his stomach ailments and love life, Ipumer proved to be the ideal scribe. He was rarely absent from his duties, late, drunk or insubordinate.'

'And, of course, he would be allowed to go where he wished?'

'Precisely.'

'So, he comes to Thebes,' Amerotke continued, 'only the Gods know for what reason. He is successful and takes up his post. Ipumer flatters and soothes his superiors on an evening, probably like this, when everyone is tired and distracted, he creeps into the Hall of Records and removes all trace of himself.'

'There was nothing,' Valu agreed. 'You know how the scribes are appointed, my lord? All the details about them are described on papyrus rolls which are stored, by the year, in large reed baskets. I have the same system, and you likewise. Unless something extraordinary happens, no one really cares. The details of a scribe in the House of War are not close to the heart of Pharaoh or the royal circle. They have no more significance than the dust motes dancing in the sunlight.'

'But, if he came from Avaris,' Amerotke declared, 'he must have brought letters of accreditation from a House of Life in a temple at Avaris.'

'I hear what you say.' Valu got to his feet and burped gently. 'However, my stomach is calling. I will send a messenger to Avaris. I am the Eyes and Ears of Pharaoh. If I cannot discover who this Ipumer is, then no one will!' He gestured at the dead man's possessions. 'My scribe will put these away. I bid you good night.'

A short while later Amerotke and Shufoy left the House of a Million Years and went down the great causeway. Here, mercenaries milled about, dressed in their distinctive armour: the Shaduana with their grotesque horn helmets; Dakkari in striped headdresses, rounded bronze shields slung over their backs; Kushites with long cloaks and embroidered belts, their dark skins covered with blue and red tattoos; Nubians, black as the night, in leopardskin kilts and feathered headdresses, their weapons piled beside them. These were Valu's guards, his escort and, if necessary, his police. They would answer only to him. If he wished to arrest someone, pluck them up in the dead of night, these mercenaries were skilled at doing it. They watched Amerotke pass. Shufoy put them at their ease by declaring in his booming voice who his master was.

The visitors went out through a gateway into the market-place. Some stalls were still open and the cookshops were doing a bustling trade, supplying food and drink to those who had worked all day. The night air carried the smell of fresh gazelle and ibex brought in that day by hunters, to be gutted, cleaned and laid out in strips over huge grills above glowing beds of charcoal. The smell had summoned the legion of beggars who plagued the city. They sat, bony fingers extended, begging for sustenance and alms. Nearby a group of drunken singers sang a hymn to Amun, 'He who listens'. A physician, a specialist, being a Guardian of the Anus, came running up, bawling that he had a sure cure for internal boils and haemorrhoids. Shufoy lifted his parasol threateningly and the man scuttled away.

Amerotke grasped Shufoy by the shoulder, forcing his way through the crowd and on to the broad basalt-paved avenue which wound down to the great city gates, its two scaring pillars dominated by watchtowers. A corps from the Ibis regiment stood on guard, their polished leather greaves and breastplates shimmering in the torchlight. From one of the towers a conch horn brayed, proclaiming how, within an hour, the city gates would be closed for the night.

Amerotke and Shufoy passed through on to a causeway fringed by trees, which ran alongside the city wall. To Amerotke's right the Nile coiled and glimmered like some huge snake, above which shone the lights of merchant boats, desperate to reach safe mooring. At night the Nile became a different place. In the papyrus groves, pirate skiffs lurked amongst the lush undergrowth, watching and waiting for the unwary.

Shufoy stopped to listen, not just to the harsh call of night birds but for other, deeper, more menacing sounds. There was nothing except the booming roar of the hippopotami and, now and again, the yip yip of scavenging jackals.

'What's the matter?'

Amerotke, lost in thought, realised he had left Shufoy behind, and came back.

Shufoy grasped his master's hand and stared up.

'I agree with the Lady Norfret. Master, we should have an escort for this road. What about Asural, the God of War, eh? He'd frighten a crocodile.'

'Are you nervous?' Amerotke asked.

Shufoy looked back the way he had come.

'I am always nervous, Master, whenever we walk here late at night.'

'There's nothing to worry about.'

Amerotke walked on. They entered the Village of the Unclean; its inhabitants were peasants who'd flocked to the city. They were too poor to buy stone so they dug mud from the banks of the Nile, dried it and built their own maze of mean, one-storeyed tenements. These housed not only workers from the quarries but fugitives from the law. Shufoy hated the place. Amerotke, however, always insisted on walking the same route and, by now, he was a common sight. People seated in doorways were busy with the cooking fires, the air pungent with the smell of salted fish, cheap beer and the harsh, tangy bread these people baked. Some looked up and called Amerotke's name, raising a hand in salutation. Amerotke cheerfully replied. Before he left, as always, he'd met a gaggle of naked, dirty children who followed him to receive their usual reward.

'Come tomorrow,' Amerotke smiled down at them, 'at the tenth hour to the side gate of my house. Food and fruit will be given you.'

Master and servant climbed the small hill which overlooked the Nile. Amerotke halted at the top to savour the cool, fresh night air. He stared back at the winking lights of the village. Time and again, at the meetings of the royal circle, Amerotke had insisted that something be done about the Village of the Unclean.

'It grows by the week,' he declared, 'the refuge for every malefactor and criminal in Thebes!'

It was one matter on which he and Lord Valu closely agreed. Amerotke stared down at the river. Criminals from the Village of the Unclean were often paraded through the Hall of Two Truths.

Yet, if the truth be known, individuals like Lady Neshratta and Ipumer caused Amerotke a deeper concern. Despite any feeling of compassion, he was determined on the truth. If Neshratta had killed Ipumer, poisoned him barbarously, then she would have to pay the full penalty. Thebes was becoming richer, more powerful; gold, silver and precious stones from the mines of Sinai poured like a river into the city. Hatusu's merchant ships sailed further and further afield. The Nubians, Libyans, Kushites, even the powerful Mitanni across Sinai, now paid lavish tribute. Such wealth brought its own demands. Crime was on the increase, not just amongst the thieves and vagabonds who flocked to the city but amongst the powerful and rich. Those professional killers, the dreaded Guild of Amemets, the Destroyers, had reappeared and, according to Amerotke's spies, were doing a flourishing trade.

Amerotke stared across the Nile towards the City of the Dead. If Lady Neshratta was guilty, an example must be set. Yet, was the case so simple? Peshedu was a very wealthy man: his daughter would have everything she asked. A man like Ipumer was beneath them and, if Neshratta wanted to murder him, why take the risk herself? And Peshedu? He must have known about the scandal the manner of Ipumer's death would cause. A simple walk along the quayside and Peshedu would find a host of killers who, for a piece of silver, would have cut Ipumer's throat. Why did Lady Neshratta take the risk herself? Undoubtedly Ipumer had been poisoned after his visit to the House of the Golden Gazelle. Someone there had met him. But who?

'And why take that risk?' Amerotke murmured.

'We are taking a risk,' Shufoy moaned. 'Master, I want to be home. My belly thinks my throat's cut.'

Amerotke glanced down.

'And I have a scheme.'

'Oh no,' Amerotke groaned. 'Go on, Shufoy. As we walk you can tell me.'

They continued on their way. Shufoy, chattering like a monkey, ignoring the growing disbelief of his master, as he explained how he would exploit the cult of Seth and make his fortune.

SETH: a War God, worshipped by the
Hyksos.

CHAPTER 4

Hepel, scribe in the House of War and self-confessed acquaintance of the dead Ipumer, struggled awake and stared in horror around him. He could not understand why his naked body was strapped out against the hard, gravelled ground his legs and arms lashed by wrist and ankle to pegs driven into the ground. Hepel tried to speak, even as he stared in terror at the starlit sky above him, and his sweat-soaked body chilled under the bitter cold of the desert wind. He struggled against the wine fumes as well as the opiate which must have befuddled his wits and clouded his mind. He moaned softly and looked over at the small fire which had been lit. A hooded figure crouched before it.

'Where am I?' He gagged on the wine and bile at the back of his throat. 'What am I doing here?'

The figure did not move. Hepel shivered at the cold. He felt as if he was going to be sick and let his head fall back, bruising himself on the hard rocky ground. Somewhere on the breeze he heard the mocking roar of the hyaenas, those great striped predators which prowled the rocky outcrops beyond the lush lands of the Nile. He closed his eyes. Surely this was a nightmare?

He recalled going down to a house of pleasure, near the Temple of Isis, just off the ceremonial causeway leading from the river. The girl he'd hired had been active and pleasure-giving, writhing under him like some oiled snake. He had drunk deep of her love, and lurched out, a garland of flowers on his head, to a nearby wine shop. A celebration had been taking place, some festival associated with Horus. Men and women cavorted, their faces covered with falcon masks. He had been invited to join them. He recalled the man, eyes glittering behind the mask, the sweet smell of perfume. A heset girl had come and sat on his knee whilst he'd watched two others perform a sinuous dance to the sound of clapping, the rattle of sistra and the haunting lilt of lute and lyre. The loving bowl had circulated, its wine thick and un-watered. Hepel recalled it being offered to him. After-wards he felt drowsy, heavy-limbed, the laughter dinning his ears. Eventually he'd left, being helped by his new-found friend. He recalled staggering down to the quay-side, the mocking cries of some sailors they passed and now this.

Hepel opened his eyes and stared down his body. Every time he moved, the rocky ground beneath scuffed and scarred him.

'Help me please!' he begged.

The figure left the fire and moved silently to crouch

beside him. Beneath the striped cloak he wore a costly white linen gown; the falcon mask still covered his face.

'You are Hepel?' The voice was soft.

The scribe nodded vigorously.

'And you are a friend of Ipumer?'

Again the nod.

'You were paid to spy on him, weren't you?'

Hepel, his eyes on that mask, shook his head. A knife came out and sliced the fleshy part of his arm. Hepel threw his head back and screamed.

'When I ask you a question,' the voice came like the hissing of a snake, 'you will always answer the truth. Look over there, Hepel. What do you see?'

'I see a fire,' Hepel stuttered.

'And beyond it?'

'An outcrop.'

'That's right, Hepel. We are out in the Red Lands on a dusty trackway above the Valley of Kings, a place of ghosts and demons. Now, look to the right of the fire. What do you see?'

The figure forced Hepel's face to turn, pushing at his cheek so the left side of his face was scored by the harsh rock.

'Look!' he ordered.

'I – I see a box and a pottery pipe.'

'Do you know anything about the Hyksos, Hepel?' the voice continued. 'They used to take prisoners and peg them out in the desert like I have you. They'd take a piece of pottery, a vase with the base removed, and strap it to the prisoner's side. They'd put a rat inside, one they'd starved, so ferocious it would attack and eat anything. I have brought a similar rat tonight. No, no –' the man covered Hepel's open mouth – 'don't scream: you can't be heard here. The fire can't be seen. But we don't want to attract the hyaenas or the lions! Now, if you continue to lie, I will do what the Hyksos did: strap the pipe to your body, place the rat inside and build a fire at one end. There will be only one way out.' Hepel's tormentor pressed his hand against the scribe's stomach. 'You understand?'

Hepel nodded.

'Good!' The tormentor took his hand away. 'Now, I shall begin again. Ipumer was your friend?'

'Yes.'

'And the widow Felima paid you,' his voice turned to a snigger, 'only the Gods know what, to spy on the love of her life, Ipumer, yes?'

'I did so. Felima is wealthier than she pretends.'

'Good! Good!' the voice soothed. 'And the night he died, he left the wine shop and you followed, yes?'

Again the vigorous nod.

'Back to Felima, then where?'

'To a house in the Street of Oil Lamps. He went inside and then came out.'

'Good! Good!' The tormentor squatted on his haunches and moved, his sandals crunching on the sand. 'And afterwards?'

'Ipumer went to a beer shop. He had a wineskin over his shoulder. I think he filled this and went to the House of the Golden Gazelle, to meet the Lady Neshratta.'

Hepel yelped as his assailant sliced at his arm with the razor-sharp knife.

'I want the truth, Hepel, not guesses. You followed him there?'

'I did but I am not too sure whom he met. I glimpsed the pedlar, the one who took the oath in court, sheltering near the wall under the sycamore tree. I didn't know what was happening.'

'I don't care about that.'

The tormentor broke off at the harsh coughing roar of a lion, followed by the eerie screech of a hyaena. To Hepel's fevered imagination they seemed closer.

'So, you are telling the truth. Let's leave the Lady Neshratta and go back to Ipumer. What did he tell you?'

Hepel started to shiver; the cuts on his arm were throbbing with pain. He turned, gagging and retching. When he looked back the man had got to his feet. He came back and threw a cloak over Hepel's sweat-soaked body.

'See,' the voice behind the mask reassured, 'you have nothing to fear, Hepel. Just tell the truth. Did Ipumer ever tell you about his days in Avaris?'

'He claimed he came from a distinguished family. He often boasted about the high office he held.' Hepel swallowed and moaned at the acid taste at the back of his throat. If he escaped here, he vowed quietly, never again would he visit a pleasure house or drink with strangers. He closed his eyes and cursed Ipumer.

'If he was so powerful in Avaris,' the tormentor continued, 'why did he travel to Thebes?'

'I asked him that once when he was in his cups. He said he had been in Thebes for two years and wished he hadn't come but there was no going back.'

'Did he tell you why?'

'Ipumer only boasted when he was in his cups.' Hepel blinked as some sand stung his eyes. 'He said he was in Thebes to perform great deeds. He said he had been brought here by the Panthers of the South—'

'Ah!' the tormenter interrupted. 'Our self-proclaimed heroes from the regiment of Seth.'

'Yes, yes, that's it.'

'Did he say who?'

'One of the commanders, one of those who have now died.'

'Good!' The tormentor looked up at the stars. 'Now, Hepel, think, and think clearly. Did he say anything else which is of interest?'

'I can't remember. He was distracted by Neshratta. Most of the time that's all he talked about. On one occasion I found him crying in a wine shop near the quayside. He said he wished he hadn't come, that he wanted to see General Peshedu, Neshratta's father.' Hepel closed his eyes. 'I can't tell you any more because I don't know any more.'

'Good!'

The masked figure seemed distracted by the horrid sounds of the scavengers of the night.

'Please!' Hepel begged. 'Please release me. I have told you the truth.'

'So you have,' the man replied. 'Tell me one more thing,

Hepel: do you think our friend Ipumer, who has gone before you into the west, was murdered by the Lady Neshratta?'

'I don't know.'

'Neither do I. But I'll give you this comfort,' the tormentor declared. 'I brought no rat out here. A cruel jest, eh, Hepel?'

The young scribed nodded vigorously.

'I am going to release you.'

Hepel let his head fall back and closed his eyes in a sigh of relief. He was about to promise solemnly, call on all the Gods that he would keep his mouth closed, but the tormentor had already decided. With one quick cut he sliced Hepel's throat from ear to ear. He coolly watched as the young man jerked and coughed up his lifeblood. The tormentor pulled his cloak away and waited till the body stopped quivering, the eyes gazing blindly up at the night sky. He cut the thongs binding the ankles and wrists, pulled out the wooden pegs and pieces of twine and rolled these up in his cloak. He went across and stamped out the fire, kicking dust over it. On the night breeze the assassin caught a fetid smell. The hunters were closing in. They'd smell the blood and, by dawn, all signs of Hepel the scribe would have vanished. The assassin didn't care. He glanced round once more and turned towards the great peak of rock which overlooked the City of the Dead, the dwelling place of Meretseger, the Scorpion Goddess. He muttered a quick prayer and swiftly left.

The assassin put as much distance between himself

and his victim's corpse as possible before stopping for a small gulp from his wineskin. Below him sprawled the City of the Dead, and the Nile glinting in the moonlight. The assassin, still wearing the Horus mask, stared up at the sky. He wanted vengeance against Neshratta's father, against those brave heroes, the Panthers of the South. He ground his teeth in fury and strode off into the night.

The Lady Norfret had made herself look as appealing as possible with pots of paint and jars of kohl. Her oil-drenched wig exuded its own perfume and, every time she moved, her gauze-like robe gave off its own fragrance. Amerotke glowered at her. She had painted her fingernails purple; round her neck hung a beautiful gorget of jasper mingled with gold and silver; matching rings hung from her ear lobes. Every time Norfret moved her beautiful hands, the silver bangles on her wrists jingled. Between her and Amerotke stood a table bearing a wide range of cooked foods: fish, quail, goose and succulent filet, all in their own special sauces; jars of butter and cream, a special jug of Charou, white wine chilled in the small irrigation pool specially dug for that purpose.

Amerotke and his wife were dining on the roof of their house. The oil lamps had been lit. Great bronze dishes of charcoal, sprinkled with incense and grains of sandalwood, provided sweet cloying warmth and drove away the flies and moths. Amerotke looked to his left. From here he could glimpse the lights of the city, the glint of the Nile, and listen to the soft sound of the night from the gardens below. Shufoy and his two sons, Ahmase and Curfay, were playing in the hallway. He could tell from Shufoy's plaintive voice how the manservant wished he could join his master and listen to what was being said.

'You are as bad as Hatusu,' Amerotke accused, keeping his face severe. 'You are a minx, a vixen and a hussy! You have adorned yourself to look as beautiful as the night, prepared a banquet that would do credit to the Fields of the Blessed and now you stare all wide-eyed and innocent at me.'

'I am worse than Hatusu,' Norfret murmured, sticking her tongue out. 'The night is yet young, my lord judge, and the pleasures which might await you are never ending.'

'Neshratta,' Amerotke retorted, picking up a piece of charcoaled fish and popping it into his mouth, 'all of Thebes is talking about Neshratta. You want to know what I know. So, tomorrow, instead of working with steward and bailiffs, supervising their accounts, or inspecting the wine press, you will be distracted. All your friends will arrive, on some pretext or other, with one purpose in mind. What does Norfret know about the case of Lady Neshratta? Is she a poisoner? Will she die? What other details can be gleaned?'

'The thought never crossed my mind,' Norfret pouted in hurt innocence. Amerotke could tell by the way she tightened her lips that she was on the verge of laughing. 'If you don't want to talk about it,' she dabbed at her pretty mouth with a napkin, 'then we don't have to talk about it. You are to leave with Karnac tomorrow?'

'At dawn,' Amerotke agreed warily.

'And Shufoy seems distracted.'

'We visited the Temple of Seth,' Amerotke explained. 'I told you why. Shufoy has what he calls this brilliant idea: to sell the shablis of the Goddess Ma'at. He is going to claim these are specially blessed by me, drenched in the Pool of Purity in the Temple of Ma'at and, if placed in the grave of a loved one, will keep him or her safe in the Hall of Judgment.'

'It's never been done before,' Norfret mused. 'But why does Shufoy—'

'He's got gold and silver enough,' Amerotke confirmed, 'but Shufoy nurses a great dream. He wants to become a rich and powerful merchant. His brain teems like a snake pit: remedies, amulets, scarabs, ingenious cures, love potions . . .' Amerotke blew his cheeks out in exasperation. 'The list is endless.'

'And the Temple of Seth?' Norfret was determined not to give up.

Amerotke sipped from his wine goblet, his fingers feeling the carvings on the side: writhing snakes, threading their way through a vine grove. The goblets were of carved silver and gold, studded with emeralds, a wedding gift from Norfret's brother. When his wife put these on the table, Amerotke always knew something was afoot. These were their loving cups which they had exchanged, full of wine, on their marriage night. Amerotke glanced across at his writing desk. A night he would never forget! Yet now the goblets provoked memories of those Scorpion Cups in the Red Chapel.

'The Temple of Seth . . .' Norfret gently clinked her goblet against his. 'I remember once,' she said wistfully, 'watching the Panthers of the South parade through Thebes dressed in full armour. Heralds went before them proclaiming their deeds, beautiful maidens throwing rose petals, gaily coloured ostrich plumes wafted around them. Now one has been murdered. Why, my Lord Amerotke?' Her tone turned icy.

'I don't know,' Amerotke replied. 'The war against the Hyksos is thirty years old. Walking back to the house, I reflected on my two probable conclusions about the killer. First, it could be someone from Avaris, who has travelled south to settle old grudges and grievances. Perhaps Meretseger had a son or daughter? Some young person who nourished vengeance and plotted revenge? But I can't see who.'

'Or?'

'Someone close to the regiment of Seth and these famous slayers, the Panthers of the South.'

'Couldn't you have questioned where they all were when Balet was killed?'

'I will do so tomorrow, but you know such men. They are busy and powerful. The killer would have covered his tracks very carefully. You see,' Amerotke moved on the cushioned seat, his fingers played with the fretted arm of the couch, 'I am also suspicious about that priest we met, Shishnak, sly-eyed as a cat. I can't understand why

Balet was killed so silently. According to the reports, the chapel was as disturbed as a battlefield.'

'And the Divine Hatusu does not like any of this?'

'No she doesn't, that's why she's as nervous as a mongoose.'

'A fitting description,' Norfret jibed.

'Hatusu wants to keep the army happy,' Amerotke replied. 'People declare how for thirty years nothing happened to our heroes of Thebes, until she succeeded to the double crown. Nothing must disturb her harmony.'

'Except the Lord Senenmut?'

Amerotke leant across and pressed a finger against Norfret's lips.

'You may talk like that to me,' he whispered, 'but never to your friends.'

'Pharaoh or not,' Norfret snapped, 'the Divine Hatusu does not frighten me.'

Amerotke glanced down at the table. His wife entertained the deepest reservations about Egypt's ruler.

'She may be Pharaoh,' Norfret scoffed, 'the Divine daughter of Ra, the Word from His Mouth, the Incarnation of His Will, but she is still a woman skilled in trickery.'

Amerotke filled his goblet and Norfret's.

'So, it is to the Red Lands tomorrow?'

'Yes.'

'And what about the Lady Neshratta?'

Amerotke smiled and sighed. 'As persistent as a mongoose!'

'And as tenacious,' Norfret agreed.

'Tomorrow morning Valu will come before the court, my

Director of Cabinet will say it is adjourned and they will have to wait.'

'Is she guilty? Come,' Norfret leant over the table, 'I promise you, the breeze is not a spy. It won't carry our words to the Lord Prosecutor.'

Amerotke knew he would have no peace. He also knew that Norfret was astute. Her tongue wouldn't wag. What he told her would remain confidential, though she would tease her friends and acquaintances that she knew more than they did.

'It's a most curious murder.' Amerotke sat back on his couch, cradling the goblet in his hands. 'On the one hand we have the Lord Peshedu, his plump comely wife and their two daughters. Apparently Ipumer met them at some banquet and, if gossip is to be believed, he and Neshratta were deeply smitten. Neshratta lives a sheltered life. We know all we do about her.'

'And Ipumer?'

'Now he's a mystery. He's also a nobody, a stranger from Avaris. He arrives in Thebes and, due to mysterious patronage, becomes a scribe in the House of War. Of course, we mustn't forget Ipumer's silver tongue was quite successful with the ladies. He was well known to the hesets and dancing girls, the whores and courtesans. He was also well liked by Felima, whilst the one he lodged with, Lamna, appeared to have had a soft spot for him.'

'What are you implying?' Norfret plucked a grape from the bowl and pressed it gently to her husband's lips. 'Are you saying,' she continued, 'that the meeting between Ipumer and Neshratta was planned?'

'I think so, but why should Ipumer seek out Neshratta? That's the mystery.'

Amerotke cleared his mouth.

'There's another one,' Norfret offered. 'Neshratta herself. Here is a young princess of the city, very wealthy, probably intended for a worthy match. Instead, she bestows her favours on a scribe about whom she must have known very little.'

'Yes,' Amerotke grinned. 'I may have to make you assistant judge in the Hall of Two Truths. The next time the court convenes I will ask Neshratta that question. Of course, she may have been smitten, she may have just fallen in love. Ipumer may have also been her way of rebelling against her parents and their wishes.'

'That's possible,' Norfret agreed. 'But then what?'

Amerotke stared at the sky. He was pleased with this conversation. It helped pull together different threads.

'Neshratta is probably her father's darling, the apple of his eye: rich and spoilt with it. She played the flirt, had her dalliance but then decided enough was enough.'

'So, if the gossip is true,' Norfret declared, 'the Lady Neshratta told Ipumer he was no longer welcome.'

'He remained insistent.'

'So what?' Norfret grinned impishly. 'In my time, my Lord Amerotke, I have had many suitors. I could even say admirers. They can insist to their hearts' content but I know where my heart lies.'

Amerotke lifted his cup in salutation.

'I have wondered that myself,' he replied. 'All Lady Neshratta had to do was keep her bedroom window closed, the postern gate to her garden locked and Ipumer would have been sent on his way. I am sure her father would have been only too pleased to release his retainers and guard dogs on him.'

'Or worse?'

'Or worse,' Amerotke agreed. 'You can hire a brigand for a piece of silver. There are men and women in Thebes who would kill their own brother or sister for the price of a good meal.'

'But perhaps that's what happened?'

'No.'

Amerotke told her in sharp, precise phrases exactly what had been established in court that morning.

'We do know Ipumer went down to the House of the Golden Gazelle. We know someone left that house to meet him and that's where he was probably poisoned. I can't imagine,' Amerotke continued, 'Ipumer knocking on the gate, an assassin stepping out and the scribe wandering off with him into the dark.'

'So, it must have been the Lady Neshratta?'

Amerotke considered his words carefully. 'Valu will have to prove that on the night Ipumer died, he was definitely given poison by Neshratta or on Neshratta's orders. If he can't prove that, then he must try to establish how, on previous occasions when Ipumer fell ill, first, that the illness was caused by poisoning and secondly, that it was the work of—'

'Neshratta or someone acting on her behalf.' Norfret finished the sentence for him.

'Now,' Amerotke warmed to his theme, 'if Neshratta's

advocate is worth his salt, he will try to cloud the issue. I think he is trying to do that. Why should Neshratta kill Ipumer? Perhaps someone else resented his love for Neshratta? The Lord Peshedu? Another member of her family? Or was it one of our jealous widows, Lamna or Felima? Or some mysterious stranger whose name we do not know?'

'Blackmail,' Norfret offered. 'Ipumer may have turned from his seduction to blackmail.'

Amerotke agreed. 'It's possible.'

'It's possible,' Norfret repeated. 'Ipumer decided that, if he couldn't have Neshratta, he would at least be paid for his pains. The person he met may have been Neshratta's mother, her father? Or their representative? You can imagine Ipumer's threats: "Fill my bag with gold or all of Thebes will know about Lady Neshratta's easy seduction by a commoner."'

'Possibly, but one thing Valu has established,' Amerotke glanced across at Norfret, 'is that Neshratta bought the venom which killed Ipumer. Valu is quick and cunning. He has two ends of a chain,' Amerotke raised his hand, 'and he is trying to clasp them together. I suspect he will use the adjournment tomorrow to continue digging like a jackal at a hole.'

'Can you question the Lady Neshratta?'

'Before the case began, yes. Now . . .' Amerotke shook his head. 'Valu would object. The matter is now before the court. It has to be settled there unless circumstances change.'

'What if she's guilty?' Norfret was no longer playful.

Amerotke pulled a face. 'Pharaoh's law is well known. A person who deliberately and maliciously poisons another must suffer the full rigour, be buried alive in the Red Lands.' He glimpsed the horror in Norfret's eyes. 'But I am sure it will not come to that. Meretel seems a good advocate.'

'And so is my Lord Valu.'

Amerotke was about to continue when he heard Shufoy's shout and hurried footsteps on the stairs.

'My lord, you have a visitor.'

Amerotke glanced at Norfret, who nodded.

'It's the priest Chula from the Temple of Seth.'

Shufoy came to the top of the stairs, Chula following. He had wrapped an embroidered shawl round his shoulders and its small hood was pulled over his head. He pushed this back, bowed deeply at Lady Norfret and glanced, hollow-eyed at the judge.

'I am sorry to disturb you, my lord, but the Divine One's orders in this matter are quite explicit.'

Norfret clapped her hands and indicated that Shufoy bring a chair to the table. She grasped the priest by the hand and gestured that he sit. She flattered him further by insisting that he eat and drink first. Chula needed no second bidding but delicately picked up a piece of roast duck. Amerotke and Norfret pretended to continue their meal. Chula took a sip of wine and cleared his throat.

'May He who listens and sees all extend His shadow over you.' Chula turned, his harsh face gently smiling. 'And may He keep you in the shadow of His wing.'

Norfret thanked the priest for his blessing.

'My lord, once again I apologise,' Chula came swiftly to the point, 'but I bear interesting news. First, the heset girl who was clubbed and thrown bound into the Nile? She was pregnant.'

He ignored Norfret's horrified gasp. Killing a pregnant mother was a hideous sin for which the Devourers of Souls would demand eternal retribution.

'You are sure?' Amerotke asked.

'I am a physician. When I began the embalming I discovered . . .' The priest's eyes filled with tears. 'Perhaps no more than two months advanced, my lord. I prayed for vengeance before the statue of Anubis. My wife and I would give years of our lives to have a child. Now, as you know,' the priest continued, 'the heset girl's corpse should be handed over for burial to the Temple of Anubis. She danced before their God. I went there this evening and made further discoveries. This heset was apparently quiet and withdrawn. In the main she kept to herself but she had one so-called secret.'

'A lover?'

'Yes, my lord, but no one knew who he was. Apparently the girl would steal away to meet him at some prearranged spot. Because the relationship was kept secret, the man must have been married.'

Amerotke nodded in agreement.

'However, on one occasion the heset girl did confess that her lover, and possibly the father of her child, was a high-ranking officer in the Divine One's army. Her friend at the temple challenged her on this, accusing her of lying.

The heset hotly replied that he was her lover, an officer and, even better, a hero of Egypt, a Slayer of Seth, one of the Panthers of the South.'

'You are sure?'

Chula nodded and sipped his wine, his eyes never leaving Amerotke's.

'I am the Keeper of the Dead, devoted to the cult of Anubis. No one in his service would dare lie to me. I asked the girl again and again and she repeated the same story. I do not think she was lying.'

Amerotke whistled under his breath. 'This is news indeed,' he murmured, 'and could explain her murder.' He glanced at Norfret. 'A young temple girl becomes pregnant. She might become insistent, even threatening. So she is killed and the child within her also dies. I do not doubt what you have said, Keeper of the Dead, but the heset was murdered as if she was the sacrificial victim of a Hyksos warrior.'

Amerotke stared up at the sky. The stars seemed closer this evening. Was that some trick of the night, or had he drunk too much wine? Or was this something the students of the heavens in the House of Life could explain? He closed his eyes and reflected on what the Keeper of the Dead had told him. It had a logic all of its own. A young temple heset, much taken by a war hero, was flattered and seduced. Joyful in her lovemaking, she had ignored the usual techniques to prevent conception. Or had she planned it to trap a lover, who had always demanded absolute secrecy about their relationship? There would have been a confrontation, her lover would have lost his temper and savagely killed her. And so was Balet's murder linked with this?

'My lord, I have other news.'

Amerotke rubbed his eyes.

'The scribe Ipumer is now ready for burial. His obsequies will be paid by the House of Silver. However, when I was preparing his corpse,' the Keeper of the Dead moved in his chair, 'I noticed a tattoo, the pigment slightly faded. I used paints to trace its outline.'

'And?'

'Two war clubs crossed.' Chula smiled at the look in Amerotke's eyes.

'But that's the symbol of a Hyksos noble. So, our scribe was not Egyptian born?'

'Possibly,' the Keeper of the Dead agreed. 'Perhaps the son of a high-ranking Hyksos warrior and an Egyptian woman. After Avaris was taken by Pharaoh's armies there would have been many orphans.'

'Aye,' Amerotke agreed. 'And anyone with any sense would try hard to conceal such a tattoo.'

'This was the case here,' Chula declared. 'From the little I know, the tattoo would have been etched shortly after his birth. When the child was probably no more than a year old, someone tried to deface it. Ipumer was a man of about thirty summers, which would place his birth about the time of the great Hyksos defeat.'

Amerotke stretched his hand across the table and touched Chula's goblet.

'You have done well, my friend.'

Despite his severe looks Chula blushed.

'You have greatly inconvenienced yourself,' Amerotke continued, 'to bring me this news. I insist that you stay here tonight as our guest. The Temple of Seth will still be there in the morning. You have other news?'

'About the heset girl, no. But I was fascinated by Ipumer. Every tongue in Thebes has a theory about his murder. Now, as you know, my lord, during the embalming process we take out the internal organs. They are cleansed and placed in Canopic jars. In Ipumer's case I studied them closely. It's my belief –' he glanced at Norfret, who sat fascinated by what she was hearing – 'but I have little evidence to prove it, Ipumer took opiates.'

'Opiates?'

'For what reason, my lord, I don't know. To sleep, to dream? Juice of the poppy or other herbs? They can change consciousness, make one feel happy. But the knowledge may be of use to you.'

'How?' Norfret asked.

'One theory I didn't mention,' Amerotke explained, 'is that Ipumer at times could be excitable, especially over Lady Neshratta. I give no secrets away, but Meretel might argue that Ipumer committed suicide, deliberately took the venom so his death would be blamed on Neshratta. He hoped his Ka would haunt her.'

'Stupidity!' Norfret snapped.

'To you, me and our guest, yes,' Amerotke replied, 'but to a man whose mind is turned and who is taking drugs for whatever reason . . . ?' Amerotke picked up his wine goblet. 'What I say is secret but the more I learn about Ipumer the more I suspect his death and Lord Balet's are connected, though I cannot see how or why. One fact is emerging. Ipumer was of Hyksos blood. I don't think it's a coincidence that he arrived in Thebes to pay court to the daughter of a warrior who helped destroy his people!' Amerotke smiled at the Keeper of the Dead. 'What I want to know is, did Ipumer come of his own accord or did someone bring him? Tell me –' he filled the priest's goblet – 'you are a physician: are there many Hyksos in this city?'

Chula pulled a face. 'The word Hyksos covers many tribes. Some were of Hittite origin and came from beyond Sinai. During the Season of the Hyaena they intermarried, some Egyptians switched their allegiance to them. It's possible. Thirty years ago a secret society flourished in Thebes, supporters of the Hyksos, who claimed to carry on a secret war against the Egyptian conquerors.'

'I have never heard of those.'

'They were secret,' Chula laughed, 'but not very dangerous. They flourished here and in Memphis. Due to Pharaoh's police, not to mention the passage of time, they disappeared like dew under the sun. Why, my lord, do you think such a society has re-emerged?'

Amerotke shook his head. 'I see all the reports of the police. They talk of assassins, smugglers, cunning men but nothing about the Hyksos. They are part of history, dry and as dead as desert dust.' Amerotke stretched. 'But tomorrow is another day.' He glanced down at Chula. 'I will not be returning to the court. I am off to the Oasis of Ashiwa.' He glanced at Norfret. 'You know what that place holds for me?' He leant across and grasped her hand.

'The Oasis of Ashiwa,' Chula said, all the good humour drained from his face. 'Are you sure that's safe, my lord?'

'Why, it is only ten miles north-east of Thebes. A watery enclave in a desert of dust and shimmering heat. Why do you ask?'

'A corpse was brought into the temple late this evening,' Chula informed him. 'A merchant was attacked and severely wounded near the oasis. He was picked up by desert scouts but died shortly afterwards. He claimed that a war band of Sand Wanderers had attacked him not far from the oasis.'

Norfret tightened her grip on Amerotke's hand.

'They may attack a lonely merchant,' Amerotke assured his wife and visitor, 'but a squadron of war chariots?'

He released Norfret's hand, walked to the edge of the roof and stared down at the gardens. Attacks and ambushes were common in the Red Lands. Amerotke's real concerns were the two mysteries which now confronted him. He wondered what he would find in the Oasis of Ashiwa. He quietly vowed that, when this court reconvened, he would take over the questioning. The key to Ipumer's murder might also resolve the mystery of those intent on killing the Slayers of Seth.

SETH: his wife was Anath, a War
Goddess armed with shield and
battle-axe.

CHAPTER 5

'You shine and are seen every day.
You are the Lord to the limit.
You sail through the night in your barque.
You are the Lord of the Waters crossing Heaven.
Under you is the horizon and you dwell behind it.
All life is yours.
You are the Lord of Light.
The sceptre shall not be taken from your hand.
You live in the Mansions of a Million Years.
You send the Four Winds so that we may breathe
    and live.
You are the Lord of Fire who lives in truth.
You are the Lord of Eternity, the maker of joy.
You are the God in your shrine, the Lord of Feasts.
The Lord of Slaughter who calms the storms.'

The priest's voice was strong and vibrant. It carried up to
the blue sky now shot with liquid gold as the sun rose in

gorgeous splendour, its rays transforming the dark rocks of the Red Lands into eye-catching colours. Amerotke and the rest knelt on the prayer carpets, heads bowed, hands extended as they worshipped the God Ra rising from his nightly journey through the Underworld, a solemn, silent moment. The cries of the desert faded; the sky was even free of vultures: Pharaoh's hens. Amerotke muttered his own silent prayers and, lifting his head, shaded his eyes. He looked to his left and prayed to Amun-Ra who sent his breath, the sweet north wind, which always came at dawn and disappeared in the searing heat of the day.

The chariot squadron was ready. The burnished armour of their carriages sparkled in the dawn light. The horses, each a magnificent pair from Pharaoh's stables, stood hobbled, their riders talking to them softly. There were thirty chariots in all, a small war squadron. Each would carry a driver and a soldier, well armed with bow and arrows, as well as the throwing spears in the brocaded sheath fastened to the side of the chariots.

Karnac got to his feet; prayer was finished. The small campfire, lit in the shade of some date trees, was quietly doused. Waterskins were filled. The Tedjens, or drivers, now checked the chariots, their wheels, shafts, harnesses and reins. News of the Sand Wanderers' recent attack was widely known. Karnac had decided not to take any chances. The general climbed into the leading chariot pulled by two magnificent black mares.

Amerotke fastened on his leather helmet with its hardened cap as protection, not so much against attack, but being jolted and thrown from the chariot. Amerotke climbed into his chariot, driven by a young, smooth-faced charioteer who smiled and winked. Amerotke grasped the bronze rail, spreading his feet on the leather floor. The driver gathered the reins, clicking gently at the horses. The chariot squadron began to move, fanning out into a long line.

The morning stillness was now shattered by the harsh grate of wheels, the neighing of horses and the shouts of their drivers. The squadron was magnificent, each chariot pulled by matching horses decorated with blood-red plumes, the insignia of the Vulture squadron, attached to the regiment of Seth. Karnac's charioteer, Nebamum, unfurled the regimental banner displaying a red-haired Seth against a black background. The morning breeze sent it fluttering bravely. Amerotke knew what was going to happen: this chariot squadron was a crack unit which prided itself on its speed and skill. As Amerotke had informed Shufoy when he had left for the city, the journey to Ashiwa would not be some stately procession. He was most reluctant to allow his manservant to accompany him. Shufoy was so small it wouldn't be the first time he had fallen out of a jolting carriage. He and Prenhoe had been given tasks, which, Amerotke hoped, would keep them out of mischief.

The driver gently snapped the reins. The chariot moved faster, keeping in line with the rest. Amerotke made himself relax. He thought briefly of the banquet the night before. He smiled on how sweet Norfret had been when they had bade the Keeper of the Dead good night and retired to their own private quarters.

'Haida!' The charioteer snapped his reins more vigorously.

Somewhere along the line the accompanying chapel priest intoned a regimental hymn to Seth.

'Who drives off the serpents?'

'The Lord Seth!' the cry came back.

'Whose face cannot be seen for fear of death?'

'The Lord Seth!' the voices thundered in chorus.

'Who is merciless in battle?'

Amerotke remained quiet as Karnac and the other Panthers of the South led the chariot squadron in this paean of praise to their patron God. After each verse the chariot line moved a little faster. His own driver now had his whip in his right hand, reins in the left, body braced, tense with excitement. The leisurely line was breaking up under the crack of whip, the rumble of wheels and the drum-like beating of the horses' hoofs.

The sun was rising. The coolness had disappeared. The rocky desert was taking on a dull, blood-like glow. The wind was no longer cool but thick with grains of sand. Amerotke picked up the white scarf round his neck and pulled it up to cover nose and mouth; the charioteer did likewise. All the time the ominous music of the squadron – the crack of whips, the crash of wheels, the quickening horses – made Amerotke's heart miss a beat. He felt a tingle of excitement and recalled the number of times he'd raced in the chariot line. No matter how many times, the effect was always the same.

Karnac's chariot sped out in front, like some bird flashing across the desert floor. The rest of the squadron followed, each charioteer determined to show he was the most expert, his horses the fleetest. Amerotke grasped the rail and held on for dear life. He felt slightly alarmed but knew the man beside him was testing his courage. Any nervousness, any fear, any word of reproach, would later make the judge a butt of jokes round the campfire. Amerotke's world narrowed to the horses thundering in front of him, the roll and crash of the chariots. He was aware of the rocks and scrubs of the desert speeding by. The dust-storm raised cut one chariot off from another in this hurried flight under a dusty sky.

Amerotke breathed a sigh of relief when the conch horn blew. The charioteer, clicking his tongue, gently eased the horses back. Little by little they were coaxed out of their charge. Amerotke looked around. Some chariots were in front, others behind. Ahead of them Karnac had stopped. The terrain had changed – no longer the flat, galloping ground beloved of charioteers but rocky, uneven, the sand much finer.

At last the squadron reached its leader. There were cries of congratulations, a great deal of teasing. Karnac, dressed as a common soldier, shouted orders that they were to follow the trackways, keep close together and be vigilant for any sign of the Sand Wanderers. Amerotke lowered the scarf round his face. The exhilaration of the charge evaporated. The slow trudge of horse and chariot became an increasing irritation as the heat of the desert made itself felt. Amerotke had no choice but to listen to the chatter of the charioteer. He stared out across the Red Lands, a bare, soulless, waterless place with rocky clefts, shrivelled shrubs and a heat haze which could play devious tricks on tired minds or eyes. Above them vultures circled as if they knew from habit that where such war squadrons went, a trail of corpses was always left behind.

'A symbol of good luck!' the charioteer quipped, following Amerotke's gaze.

Amerotke agreed. He quietly hoped that the journey would be uneventful. Now and again they stopped to eat their rations and drink from the waterskins. They must have travelled for two or three hours before the soaring date and palm trees of Ashiwa came into sight. Despite the heat Amerotke felt a clammy cold. He'd always hated this place. He had travelled here as a young man to pay his respects to his brother's Ka. The Oasis of Ashiwa was nothing more than a dense clump of palm trees with desert grass sprouting around a deep pool. Nevertheless, it was an important staging post for both merchants and Pharaoh's army. In Amerotke's mind it had not changed a whit since his last journey fifteen years previously: the coarse grass, the ancient twisted palm trees, the rocky outcrops at one end and the shimmering, inviting pool which lay at its heart. The chariot squadron rested in the shade of the trees: the horses were led away and hobbled under the care of their grooms.

Karnac, Amerotke and the Panthers of the South squatted under a palm tree. The six warriors looked as if they were enjoying themselves. Apart from the rich bracelets, they were all dressed in the simple leather corselets and kilts of the common soldier, though they also wore white gauze robes to protect their heads and shoulders against the sun. Like Amerotke the Panthers wore marching sandals with thick soles and heavy thongs with a leather guard to protect the ankle and heel. Nebamum was different: he wore strange leather boots up to his knees. Squatting down with the rest, Karnac's manservant caught Amerotke studying him.

'They protect the muscle,' he declared, tapping the boots, 'and support the leg.'

'How is your wound?' Amerotke asked, passing the waterskin to him. The others were still discussing the oasis and the memories it provoked.

'Until two years ago,' the servant scratched the side of his head, 'it was almost healed but then I fell. The physicians say my wound went deep, shattering muscle, bone and flesh. I began to favour the right leg and that, too, brought problems. Ah well.' Nebamum lifted the waterskin and poured the contents into his mouth, allowing some to splash over his face. 'Such is the life of a soldier, my lord.'

Karnac called for silence. He held up a scroll of papyrus.

'After our great victory against the Hyksos,' he remarked to Amerotke, 'we seized their camp and all their possessions. What a day!' His eyes held a faraway look. 'Not like now, eh? We were lean and as hungry as wolves. We took our share of plunder; that's where we found the medallions.' He grinned.

Amerotke noticed how Karnac's teeth had been deliberately sharpened. A killer, Amerotke thought, a man born for slaying, a warrior to his very heart. He watched Karnac's dark eyes: this man could be cruel and implacable. Amerotke glanced round at the rest. They were all the same, Nebamum included, not a touch of softness in any of them. Despite the sweat and the folds of skin, these men saw themselves as slayers – not soldiers doing their tasks but warriors who exulted in the glory of battle, the splashing of hot blood and the division of spoils. In his heart of hearts the judge concluded that none of these would blink an eye or flinch at killing anyone who threatened them.

He glanced away, staring out across the desert. He welcomed the shade of the palm tree: the real journey was yet to begin. Karnac, however, was still staring at the map as if lost in his own memories. His companions gazed silently as wolves would at the leader of their pack.

'Continue, my lord,' Nebamum gently chided him.

The general glanced up. 'This, Amerotke, is a map drawn by one of Pharaoh's scribes who has now gone to the Far Horizon. As I have said, we found Meretseger's medallions as well as her corpse. Pharaoh entrusted both to me and my companions.' He gestured to the west. 'The battlefield is about half a day's march. We decided to bring Meretseger's corpse here.'

'To the oasis?' Amerotke queried.

'No, we ate, drank and refreshed ourselves at Ashiwa but we decided that the filthy sorceress's corpse should rot out in the dirt of the desert.'

Karnac got to his feet, shouting at the grooms to bring

bows, arrows and the throwing javelins from the chariots. These were distributed amongst the Panthers of the
South.

'We are going alone?' the judge demanded.

Karnac's sombre eyes held his. 'Of course, my lord judge.
Meretseger's burial place is a secret. You are not afraid,
are you?' He smiled bleakly. 'We must do this. We have to
see if Meretseger's grave has been disturbed. If the killer
is one of hers, he or she would not ignore such a hideous
shrine. We must march and not be afraid.'

'How far?' Amerotke decided to ignore the comment.

'About an hour's walk.' Karnac gestured at the weapons
and the waterskin Amerotke carried. 'If you want, you can
stay here with the rest of the lads.'

'The Divine One,' Amerotke replied, 'instructed me to
come, so come with you I shall. But I'll confess, my lord,'
Amerotke grasped the javelin he carried like a walking
stick, 'the Red Lands terrify me.'

'That's why we buried her out there.' Karnac smiled
round at his companions. 'And you are in good company,
my lord judge. Only a fool would wander here without a
worry in his heart.'

Karnac led them out of the oasis. Amerotke pulled his
hood up, checked the waterskin was safe and followed
behind the rest. They climbed a small hill and, even
though they only went a few paces, Amerotke felt the
breathless, burning heat. They were now in the desert
proper – sand dunes broken by the occasional rocky outcrop which reflected the heat and brilliance of the sun.
Amerotke kept his head down. Using the javelin as a

walking stick, he faithfully followed in the halting steps of Nebamum. Karnac and his companions were now quiet, a silent file of men trudging under the glare of the sun. The only sign of life was vultures hovering high above them, waiting expectantly. Now and again the line would stop. Amerotke recalled his training as an officer. He used the water sparingly to wet his throat and lips; he dabbed his brow and the back of his neck. The heat was stifling. Amerotke realised that the only guide to where they were going was the occasional cluster of rocks. He quietly prayed that Karnac, over the years, had not lost his sense of judgment or direction.

Amerotke tried to distract himself by thinking about Norfret and the boys. He contrasted this journey through the burning sands with the cool, calm elegance of the Hall of Two Truths.

Now and again Nebamum, leaning heavily on his staff, would stop, turn and ask the same question: 'Are you all right, my lord?'

Amerotke would reassure him, the servant would turn and they'd continue their march. Amerotke felt as if he was in a nightmare, walking for ever under a relentless sun, the hot sand searing the skin of his feet. The bow and quiver of arrows seemed to grow heavier. Now and again the javelin slipped from the sweaty palm of his hands. Amerotke became tired, slightly nauseous. He took another slurp of water.

Nebamum turned. 'Thanks be to Ra, my lord judge! After we buried Meretseger we were trapped in a sand-storm. At least we're free of that!'

Amerotke grimaced. He was about to ask Nebamum how much further when Karnac shouted, pointing with his finger. Amerotke shaded his eyes and glimpsed where the sand dunes rose to a gnarled rocky outcrop. Karnac led them across to it, his companions chattering amongst themselves. Karnac was walking faster and, even before they caught up with him, Amerotke heard his quiet curse. The incline to the rocky outcrop was slippery. Karnac had scrambled up and was crouching in the shadow of its jutting spur. The rocks formed a small cave which had been blocked by a boulder. This had now been pulled aside and the dark tomblike cavern inside appeared empty.

'This is where we put her!' Nebamum hissed.

The rest of the group clustered round, staring at the boulder which had been pulled away.

'It can't be!' Heti exclaimed, crouching and peering inside.

Karnac, grasping his javelin, pulled Heti back and squeezed himself in.

With any other man Amerotke would have found the sight ridiculous but Karnac reminded him of a savage animal intent on its prey.

Karnac, cursing quietly, withdrew, a scroll in his hands.

'The body has gone!' he declared. 'Only this remains.' He opened and read it, then tossed it angrily at the judge. 'Meretseger has risen from her grave!' he rasped.

'The dead don't walk,' Amerotke retorted. 'Perhaps the body decayed.'

'Not in this cave,' Karnac replied.

'Was this buried with her?'

'Read it!'

Amerotke did so. The papyrus was thick, of good quality. The drawing and hieroglyphics it contained were the work of some itinerant scribe. He studied it quickly, fending off the hands of his companions.

'Out loud!' Karnac demanded.

'"You will be caught in the net which catches the dead."' Amerotke glanced up. 'My lord, it's a curse. The ink is red, possibly the blood of some animal.'

'Continue,' Karnac demanded.

'"The Devourers of Souls will snatch you all,"' Amerotke read. '"You shall fail the test before Osiris in the Hall of Truth. You shall be eaten alive by the Devourers of Souls. You shall be beheaded and packed, burnt like sacrifices! Meretseger has returned!" Nonsense!' Amerotke threw the curse back at Karnac. 'My manservant, Shufoy, could buy you similar curses in any marketplace in Thebes. Meretseger is dead and she will remain so. Whoever removed her corpse came out here to frighten you, to provoke memories. In the early hours of the day, or when you lie in bed at night, you will recall her death and tremble. But you are warriors,' Amerotke continued. 'Such curses do not frighten you.'

He stared round this group of hard-faced men. In truth, they were frightened – warriors who could withstand the charging battle line of Hyksos chariots or steal courageously into the enemy camp at night. Nevertheless, they were highly superstitious, more frightened of what they couldn't see than any visible enemy.

'Who removed the remains?' Nebamum broke the silence.

'My Lord Karnac, how many people in Thebes knew where Meretseger was buried?'

Karnac blew his cheeks out, and wiped the sweat from his face with the back of his wrist.

'We do,' he smiled bleakly, 'and whomever we may have told over the years.'

His statement was greeted by protests and denials.

'Someone came here,' Amerotke declared loudly, 'and our journey hasn't been in vain. Meretseger is nothing but a sack of bones. At least this proves that Lord Balet's murder, as well as the dispatch of those medallions to each of you, are somehow linked with your glorious exploits thirty years ago.'

'Where could her remains be?' Heti demanded.

Amerotke stared across the burning sands. Asural often hunted the Scorpion Men, the creatures of the night who dabbled in the black arts, wrote the execration texts to curse enemies and so wreak havoc in the world of men. One of the great powers such creatures claimed was their ability to call on the Akh, the ghosts of the dead. A female ghost particularly, like Meretseger, would be regarded as highly powerful and malignant. Whoever was behind these murders, Amerotke reflected, knew the warriors well: their superstition, their fear of the unknown, their awareness of invisible, malignant forces only a breath away from intervening in their lives.

'Perhaps it has already begun.' Nebamum nursed his wounded leg. 'This was getting better; now it's worse.'

Karnac gripped his manservant by the shoulder. 'It was good of you to come, Nebamum.'

It was the only time Amerotke had seen the leader of these warriors show any gentleness or compassion.

'Are you sure it's not hidden away elsewhere?' Thuro demanded, glaring at Amerotke. 'You seem to know a great deal about these matters, my lord judge.'

'I know very little,' Amerotke retorted, 'except that I am hot, sweaty and tired, whilst the desert dust seems to be in every orifice of my body.'

A murmur of laughter greeted his words. The sun was now at its zenith, beating down on the rocky outcrop like a sword on a shield. Amerotke felt a little giddy. He stepped away, and as he did so he glimpsed a movement where a sand dune soared up to the sun-drenched sky. Was that a man? He grasped his water bottle and drank quickly. Nebamum followed his gaze.

'I thought I saw something,' Amerotke murmured. 'In fact, I am sure I did.'

'Nonsense!' Ruah declared. 'The desert sun plays tricks.'

Amerotke was not so convinced. He felt a shiver of apprehension. His elder brother had been killed out here: the judge had a sinister premonition of danger.

Karnac, however, was now busy searching the rocky enclave, making sure that Meretseger's remains were not hidden nearby. Amerotke kept staring out across the sands. He closed his eyes and quietly prayed to his brother's Ka and to his patron, Ma'at, that he and the veterans had not been lured into an ambush. He was relieved when Karnac gave the order to return. The tomb was examined once again and they began the long trek back.

Amerotke felt better now he was moving, even though

the heat was intense and the glare from the sand hurt his eyes. He tried to relax by thinking of the cool serenity of his own garden: Norfret's impish face, the boys chasing Shufoy around the pool. He heard a sound and looked up. The vultures had clustered again. He was aware of Nebamum striding in front of him; the sand-duned horizon was empty. He heard a shout and looked again. A line of figures had appeared. Amerotke cursed. Their dromedaries made the sinister statues garbed in black look like some grotesques spat up from the Underworld. They stood in a long, silent line.

Desert Dwellers? Sand Wanderers? Amerotke wondered. Perhaps a peaceful group of bedouins looking for an encampment? Amerotke remembered the old proverb: 'One never meets a friend in the Red Lands, only an enemy.'

The figures moved. Karnac shouted orders. Amerotke and the rest threw themselves flat on to the hot sand as their attackers brought up short-horn bows. A volley whistled over their heads. Karnac was bellowing at Nebamum. Amerotke forgot his fear. Because of their mounts, the Sand Wanderers had been unsure in their aim, whilst their bows were not as powerful as the ones Amerotke and his companions carried. Amerotke fumbled about and grasped his bow. He notched a sharp, bronze-tipped arrow with a flight of vulture feathers. He chose a target and, kneeling on one knee, loosed as the others did. Three, four figures toppled from their mounts. Karnac urged them on. Amerotke grasped his bow and followed. Arrows whistled over their heads.

The Sand Wanderers were now moving, crawling like black spiders down the dunes towards them. Thankfully the ground underfoot, thick and heavy, prevented any charge. Karnac and Nebamum were superb archers: more attackers tumbled from their mounts. The Sand Wanderers' line broke up in disarray.

Karnac shouted at his companions to follow. They forgot the heat, the searing blast of the desert, and charged. Amerotke could tell from their faces how the Panthers were back in time. They did not regard this as some attack by bandits. They were reliving, re-enacting, their own heroic exploits against the Hyksos. Shawls and robes were thrown away. Time and again they stopped, a cluster of archers, their composite bows bent right back to their ears, arrows loosed. The Sand Wanderers grew desperate to close. Amerotke glanced to his right. He could see the distant fronds of the Oasis.

'Surely,' he shouted at Nebamum, 'someone will see us?'

Nebamum grinned. He stepped back as an arrow pierced him in the soft flesh of his shoulder. He winced but plucked up the conch horn slung on a piece of leather around his shoulders and blew a low throaty blast, which he repeated time and again. Amerotke tried to help. He heard shouts and screams. The Sand Wanderers were closing in. Amerotke stepped in front of Nebamum and loosed one arrow. He'd left his javelin, so he used the bow shaft as a spear. The attackers came crashing in.

A dromedary charged, gait ungainly, its rider swaying from side to side. Amerotke watched intently. The Sand

Wanderer was dressed in black, nose and mouth covered by a band, eyes gleaming. He raised a curved sword, only to recoil in the saddle as an arrow struck him high in the chest. Amerotke jabbed the animal in the neck. It screamed and collapsed to its knees. Amerotke ran forward; the rider was trapped beneath the dromedary. He pulled the sword from its wounded owner and turned as another Sand Wanderer slipped from his high saddle and came running towards him. They met in a clash of swords. Amerotke's opponent was ungainly, unsteady on his feet after the swaying movement of the dromedary. He slipped and slithered, gave up the fight and ran.

All around Amerotke similar attacks were taking place. The Panthers of the South were holding their own with sword, dagger and whatever weapon they could grasp. Amerotke heard the bray of trumpets, the rumble of chariots. Their powerful squadron swept towards them. The Sand Wanderers broke off and retreated, leaving the ground littered with dead and dying, both men and animals. The chariots, because of the sand, found progress difficult. Karnac ordered them not to proceed any further.

'Your wheels will become clogged!' he shouted. 'They'll turn and pick you off one by one.'

For a while the battle scene was confusion. Amerotke sank to his knees. He was aware of his charioteer beside him, offering him a waterskin. He took it and poured the rest over his head and the back of his neck.

'You'll come to no harm, sir.' The charioteer, a cheeky grin on his face, squatted down beside him. 'Sir, are you well?'

Amerotke blinked and prayed he wouldn't vomit. If the truth be known he was terrified. He felt like springing to his feet and screaming at the Sand Wanderers, at Karnac, even Hatusu for sending him out here.

'I am a judge, not a warrior,' he murmured.

'Well, I don't know about that,' the fellow replied mischievously. 'Come on, sir. You've been out in the sun too long.'

He helped Amerotke to his chariot. The judge climbed in and looked round. The rest were pressing round Karnac, shouting and laughing like a group of boys after some mischief.

'Apart from Nebamum,' the driver pointed with his whip, 'there are no injuries. My Lord Karnac and the rest will be celebrating for days.'

The driver was correct. Karnac and the rest began their rejoicing as soon as they reached the Oasis. Guards were posted, cuts and wounds attended to. They stripped naked and washed the sand and the sweat from their bodies. A temple healer amongst the chariot squadron checked them once more. He said that, apart from Nebamum's wound, which would heal in a few days, everything was well. Once they had dressed, Karnac insisted that the accompanying priest lead them in a prayer of thanksgiving to Seth. The supplies were opened and an offering made to Amun of bread, wine and fruit.

'We'll stay here till dusk,' Karnac declared, ignoring Amerotke's look of protest. 'We'll rejoice and we'll feast.'

Amerotke had no choice but to agree. Although now refreshed, he still felt tired. Karnac was correct: they had borne the heat of the day and the brunt of battle; it would be better to travel back to the city in the cool of the evening. The rest of the heroes congratulated themselves, recounting details from the battle. Only when they sat round the makeshift fire, and the food and wine was shared out, did Karnac clap his hands for silence.

'That was no accident, my lord judge, was it?'

Amerotke stared down at his bronze beaker and swilled the wine around.

'It was no accident,' he agreed.

'What do you mean?' Heti declared, already half drunk.

'They were a gang of Sand Wanderers looking for easy pickings.' Karnac cuffed him gently round the ear.

'By a maiden's tits!' Heti bellowed playfully. 'What pickings? A group of old soldiers and a judge?'

'We had our bracelets and weapons.' Thuro spoke up.

Ruah was now staring narrow-eyed at Amerotke. The laughter and talk died as Karnac's words sank in.

'You mean they were waiting for us, don't you?' Ruah demanded.

'Of course they were.'

Amerotke tried to keep the jibe out of his voice. He felt tired and bad-tempered. He didn't like being with these men. They were secretive, blood brothers, with their own code; a tightly knit group who clearly resented outsiders. He gazed round. Despite his share in the battle there was no feeling of camaraderie towards him. No wonder Hatusu had intervened. These were very dangerous men, powerful warriors who held considerable sway amongst the different regiments of the army. Balet's death was not only murder but a gross insult to them. They would demand both vengeance and justice. They looked to Hatusu to provide it.

Amerotke sipped from his beaker. 'I am not a soldier,' he confessed, ignoring the sarcastic grunts of approval, 'but Meretseger's burial site is a lonely, hot, dusty place out in the desert. You probably chose it thirty years ago because of that. It's no coincidence that the very time we go there, we discover Meretseger's corpse has been removed, and a powerful band of Sand Wanderers, Desert Dwellers, whatever they were – Libyan marauders or even hired assassins – suddenly appear on the skyline. They were waiting for us.'

'Of course they were,' Karnac interrupted. 'And they timed their attack well. We marched to the tomb, discovered what we did. We were on our way back, out in the open.'

'True,' Ruah agreed. 'If they had attacked whilst we were at Meretseger's grave, we could have held them off amongst those rocks.' He raised his beaker mockingly in Amerotke's direction. 'I agree with our learned judge. It was a well-planned ambush.'

'Don't be harsh with him, my lords,' Nebamum broke in. 'What the judge says is correct.'

He glanced at Karnac, who indicated that Amerotke speak whilst his companions held their peace.

'It was no coincidence.' Amerotke kept his voice level. 'They knew where we were, they realised we were vulnerable. Someone hired them to launch that attack—'

Karnac bellowed for silence at the loud protests.

'Continue, my lord judge.'

'Of course, I must ask who.' Amerotke smiled round. 'But, to be fair to all of us,' he gestured towards the edge of the encampment, where the rest of the escort were either tending to the horses or relaxing, 'our destination was no great secret. However, to hire an enemy like that – what my lords, fifty, sixty men? – it must have cost a great deal of gold and silver. One thing they weren't told,' he smiled tactfully: 'that their intended victims were the formidable Panthers of the South.'

Nods and grunts of approval greeted this. Flattery, Amerotke reflected: these heroes love it as a cat does milk.

'Explain!' Karnac insisted.

'Back in Thebes,' Amerotke continued, 'you have the great waterfront. Everybody, sooner or later, comes to the quayside: Nubians, Kushites, Hittites, travellers from Pont, Libyans, Sand Wanderers, Desert Dwellers. All the dark creatures will pour in from the Red Lands. They come to buy supplies, see what they can steal or, as in this case, be hired.'

'It's a pity we didn't take prisoners,' Nebamum broke in.

'Even if we had,' Amerotke retorted, 'I doubt if they'd know their paymaster. A shadowy corner in some wine shop? Gold and silver offered, more promised when the deed was done?'

'But why didn't they just keep the money and go?'

'Ah.' Amerotke held out his copper beaker to be refilled. 'Their hirer then played them false. We were depicted as middle-aged men, probably powerful noblemen on some secret mission for Pharaoh. Perhaps the Sand Wanderers weren't going to kill us, but hold us to ransom? My lords, it's quite common enough.'

This time they didn't disagree.

'Now I have your attention,' Amerotke declared, 'let me continue my questioning. What have we discovered?'

All eyes were on him.

'The medallions taken from Meretseger some thirty years ago must have been stolen by someone here, some high-ranking officer in the army or an official in the royal circle. Agreed?'

There was no dissent.

'Secondly, Balet's murder. He was by himself in the Red Chapel at the Temple of Seth. Very few people – and most of them are here – knew your comrade's routine and his preference for visiting the chapel alone. Thirdly, whoever entered that chapel was no stranger. We have not received reports that anyone untoward was seen in the Temple of Seth. Any of you could have entered its precincts and no one would have given it a second thought. Fourthly, Balet was a warrior, skilled in arms, though not as proficient as his assailant. Fifthly, it wasn't just an ordinary murder but a ritually blasphemous act. Balet's body was deliberately mutilated. Sixthly,' Amerotke was enjoying himself. He felt like a teacher with a group of young scribes, 'Meretseger's corpse was a matter for the House of Secrets. Very few people knew where she lay. Until this day I didn't, but all of you did. Someone came out and removed that hideous corpse. Finally, we have the attack. Whoever arranged that enjoys considerable wealth, but that is not all.' He pointed across at Peshedu, who, throughout the entire journey, had been quiet and withdrawn. 'My lord, you know the conventions. During this journey I have not talked to you about the case before me in the Hall of Two Truths. I only speak now in the presence of witnesses. You, too, are under attack. Your daughter is accused of hideous murder.'

'What are you saying?' Karnac asked. He gestured at Peshedu. 'We all feel for our comrade. Are you saying that these matters are entwined like some creeper round a vine? That Ipumer's death is connected somehow with Lord Balet's?' His voice took on a sneering tone. 'What proof do you have?'

'Did you know that Ipumer – if that is his true name – might have been a Hyksos prince?' Amerotke retorted.

His companions gazed speechlessly back.

'Impossible!' Peshedu snarled.

'I am not showing bias,' Amerotke declared. 'This will become common knowledge. More importantly, did you know that I went through Ipumer's possessions? I found one of the medallions such as were sent to you.'

Peshedu sprang to his feet. 'I don't believe this!' He walked away from the group, then turned and came back. 'He was a scribe!' he shouted. 'A mere worm of a man who tried to seduce my daughter!'

'Sit down!' Karnac ordered. 'Keep your voice low.'

'I think he was more than that,' Amerotke declared softly. 'So, I have two questions for all of you, my lords.

Apart from my Lord Peshedu, did Ipumer ever approach any of you?'

A chorus of denials greeted his question.

'Did you know him?'

Amerotke received the same reply.

'Then, finally,' he sipped from the beaker, 'did any of you, in any way, recommend that Ipumer be given a post in the House of War? I ask this because we have checked with the Hall of Archives. Ipumer's records have disappeared – either taken by himself or by the person who hired him, opened doors for him in the city of Thebes.'

In other circumstances Amerotke would have enjoyed the consternation his statement caused. Each of these powerful officers loudly protested his innocence. They had no knowledge of Ipumer and certainly had no hand in his appointment as a scribe in the House of War.

'My lord . . .' Karnac was chewing something, studying the judge, as if seeing him for the first time. 'My lord, I had you wrong. Oh, I have heard of your exploits with the Divine One's army. I thought you were lucky, a soft-skinned man, good at asking questions in the Hall of Two Truths. Yet you can march and fight, even though your heart's not in it.' His smile widened. 'More importantly, you possess a wit as cunning as a mongoose.'

Amerotke bowed at this back-handed compliment. 'I will have to ask you blunt questions,' he declared, 'about where you all were when Balet was killed. However, this is my theory. Ipumer was of Hyksos descent: there is some connection between him and the cult of Meretseger. He came to Thebes to do you all ill. Somehow,' Amerotke shook his head, 'he became distracted, possibly by the Lady Neshratta. That is a separate case. What concerns me more – and this is of greater danger to you – is not so much Ipumer – he is dead and gone – but the person who hired him. Now, my lords, we deal with a soul as black as night, as malicious as a roused viper. I say "he", but it could be a woman. Whatever, this person who controlled Ipumer and secured him a post in Thebes means to wreak a terrible vengeance on you. He first tried to do this through Ipumer but failed. I suspect he, or she, has now decided to act alone. Balet's death was the first blow. The attack on Nebamum the second. Today, the third. Believe me, lords, this viper will strike again and again!'

SETH: God of violence and turmoil, who
entered the world by bursting through his
mother's side.

'I'm sorry,' Prenhoe had apologised.

Shufoy had grinned wickedly and grabbed the end of Prenhoe's nose. 'I can always take yours. But, come, I want you with me.'

Prenhoe's remorse at the cruel jibe had soon evaporated as his temper returned. Shufoy, ever enigmatic, holding his parasol like a staff of office, had bade goodbye to Lady Norfret and pompously walked along the earth-beaten trackway: the mansions of the nobles to their right, the slow moving Nile to their left. Prenhoe had asked questions. Shufoy, imitating his master, had just shaken his head murmuring: 'You'll see. You'll see.'

Prenhoe had thought they were going into the city. Instead, Shufoy had stopped at the soaring gateway of one of the great mansions. The porter had been most offensive.

'The widow Aneta,' he'd declared, 'is not taking visitors.'

Shufoy had produced Amerotke's cartouche and pushed it into the man's face. After that there were no problems. They'd been led up the pathways, past the ornamental pools, with their pavilions and kiosks, along the broad, sweeping steps and into the entrance portico. A house servant had escorted them into this beautiful reception hall with its wooden pillars of dark red, their ends carved in the shape of green and gold papyrus stems. The walls were a light yellow with a frieze along the top, showing ducks and geese flying up out of the papyrus beds. On each side of the doorway, leading deeper into the house, was a carving of the red-haired God and, above the door, a ceremonial shield depicting the arms of the Seth regiment.

'Why are we here?' Prenhoe asked after the servant had

washed their hands and dabbed their foreheads with oil. He had also served cups of beer and small date cakes covered in almonds. Prenhoe had nibbled at his but Shufoy had scoffed the rest.

'My Lord Amerotke's business,' Shufoy declared sonorously.

'The Lady Aneta,' the house servant announced.

The visitors shot to their feet. Prenhoe had to keep his face straight at the woman who swept in: she reminded him of a hippopotamus. She was small, very fat and waddled rather than walked. Despite her best efforts, her black wig hung slightly askew. Her face had more paint than the walls of her house whilst the transparent gown she wore billowed out like the sails of a ship. Prenhoe felt almost giddy at the clouds of perfume which wafted towards him.

'Visitors,' she cooed, her little black eyes studying Prenhoe from head to toe. She licked her lips, then glanced distastefully at Shufoy. 'You say you are from the Lord Amerotke? I met him once, such a handsome man.' She peered down and sniffed. 'I think you'd best stay here. Bring me a chair!'

The servant came back, muttering and groaning at carrying a heavy, leather-backed chair which he placed before the marble bench. The widow Aneta slumped down on this. Shufoy giggled, and Prenhoe kicked him sharply on the ankle. Even so, the scribe found it hard to keep his face straight. The Lady Aneta wore so much jewellery on her hands, wrists and fingers, it was a wonder she didn't topple over.

'Well, sit down! Sit down!' she cooed, beckoning the servant. 'Bring me wine and date cake. Oh yes, and some cherries. When you have served them close the door and don't be listening.'

Shufoy and Prenhoe sat, hands in their laps, until the servant returned with a small table and tray on which he placed food and drink. Lady Aneta picked up one of the cherries, popped it into her mouth and sucked noisily. The doors were closed. Lady Aneta demanded to see Amerotke's cartouche again. She took a generous gulp of wine, smacked her lips and glared at Shufoy.

'I can't take you deeper into the house,' she lied. 'The chambers are all being painted. I am preparing for the festival of Opet. Now, what does my lord judge want?'

'Your late husband?'

Shufoy still found it difficult to speak. He had this overwhelming urge to imitate the woman who flounced before him: he had taken as deep a dislike to her as she to him.

'Well, he's gone into the Blessed West,' Lady Aneta sighed. 'He died almost a year ago in the Season of Planting.'

'Of what, my lady?'

'Lack of breath.' Lady Aneta had apparently become bored with these questions.

'Lord Amerotke could summon you to his court,' Shufoy replied sweetly.

'The widow of one of the Panthers of the South!' she jibed.

'Lord Peshedu's daughter is already there.'

Lady Aneta almost choked on the cherry. She took another mouthful of wine.

'My husband, the Lord Kamun,' she replied, as if she was going to behave herself, 'was a soldier born and bred. After the great victory against the Hyksos, he served in the Delta. He caught malaria, which weakened him, as he suffered from recurrent bouts. Over the years he grew worse.' She shrugged. 'He died,' she glanced doe-like at Prenhoe, 'and now I am a poor widow.'

'And your husband's companions?'

'Oh, the other brave heroes of Pharaoh. Lord Peshedu can tell you all about that: this festival, that festival, that parade, this parade.' She moved her hands from side to side.

'Does the name Ipumer mean anything to you?'

Lady Aneta opened her mouth to reply. Her black eyes blinked. Shufoy saw the quick change of mood.

'My lady, I am here on the business of the Hall of Two Truths. To lie to me,' Shufoy grew pompous, 'is to lie to Amerotke, who is the Word which springs from Pharaoh's mouth.'

'I . . . I . . . er,' she stuttered, 'yes. I have heard about the case against the Lady Neshratta. Ipumer was a visitor here.'

'Before your husband's death?'

'Of course, not afterwards!'

'And why did he come?'

'I don't know. My husband,' she gabbled on, 'used to entertain him in one of the garden pavilions. I suppose they chattered about the only thing my husband was interested in: fighting! Ipumer was a scribe in the House of War.'

'But how did they meet?'

'I don't know. I once asked my husband. Of course, he never deigned to tell me anything. He was always glad to see Ipumer and the scribe was personable enough.'

'Did he ever bring your husband presents?'

'Oh, of course – a flask of wine, something special brought from the quayside. Then my husband grew—'

'Ill and died.'

'He was always ill. He simply had one bout too many.'

'My lady, what are you doing here?' The door to the reception hall was flung open. A young man stood in the entrance. Shufoy could tell from Lady Aneta's cloying glances he was not some ordinary servant.

'I'll be with you soon,' she cooed.

The young man pouted and flounced out, slamming the door behind him.

'My manservant,' she explained. 'He gives himself such airs and graces. Now, Shitai—'

'Shufoy!' the dwarf barked.

'Ah yes, Shufoy. Are there any other questions?'

'So, your husband died and his body was . . . ?'

'Taken to his tomb across the river. I have to look on the bright side of life,' she continued. 'Since his departure the Panthers of the South no longer bother me. I certainly don't bother them. Well,' she eased herself out of the chair, 'if there is nothing more . . .'

Once they had been let out of a side gate, Shufoy and Prenhoe collapsed with laughter.

'Can you believe it?' Prenhoe wiped his eyes on the back of his hand. 'She couldn't care if her husband lived or died.'

'I think she was more interested in Little Poutface's bottom.'

'But what was Ipumer doing there?'

Shufoy wiped the tears from his cheeks on the hem of his robe. He didn't answer Prenhoe but began to imitate, what he called The Sacred Hippopotamus, making Prenhoe act the role of the pouting manservant. Laughing and joking, they made their way back to the highway and stood for a while looking down at the Nile.

'Why didn't you let me come with you this morning?' Prenhoe asked.

'Last night,' Shufoy explained, 'my master took me for some wine in one of the garden pavilions, just before he and the Lady Norfret retired.' Shufoy's face was a mask of sanctimonious solemnity. He grasped the parasol as if it was the source of all power. 'He confided in me. I agreed with his suspicions.'

'Oh, sacred bull!' Prenhoe moaned. 'Won't you come to the point?'

'By the sacred bull's balls, I will!' Shufoy grasped Prenhoe's arm and led him back towards Amerotke's mansion. 'Our master must be cunning and astute. He cannot openly question those involved in the case before him in court but he can make discreet enquiries. Ipumer was of Hyksos origin. Over a year ago he was brought to Thebes and given a job as a scribe in the House of War.'

'For what reason?'

'To wage war against the Panthers of the South. Now,' Shufoy warmed to his theme, 'my Lord Amerotke and I believe that Ipumer obtained his job due to influence in high places. Who better than one of the Panthers of the South?'

'You mean the dead General Kamun?'

'The same. Let me explain.' Shufoy moved the parasol from one hand to another. 'Kamun was only a cat's-paw. You know how it is, Prenhoe. Someone goes to an old veteran like him and says a friend wants a job. Kamun agreed and Ipumer, whoever he was, arrived in Thebes. He then does two things. First, he has to silence General Kamun so he goes to thank him. The old soldier is sickly, eager for company. Ipumer has a silver tongue; he'd lavish praise upon our hero. He becomes a regular visitor. One day he brings a flask of poisoned wine and Kamun is no more. Secondly, Ipumer removes his own records from the House of War so that Kamun's involvement in his appointment is cleverly destroyed.'

'But Ipumer didn't do this of his own accord?'

'Oh no, someone else was directing him. That person is the assassin.'

'Could this assassin have killed Ipumer?'

'Possibly.' Shufoy dropped his pompous stance. 'Though, if the evidence is believed, Ipumer was poisoned by someone in Lord Peshedu's household.'

'This is a deadly labyrinth,' Prenhoe mused. 'If I understand you correctly, Shufoy, Lord Amerotke is now following two strands that are connected: on the one hand, Ipumer's murder; secondly, somehow or other, the dead scribe had something to do with the murder of Lord Balet.'

'Yes, you are correct.'

'Now, that's strange,' Prenhoe mused. 'Because . . .'

Before he could continue they had to stand aside, as round the bend came chariots and, behind these, a cart carrying water jars, boxes and baskets, pulled by oxen. A surveyor from one of the estates was leading out his workers, followed by their women and children: a noisy gaggle of workers and retainers dressed in short-sleeved tunics over their loincloths. They were going down to one of the fields, the surveyor busily shouting instructions. Shufoy and Prenhoe waited under a palm tree until they passed in clouds of dust. Hordes of flies hovered, attracted by the food they carried. Shufoy watched them go. He idly speculated how, if he had not been falsely accused, that would be his life: a horde of children and work on some estate.

'This has broken my dream,' Prenhoe declared.

Shufoy closed his eyes: Prenhoe's dreams were famous.

'I was by the Nile and a crowd of farm workers passed by. They raised a lot of dust, which swirled towards me. A beautiful heset came out of it. She was naked except for a loincloth, a thick necklace of beads round her neck. She had a long, perfume-drenched wig which framed the sweetest face I've seen in many a dream.'

'Someone I know?' Shufoy asked soulfully.

'She beckoned me over and, before I knew it, I was in the Red Lands. She took me out to a small oasis. We lay in its soft grass in the shade but, when I drew her close, she turned into a scorpion. I woke screaming. What do you think that signifies, Shufoy?'

'Don't eat cheese just before you go to sleep,' Shufoy grumbled, plucking at his companion's sleeve. 'We have got to go! It's about the fourth hour, isn't it?'

Prenhoe wouldn't be put off. He started describing other dreams and was still chattering when they reached Amerotke's house. Shufoy half listened as they took off their sandals and washed their feet and hands. The boys were out swimming in the pool with Lady Norfret. Shufoy and Prenhoe put on their house sandals.

'Come on,' Shufoy grinned as Prenhoe described another dream, 'we are expecting a visitor and, for goodness' sake, shut up!'

They went down a long, cool corridor to Amerotke's writing chamber at the back of the house. The door was unlocked. Shufoy opened it and dragged Prenhoe in.

'Are we supposed to be here?' The scribe gazed, wide-eyed.

This was one of Amerotke's sanctuaries: cushions piled high on the far dais where the judge could sit and relax; a large, oaken desk inlaid with strips of silver; a comfortable quilted chair; stools; an ivory-coloured writing cabinet, and baskets where papyrus scrolls were stored. Shufoy went and pulled back the shutters of the large window overlooking the vegetable garden. The sweet smell of lettuce and radishes seeped into the room as well as the fresh black soil specially dried from the black mud of the Nile, in which any plant would flourish. Shufoy sat on a stool, Prenhoe on the edge of the dais. The dwarf put his parasol on the ground beside him.

'What are we doing here?' the scribe insisted.

'I told you, we are expecting a visitor.'

Prenhoe glared across. 'Do you think the Lady Neshratta is guilty?'

'I don't know,' Shufoy replied absent-mindedly. 'Anyone could have killed Ipumer: the person who brought him here from Avaris, one of his widow friends, Neshratta's father. Anyway, that's for Lord Amerotke to decide. What is the matter?'

Prenhoe sat horror-struck. They were no longer alone. A figure stood by the window. Prenhoe got to his feet. Shufoy chuckled.

'How dare you?' Prenhoe advanced threateningly.

The figure stepped out of the shadows.

'Sit down,' Shufoy ordered. 'This is our visitor.'

Prenhoe remained unconvinced. The stranger was of medium height, thin and wiry, his head completely shaven, a long, lean face with high cheekbones and sunken cheeks, thin, bloodless lips and darting, glittering eyes. He was dressed in a dyed linen sleeveless shirt above a leather kilt, sandals on his feet, and laced-up leggings, like those worn by peasants who didn't wish to be pricked by sharp blades of grass, protecting his calves. He stood all tense and watchful, hand on the dagger stuck into the leather belt round his waist. He turned his head; one ear was missing. He wore no jewellery, only a leather pouch on a piece of cord slung round his neck.

'Shufoy, is your friend going to attack me?' The voice was soft, cultivated.

'No, he's not.' Shufoy sprang to his feet. 'Prenhoe,' he poked the scribe in the chest, 'sit down. Greet my friend.'

He brought a stool and gestured to his visitor to sit. 'Do you want some wine?'

The man shook his head. He gazed admiringly around the room, his attention drawn by the beautiful leather cases on Amerotke's desk which held the judge's styli and writing instruments.

'Your master won't object?'

'As long as you don't touch anything,' Shufoy replied. 'Prenhoe, may I introduce a colleague of mine?'

'What's his name?'

'I don't know. We call him the Mongoose.'

The Mongoose shifted a stool so he could stare directly at Prenhoe.

'Who I am and where I come from is none of your business.'

'He's called the Mongoose,' Shufoy hastily intervened before Prenhoe took offence, 'because of his cunning and the way he can enter and leave without anyone noticing. He's well known to the Maijodou,' Shufoy grinned, 'our old friend the market police. He's also wanted for questioning in a number of nomes, from the Delta to the Third Cataract. Most of the time, however, he hides in Thebes.'

'Does Amerotke know he is here?'

'My Lord Amerotke keeps the Mongoose close to his right hand,' Shufoy replied, 'so he can use him for his own special purposes.'

'He's a thief,' Prenhoe declared, holding the Mongoose's gaze.

'I wouldn't say that,' Shufoy replied. 'He just finds it

difficult to distinguish between his property and every-body else's. He also collects information. Our master,' Shufoy added warningly, 'has never had any evidence placed before him against my friend.'

'What's that he's wearing round his neck?'

The Mongoose tapped the side of his head. 'My ear. An assailant once bit it off. It can't be sewn back and it's too precious to throw away.'

'Why all this drama?' Prenhoe demanded.

'Because I wanted to convince you and the Lord Amerotke that the Mongoose is as good as his word. So, what have you found?'

The Mongoose winked at Prenhoe and turned back to Shufoy.

'I have been down to the House of the Golden Gazelle. Lord Peshedu is away but his wife and two daughters are enjoying the shade of the garden. The household is subdued.'

'And you climbed into Lady Neshratta's bedchamber?' Shufoy asked, enjoying Prenhoe's gasp.

'Oh yes, a veritable treasure house. I took nothing. The wooden lattice framework can be taken away and there is a rope ladder.' He pulled a face. 'For a young, vigorous woman like Lady Neshratta it would be easy to move the lattice and climb down. Bushes grow near the base of the wall to hide footprints, whilst it's an easy journey across the gardens to the postern door. I went through that and out on to the trackway. There are trees, a small grove. You only have to be wary of a nearby irrigation canal.'

'And how did you find the Peshedu household?'

The Mongoose smiled; his eyeteeth were sharply filed, giving him a hungry, predatory look.

'I eavesdropped on the servants. They were, of course, discussing the Lady Neshratta. One thing I did learn. Do you know, or does your master, that on the night the Lady Neshratta was supposed to be meeting her lover, the Lord Peshedu was absent?'

He saw Shufoy's look of surprise.

'There's nothing wrong with that!' Prenhoe snapped. 'Peshedu is not on trial.'

'Ah yes.' The Mongoose glared. 'But did you also know that Peshedu has a soft spot for the hesets, the dancing girls in the Temple of Anubis? It is common chatter in the good general's household.'

Shufoy leant forward, eyes gleaming. 'You have done very well, Mongoose. And what else?'

'I visited the Temple of Seth. It is easy to enter the Red Chapel from an adjoining, lonely garden. A stealthy slayer would be hard to detect.'

'And?'

'I also chatted to my tavern friends, including a guard who does a tour of duty at the House of War. Ipumer was a conscientious scribe.' He glanced sideways at Prenhoe. 'A little like your good friend. He also liked the ladies.'

'How do you know that?'

'He started work just after dawn but always left just around the eleventh hour.'

'So?' Prenhoe queried.

'The same hour,' Shufoy observed, 'that the ladies of the city go down to the market.'

'More remarkable,' the Mongoose continued, 'his friend Hepel never accompanied him. Oh, by the way, Hepel has disappeared from his duties.'

Shufoy rubbed his hands together. His master would be pleased at what he had learnt: the Mongoose made sense.

'Go on!' Prenhoe urged crossly. 'You were telling us about your friends.'

'Well, Ipumer never broke his fast with anyone, nor did he ever visit the cookshops, the barber's chair, the wine houses.'

'The only explanation for that, my learned scribe,' Shufoy gloated, 'is that our good friend Ipumer was meeting someone secretly almost every day or, at least, during the few months before he died.'

'And the Hyksos?' Prenhoe demanded. 'My master talked about a secret society linked to the Hyksos.'

'Nonsense!' The Mongoose picked at his teeth. 'Thebes has more secret societies than a dog has fleas. You know how it is: this cult, that cult! True, thirty years ago there were people in Thebes who had a lot to hide, having collaborated with the invaders, but they are all dead and gone. The Hyksos are history.'

'General Balet wouldn't agree with that,' Prenhoe declared.

'Well, they are gone! Sand in the wind, nothing else.' The Mongoose got to his feet. 'I've stayed in this chamber long enough. I want to show you something.'

'What about the Street of the Oil Lamps?' Shufoy demanded.

'Oh yes, that as well.'

Shufoy and Prenhoe collected their walking sandals and the dwarf took his parasol. It helped him keep up with the others whilst, if they met trouble, the sharp and pointed end was as good as the dagger hidden under the folds of his robe. The Mongoose insisted on leaving the way he had come. The others met him outside the main gateway and hurried along in the direction of the city. Every so often the Mongoose would stop and take his bearings.

At last they reached a trackway which ran down the side of one of the great mansions. Prenhoe looked further along the wall. He glimpsed a polished wooden main gate and the glint of the golden gazelles carefully painted there.

'So.' Shufoy stood at the top of the lane and stared down. 'Yes, I can see the palm tree where the pedlar stayed, the grass and bushes.'

Prenhoe followed the direction of his gaze.

'He'd have to be careful,' Shufoy warned, pointing to the canal which snaked down the centre, almost hidden by the overgrown grass and bushes.

'Lead on!'

The Mongoose, keeping close to the wall, scurried down.

They reached the postern door; the ground around it was trodden down.

'It looks as if it is used often,' Shufoy joked.

He stared to his right where a makeshift bridge crossed the canal into a palm grove. He glimpsed terebinth and sycamore, wild grass and bushes – a cool, inviting place. He and Prenhoe followed the Mongoose as he led them into this. The trackway forced them to go single file.

At last they reached a small clearing which contained a green-skinned pool fringed by willow trees.

'Be careful of the snakes,' Prenhoe warned.

The Mongoose ignored him and led them over to a willow tree. The ground around it was soft and even.

'Wouldn't you agree, Shufoy,' he said, squatting down, 'that if you were meeting your beloved at the dead of night, this is the best place to rest? Behind you is nothing but wasteland and the wall of the next mansion whilst, if you stay here, you can watch anyone who might approach.'

Shufoy agreed.

'Look!' The Mongoose got to his feet. The roots of the willow tree jutted out slightly above the ground; one of them was stained quite thickly by grease from an oil lamp. 'And over here.' The Mongoose drew something from beneath a bush: a piece of linen, dirty and soiled, the type used to cover food.

'If I remember correctly,' Shufoy declared, 'on the night Ipumer was murdered, someone came out of Peshedu's house after Ipumer left, either the same person who met the scribe or someone else.' He looked back towards the House of the Golden Gazelle. 'It certainly looks bad for the Lady Neshratta. Someone came out here early in the day with a food basket. Neshratta later slipped out to meet Ipumer. They lay together in the moonlight, ate the food and drank the wine. That's when the scribe was poisoned. Afterwards Lady Neshratta came out and either brought the cups and platter back, or,' Shufoy pointed to the pool, 'dumped them.'

'Why are you doing all this?' Prenhoe asked.

The Mongoose embraced Shufoy and squeezed him tightly.

'Some days are fortunate, my friend, others not so. You never know when a man like me will have to beg for Pharaoh's mercy. But come, I have other things to show you. We must go into the city.'

Shufoy and Prenhoe followed him. The heat was ebbing as the sun dipped, changing the colour of the stone, the trees, even the Nile. Peasants and traders were leaving the city, chattering noisily, scolding their children, lashing the lazy oxen to go a little faster. Shufoy always loved such sights. He kept a sharp eye out for the Scorpion Men, those wandering pedlars who were a constant source of new ideas for him. He was still excited about plans to sell sacred amulets and statues, particularly to the devotees of the Temple of Seth. The Mongoose, however, was striding ahead as if eager to finish his business.

They entered the gates, pushing their way through the throng. The ladies of the night were already gathering, hoping to solicit the soldiers. They wore oil-drenched wigs. Little bells hung from their nipples; red and blue tattoos decorated their arms and thighs; silver studs gleamed in their navels above the gaudy cloths which covered their groins. They lounged in the shade and called softly across to passers-by. Next to them, in sharp contrast, a corpse-carrier from the Necropolis had set up a makeshift stall and was bawling for custom.

'I shall show you,' the fellow cried, 'the tombs of the great as well as the mysterious cave of darkness where long ago a man was buried alive!'

Beside him a wandering storyteller had decided that people interested in the Necropolis might pay to listen to his tale of wandering across Sinai, the exotic creatures which lived in the mountains or the savage tribes which hunted them.

Shufoy would have loved to have stayed but Prenhoe plucked him by the arm. They turned left off the main road leading to the temples and palaces and towards the quayside. Droves of people flocked here, either seeking passage across the Nile or to do business in the makeshift market which always sprang up in the evening. The air was rich with different smells and flavours: goose flesh grilled over charcoal; gazelle meat turned on a small spit outside a wine shop; the nose-tickling fragrances from the perfume stalls and, as they went down the needle-thin alleyways, the pervading stench from midden heaps and open latrines.

The Mongoose walked purposefully. The only time he paused was to step into a doorway, away from the sharp-eyed market police who came swaggering along swinging their cudgels.

The three crossed different quarters; the dyers and fullers, the linen-makers, potters and carpenters. At last they reached the small oil market in the southern corner of the city. The Mongoose certainly knew his way. They went down a broad road, flanked either side by houses, and stopped at a shop where a stall had been set up under a great open window which looked into the house. The stall was covered with different types of lamps: bronze, copper, precious alabaster, rough stone. Some were gaily decorated and exquisitely carved in the form of duck, geese or resting deer. The Mongoose grabbed the arm of one of the apprentices.

'Can I see your master? We have business.'

The boy ran into the house and returned with a small, fat man, mopping his sweaty face with a rag.

'You have business, sir?'

The Mongoose glanced at Shufoy. The dwarf opened the purse hidden under the folds of his robe and brought out a small deben of copper. He gazed up at the two-storeyed house, its top room approached by an outside stair built into the wall.

'Do you know the scribe Ipumer?'

'Why yes, he hires a room here. The one you are looking at.'

'Can we see it?'

The merchant scratched under his chin, a sign he was impatient to trade. Shufoy held out the deben of copper.

'We just want to look and ask questions.'

The shrewd eyes of the merchant studied Shufoy. He glanced quickly at the Mongoose.

'I have seen you before, haven't I? You were asking questions.' He tapped the circle of keys which swung from his leather belt, a sly grin on his face. 'I'll show you: two deben of copper.'

Shufoy agreed. The merchant grabbed them. Huffing and puffing he made his way up the steps. When he reached the top, he pushed the door open and mockingly waved them forward. Shufoy stepped inside and gasped in astonishment. The room was empty. Nothing but hard stone floor, a timber and plaster ceiling and lime-washed walls.

'Ipumer rented this?'

'Why yes,' the man smirked.

'Well, where are his possessions?'

'He moved them out.'

'When?'

'Oh, about eight days ago.'

Shufoy glanced at Prenhoe.

'That was after he was murdered.'

'Murdered! Ipumer wasn't murdered!'

An angry debate took place. Shufoy felt the merchant was tricking him but the fellow remained adamant.

'I told you,' he almost shouted, 'Ipumer came here and removed all his possessions.'

'But he can't have,' Shufoy riposted. 'Ipumer was murdered ten days ago but, according to you, two days after his corpse was taken to the House of Death, he returned to clear this room out. What did this Ipumer look like?'

'I don't know.'

Shufoy lifted his parasol threateningly.

'Now, don't start on me.' The man backed off.

Shufoy kicked the door shut. The Mongoose moved sideways, a thin, ugly knife in his hand.

'My friend is right. We paid a good price for useful information,' he said threateningly.

'All right. All right.'

The merchant went and sat in the corner, gesturing at them to come across.

'About a year ago,' he began, 'a man called Ipumer – he

said he was a scribe in the House of War – came along the street. I had advertised that the room above was vacant. Trade is good: we own the house next door and use the bottom floor of this as a warehouse and shop. He said he needed a place where he could meet certain ladies,' the merchant's fat face creased into a smile. 'So it was best if I knew as little as possible—'

'But he had a face!' Prenhoe broke in.

'No, he didn't. He dressed in a white, flounced linen robe with sleeves down to his wrists. He had a white shawl with a hood over his head and wore one of those Horus masks – you know, popular amongst the young bucks.'

Shufoy closed his eyes and groaned.

'Weren't you suspicious?' Prenhoe asked.

'Why should I be? He paid a good price. He claimed he would be no bother and the least I knew the better. We spat, clapped hands, he handed the price over, and a great deal more, so I gave him the key.'

'Did he come here often?'

'No.' The merchant shook his head. 'In fact, that surprised me. He gave me the key back because he hired a locksmith to make a new one. I don't think he trusted me. He brought some furniture, not much. I very rarely saw him.'

'And did his ladies come visiting?'

'I never saw one. On the few occasions he came, it was always dusk and he always wore that mask. You'd never know he was there. My wife objected but he paid well and caused no trouble.'

'Did anyone else come?'

'A young man. I could tell from his fingers he was probably a scribe – you know, ink-stained. He always looked a bit anxious. On the few occasions I glimpsed him, he had his head and face covered by a hood.'

Shufoy sat rocking backwards and forwards.

'I've told you what I know,' the merchant declared, getting to his feet. 'I can say no more.' He pushed his way by them and went across to the door. 'I think you should go now.'

Shufoy gestured for the rest to follow. They went down the steps and across the street into a small beer shop. The place was empty except for two porters who had placed their bundles on the floor and were angrily demanding jugs of ale. Shufoy told them to shut up. He ordered drinks for his friends and they went and sat on a stone bench at the back.

'I've done what you asked,' the Mongoose said. He picked up the stone jug and took a mouthful of beer. 'And more than that.' He patted Shufoy on the head and disappeared through the doorway.

'That wasn't too good,' Prenhoe opined.

'No, it wasn't.'

Shufoy moved restlessly and stared out as if fascinated by a bee buzzing from one flower to another. He sat listening to the sound of the streets, the cries of the vendors.

'My master thought Ipumer had another chamber somewhere in the city. What I think happened is this. Ipumer was brought into Thebes by a man who planned to murder as many of those Panthers of the South as possible, only

Ma'at knows his reasons. Now, this assassin,' Shufoy sipped at the beer, 'was going to use Ipumer. So he hired a chamber in the scribe's name but did so masked and disguised. As you can see, our oil lamp merchant didn't blink an eye. The chamber was used so he could meet Ipumer. Once the scribe was dead, the room was cleaned, everything in the room removed and this Horus-masked assassin disappears.'

'Well, who could it be?'

'I don't know.' Shufoy stared up at the streaks of red-gold in the sky. 'I hope my master is safe. He said he would be back late in the evening. He'll make sense of this.'

'But listen to my theory.' Prenhoe preened himself. 'Ipumer was no more than a trained dog. He came to Thebes but wasn't fitted for the task. He was introduced to Lord Peshedu and decided it was more worthwhile to pursue the Lady Neshratta. The person who hired him grew tired, murdered Ipumer and began his own campaign.'

'Yes, but Ipumer died immediately after visiting Neshratta?'

'You heard the Mongoose,' Prenhoe countered. 'The man who hired the chamber could have been waiting for Ipumer at the House of the Golden Gazelle.'

'But the pedlar saw them kiss.'

'Perhaps Ipumer liked both sides of the platter,' Prenhoe joked. He glimpsed the disbelief in Shufoy's eyes. 'All right, that sounds fanciful,' he conceded, 'but what if Ipumer and Neshratta lay in the grass and ate some food and wine, all innocent, but Ipumer, on his way home, met someone else who administered the poison?'

Shufoy drained his beer jug and got to his feet.

'It's too simple,' he murmured. 'But you've put your finger on it, Prenhoe. The court will have to decide, or discover, if our strange scribe, after he left the House of the Golden Gazelle, visited anyone else?'

They walked back into the beer shop, said farewell to the owner, and stepped into the street. Prenhoe noticed Shufoy was agitated. The dwarf grasped the parasol and walked swiftly down the street; he turned a corner where he grabbed Prenhoe by the arm and pulled him into a doorway.

'Shut up and wait!' he whispered.

Prenhoe was about to berate Shufoy when a small, wizened man padded into sight. He paused just near the doorway, looking expectantly around.

'We are here,' Shufoy called softly.

The man started; he would have run away but Shufoy was faster. He darted from the doorway, caught the man by the wrist and held him tight. The man struggled but Shufoy refused to release him, pushing him up against the wall, raising the sharp tip of his parasol under the man's chin, forcing back his head.

'You've been following us all the time, haven't you?'

The man stretched out his hand. Shufoy glimpsed a small signet ring, a circle of copper emblazoned with the eye of Horus.

'So, you are from the Lord Valu, the Eyes and Ears of Pharaoh,' Shufoy mocked. 'And why do you find the servants of Lord Amerotke so interesting? You are very good,' the dwarf continued, 'but I saw you near the House

SETH: often associated with the pig
which, in turn, was regarded as unclean.

CHAPTER 7

For years to come, in the Perfume Quarter of Thebes, people would remember that night! A time of fire and brutal murder! Some of the ancient ones whispered the red-haired God Seth prowled the alleyways, a battle-axe in one hand, a sword of judgment in the other. Others dismissed this as fanciful nonsense.

The night in question started peacefully enough – a dark blue sky, stars hanging heavy with a full moon above the city. Intef the physician had waited for darkness. Dressed in his best robe, he quietly left his house and made his way through the overgrown garden out by the back gate. He crossed the square where the Perfume Market was held and hugged the wall like a shadow until he reached the house of his good friend and colleague, the widow Felima. He went down the side, through the wicket gate and knocked on the rear door, the prearranged signal. A light glow followed by the crash of bolts being pulled back. Felima, dressed in a white robe and embroidered sash, sandals on her feet, greeted him with open arms. Intef slipped in whilst she locked and bolted the door behind them.

'Are we alone?' he asked teasingly.

'The servants are all gone,' she smiled, 'and everything is ready.'

She led him along the corridor into the central pillared hall of the house, a lofty apartment with gaily decorated wooden pillars, in the centre a small raised stone platform where a brazier was crackling merrily. The dais at the far end had already been decorated. Finely embroidered curtains covered the wall. Carpets and cushions were strewn around the two small tables, which bore bowls and platters of fruit, cooked meats, dried salted fish and deep bowled beakers of wine.

Intef groaned with pleasure. He allowed Felima to undress him and he did the same for her. Both naked, they climbed on the dais and lay down on the cushions, touching each other, kissing, even as they exchanged food and drink. It was always the same – what Intef called his 'secret nights of pleasure' with this respectable-looking widow, who was more skilled in the arts of love than any trained heset or courtesan. Intef drank deeply of the wine and watched Felima's pet monkey scamper about. He turned and admired the pale green paint of the wall friezes, the wooden pillars, freshly done in black and red, the handsome wine jars.

'You've been spending some money,' he murmured.

Felima drew closer, hand rubbing Intef's stomach, crawling enticingly down to his groin.

'Profits are good,' she replied. Her face grew serious. 'But are we safe?'

'Ah, you mean the bitch Neshratta?' Intef raised his cup. 'She'll pay for her crimes.'

He fondled one of Felima's breasts and sniffed at the heavy perfume which drenched her embroidered wig. Felima pushed him away and, turning to a small bowl, took out a phial of precious perfume and, running it between her fingers, began to anoint his head, eyes, cheeks and chin.

'Do you think they'll find out?' she asked, pulling away.

'Find out what?'

'That Ipumer visited your house before he returned to fat Lamna?'

'What can they say?' the physician retorted. 'If I am called to speak on oath, I'll just say he felt unwell, which is the truth.' He took another sip. 'But what happens if they ask you questions?'

'Such as?' Felima demanded.

'Well,' Intef cradled the cup, enjoying himself, 'they might start asking how you came to know someone who has been in Thebes only over a year. Why you were so generous with your money and favours to a stranger.'

'That's no problem.'

Felima pouted and rose rather angrily to fetch another jug of wine.

'He was a young man and handsome with it. I met him in the marketplace.' She giggled, looking at Intef from under her eyelashes. 'He was quite a stallion and you didn't object, did you? You liked to hear about my exploits. He came looking for lodgings so I recommended him to the widow Lamna.'

'Amerotke's sharp,' Intef snarled. 'He'll ask why you didn't take him in.'

Felima, now tipsy, waved round the chamber.

'I don't take lodgers, that's well known. If Lamna hadn't given him a room upstairs, perhaps I would have reconsidered.'

Intef didn't seem convinced. He stared narrow-eyed at the brazier, crackling noisily and sending up small spirals of smoke.

'I don't know . . .' Intef whispered. Shadows danced against the wall and a cold finger of fear pricked his back. Amerotke worried him. At first Intef thought the matter was closed and sealed. Valu would present his case and Neshratta would be condemned. Not that the physician really cared. Ipumer's murder had nothing to do with him. Well, not really! But if Amerotke continued his questions . . . ? Intef sighed and took another gulp of wine. He and this widow woman had a great deal to hide.

'Why did Ipumer come to you?' he demanded.

'I've told you, it was a chance meeting.'

'Do you think Neshratta will talk?'

'How can she?' Felima laughed. 'A matter like that! She'll keep her mouth closed. Anyway, she has no proof.'

Intef was about to continue the conversation when he heard the faint sound of a conch horn not too far away. The alarm had been raised. He got up, went to the window and glimpsed the red glow against the sky.

'A fire has broken out,' he declared. 'I can see a glow of flame.'

'Well, it's not here, is it?' Felima slurred. 'Come back!'

Intef reluctantly obeyed. He had drunk deeply, yet he was sure the fire was in the same direction as his own house. But it stood in its own grounds and he had doused any oil lamps, any lights.

Felima was now becoming insistent. She edged along the cushions, heavy-eyed, lips slobbering, wig slightly askew.

'Shall we play? Shall we frolic?'

She broke off as her monkey raced to the end of the dais and began chattering noisily.

'Shut up!' she shouted, and, picking up a cushion, threw it angrily at the animal. The monkey scampered away. Felima stared into the shadows at the far end of the hall. Was someone there? The monkey only chattered if someone approached.

'Leave it!' Intef murmured. Now aroused by Felima's wandering fingers, he pulled her closer. 'Let's play,' he grinned. 'Let's eat and drink.'

'And then die!'

Intef and Felima sat up so suddenly they knocked one of the tables over, the jug crashing to the floor, the red wine spilling out. They gazed in horror: a movement amongst the shadows. A figure came forward, silently, as if gliding across the polished floor yet this was no fantasy. He was dressed in the leather shirt and war tunic of a soldier, sandals on his feet, leather guards on his wrists. The war belt he wore held sword and dagger, and he carried a bow with a quiver on his back. He brought his head up, but all Intef and Felima could see were eyes glittering behind the Horus mask.

'What are you? What are you doing? Why?'

'Come to deliver judgment!' the masked figure declared.

'Judgment! What have we done?'

'This!'

The bow came up, an arrow notched. Felima sprang drunkenly to her feet. She tried to run but the assassin was quicker. An arrow was loosed. It caught her full in the throat and sent her clattering back against the wall. Intef, on hands and knees, crawled towards this hideous figure of death, the assassin notching another arrow to his bow.

'Stand up!'

Intef obeyed.

'Die like a man,' the intruder continued, 'with your face towards your enemy!'

Again the bow twanged. The arrow took Intef clear through the heart, so sharp, so deep, he was dead before his head smacked against the hard, glass-like floor. The assassin, still holding the bow, went and checked both Intef's corpse and that of Felima. He grunted in satisfaction and, going back down the hall, brought up the bulging wineskins. Taking out their stoppers, he emptied the oil. It seeped everywhere. The assassin took a second wineskin and did the same along the passageway. Opening the door to the cellars, he threw the wineskins down. Carefully, silently, he took the lamps from their niches. Some he threw on cushions and, when he was satisfied, ripped a piece of tapestry from the wall. He soaked this in oil and threw it into the dining hall, its floor shimmering with oil and the blood of his victims. The flame took hold. A sheet of fire raced along the floor. The assassin stopped, watching the effect of his handiwork, before slipping through the back door and out across the gardens.

The widow Lamna was in her counting house. She had decided to distract herself by once again going over her accounts, taking pleasure from the profits she'd made. She dreaded being called back to the Hall of Two Truths. As she'd confided to her neighbours, she had never been so petrified in her life: the great open space before the judgment chair; that sharp-eyed Valu the prosecutor; Meretel the advocate listening to her every word; the young woman Neshratta, immobile as a statue, and, above all, that keen-eyed judge studying her intently, weighing every sentence and phrase she uttered.

Lamna had really racked her memory. Did she have anything to fear? She had done nothing wrong, except offer Ipumer a chamber. Lamna, despite her podgy looks and slow ways, was still sharp enough to recognise hidden dangers. The widow Felima had been most uneasy, whilst physician Intef apparently knew Ipumer better than she'd thought. Lamna anxiously chewed her lip. What had she to do with murder, secret love meetings? Had she been used? Ipumer had come here on Felima's recommendation. Lamna moved the oil lamp closer.

She heard the conch horn blowing and wondered where the fire had broken out. That was a common occurrence and there was no strong wind. The market police would take care of it. Lamna glanced at the ointments and perfumes and, above them on the shelves, the little baskets of herbs and powder which provided the ingredients. Lamna was sorry Ipumer was dead but she wanted to forget him.

She heard a sound outside and pushed back the stool, got to her feet and went out. The passageway was empty. Lamna went back and sat down. She was about to roll the piece of papyrus up when she heard her name called. Her head came back in surprise and, as it did so, the strangler's cord wrapped round her throat. Lamna struggled but her assailant was strong. The cord tightened, dug deep into her throat and, after a short while, Lamna's struggles ceased. Only then did the assassin lower her corpse gently to the ground.

Amerotke was in the Silver Room, a small antechamber in the House of a Million Years near the Great Mooring Place on the Nile. He sat on a marble ledge built against the wall, and grasped the goblet of chilled grape juice a chamberlain had brought. He felt tired. Despite bathing, relaxing for a while, Amerotke still ached from the jolting chariot ride back into the city. He was glad to be away from the Panthers of the South. They had grudgingly accepted him but he had made little headway. Time and again, before they had left the Oasis of Ashiwa, he had tried to discover if there was any acrimony between them, resentment, hidden grudges. He had discovered nothing.

'We are a band of brothers. We stood in the battle

line together and faced the furies of Pharaoh's enemies,'
Karnac had declared. 'Why should we murder a comrade?
No, no, my Lord Amerotke,' Karnac had raised his hand
as if taking an oath, 'the killer of Lord Balet, the assassin
who stalks us, is not one of us.'

The rest had supported him in this, yet the mystery remained. Who had hired those Sand Wanderers to
attack? Who had removed Meretseger's grisly remains?
And, above all, who had threatened these soldiers, then
carried out that threat with the bloody execution of
Lord Balet?

In the short but furious journey home Amerotke had
tried to marshal his thoughts. He'd returned to his house
tired and irritable. He had to apologise profusely to
Norfret, who chided him gently at the way he scolded his
sons. He had bathed, rubbed oil into his body and relaxed
on a roof couch until Shufoy appeared. Amerotke had
listened carefully to what his manservant had discovered
and his heart had softened at the excitement in the little
man's eyes.

'We have done well, haven't we, Master?'

Shufoy had looked over his shoulder at Prenhoe; a rap-
turous smile had transfigured the young scribe's face.

'You have done well,' Amerotke had agreed. 'More pieces
to the puzzle but no clear picture.'

He had gone back to his musings. He'd even tried
to write down his thoughts, but Shufoy's discoveries,
as well as those they had learnt from Valu's 'eyes and
ears', were interesting, relevant, but only deepened the
mystery. Amerotke had been about to retire for the night

when the messenger had arrived bearing Hatusu's cartouche.

'The Divine One,' the envoy had declared, handing across the seal, 'has deigned to show Her face and smile on you. Your presence is required in the Amethyst Chamber in the House of a Million Years.'

Amerotke had groaned but a summons was a summons. Hatusu and Lord Senenmut would have been informed what had happened at Ashiwa. If the Divine One wanted to discuss it, the Divine One would do so, whatever hour of the day or night. Amerotke had apologised once again to Norfret, kissed her and, accompanied by Shufoy and Prenhoe, made his way back into the city.

The curfew had not yet sounded; the guards had been concerned about a fire raging in the Perfume Quarter.

'Isn't that where Ipumer lived?' Shufoy had asked.

Amerotke hadn't had time to answer. A contingent of archers from the Ibis regiment had been waiting impatiently and promptly escorted them down to the Divine House. Shufoy and Prenhoe were left to kick their heels in the kitchens whilst Amerotke was to await Pharaoh's pleasure.

The judge stared through the half-open door at the passageway outside and wondered if the palace ever slept. Chamberlains and stewards scurried by – servants bearing trays of food and wine, their flavour so enticing Amerotke's mouth watered. The stream of attendants and servants was constant: the Keepers of the Divine One's perfume, the Director of Her Cabinet, the Holder of Her Fan, the Imperial Sandal-Bearer, all passed by, chattering excitedly. Amerotke heard the faint singing of the imperial choir practising a hymn, one of Hatusu's favourites.

> 'The voice of the swallow haunts me.
> The lands are alight when you are away!
> No, little bird, you cannot entice me,
> I follow the path of the one and only.
> I peer through the morning mist
> And seek his golden face.
> I turn my hot cheek to catch his cooling breath.'

Amerotke's eyes grew heavy. He started awake and prayed he wouldn't shame himself by falling asleep. He wondered what mood the imperial lady was in. She would demand answers. She would know that Amerotke had informed Karnac's group how the death of Ipumer was linked to that of Balet and so they all may have to be questioned in open court. They had not liked this; neither would Hatusu.

'Have you been waiting long, my lord?'

Amerotke glanced up. Valu, the lord prosecutor, stood in the doorway, head and face shining with oil. He was dressed in elegant white robes with silver sandals on his feet. He had painted his eyes and lips; his finger- and toenails were dyed a deep purple.

'I have received a summons too.'

Valu came over and sat beside him, his eyes crinkled in amusement.

'You look tired, Amerotke. Tomorrow, when I face you in court, you will be attentive?'

'Where you are concerned, my Lord Valu, I am all "eyes and ears".'

Valu laughed.

'I understand that your servants and mine have been very busy,' Valu declared. 'You know what I have found? A good witness, a soldier who stopped Ipumer on his return to the city that night. He was apparently admitted through a postern gate. Ipumer claimed to be unwell. He joked that he didn't know the pleasures of love could affect his stomach. The soldier thought Ipumer was rather drunk or at least tipsy. "Where have you been, sir?" he asked. "To the House of the Golden Gazelle," Ipumer answered.'

'It still doesn't prove the Lady Neshratta is a murderer!' Amerotke snapped.

The debate would have continued but the cedar doors swung open.

'The Divine One,' the pompous chamberlain declared, 'has deigned to smile on you. You may enter the House of Adoration!'

Valu glanced at Amerotke and raised his eyes. They followed the chamberlain in. The Amethyst Chamber was circular, ringed by pillars, in between which were windows overlooking Pharaoh's private garden. The walls, ceiling and floor were of a rare shiny stone which glowed like amethyst. Silver and gold decorated the top and base of the pillars. The oil lamps, hidden behind transparent panels in the walls, gave the impression that the room was being heated and lighted by some mysterious fire.

Hatusu was waiting for them on the gold and silver

throne on the dais at the far end of the chamber. Amerotke and Valu advanced halfway, knelt and pressed their foreheads against the ground. The floor, with its gold and silver motif, felt cold. Amerotke looked quickly to his right. An eating place had been set up beneath a window: a ring of cushions with tables bearing fruit, meat, bread, goblets and jugs of wine. The chamberlain coughed.

'We rejoice,' Valu intoned, remembering protocol, 'that we are summoned to your presence, for your smile, Divine One, is better than a thousand days of pleasure. Your presence warms us like the sun.'

'Amen!' Amerotke added hastily.

The doors closed behind them as the chamberlain left.

'You may approach,' Senenmut, standing beside Hatusu, proclaimed.

Amerotke sighed and got to his feet. Hatusu was in one of her imperious moods! Going forward to the steps covered with cushions, they prostrated themselves once more and kissed the silver sandals embroidered with gold rosettes.

'Your face is beautiful,' Valu intoned.

'I think we've had enough of that!' Hatusu remarked sharply. 'You may stand!'

Amerotke and Valu got to their feet. Hatusu grinned at them. She was dressed in a purple dyed gown, a gold gorget studded with different jewels round her throat. Amethysts gleamed at her ears and on her fingers; her bracelets were of pure ivory.

'Do you like my face? I've used new paints and powders.' She glanced quickly at Senenmut standing behind the chair, one hand resting on the gold carved lion. 'Senenmut thinks that the rouge is too heavy, whilst I should use green not black kohl round my eyes.'

'You look beautiful,' Valu replied.

'You are a flatterer.' Hatusu got to her feet and stood on tiptoe, peering down the hall. 'Good, they have closed the door.'

She moved and Amerotke smelt her beautiful perfume.

'It's a mixture,' she explained as if she had heard his sniff. 'Cinnamon, bitter almonds, frankincense and myrrh. You look tired, my lord. How are the Red Lands?'

'Better now I've left them.'

'I suppose that was stupid,' Hatusu sighed.

She grasped Valu by one hand and Amerotke with the other and led them down the steps. She tripped slightly on the bottom one and swore under her breath.

'If I was holding an audience that wouldn't do, would it?' She turned and kicked the offending cushion. 'I thought I'd dress to suit the room. My father used to meet his courtesans here. Their squeals of laughter used to ring through the palace.'

She led them across to the tables and plumped down in the centre, fluffing the cushions out, crossing her legs and helping herself to food and drink.

'Come on!' She gestured at Senenmut. 'You haven't said a word, my lord. I'm starving, whilst Amerotke looks as if he is going to fall asleep. There's nothing like a foreign ambassador droning on for hours to give you an appetite.'

Hatusu distributed the food, broke up the bread and

placed portions on jewelled silver plates. Using a gold prong, she scooped out the chunks of fillet steak cooked in a wine sauce and heaped each plate with cucumber, lettuces and other vegetables.

'We'll eat with our fingers.' She smiled round. 'And, my Lord Valu, no more courtesies. I want to swim in the Pool of Purity before I –' she grinned at Senenmut – 'we retire.'

Amerotke made himself comfortable. Senenmut was taciturn. Amerotke could tell by the way Hatusu was flirting with him and Valu that she and her lover had quarrelled over something. Hatusu ate daintily, smiling between mouthfuls.

'I do admire the paint on your fingernails,' Hatusu cooed at Valu. 'I really must have something of the same.'

'It's a personal mixture, my lady.'

'Not any longer,' Hatusu laughed. 'Well, well, well.' She lifted her goblet. 'This wine is from across Sinai, the best vineyard in Canaan. My Lords, I give you a toast: to the House of Adoration and the Glory of Ra!'

'May she live for a million years!' Valu added.

'Right!' Hatusu put down the cup and patted her stomach. 'I see that I am going to be the life and soul of this party. Amerotke,' she leant across and poked him playfully on the shoulder, 'don't you dare go to sleep.' The smile faded from her face. 'I heard what happened at the Oasis of Ashiwa. I have told my Lord Senenmut bluntly, a military escort should have accompanied you.'

'But Karnac insisted and you agreed,' Senenmut broke in angrily.

Hatusu turned and blinked. 'I don't remember that.'

Senenmut glowered and lifted his goblet.

'Amerotke, we are waiting,' Hatusu went on. 'What did your quick wits learn? Is it true,' she continued, 'what Peshedu suspects? Are you going to question him in court?'

'My lady, for one moment let's put Peshedu aside. What I tell you now is conjecture. I have very little proof. The Panthers of the South are heroes of Thebes. True, my lady, they could have been killed and captured, together with your unworthy judge.'

'I would have become a laughing stock.' Hatusu's eyes blazed with anger. 'I'll have the balls wrenched from the man responsible!'

'The Panthers of the South,' Amerotke continued, 'are heroes. They are the glory of Thebes. For thirty years they have enjoyed the fat of the land. Now there's an assassin amongst them. I call him the Sethian because he is a true devotee of that God. I suspect that, eighteen months to two years ago, there was a shift in this noble company of warriors: a terrible breach which either all of them haven't recognised or have kept silent about. One of them is the Sethian. I truly believe that.'

'But my Lord Amerotke,' Valu gestured with his cup, 'all of them were out in the Red Lands at Ashiwa. If the Sand Wanderers, the attackers, had been successful, he too would have been captured.'

Amerotke wiped the rim of his goblet. 'My conclusion is that he doesn't care. Like a warrior who throws himself into the battle, he doesn't worry if he will win or die—'

'As long as his enemy loses.' Hatusu finished the sentence.

'Precisely, my lady: that's the true gauge of his malice. His heart has turned to evil, his mind bent solely on vengeance, for what reasons I don't know. He decides to strike at the very heart of this company of heroes. He was at Pharaoh's great victory against the Hyksos. He knows all about Meretseger. He has obtained some of her medallions and knows where her corpse was buried. Indeed, he may have learnt more about Meretseger's family than any of us here. He plots a subtle and cruel revenge. Somehow or other he finds that the scribe known as Ipumer, a son, perhaps a kinsman, of Meretseger, is alive in Avaris. Ipumer is Hyksos, probably the son of one of their princes.'

'Could he be Meretseger's child?' Hatusu asked.

'Possibly,' Amerotke replied. 'Born just before she died, Ipumer was the right age. He certainly has the sacred tattoo of a Hyksos noble. The Sethian bribes, encourages, motivates Ipumer to come to Thebes. He is going to be the knife with which the Sethian will strike at his companions.'

'Why would Ipumer agree?' Senenmut asked. 'It's a dangerous task.'

'Perhaps he wanted revenge, to make mischief? Ipumer was a venal man. Perhaps the bribe was so enticing he couldn't resist?'

'But wouldn't Ipumer discover who the Sethian was?' Valu demanded.

'No, I think they met in shadowy corners at the dead of

night whilst the Sethian disguised his face behind a Horus mask.' Amerotke shrugged. 'That's not too extraordinary. Wander round Thebes, you'll often pass devotees of a particular cult or members of a certain society wearing the mask of their God.'

Hatusu dug under the cushions and brought out a mirror, its handle of mother-of-pearl. She examined herself carefully.

'I always keep one nearby,' she murmured. 'And, by the way, Amerotke, you are correct. My Lord Senenmut and I always wear masks when we wander round Thebes at night.' She grinned at Valu's surprise. 'This Sethian intrigues me.'

She gripped the snow-white crown bearing the golden Uraeus, the striking cobra, gently extricated it from her perfume-drenched wig and placed it on the cushion beside her.

'Too tight,' she murmured. 'I'll have my Keeper of the Diadem look at it. Continue, Amerotke.'

'The Sethian hires a chamber in the Street of Oil Lamps. He used Ipumer's name but really it's for himself. He will meet Ipumer there. At the same time the Sethian has persuaded General Kamun to appoint Ipumer to the House of War. It can be easily done. Kamun wouldn't be suspicious. Such patronage is commonplace. The Sethian would ask Kamun to keep the matter secret, yet he has nothing to fear. One of Ipumer's first tasks is to visit General Kamun, thank him, flatter him and poison him.'

'You believe that?' Senenmut asked.

'Yes, I do. The Sethian, or Ipumer, then removed the

records from the Hall of Archives. No one now knows who brought Ipumer to Thebes. No one knows anything about his past.'

'I have sent my spies to Avaris,' Valu interrupted. 'It might take them weeks . . .'

'By which time,' Amerotke continued, 'the Panthers of the South will have been killed. Anyway, the Sethian introduces Ipumer at some banquet or festival. Again it wouldn't be difficult. Ipumer worked in the House of War. Why shouldn't he attend a military gathering?' Amerotke paused. 'I can only surmise but this is where the Sethian's plot went wrong. Perhaps Ipumer was meant to seduce and degrade Neshratta, cause scandal, besmirch her family name. Or it could be even simpler . . .'

'Ipumer fell in love with Neshratta?'

'Yes. Whatever happened, Ipumer became distracted. Perhaps he grew tired of the task – objected, dragged his feet. One thing was on his mind: Neshratta. Everything else was ignored.'

'Why didn't the Sethian just kill Ipumer?' Valu asked.

'He might have done,' Amerotke smiled. 'That is the case before me in the Hall of Two Truths. Or perhaps the Sethian was quite content to see Lady Neshratta make a fool of herself. Such an affair was bound to end in tears and disgrace.'

'I agree,' Senenmut declared. 'Peshedu is a laughing stock with his daughter acting like a heset, going out in the dead of night to lie with her lover in some muddy spot.'

'And there's more.' Amerotke sipped from his cup.

'Now Ipumer is dead, under mysterious circumstances, Peshedu's family and all their secrets are open to public gaze. General Peshedu's love for heset girls and courtesans will soon become public knowledge. He will be shamed and so will his wife. We have yet to find out what secrets she possesses.'

'Ah, the heset girl who was murdered!' Valu exclaimed. 'Oh yes, Amerotke, I, too, have spies in the House of Death. The one who was pregnant.'

'Pregnant?' Hatusu demanded.

Amerotke quickly told her what he had learnt.

'What are you saying?' Hatusu demanded. 'Could Peshedu have murdered that temple girl? Perhaps he was involved in Ipumer's murder.' Hatusu groaned. 'Whatever, I follow your logic. Peshedu is going to be dishonoured, the laughing stock of Thebes. He'll even have the finger of suspicion pointed at him. Could he be the Sethian?'

'Any one of them might be. But,' Amerotke shook his head, 'I am not yet into the mind of the killer. I do believe he tired of Ipumer's games and decided to take matters into his own hands. I have tried to establish where everyone was when Lord Balet was killed but it's nigh impossible. The Sethian must have known that: the heroes all have different households. I can't determine what they told me is true or false.'

'How did Balet's killer get in to the Red Chapel so silently?' Senenmut asked.

'Through a window from a garden. A man I know,' Amerotke smiled, 'one of Shufoy's friends, found he could enter the garden, climb up through a window and cross the passageway to the Red Chapel. He was through the door before the guardian priest or his wife could detect anything was wrong.'

'But there was no noise?' Senenmut asked. 'No alarm raised? You said Balet wouldn't give up his life easily.'

'He was struck from behind; died before he even knew. I believe the killer turned over stools, created disarray, to make it look as if a struggle had taken place. That only deepened the mystery; heightened the impression that Balet's murder had more to do with vengeance from the Underworld than the malice of man. He emphasised this by removing Balet's eyes, tying red twine round his ankles and wrists and sprinkling the cups with the poor man's blood. Afterwards he left quickly and silently. The guardian priest was probably sleeping with his wife. From what I gather they are a precious pair, more concerned about their own pleasures than prayer and sacrifice.'

Hatusu muttered something about having both removed.

'And Meretseger's corpse?' Senenmut demanded.

'Oh, that was easy enough. The Panthers of the South have chariots. The Sethian went out to the Oasis of Ashiwa. It's a lonely, desolate place. The grave was opened, the bones, or whatever was left, placed in a casket and he returned to Thebes. Chariots leave this city by the score every hour of the day. It could have been done months ago.'

'I wonder where those remains are,' Hatusu mused.

'Some secret place out in the desert. Perhaps the Sethian built a shrine to her. He's certainly full of hate.

He realised, once these murders began, Meretseger's grave would be revisited and, of course, the only people who know where it is are his fellow heroes. Bandits, outlaws and mercenaries are easy to hire. A sudden brutal attack and the Panthers of the South could be kidnapped, killed or humiliated and he has his revenge. One thing he overlooked: whatever we may think about Karnac and his companions, they are just as good at killing as he is. Believe me, my lady, I spent a day with them: those men were born for fighting. They relish it.'

'And now?' Senenmut demanded.

'The Sethian is frustrated so he will try to kill his companions one by one. He'll strike quickly and ruthlessly.'

'But why?' Valu demanded.

'If I knew that, my lord, I'd trap the killer.'

'And you must question Peshedu?' Senenmut demanded. The Grand Vizier leant over and filled each of their goblets.

'Yes, I must.'

'I agree,' Valu spoke up. 'We have to establish just exactly what happened in the House of the Golden Gazelle the night Ipumer died.'

'But, my Lord Amerotke,' Hatusu teased, 'you pick at loose threads, you pull them loose – is there anything else?'

'I am curious,' Amerotke replied, 'how Ipumer managed to secure lodgings with the widow Lamna. And why he became so friendly with another, Felima, as well as his relationship with the physician Intef. My Lord Valu, you'll agree, Ipumer came home ill early in the morning. Everyone has sworn to that. Why didn't he go to Intef's house? He must have passed it on the way.'

Valu clicked his tongue. 'If only Neshratta had confessed,' he replied ruefully. 'If we could only discover just whom Ipumer met that night. Yet her maid and younger sister are unshakeable: they claim that Neshratta never left her bedchamber that night.'

He was about to continue when there was a loud rapping on the door. An anxious-faced chamberlain slipped through and prostrated himself, forehead against the ground.

'What is it?' Hatusu declared.

'Oh, Divine One, an urgent message for my Lord Valu.'

Hatusu indicated with her fingers that Valu could leave. Whilst he was gone Hatusu leant over.

'Should Neshratta's case be closed, Amerotke? Why don't we just dismiss it?'

The judge held her gaze. 'My lady, you know what will happen. Is Pharaoh's justice for all or just for some? They would claim I am your creature, a judge bought and sold like a bullock in the market.'

'It was worth a try.' Hatusu sighed in exasperation. 'But you know the old song, Amerotke. I won't repeat the words. Karnac and the others are much beloved. They hold great sway with the army. Balet's sacrilegious death was enough, but to see one of their company have his reputation picked to pieces like buzzards do a carcass . . .' She broke off as Valu returned.

The prosecutor squatted back on the cushions.

'I had my suspicions,' he murmured.

'What?' Hatusu demanded.

'Oh, rumours, picked up by my spies that the widow Felima and the physician Intef were not what they appeared.'

'Be precise!' Hatusu snapped.

'I would love to, my lady.' Valu's voice was tart. 'And, perhaps in time, I could have been. Fresh murders: the widow Lamna has been found garrotted in her chamber. The remains of Intef and Felima have been found in her burnt house – both of them apparently killed by some mysterious archer. The arrows were still embedded in their charred corpses. The assassin burnt Felima's house; he also destroyed Intef's the same way.'

Amerotke closed his eyes. One path out of this maze was now blocked.

'Why?' Senenmut demanded.

'The Sethian,' Amerotke declared, 'is protecting himself. Ipumer has gone and he wants to make sure that no thread can be found to lead us back to him.' He glanced at Valu. 'You said that the widow Felima and the physician Intef were suspect?'

Valu pulled a face. 'Just rumours, gossip. They lived as if they had little, yet they were wealthy enough. Fine linen beneath the dirty robes,' he joked. 'But the source of their hidden wealth?' He shook his head. 'My lord judge, your guess is as good as mine. Potions, powders, drugs to provide dreams? Whatever?' He waved his hands.

'They were certainly murdered,' Amerotke murmured, 'and for the same reason that poor heset girl was. The

Sethian is ruthless. He's putting as much distance between himself and Ipumer as possible.'

'If that's the case,' Valu observed, 'there might be another victim whose corpse has not yet been discovered. Ipumer had a friend, an acquaintance in the House of War, the scribe Hepel, a conscientious man. He didn't turn up for work today and has been absent from his chamber. He was last seen roistering in the wine shops along the quayside.'

Amerotke grasped his cup. 'He'll kill soon,' he murmured. 'I tell you this, my lady: before that moon rises again, this Sethian will have claimed another victim.'

SETH: opponent of Horus, the God of
Light.

CHAPTER 8

The assassin, whom Amerotke called the Sethian, could find no peace. He'd crossed the Nile, robed and hooded, and stopped for a while before the soaring statue of Osiris, Foremost of the Westerners. The shrine made him think, pricked his heart and conscience and brought back memories of happier days. Although darkness had fallen, the air was still heavy with the pungent smells from the mummers' shops and embalming houses, the bitter-sweet smell of myrrh and frankincense mixing with a heavy salty tang of natron, reminiscent of his days in the Delta near the Great Green. He stared up at the sky and watched the moon, so clear, so near he felt he could stretch out and touch it. Visitors to the Necropolis hurried by. They didn't spare the Sethian a second glance. Most of them had been shopping, purchasing caskets, jars and other funeral objects. Others had been visiting the family tombs, enjoying the warm evening whilst they ate and drank with friends and discussed loved ones who had passed to the Far Horizon.

Candlelight and oil lamp beckoned at windows and doorways. Torches of pitch and tar had been lit and spluttered bravely against the darkness. Along the broad quayside a chariot clattered by: one of the squadrons returning from patrol in the Red Lands. A Sand Dweller, his hands bound, lashed to the rear of one chariot, stumbled along, groaning and yelling at his cuts and bruises. Children flung pieces of dirt at the malefactor, who would spend the next day in the House of Death before being punished on the execution ground. A group of Necropolis guards, dressed in black leather armour, their faces hidden by jackal-headed masks, made their way down the main road, preceded by two young boys carrying flaring torches.

The Sethian put on his own Horus mask. He made his way up the winding, narrow streets. Beggars, their sightless eyes white, milky pools, stood and begged for alms on the corner of alleyways. Cripples, and idiots with twisted faces, scrounged amongst the rubbish heaps still thick with black clouds of flies. Two prostitutes, arm in arm, naked except for faded loincloths, their bodies shining with cheap oil and perfume, pointed their fans enticingly at the Sethian, beckoning him over. The assassin walked on. A dog came yapping out. He raised his stick; the creature slunk away. Children danced and played in the streets outside open doors. Inside, their parents, workers in the City of Funerals, prepared to close their shops for the night, counting their profits and stowing away their goods. Women on the flat rooftops chattered and talked to each other. Somewhere a lute played and a child's

voice, surprisingly strong, sang about the wonders of the
Nile and a journey to the Third Cataract. The Sethian
kept on walking, swinging his stick; his mask drew little
attention. This was the City of the Dead. Night had fallen.
Strange creatures now prowled its streets. He covered his
mouth as he passed an embalming shed. Clouds of steam
rolled out and the workers' bodies, laced in sweat, still
crouched over corpses, preparing them for burial just
after dawn.

At last the Sethian was free of the city. He made his
way along a pebbled, sand-strewn path, beneath broad
cliffs which overlooked the City of the Dead. Few people
came here. This was the edge of the Red Lands. The
pathways would lead out into the desert or twist and turn
into sombre, shadow-filled valleys. The Sethian paused to
make sure he was following the right direction. A lonely,
haunted place, yet, because of the nearby Valley of the
Kings, it was patrolled and guarded by Pharaoh's desert
troops.

The Sethian climbed slowly. He stopped and looked
round. The lights of the Necropolis glowed like myriad
fireflies; beyond them, the Nile glinted under the moonlight.

The Sethian reached the spot where Hepel had died.
He crouched down, gathered some dried gorse and made
a makeshift fire. He examined the ground carefully and
grunted in satisfaction. No sign of Hepel's corpse: the
scavengers of the night had seen to that. He kicked dust
over the fire and continued climbing.

He entered a narrow ravine and made his way to the

mouth of a small cave, one of the many which honey-combed the rock face. He clambered quickly up into its darkness. Like an animal he crouched at the entrance and listened to the sounds of the night. He recognised the dangers of marauding lions: desperate for food, these huge cats would slip out of the Red Lands to scavenge, even attack the unwary along the edges of the Necropolis. Even more fearsome were the ravenous packs of huge, striped hyaenas, which smelt their prey from miles off. Yet, apart from the cry of a night bird, the Sethian could sense no danger. He fumbled in the darkness for tinder and lit one of the pitch torches hidden by the entrance. He thrust this into a crevice and crawled deeper into the cave.

Meretseger's skeleton lay at the back, blackening with age. He'd seated it against a rock. The severed skull, tied on with a piece of twine, turned a collection of darkening bones into something grisly and grotesque. The Sethian, as a macabre joke, had placed Lord Balet's eyes into the empty sockets but these had now fallen out. The Sethian squatted before the skeleton, removing the Horus mask the better to study this monstrosity. He wasn't frightened of the pathetic remains of a dead witch: he just needed her powers, her malice. After all, she had begun all this. Again he felt a twinge of compassion. He recalled the glorious night when they had burst into the Hyksos camp and taken this wretched's head. Now, other deeper shadows held his soul. He could never pardon the great wrong done. He took the small, leather bag off his sash and shook the counters into his hand. He let them fall on the ground, closed his eyes and picked one up. He felt the hieroglyphic it contained and smiled. He had chosen his next victim.

Dawn was breaking when, as usual, General Ruah rose early. Despite his journey into the Red Lands, the fierce fight with the Sand Wanderers and the dangers which now threatened, General Ruah was determined that his daily routine would not be disturbed. He walked into the bathroom, where his slave poured jugs of cold water over him. He then sat on the stool whilst the same manservant carefully shaved his face and head, rubbing in the oil and faint aromatic perfumes Ruah so liked. He then dressed in a simple white robe with a sash embroidered with the emblem of the Seth regiment, slipped his feet into sandals and went on to the roof of his great mansion. He knelt on a padded cushion and faced the east, extended his hands, bowed his head and murmured prayers to the ever victorious, ever eternal, ever holy, supreme Amun-Ra. He turned to the north and felt the cold refreshing breeze which always sprang up just as the sun rose. The general closed his eyes and leant back on his heels. He muttered the regimental prayer to the red-haired Seth. He called on all the guardians of his house and regiment to protect him and his family that day.

General Ruah opened his eyes and watched that miracle of the sky as it changed to a dizzying variety of colours as the sun rose. Different hues of red-gold as the liquid light of the sun poured over the Far Horizon. One day Ruah would take the journey to it but he was prepared. He had read the *Book of the Dead* and the *Book of the Gates*. He knew how to answer the different Gods he would meet at the entrance to the Underworld. When he reached the Hall of Judgment, he was sure his soul would be weighed rightly on the scales of Ma'at. He would enter the beautiful fields, the land of eternal day. He had kept faith with Pharaoh. He would join his companions.

Ruah felt the sadness biting at his heart. He had loved General Balet more than a brother. Who could have slain him in such a hideous, grotesque way? Who had gone out, plundered Meretseger's tomb and stolen that malevolent woman's remains? He did not like the gimlet-eyed judge Amerotke, with his sharp questioning and watchful silences. Who was he to sit in judgment on the Panthers of the South? What proof did he have that one of them was a murderer? Ruah had known these men since they were striplings. As he'd confessed to his wife, as well as to his chapel priest, he could recollect no grudge or grievance which might provoke such heinous acts.

Ruah sighed. He loved this part of the day; such dark thoughts should not blight it. He quietly went back down the stairs, broke his fast on bread, wine and fruit and made his way out into his spacious, ornately planned garden. This was his paradise. Ruah had used his wealth to import plants and trees from every part of the empire: willows, pomegranates, sycamore trees, as well as rare flowers like the poppy. He particularly loved the tamarisk tree, dedicated to the sky Goddess Nut, as well as those medicinal plants and herbs which he sold in bulk to the army physicians.

General Ruah made his way across the grass, his manservant and bodyguards following him to the edge of the lake. This was Ruah's pride and joy. Man-made, it stretched to a small island at the far end. Ruah breathed in deeply. Ah, the fragrance of the papyrus groves! The glassy surface of the lake was rippled now and again by the carp rising to nudge the dainty, floating lotus blossom. Ruah had brought in the best architects from Thebes. Water had been diverted from the Nile and the island had grown with blossoming grass and flowers. In the centre of the island, stood a gorgeously built pavilion where Ruah could shelter to write his memoirs, drink wine and reflect upon the glories of the past.

The lake was coming to life. Birds swooped over the surface, the lotus opening to greet the sun. The water itself was changing, reflecting the bursting light of the rising sun.

'You will cross, Master?'

'I will cross now.'

The manservant snapped his fingers. The bodyguards went to their appointed places around the huge lake. Ruah had decided on this. If an assassin was hunting him, what safer place than his island, where its every approach was watched and guarded by trusted men? Helped by his manservant, Ruah stepped into the long, narrow punt and picked up the pole. He issued an order and the servant pushed out. Ruah, deftly using the pole, watched it nose its way through the lotus blossoms towards his own private paradise. The punt moved effortlessly, Ruah, skilfully using the pole. He nudged the punt in, clambered ashore, grabbed the rope, carefully tethered it to the mooring post and walked up the specially laid-out path to his pavilion.

Fashioned out of precious woods on a stone base, the pavilion was circular, the wood painted green and gold with a small pyramid top. Its windows, protected by shutters, opened out so Ruah could enjoy every aspect of his island. The general climbed the steps, opened the door and walked in. Everything was in order: his desks, his chairs, his coffers, the panther-headed couch which he used for his rest. Ruah savoured the sweet smell of sandalwood. Yes, he'd write first . . .

He had barely taken three steps forward when he heard the sound, half-turned, but it was too late. The vicious war club smashed the side of his head, crumpling flesh and bone. General Ruah staggered and, with a groan, collapsed to the floor.

On the edge of the lake his manservant and guards had detected nothing wrong. They settled down to their usual duties. Some had brought food and wine; others games, playing Senet against themselves, rolling dice. Others just watched and waited. The general would always spend the first three hours of the day on the island and return across the lake to greet his wife and family. The routine was fixed. One could almost mark the hours of the day by it, so the manservant was alarmed when he saw the first tendrils of grey smoke rise above the trees. Other sentries glimpsed this and sprang to their feet, wondering what to do. General Ruah was eccentric. Sometimes he liked to play the role of the old soldier and light a campfire. On occasions he would weed the garden and vegetable patch on the island and burn what he'd cleared. Yet the manservant knew there was something wrong. The sweat on his back turned to a prickling cold: the smoke was denser, thicker than it should be. Moreover, from across the stillness of the lake came the crackling of burning wood.

'Something's wrong!' he shouted.

Joined by the others, he went down along the small jetty where other punts were tethered. The men hurriedly clambered into these and poled their way across the lake. By the time they reached the island, they could smell and hear the fire. They ran up the path and stopped in horror. General Ruah's gorgeous pavilion had been turned into a raging inferno. Even as they watched, the flames burst through the ornate roof which collapsed in a shower of fiery sparks and leaping flames. The walls began to buckle. The manservant, shading his eyes, tried to draw closer but the heat was too intense.

'General Ruah! General Ruah!'

Perhaps the general hadn't gone inside? The manservant ordered a hurried search. The retainers milled around, desperately hoping the fire was some unlucky accident and their master was elsewhere. Confusion and chaos reigned. Some servants stood and watched helplessly, others continued their fruitless search. A few ran back to the punts, eager to alert the rest of the household about this calamity. Ruah's manservant, however, refused to leave. He tried to organise carriers to bring water from the lake but this was futile. The raging conflagration began to die. Apart from the stone steps and base, the beautiful pavilion had ceased to exist. The manservant knew that his master had died inside.

'A terrible death!' he murmured.

No corpse, no gracious, hallowed and ornate funeral, no preparations for the general's journey through the Underworld. The manservant put his face in his hands and sobbed uncontrollably whilst the raging fire, bereft of anything left to destroy, sank and died.

Amerotke was in his writing chamber when the dreadful news arrived. He and Valu had left the House of a Million Years in the early hours. Both had agreed that the court could not be reconvened until the following day. When the messenger described what had happened to General Ruah, Amerotke recognised his prophecy had been proved correct: the Sethian had struck and would do so again until he was satisfied.

The judge and Shufoy arrived to find Ruah's mansion in uproar. The general's widow had been sedated by a physician whilst his two daughters and son clung tearfully to each other in the entrance hall. Servants rushed around. Asural was already there, having received Amerotke's summons.

'It's a mystery,' he declared as they walked through the gardens to the edge of the lake.

The sun had now risen full and strong, shimmering in the lake's surface. Amerotke stared across the water.

Tendrils of grey smoke still wafted amongst the trees. The wind carried the stench of burning wood and something else, like the odour of oil burning on a skillet. Amerotke pulled the white hood of his linen shawl across his head and shaded his eyes. The backs of his legs hurt and his stomach felt slightly uneasy after the late night banquet at the palace. He had looked forward today to teaching Curfay the finer points of the lute and examining some exotic fish Norfret had bought for their own ornamental lake.

'It's a mystery,' Asural repeated.

'I know . . . I know . . .' Amerotke wetted his lips. 'Well, come on, Shufoy. Asural, you can manage a punt, can't you?'

All three clambered in. The punt swayed dangerously from side to side but Asural pushed away and expertly guided it across. By the time they reached the island the smell of burning was offensive. Servants still milled about, gossiping quietly to each other, watched by members of Asural's temple police. The pavilion was completely gutted. Most of the timbers had collapsed inwards; some of these still glowed in the smoke. Manservants were trying to pull them apart, treading warily as sparks jumped up, until the curling smoke made them drop their poles and sent them off coughing.

'They are looking for what is left of Ruah's corpse,' Asural said.

'You are certain he died there?' Amerotke demanded.

'Well, he's nowhere else.'

Amerotke smiled grimly. He stopped by a water jar,

wetted his mouth and face, made a makeshift mask out of his linen shawl and climbed the steps.

'I've told them to be careful!' Asural shouted.

The fire had been so intense that the pavilion and everything in it had been consumed, reduced to charred ash so it was hard to distinguish what had been a coffer, a chair or a table. Amerotke walked away. Asural now had Ruah's manservant beside him. The man was still sobbing. Eyes red-rimmed, he was unable to express himself coherently but, after a spate of gentle questions, Amerotke learnt what had happened.

'It is murder, isn't it?' the man whimpered.

'I think so,' Amerotke replied. 'If I understand you correctly, General Ruah had scarcely entered the pavilion when the fire started. I suspect he was killed immediately. A fire of such intensity must have been deliberately started.'

'But how?' Asural demanded.

Amerotke glanced back at the smoking remains. 'The island was guarded once General Ruah crossed,' he explained. 'The assassin must have been there already. He probably scaled the garden walls and swam across. One of my sons could do that easily. It would be no obstacle for a fully grown man, a trained soldier.'

'And escape?' Asural demanded.

'Look around you. Tell me, can you distinguish one retainer from another?'

Asural agreed. Each of the servants was dressed in a simple white tunic edged with red, which fell just below the knee.

'Imagine the confusion,' Amerotke continued. 'The pavilion's ablaze. General Ruah has disappeared. Some servants want to douse the flames, others search for the general—'

'And a few,' Shufoy interrupted, 'took the punts and crossed the lake to raise the alarm.'

'And that's precisely what our assassin did.'

He was about to continue when they heard shouts from those clearing the pavilion. Asural hastened across.

'It's General Ruah's corpse,' he called out. 'What's left of it!'

Sheets were brought. Servants, wearing the thick gloves used by gardeners, picked up the mangled remains and placed them gently within, amidst loud cries and wails of lamentation. They carried the charred remains over to Amerotke.

'We could smell oil.' One of the servants who had been in the pavilion pulled down the mask covering his nose and mouth. 'My lord judge, the place reeks of oil.'

Amerotke pointed to the ugly rent in the charred skull. 'General Ruah was slain by the assassin who drenched his corpse in oil.' Amerotke wafted away the buzzing flies. 'Hence the inferno.'

He placed his hand on the skull; it was still warm. With his finger he sketched an Ankh, the sign for eternal life. He heard shouts across the lake and, turning round, glimpsed Karnac and the other Panthers assembling near the small wooden jetty. He left Asural to supervise a further search of the pavilion, and he and Shufoy crossed the lake.

The Panthers of the South had retreated into the shade of an ageing sycamore tree. They all squatted on the ground, Nebamum just a little behind his master. Karnac was as stone-faced as ever. Heti and Thuro, however, looked agitated as did Nebamum, plucking at the grass, staring across at the island.

'Where's General Peshedu?' Amerotke asked, sitting down.

'He doesn't know yet,' Karnac snapped, his black eyes scrutinising Amerotke. 'He goes hunting on the river in the mornings. I sent a messenger.'

'I told you all to be careful,' Amerotke warned. He stared at the stubborn faces of these veterans. 'Do you think,' he tried to keep a taunt out of his voice, 'that because you are Panthers of the South, you are invulnerable?'

'What's he doing here?' Karnac pointed insolently at Shufoy, standing behind Amerotke. 'I have heard of your disfigured servant. Can he be trusted?'

Amerotke heard Shufoy's sharp intake of breath. He raised his hand.

'I will answer for Shufoy. I'd trust him with my life. The problem is, General Karnac, one of you can't be trusted!'

'Ridiculous!' the general retorted.

'I call this assassin the Sethian,' Amerotke continued, 'because he is Seth's true son. Somebody entered General Ruah's estates just before dawn and swam across to that island. He was waiting for General Ruah in the pavilion, killed him with one blow to the head and burnt both the pavilion and the general's corpse. The embalmers will have the greatest difficulty preparing him for his journey to the Blessed Fields. Can't you see what's happening?' Amerotke insisted. 'Your companions have not only been murdered but deliberately disfigured, bereft not only of life but of a good death.'

Karnac remained unmoved. Nebamum and the rest were now agitated.

'You must arm yourselves,' Amerotke insisted quietly, 'turn your mansions into fortresses. Never go anywhere by yourselves. I ask you again, do you know of any grudge or grievance against any or all of you?'

All he received were blank stares. Amerotke closed his eyes. The sun was beginning to strengthen. He ignored the birdsong in the tree above him, the bees buzzing in the nearby flowerbeds, the shouts of servants and the slap of water from the lake. He tried to concentrate. Faintly, on the breeze, rose a hymn of lamentation as General Ruah's remains were taken into his mansion.

> 'Oh, Anubis, Lord of the Underworld!
> All hail to thy great shadow
> Under which every soul must fall!
> All hail to thy secret face
> On which every soul must look!
> All hail to your sacred hands
> Which weigh the soul of every man!'

Amerotke opened his eyes. 'All hail to the great Lord Anubis! If these murders continue, sirs, I assure you, within the week, similar cries of lamentation will be heard in each of your mansions.' He joined his hands together in supplication. 'I must beg you to reflect. I am here to protect you.'

'We are the Panthers of the South,' Karnac whispered hoarsely. 'We can protect ourselves. We also look to Pharaoh to extend her hand and shelter men who won great glory for her house.'

Amerotke recognised the threat. 'The Divine One,' he retorted, 'has this matter close to her heart. I am to meet Lord Valu today. Both of us will question the Lady Neshratta on what she knows about Ipumer. It was with him that this killing started. But I must ask you, before you leave,' he gestured as Karnac made to get up, 'where you all were this morning?'

'I slept late,' Karnac declared offhandedly. 'As did my servant, Nebamum. It was he who aroused me with the news of General Ruah's murder.'

Amerotke looked at the manservant. His lean face was unoiled and unshaven, his eyes slightly red-rimmed from the hasty journey across the desert the previous evening.

'My master has answered for me,' Nebamum smiled, echoing Amerotke's words about Shufoy. 'I have my own chamber near his. Make enquiries amongst the servants. A messenger from General Ruah's house roused me and I woke my master.'

The other two gave similar stories, pointing out that all their mansions were a mere walk from this one. Amerotke could see that they still wouldn't accept that one of their party could be the assassin.

'Lord Amerotke,' Karnac got to his feet, tightening the colourful regimental sash round his waist, 'I see that your interest is really in us.' He turned and grasped Nebamum by the arm. 'After yesterday, I decided that Nebamum will tell you all about us. He will explain everything – the history of our regiment, the Panthers of the South. He will take you to the Red Chapel and show you the pictures which record our history. Any further questions you may have, ask him!'

And, turning on his heel, Karnac and his two comrades marched across the grass towards the mansion.

'Is he always so difficult?' Amerotke asked.

Nebamum's face creased into a lazy smile. 'His bark is much worse than his bite.'

'And you've been his servant . . . ?'

'For many years, my lord.'

Amerotke studied Nebamum. The man was dressed very like his master, except for the leather boots he wore, and the sash round his middle was different.

'I was a mere stripling,' Nebamum continued as they walked across the garden to the main gate, 'a pageboy in Karnac's household. We grew up like brothers. When he joined the army, that continued.'

'But you are a free man?' Amerotke asked.

'Who's free, my Lord Amerotke?'

'And you've never been married?'

'I never had the desire.' Nebamum paused to shade his eyes, watching a gaily coloured bird swoop above the sunken garden beds.

'But your master rewards you well?'

'Whatever I want: my needs are few.' He pointed at Shufoy, who was trailing behind, lost in his own thoughts.

'The same can be said for your manservant? Faithful service is a rare commodity. But come, my lord, let me tell you about the regiment.'

They left the gardens and turned on to a busy thoroughfare which would take them down to the city. Nebamum had a sharp memory and was a good talker. He explained how, after the great victory against the Hyksos, Karnac and his companions had been quickly promoted. They had fought valiantly against the invaders, smiting them, hip and thigh. Then, afterwards, against the Libyans, Nubians, even the strange sea-going people who poured in from the Great Green to raid the towns of the Delta.

'I have never seen the like before,' Nebamum declared. 'We took captives. Some had fair hair and blue eyes.'

'I've heard of them,' Shufoy piped up. He had been avidly listening to Nebamum's tale, quietly vowing that, if he ever became a professional storyteller, he would remember such a story.

'At one time,' Nebamum continued, 'Pharaoh sent us into the Great Green. We attacked pirates, found their lairs and burnt them. On one occasion a great wind swept our galley north to the islands. Strange people . . .' He mused shaking his head.

'Is it possible,' Amerotke broke in, 'that the Panthers of the South are being hunted by survivors of the clans and tribes they destroyed?'

Nebamum shook his head. They had now reached the gateway leading into Thebes.

'We were soldiers, my Lord Amerotke,' he replied slowly. 'We fought for Pharaoh and carried out his orders. To answer your question bluntly, apart from the witch Meretseger, I can't think of any incident which could provoke a blood feud like this.'

'Do you think one of your companions is the Sethian?' Amerotke asked.

'No.' Nebamum's response was quick and vigorous; his face had the same stubborn look as his master's. 'You forget, my Lord Amerotke, we have been together as a group for decades. Why now?'

Amerotke couldn't answer the question. They walked through the gateway into the busy, teeming city. They decided to go by the back streets, well away from the throng. Occasionally they were besieged by beggars and had to pause and stand in a doorway, away from a slow-moving cart pulled by large, plump oxen. These were managed by the Scavengers, who cleaned the streets every week and removed the mounds of evil-smelling refuse and rubbish. Dressed in black from head to toe, their faces masked, the Scavengers also carried mongooses in cages to hunt the rats which teemed along these narrow alleyways.

Amerotke watched this noisy parade pass – the cart piled high, over it a black cloud of flies swarming noisily.

'What's the matter, my lord?' Nebamum asked.

Amerotke pointed to a dead dog thrown on the back of the cart.

'Death,' he declared. 'It comes in many forms: a dog, dead of starvation or crushed under the wheels.' He gestured at a beggar sleeping in the shadows. 'Illness or infection.'

They left the alleyway and entered the Avenue of Rams. Amerotke paused in the shadow of one of these great statues.

'My lord?' Nebamum's voice was testy.

'One thing I never asked Lord Karnac,' Amerotke mused. 'This Sethian, the assassin, is determined to kill you all. Now, death in Thebes comes in many forms. Murder is just as varied.'

Shufoy was jumping from foot to foot in exasperation.

'What I am saying,' Amerotke continued, walking, 'is that Generals Balet and Ruah could have been murdered less dramatically. A cup of poison? An arrow? An assassin striking in the dark? But that didn't happen.' Amerotke paused, fingers to his lips. 'The assassin took terrible risks. He struck Balet and Ruah quickly, ruthlessly, yet the slightest slip, the odd mistake and it may have been a different story. He could have been seen in the Red Chapel or on the island, captured and held. So why expose himself? Why take such risks? Neither Balet nor Ruah, nor any of the Panthers of the South are sacrificial lambs.'

Nebamum, mystified, shook his head. 'My lord, I cannot answer that.'

They went through the pylon-dominated gateway of the temple, across the main concourse and up into the porticoed entrance. Amerotke was still lost in thought. Despite Karnac's protests he was certain he had met the Sethian. Perhaps it was Peshedu? Had he gone boating on the Nile? Or had he first called off at his old friend's house and been waiting for him on that lonely island?

They went along corridors and galleries. Amerotke was aware of priests hurrying by, crowds of worshippers, the air reeking of incense, food, as well as the blood of slaughtered animals. Now and again he would stop and look at the pictures which covered the walls, all recounting the marvellous exploits of the great God Seth. Shufoy was all agog, drinking in the sights, quietly promising that, when time was not so precious, he would order his friend the amulet-maker to fashion special statues which he would sell to the devotees of this angry, awesome God.

They reached the passageway which ran down beside the chapel. Amerotke paused and stared up at the windows. He climbed on a bench and, standing on tiptoe, looked out on to the small, square garden – a lonely, quiet place. He stepped off and patted Shufoy on the shoulder.

'Your friend the Mongoose,' he murmured, 'is correct. Lord Balet's killer could hide behind this.' Amerotke touched the wall. 'He would hear his victim arrive, the chapel priest come and go, then strike.'

'Can I help you?'

Amerotke turned. Shishnak, a servile smile on his face, came tripping along the gallery. He paused, hands together, and bowed.

'My Lord Amerotke, you are most welcome. Can I be of assistance?'

The judge pointed to the window. 'The day Lord Balet was killed, the assassin came through there. Where were you?'

Shishnak, his eyes all a-flutter, pointed back in the direction he'd come.

'We have our retiring chamber, my wife and I, once our duties are completed . . .'

'Were you sleeping?' Amerotke demanded harshly. 'You were, weren't you? Lord Balet did not require you, so you and your wife drank some wine and went to sleep, as you do every day.'

Shishnak's eyes widened. 'How do you—'

'It's a matter of logic and routine,' Amerotke retorted. 'I am sure, if I studied your movements, I'd discover that, and so did Lord Balet's murderer. I do not need you,' he declared flatly, 'but make yourself available just in case!'

Amerotke pushed open the door of the Red Chapel. Nebamum laughed as he followed him in.

'I am sorry, my lord judge.' Karnac's servant closed the door behind him. 'I've never seen a priest so frightened. He probably thinks you can read minds: the all-seeing eye of Pharaoh!'

Amerotke looked round the chapel. The doors to the naos shrine were closed. The morning sacrifice of bread, wine and food had been removed.

'I said before,' Amerotke walked across to the paintings on the wall, 'that Balet and Ruah were not easy victims and yet, at the same time they were – typical soldiers with a set routine. The assassin simply studied this.'

Nebamum led them to the far wall. Amerotke ignored the legends of Seth, but listened attentively as Nebamum described the attack on the Hyksos camp and the other great exploits of the Panthers of the South. Shufoy grew bored and sat down on a cushion to doze. Nebamum was full of the glories of the regiment, recalling events and dates. Amerotke studied the paintings. They were not true depictions: the Panthers of the South had been given the red wig of Seth, their faces looked identical to each other and they were all dressed the same – except for Karnac, who carried an imperial staff. The more he listened the more convinced Amerotke became.

'Can't you see?' he broke into Nebamum's description. 'The assassin is imitating your great exploits in his own murderous campaign. Look!'

He went back to the picture depicting the attack on the Hyksos camp.

'According to this, Karnac stole into Meretseger's camp and took her head. That's what the assassin did: he came into your holy place and clubbed Balet to death, not taking his head but plucking out his eyes. And here,' Amerotke walked further down the wall, 'the campaign against the Sea People. The Panthers of the South stole across to one of the islands in the Delta, slaughtered the enemy and burnt their camp to the ground. Yes? And here.' Amerotke pointed to a third picture. 'Look, this is the Nile, here are enemy warships. What is this story?'

'It was after our great victory against the Hyksos,' Nebamum explained. 'We drove them out of Avaris. Some fled across the desert, others took refuge in their war galleys and tried to flee up the Nile.'

'And you followed?' Amerotke demanded.

'Yes. Karnac led the fight. We killed their admiral and captured most of their captains, a great victory. By then the Hyksos had lost all will to fight. They were determined on one thing: to put as much distance between themselves and Pharaoh's war chariots as possible. But, if you are correct . . . ?'

Amerotke stepped back and gestured at the paintings which covered the walls from ceiling to floor.

'If I am correct – and you may tell this to Lord Karnac – he and his companions have their murders described here in the very heart of their sacred chapel.'

Amerotke went back to the wall. He pointed to a painting of a house. On its steps was a crudely depicted Hyksos warrior with moustache and beard, his long hair tied at the back. He held a jug of wine in one hand, a cup in the other. In the next painting the Hyksos lay sprawled on the steps, the cup had rolled away. Instead of wine spilling out, the painting depicted dark-green liquid indicating poison.

'No one has been poisoned,' Nebamum declared.

'Where was this?' Amerotke insisted.

'A Hyksos fort near the Second Cataract, an outpost. General Karnac,' Nebamum nodded proudly, 'took it by subterfuge. He and I pretended to be merchants fleeing from Pharaoh. We brought in poisoned wine. The Hyksos garrison were only too eager to drink it. They had been cowering in their fort for weeks.' He pointed to another picture. 'The rest you know. They became drugged or drunk. Before they realised what had happened, Karnac and I opened the gates.' He shrugged. 'The fort was taken.'

Amerotke wondered if Ipumer's death reflected that story. He looked again at the scene depicting the attack on the Hyksos war galleys and thought of General Peshedu, who had gone fishing on the river earlier that morning.

SETH: the face of the sky at night, a
Deity of darkness and terror.

CHAPTER 9

Amerotke and Nebamum, Shufoy forlornly trailing behind, left the city by the Lion Gate and made their way along the highway. Amerotke explained how, shortly after midday, he was to meet Lord Valu at the House of the Golden Gazelle; it was the same direction as General Karnac's house so Nebamum accompanied him. Amerotke felt quite excited by what he had discovered in the Red Chapel.

'Though,' he added wistfully to Nebamum, 'the exploits of the Seth regiment had been so extensive it might be sheer coincidence. Yet there is a resemblance between the murder of those of your group and some of the exploits of the Panthers.'

'Perhaps, my lord judge.'

'Is your master married?' Amerotke asked Nebamum, curious to find out more about that stone-faced commander. Of all of them, Karnac seemed the least moved by the hideous murders of his companions.

'Lord Karnac is a widower,' Nebamum declared. 'His wife died of the sweating sickness some six years ago.'

Amerotke stepped out of the road, pulling Nebamum with him as two chariots thundered by in a cloud of dust. He waited until this had settled before continuing.

'He's a hale and hearty man,' Amerotke insisted. 'Hasn't he thought of marrying again?'

'My master is a man who needs very little.' Nebamum wiped the sweat from his face. 'You have seen Lord Karnac in battle, that's what he loves. In theory, he has retired from the army; in practice he loves nothing more than to lead a war squadron thundering across the desert in pursuit of Pharaoh's enemies.'

'And Lord Peshedu?' Amerotke asked.

'I'm here to talk about the regiment,' Nebamum replied. 'Lord Peshedu is his own man and his personal affairs are his own business.'

Amerotke accepted the rebuke. At least Nebamum's evasive answer had provided some insight. Peshedu was a shadowy man who loved to hide, possibly not liked by the others, especially after his daughter's public affair with a mere scribe.

He glanced over his shoulder. Shufoy had taken the parasol down but had stopped, looking back along the highway.

'What is it?' Amerotke asked. He could see nothing untoward, just carts, people passing to and from the city. The sun had grown stronger so most people were now seeking shade and shelter from the heat of the day. 'Shufoy, what is the matter?'

His manservant just shook his head, hawked and spat.

Amerotke shrugged and they continued their journey. According to the water clock in the Temple of Seth, it was just before noon. Lord Valu would be impatiently waiting for him. They reached a crossroads where the highway divided into trackways, the entrance to each shaded by date, sycamore trees and high coarse grass. Nebamum offered to go further with them. Amerotke was about to reply when an arrow sliced the air above Nebamum's head. The manservant immediately threw himself into the long grass beside the trackway. Amerotke and Shufoy, astonished, exchanged looks.

'My lord,' Nebamum whispered hoarsely.

Amerotke and Shufoy joined Nebamum in the shade of a tree, even as another arrow thudded into its trunk.

'Outlaws?' Amerotke whispered.

'Not so close to Thebes,' Nebamum retorted. 'The first arrow was intended for me.'

Shufoy was cursing: the parasol had snapped. He hissed threats against the mysterious archer. Amerotke felt both uncomfortable and slightly ridiculous. Here he was, like a child hiding in a grove, not too far from his own house. He parted the grass. The gap between the arrows meant there was only one archer. Nebamum also raised himself up, then threw himself down. Another arrow whistled above the grass, clattering into the grove behind him.

'I wonder who,' Nebamum whispered. 'The Panthers of the South are known for their archery.' He leant towards the judge. 'You will say this is reflected in those paintings in the Red Chapel.'

'We can't stay here,' Shufoy whispered hoarsely.

'This is what we will do,' Nebamum declared. 'The archer is after me. If I get up and flee . . . ?'

Amerotke recalled the man's awkward gait, the strange leather boots he wore. Nebamum seemed to read his mind.

'I am not as fleet as a gazelle but I know this place. My lord, it's the only thing we can do. If he's hunting me, he'll follow me.'

And, before Amerotke could object, Nebamum sprang to his feet. He showed himself slightly, then fled at a half-crouch. Arrows whipped through the air. Nebamum was gone, a mere scuffling in the undergrowth.

'Shall I follow him, Master?'

Amerotke pushed himself up. He glimpsed a figure flit like a shadow across the trackway. Nebamum had been correct. The assassin was ignoring them, intent on pursuing his quarry. Apart from the occasional call of the birds and the distant shout of someone passing along the highway, the judge could detect nothing wrong.

At last the creaking wheels of a cart broke the silence. A young boy approached, leading a fat, sweaty bullock pulling a cart on which the boy's father sat, his long whip extended, the pots inside clattering and jarring. The boy stopped as Amerotke and Shufoy suddenly appeared out of the grove and stepped on the trackway. Shufoy raised his hand in a gesture of peace. The boy stared, owl-eyed, his father shouted something but Amerotke and Shufoy ignored him. Using the cart as protection, they continued down on to the main highway. Only then, when they were protected by other travellers, did Amerotke glance down at his manservant.

'You were uneasy, weren't you, Shufoy?'

The little man, cradling his broken parasol, nodded. 'I felt that in the city,' he replied. 'I am your dog, Master,' he grinned. 'Once or twice I turned and glimpsed a figure dressed in dark-brown or black.'

'His face?'

'No more than a shadow. When we left the city I thought it was my imagination. I hope Nebamum is safe,' he added wistfully.

'I'll buy a new parasol, Shufoy. First, we have Lord Valu to meet.'

The Eyes and Ears of Pharaoh was already in the reception hall at the House of the Golden Gazelle, pacing up and down, watched by two of his frightened scribes, who sat clutching their leather writing satchels. The chamberlain who ushered the visitors in offered to bathe their feet and hands. Amerotke decided to forgo these courtesies.

'My Lord Valu, my apologies.'

Valu indicated with his finger down the gaily painted corridor. 'The Lady Neshratta is already waiting,' he snapped. 'And, before you tell me, I have heard of Ruah's murder. Do you know something?' Valu's voice dropped to a whisper. 'I truly believe Lady Neshratta is guilty of Ipumer's death.' He gestured with his hands. 'I have the two pieces of rope,' he raised his hands, 'Ipumer and Neshratta. If I could only put them together . . . ?'

'Has General Peshedu returned from the river?' Amerotke asked.

Valu raised his eyebrows. 'The general's whereabouts are his own concern. I am more interested in his daughter.'

'No, no,' Amerotke disagreed, 'we need to find out a little more from Peshedu. Is he the one who brought Ipumer to Thebes in the first place? Where was he the night Ipumer died? By the way, have you met the general's wife?'

Valu shook his head. 'I was greeted by Neshratta. That young woman is very self-possessed. I explained we were here on the Divine One's orders: she was to answer our questions as if she was on oath in court.'

'And her response?'

'She didn't seem to care.' Valu stared down the gallery. 'It's almost as if her own honour and that of her family are matters of little concern.'

He paused as the chamberlain returned.

'The Lady Neshratta will see you now.'

Amerotke told Shufoy to wait with the scribes, and followed the chamberlain down the passageway. Peshedu was a very wealthy man. Beautiful paintings covered the walls, most of them hunting scenes rather than the exploits of the regiment of Seth. The delicate acacia wood furniture was inlaid with ebony, ivory, silver and gold: precious figurines, statues and vases perched on niches or ledges. The room they were shown into was box-like but spacious and airy. Its folding doors were drawn back to let in the warmth and fragrance from the garden. The ceiling was supported by gaily coloured cedarwood columns, its walls covered with paintings, family scenes: a man sitting in a highly ornate chair, beneath this, a cat and a goose sat amicably together whilst a monkey dozed on the footstool.

Neshratta was studying this as the chamberlain introduced them. Lady Neshratta walked quickly over. Valu was correct: she looked calm and self-possessed. She was dressed in a brilliant white, sleeveless robe, a simple gold pendant round her neck with matching earrings and bracelets. Her face was smooth and painted, her gaze clear and calm. A woman of implacable will, Amerotke concluded. Neshratta didn't seem the slightest put out but gestured at the three chairs placed in the centre of the room, as if she was mocking the court in which she had appeared. She took her seat and nodded at the chamberlain to leave.

'Does this suit you, my lord?' she whispered.

Valu coughed and shuffled uneasily. Amerotke stared at her.

'You do not object to this?' Valu asked.

'Why should I object?' Neshratta's sloe eyes crinkled in amusement. 'I expected it.'

'Expected?'

'Well, the Divine One would hardly wish to see one of her beloved generals dishonoured in court. Indeed, this questioning should take place in the Hall of Two Truths where my advocate would be present.'

'And it may well do so,' Valu snapped. 'But the death of Ipumer masks other matters, such as the murders amongst your father's companions.'

'Of course,' came the calm reply. 'And the Panthers of the South must not be embarrassed.' She glanced at Amerotke. 'My lord judge, shouldn't my advocate, Meretel, be present?'

'If you wish,' Amerotke replied, 'that can be arranged. But we are not really here to discuss the case, more the personality of the victim. You know, my lady – and if your father was present he would confirm this – Pharaoh's justice is not limited to the Hall of Two Truths. We have every right to question you on your own. On one condition: what is said here by anyone only becomes evidence when it is repeated in court.'

'So, I could confess to Ipumer's murder but I would have to repeat that in the Hall of Two Truths?'

'Precisely.'

Neshratta turned her head slightly, playing with one of the tendrils of her perfume-drenched wig.

'But the Divine One is protecting my father.' Again the smile. 'And he has a great deal to hide.'

'Such as?'

Neshratta shrugged daintily. Amerotke watched her pretty face. Once again he was struck by the close resemblance between this woman and Norfret: the same smooth skin, the high cheekbones, the expressive eyes; above all her poise and calm demeanour which, he suspected, concealed a hot temper and a stubborn will.

'Do you love your father, Lady Neshratta?'

'I am, in all things, my lord judge, a good daughter.'

'Was your father here the night Ipumer visited the House of the Golden Gazelle?'

'Did Ipumer visit this house?' She raised her eyebrows. 'I did not see him. You've heard the sworn testimony,' she continued. 'Both my servant and my younger sister, Kheay, have sworn great oaths. I retired early, I slept well, except just before midnight my sister joined me. I have sworn an oath: I never left my bedchamber.'

'You could be questioned more closely,' Valu retorted, leaning forward. 'According to the law your servant could be put to the torture.'

'Then put her to the torture, my lord, and my advocate, Meretel, will reject such evidence as forged, contrived. Indeed, you could torture me. I would still tell the truth.'

'Was your father present at the house that night?' Amerotke demanded harshly.

'Of course he wasn't, my lord. You have probably discovered where he was – with his whores. That's where he often goes, to drink wine and dance with them; couple like a goat.' Her eyes were hard.

'And your mother?' Amerotke demanded.

'Oh, she was here, probably drinking and crying as she often does.'

Amerotke glanced away. Had Ipumer come to meet Neshratta's mother? What was her name? Ah yes! The Lady Vemsit. It was possible. Was she the person Ipumer left to meet during his working hours at the House of War? The Peshedu household was a strange one.

Ipumer came across as a born philanderer. Amerotke had heard similar stories of both mother and daughter being suborned by the same seducer.

'Your mind teems like a nest of snakes, my lord, I can see that.' Neshratta leant forward. The front of her gown hung open, exposing a generous full bosom.

'We are puzzled,' Amerotke replied. 'My Lord Valu will produce a sentry at the gates who will swear that Ipumer claimed he had been down to the House of the Golden Gazelle and drank deeply of a loving cup.'

'We have servants enough,' came the harsh reply. 'Perhaps Ipumer had fallen in love with one of those?'

'Let's start from the beginning,' Amerotke declared. 'Ipumer interests us.'

'Why?'

'Because, my Lady Neshratta, he was not what he claimed to be.'

'Oh, I could have told you that.'

'Then do so. What do you know of him?'

'Well, he once told me—'

'No, from the beginning,' Amerotke interrupted.

'Very well, my lord,' she sighed. 'I shall be repeating myself. You know General Peshedu and the brave Panthers often meet. If there is an army festival or regimental banquet, we all have to go along so we can glory in their prowess and their feats.' She raised her eyes to the ceiling. 'Have you ever been to such occasions, my lord? Don't you feel the backs of your legs ache, your jaw become numb from stifling so many yawns?'

Amerotke couldn't hide his smile. She grinned back.

'Do you know, if I hadn't protested,' she gestured at the wall, 'every gallery and room in this house would be full of the glory of the Panthers of the South.'

'Your father was a brave man,' Valu interrupted, 'a war hero.'

'Aye, my Lord Valu, but I too should be given the golden bee for valour by the Divine One. For I am now in my twentieth summer. I have had the glories of the Panthers of the South morning, noon, eventide and night for as long as I can remember. Am I not a person in my own right? Oh no!' Spots of anger appeared high on her cheeks; her eyes sparkled. 'I must remember, my mother must remember, my sister must remember and the servants must remember the glorious exploits of the past. For the love of Seth!' she rasped. 'There is more to life than that! However, there I am, seated with the ladies at this banquet, with cramp creeping up my thighs and this handsome young scribe introduces himself.'

'Did you love him?'

'I found him very amusing.'

'Why him?' Valu interrupted.

'You are the Eyes and Ears of Pharaoh,' she mocked. 'You should know, every handsome young man is scared off! May the Gods help any officer brave enough to approach the great Peshedu's daughter!'

'But Ipumer had no such scruples?'

'None whatsoever. He had the cheek of a monkey. I couldn't resist.'

'Your father must have objected?'

'Father didn't find out until it was too late. He tried

to give me a lecture on morality; I asked him about his temple girls.'

'And what did he say?' Amerotke found it hard to conceal his admiration.

'Why, my lord, he hit me full in the face as if I was some quarrelsome recruit. I told him that if he hit me again I'd . . .'

'You'd what?'

'I'd show him greater humiliation than he could ever think of.'

'So, you continued your relationship with Ipumer?'

'Of course. Sometimes we'd meet when I travelled to Thebes. Now and again we are let out of the house to shop and walk, make our devotions in the temple.'

'So, your servant can easily be bribed?' Valu asked sharply.

'My servant didn't come, only Kheay and myself. However, that became too dangerous,' she added hurriedly. 'So Ipumer came at night. I would steal out of my bedroom and meet him in the groves beyond the walls.' She smiled demurely. 'I am sure you have found the exact location.'

'Were you lovers?'

'Oh yes! A virile man, Ipumer. I think he took great delight in enjoying the daughter of one of the great ones of Thebes.' She breathed out and sat with her hands in her lap. 'I was Ipumer's lover.' She spoke as if she was chanting. 'And Ipumer was mine.'

So casual, so rote-like, Amerotke wondered if she was telling the truth.

'And then you tired of him?'

'Of course. I mean, he was gallant enough but in the end . . .'

'And you bought the poison? For domestic use?' Amerotke added hastily.

'Yes, for domestic use.'

'And no other reason?'

'You had my answer in court. I didn't tell the full truth.' Neshratta paused. 'Ipumer became importunate. I threatened, if he didn't leave me alone I'd commit suicide.'

'Why didn't you tell us that in court?' Valu asked. 'Suicides are blasphemy.'

'I didn't really mean it. I wanted to frighten him.'

'Ah! And that's why Ipumer bought the same venom?'

'Of course, my lord judge. We were playing a game like Senet. I moved a piece so he moved one.'

'Yet Ipumer fell ill. According to some of the evidence,' Valu chose his words carefully, 'Ipumer is reputed to have come down to this house on other occasions. He met you, shared food and drink, and was later ill.'

'How do you know that, my lord prosecutor? Ipumer could have taken it himself. He had a weak stomach and—'

'And what?'

'Ipumer was like many men, a goat on heat. He may have had other lovers scattered round Thebes, not to mention the courtesans and dancing girls, the hesets in the temples.'

'Was Ipumer friendly with these?'

'Oh yes.'

'Could he have murdered one?' Amerotke asked. 'Did Ipumer have the mind of an assassin?'

'He was two people. He was excitable, volatile but deep in his heart he didn't really care about anyone but himself.'

'And you?'

'My lord judge, my father is a very wealthy man. Ipumer had high hopes, dreams of a successful match.'

'But your father found out?'

'Well, of course. In a household such as this, servants are willing to betray for rewards. General Peshedu,' she added sardonically, 'became furious. He threatened to beat me, send me away or incarcerate me in one of the temples.'

'And you?'

'I told him I had no objection.'

Amerotke watched her eyes. Neshratta was cool and strong-willed. A daughter who intensely resented her father, she was only too pleased to use a man like Ipumer against him.

'Do you deny Ipumer came down here the night he died?' Valu asked.

'He may have done. There are at least forty serving girls working in this house. Any one of them could have been seduced by Ipumer, so he could find out what was going on.'

'And you think that's what happened?'

'Perhaps.'

'You say you are in your twentieth summer?' Amerotke

gestured at the domestic scenes depicted on the wall paintings. 'Hasn't anyone asked for your hand in marriage? Haven't you fallen in love? Surely there must be a stream of would-be suitors? By your own admission . . .' Amerotke paused; for a few seconds he'd glimpsed a change in Neshratta's eyes, a blink, a shift in expression, a moment of sadness. 'By your own admission,' he continued, 'you are a very wealthy young woman, a daughter of one of the great heroes of Thebes.'

'General Karnac asked for my hand.'

'What?' Valu leant forward.

'Oh yes, about two years ago.'

'And what happened?'

Neshratta pulled a face. 'The negotiations, as my father said, came to nothing. It's not a great surprise, Lord Amerotke. If you have met General Karnac, you'll know he believes the only people worth talking to are the Panthers of the South or officers from his own regiment.'

'Were you disappointed?'

'Not to fall from the pot into the fire?' Neshratta jibed. 'Another life full of the glories of the regiment of Seth? I would gladly have drunk the venom.'

Valu laughed abruptly. 'And where is your father this morning?'

'Out hunting with his servant. He has a skiff at the mooring place near the ruined Temple of Bes. Once he's killed enough he'll come home. No, no, that's wrong, he'll go to a wine shop and, flushed with his victories, visit one of his temple girls.'

'Could your father kill?' Amerotke asked.

'In the blink of an eye, my lord judge. They all like killing. It's part of their nature.'

'Then why didn't he kill Ipumer the upstart? After all, Thebes is full of murderers and assassins.' Amerotke nearly added that he had met one this morning but he decided to remain silent.

'Oh, but he tried to, didn't you know?' She laughed at their surprise. 'He often threatened Ipumer. On at least two occasions Ipumer narrowly escaped being attacked by footpads.'

'Why wasn't your father successful?'

'Ipumer had quick wits and even faster feet. I think my scribe from the House of War was well protected.'

'Ah, let's come to this. Ipumer courted you for almost a year. You shared food and drink. You must have learnt more about him?'

'Yes, he said he came from Avaris and had been given this post by someone important. Perhaps that's why my father never really had him stabbed, garrotted or drowned.'

Neshratta played with one of the rings on her fingers. Amerotke noticed it was carved in the shape of two writhing snakes locked together, with a small amethyst in the centre.

'Ipumer,' she chose her words carefully, 'was a boaster. He claimed to be of noble blood, part Hyksos, that he came from a line of warriors just as powerful as the Panthers of the South.'

'Did he tell you anything about his family?'

'Nothing except that his mother had once been powerful.'

'You have heard of Meretseger?' Amerotke asked. 'Would it surprise you to learn that Ipumer may have been her son?'

Neshratta threw her head back and laughed. 'He once mentioned the cult of Meretseger. Of course, I know the story. I had it drummed into me since I was old enough to listen. He made reference to the name on a few occasions but Ipumer was a storyteller, a gossip-collector. He seemed more interested in getting between my thighs than anything else.'

'And his friends?'

'Oh, he talked about Hepel—'

'You know he has disappeared?' Valu interrupted.

'Has he now? Perhaps he's fled.'

'And you've heard of the deaths of Lamna, the physician Intef and the widow Felima?'

Neshratta pulled a face. 'Lamna he dismissed as fat and lecherous. I think he was much smitten by Felima. He even tried to use her against me, not that I cared.'

'Anyone else?'

'Nobody. I asked him if he had a patron in Thebes but he said no.'

'He did,' Amerotke retorted. 'There was someone he met in the Street of the Oil Lamps. A man who wore a Horus mask.'

'But that was me!'

Amerotke scraped back the chair. 'My lady, that's a lie!'

'My lord judge,' Neshratta's voice imitated that of a man, 'I may have a beautiful body,' her eyes danced with merriment, 'but I have listened to my father enough.' Her voice remained low. 'And if I wear a robe, a mask, remove my wig and have my head covered, why can't I be taken for a man?' She leant forward. 'I can be more of a man than many of those I have met. Oh yes, my Lord Valu.' Neshratta's gaze lingered on the prosecutor's long painted fingernails.

'Why should you hire a shop in the Street of Oil Lamps?'

'Why, to meet my lover, of course. It's not difficult. Look at our household. Mother is lying on her bed with at least half a jug of wine inside her. General Peshedu is out killing every bird which catches his eye. Who will miss me if I slip away for an hour or two?'

Amerotke got to his feet to ease the cramp in his leg. He walked to the open doors leading out into the garden. Servants were weeding the flowerbeds. Another group were busy amongst the pomegranate trees. He closed his eyes and smelt the warm sweetness.

'My lord judge!'

Amerotke ignored Valu. He stared up at the brilliant blue sky. What if, he thought, this young woman, who hated her father and everything to do with his military life, was responsible for these murders? Neshratta was strong-willed, resourceful. She could have attacked Nebamum in that alleyway, slipped into the Red Chapel or swum General Ruah's lake. She could even have donned a black gown and hood and been that mysterious archer. By her own admission she could slip in and out of this house whenever she wished. She could have killed Ipumer because she was tired of him. But why kill Balet and Ruah? Some secret grudge or grievance? She detested her own father and was only too relieved that the marriage negotiations with Karnac had come to nothing, but why? Amerotke turned and walked slowly back to his chair.

'My lady, you met your lover in that room above the oil-lamp shop, or out in a grove of trees in the dead of night. What did Ipumer talk about?'

'What men always do. How good he was! How virile he was! How clever he was! What a marvellous lover! At first I found such chatter delightful. He was even arrogant and stupid enough to talk about our future together – how he would approach my father. I told him not to be a fool.'

'So,' Valu tapped his hands in his lap, 'it must have come as a shock to him when you decided to reject him?'

'Of course it was.'

'He must have threatened, blackmailed?'

'Of course he did.' The reply was tart. 'I laughed in his face. Whom was he going to blackmail? My father who knew everything?'

'But he still came back?'

'Of course, my Lord Valu! He thought I would change my mind.'

You had no reason to poison Ipumer, Amerotke reflected. You really didn't care.

Neshratta sat in her chair, picking at a loose thread on her gown.

'Ipumer's threats –' the judge declared – 'you welcomed them, didn't you?'

Neshratta lifted her head and winked at Amerotke. 'Of course. Anything to embarrass Father.'

'Let's go back to Ipumer. He told you nothing about his past life?'

'Very little, apart from his boasts: that he had been a scribe, that his parents were dead and that he'd come to Thebes to seek his fortune.'

'But you must have talked about other matters? Ipumer was a scribe in the House of War, your father was a famous general.'

'Oh yes, he talked about the Panthers of the South,' she jibed. 'How do you find them, my Lord Amerotke? You know my father dislikes you. He fiercely resents your intrusion, as do the others. They believe that the Divine One,' she spat the words out, 'should never have allowed Ipumer's death to be brought to the Hall of Two Truths.'

'They are not above the law?'

'They think they are.' She leant forward. 'Shall I tell you something, my Lord Amerotke? They absolutely hate being ruled by a woman.'

Amerotke ignored Valu's sharp intake of breath. Neshratta had led them on to possible treason.

'You know that, don't you?' Her eyes widened in mockery. 'The likes of Karnac, having to bow and kiss Hatusu's pretty toe? They were lukewarm in their support when she succeeded to the House of Adoration.'

'Some sections of the army were,' Amerotke replied

tersely, 'but the Divine One showed them that she was as great a warrior as her father.'

'Oh yes, and that saved her pretty neck. One of the greatest victories against the Mitanni ever. They still dislike her.'

'They are loyal subjects,' Valu countered.

'Erm . . .' Neshratta moved her head from side to side to indicate ambivalence. 'They are not the band of brothers they pretend to be either. I have heard their discussions. You know, they dine each month in one of their houses? The wine flows and tongues wag. You've heard of the legend, haven't you?'

Amerotke shook his head. 'My lady, what has this to do with Ipumer?'

'Oh, everything.' She waved her hand. 'There is a legend about the Scorpion Cups taken from the Hyksos camp. Well, when Father dies his cup goes back to the Temple of Seth. However, a prophecy exists that all those cups will come together, and be given back to Pharaoh when a mighty woman rules Thebes.'

'I have never heard of that.'

'No, no, you wouldn't, but Ipumer did, being a scribe in the House of War. Did you know that General Karnac wanted the tradition to end? That when Balet was murdered they even thought the Divine One had a hand in it?'

Amerotke hid his surprise and annoyance. Now he knew why Hatusu was so interested in this case. If these deaths continued, the finger of suspicion would be pointed and the ever-ready tongues of the priests would wag. 'Why were these heroes of Thebes allowed to live and die with dignity during the reigns of Hatusu's grandfather, father and half-brother,' they'd ask, 'but as soon as Hatusu succeeds, their hideous murders begin?'

'How do you know all this?' Amerotke demanded.

'Ipumer saw certain letters, confidential reports. He was a nosy one, my gallant scribe. General Karnac apparently wrote to the Divine One asking that the cups be given back to the families of the heroes.'

'And I suppose Ipumer read the Divine One's response?'

'Well, not hers, more that of her lover, the stonemason Senenmut.'

'Watch your tongue!' Valu interrupted harshly.

Neshratta pulled a face. 'Why, my Lord Valu? Will I get into trouble?' She threw her head back and laughed.

'Did Ipumer ever talk about the Panthers of the South, the exploits of the Seth regiment?'

'Oh yes, he once said that their exploits were founded on the death of a woman.'

'Did he resent them?'

'Sometimes he'd talk in a mocking way, but nothing serious. He wasn't a spy or someone opposed to the Divine One. Ipumer was a man who liked his pleasures. He was a monkey looking for mischief. He told me about Shishnak, the priest at the Red Chapel – how he liked to offer his wife as a handmaid to visitors; that it was not unknown for some of our great heroes to take advantage of this offer. My father was one of them. So, my lord,' Neshratta trailed her fingers across her forehead, 'I can tell you no more. Ipumer once loved me. I dallied with him and he died.'

Amerotke felt the young woman was leading them round in circles. She had told him the best lie, one mixed with a good dose of truth. How could he sort the wheat from the chaff? He glanced sideways at Valu: the Eyes and Ears of Pharaoh looked similarly bemused.

'My lord prosecutor,' Neshratta declared. 'I am thinking of making a direct appeal to Pharaoh. Ipumer may have come here, he may have met a woman of this household, but there is no proof that I met him, kissed him or gave him venom to eat or drink. Ipumer had other friends in Thebes. How do we know he did not visit the physician Intef or . . .' she paused, biting her lip, 'the woman Felima?'

Amerotke was sure that she had nearly called Felima a bitch but had caught herself just in time. He wondered what the source of this resentment was.

'Did you ever meet Felima?' he asked abruptly.

'Never.'

'Or the physician Intef?'

'Why should I?'

Amerotke got to his feet. 'My lady, if you could leave my Lord Valu and me for a while?'

'Happily,' she replied.

Neshratta rose, bowed at both of them, and slipped through the door leading to the garden.

Valu sighed noisily. 'We are going to have to withdraw this case. She's a minx with a tongue as sharp as a cobra's. We cannot link her to Ipumer's death. By her own admission she couldn't care if the scribe lived or died. She seems only interested in humiliating her father.'

'She's lying,' Amerotke declared. 'There's nothing she said which we can prove. For all we know,' Amerotke lowered his voice, 'she could have been the one who brought Ipumer to Thebes. What better way of humiliating Peshedu and the rest than giving yourself to the son of their great enemy? And what she says is logical. Ipumer was a handsome young man with a silver tongue. He came to this house for almost a year. One of the serving girls may have taken a liking to him. Ipumer accepted her offer, an excellent way of Neshratta spying on her former lover.'

'We'll see. We'll see.' Valu's voice grew testy. 'My Lord Amerotke, let us review the evidence. Call back the serving girl.'

Amerotke went out into the garden. Neshratta was sitting in a flower-covered arbour. She quickly agreed to his request. The young maid was summoned and brought in. Amerotke sat and watched as Valu interrogated her. The girl was apparently terrified but she held to her story. Bribery, cajolery and threats all failed: her mistress had not left her bedchamber that night. She had been joined by her younger sister, who had been suffering from a nightmare. On a number of occasions the maid had opened the door and locked it. Neshratta was fast asleep on the side of the bed near the door. Valu had to give up and the girl was dismissed.

'Any more?'

'It's time we spoke to the Lady Vemsit and Neshratta's younger sister, Kheay.'

Again Neshratta agreed but, just as she was about to leave, a chamberlain knocked and hurriedly came in, announcing General Karnac had arrived.

SETH: the God who, aided by the seven
stars which make up the Great Bear
constellation, attacked Horus.

CHAPTER 10

General Peshedu was going to die. He did not know it and, perhaps, that's why the Gods allowed him a brief period of happiness, before his Ka made its troubled journey into the West. General Peshedu loved nothing better than to dress in a simple tunic and sandals and go hunting in a skiff along the lonely reaches of the Nile. The skiff was broad, low in the water, paddled gently by his manservant sitting in the prow. Peshedu stood in the middle, surrounded by his nets, hunting baskets and the curved, flat wooden throwing sticks inscribed with prayers to Seth, Osiris and the other Gods who would bless his enterprises. Peshedu had enjoyed the morning. The skiff had journeyed quite a distance from the city until he had reached his favourite place opposite the ruined Temple of Bes. The restful silence was broken by the occasional roar of the hippopotami deep in the papyrus thickets, the slop of water and the occasional splash of the crocodiles. These left the Nile to bask on the bank and, when heated enough, crawled under the shadowy willow trees.

Peshedu recalled his days as a boy. How his father used to bring him down here and show him how to use the flat throwing stick. They even had a cat, trained to retrieve the downed birds. Peshedu closed his eyes. Long, sun-filled days! If the truth were known he preferred the harmony and stillness of his youth to the glorious turbulence of manhood. Peshedu grasped the throwing stick and shaded his eyes against the sun. He really should have sailed to the bank and sought shelter. Yet he was so enjoying himself, away from his tearful wife, the silent reproaches of his comrades and, above all, that fearsome vixen, his hard-hearted daughter Neshratta. If Peshedu cursed anything, he cursed the day she was born. They had been in conflict ever since she was a child: obstinate, rebellious, constantly poking fun at his achievements. The glories of the regiment of Seth, the triumphs of the Panthers of the South meant nothing to her. Ever since her courses had started she had proved to be a blight and a nuisance. Flirting with this one, teasing that one, making cow-eyes at every unsuitable young man she met. Karnac would have brought her into line. He would have made her submit but, of course, there was the great scandal, the humiliation, the promises of secrecy and, finally, that wretch Ipumer. Peshedu waved away buzzing flies, eager to feast on what he had already killed.

'Master?'

The manservant broke into his reverie. He pointed towards the thick papyrus grove, their shrubs rising high out of the water, feathery tufts bending in the slight breeze. It always reminded Peshedu of a floating forest.

'What is it?' the general snapped.

'Shall we go in closer?'

Peshedu agreed. He steadied his feet against the floor of the skiff fashioned out of tightly bound papyrus leaves. He watched a cloud of marsh birds rise. His eye caught one, chasing the great butterflies fluttering above the waving tufts, only to be distracted by another bird, with a long pointed beak, probing the mouth of a flower.

'I wonder what startled them, Master.'

'Probably a weasel,' Peshedu grunted.

He'd stalked his quarry and now he released the throwing stick. It caught the bird full in the body and returned with a graceful curve. Peshedu prided himself on his skill. The manservant would mark where the bird fell and he grunted with pleasure as he caught the throwing stick in his left hand. The manservant paddled the skiff and, using a large net, scooped up the corpse. He handed it to Peshedu, who examined it, admiring its brilliant plumes before placing it with the rest.

'Shall I go mid-stream, Master?'

'In a while.'

Peshedu smiled grimly to himself. His manservant seemed nervous, probably wary of the hippopotami basking in these groves as well as the great, long-snouted crocodiles. These had eaten well and would not return to the river until they were warm enough or brought there by prey. It was cooler in the grove.

Peshedu balanced himself carefully. He could stay

here all day. Perhaps he would? Who could threaten him here? He was well armed, strong and brave. He recalled Amerotke's warnings; his lip curled. He wouldn't take orders from that bureaucrat. Peshedu, to relax the tension in his legs, crouched down. On one thing he had agreed with Amerotke or, at least, half agreed. The killer who was stalking them must have something to do with the regiment of Seth though Peshedu found this difficult to accept. He placed the straw hat on his bald head as protection against the sun. Yes, he would stay here all day, then he'd go back upriver and visit the Temple of Anubis. His eye had been caught by a young, lissom heset: her long legs, narrow waist and those lovely sculpted breasts! Yes, he would bathe and change and she would help him. They'd share a jug of wine in one of those small eating-houses near the temple.

A roar of a hippopotamus made the general start. There was a crashing and commotion deeper in the papyrus grove. The manservant looked over his shoulder in alarm.

'General Peshedu, we should move back into mid-stream.'

Peshedu agreed. The man deftly turned the skiff; it nosed its way through the water. The manservant paddled vigorously. They cleared the papyrus grove. Peshedu looked to his left and his skin went cold. Another skiff was cutting through the water parallel with his, only a few yards away. One man paddled, the other was kneeling, facing his direction. Peshedu gazed in horror as the man raised his horn bow. An arrow was notched and sliced the air between him and his manservant. Peshedu scrambled about in the bottom of the skiff. He grasped his own bow and glanced up. Those two dark figures were like Devourers from the Underworld. Another arrow whirled through the air and pierced the throat of Peshedu's manservant. The man's convulsions made the skiff rock. Peshedu tried to grasp the paddle from the man's nerveless fingers. Too late, it fell into the river and the manservant collapsed back, eyes staring sightlessly up at the sky.

Peshedu grasped his bow but the next arrow took him full in the chest with such force he toppled into the water. The pain was intense. He could already see his own blood flooding out, his mouth was filling with water, his arms and legs were weak. He tried to turn on his stomach and glimpsed crocodiles aroused by the commotion and the smell of blood. They were already sliding down the banks, slipping silently into the waters of the Nile.

Amerotke and Valu met General Karnac and Nebamum in the same chamber they had questioned the Lady Neshratta.

'I heard about the attack on you.' Karnac sat down in the chair gesturing at Nebamum to bring a stool for himself. 'Who could it have been?'

'What is this?' Valu demanded.

'We were attacked on our way here,' Amerotke explained. 'Some hidden assassin. He loosed three or four arrows.'

'At you?'

'No, my lord prosecutor, at Nebamum.' Amerotke smiled as the manservant took his place next to Karnac. 'He escaped unscathed.'

'No real feat,' Nebamum replied. 'The undergrowth is

tangled, the trees close together; I was soon away without sight or sound of our assailant.'

'Who could it have been?' Karnac repeated.

'I don't know,' Amerotke replied in exasperation.

'Well, it proves one thing.' Karnac played with the end of a tasselled sash. 'I, Heti and Thuro were in my house when this happened. Nebamum was with you . . .' His voice trailed off. He gazed accusingly at Amerotke.

'There is General Peshedu.'

'He's hunting on the Nile,' Karnac replied languidly. 'The fool has gone so far away we couldn't find him.'

'There's his daughter,' Valu added meaningfully.

Karnac made a rude sound with his lips.

'The Divine Hatusu is a warrior,' Valu teased.

'I came here looking for Peshedu but you want to question me again, Lord Amerotke?'

'I'll do so again and again, my lord, until the truth is known. Were you once betrothed to the Lady Neshratta?'

'I was considering it.'

'And?'

'I changed my mind.'

'Why?'

'I didn't like her.'

'Why not?'

Karnac smiled to himself. 'I can judge a good horse and a good woman: my judgment is never wrong. She did become involved with Ipumer . . .'

'And you resented that?'

'Of course. One is either a lady or a temple girl. Every one has to make choices, Amerotke.' Karnac spread his hands. 'She did meet with Ipumer, didn't she? She did lie with him? Is that not true, Eyes and Ears of Pharaoh?' Karnac turned on Valu.

'According to her own admission,' the prosecutor replied tactfully. 'She met with him here and adopted a disguise, pretending to be a man, hiding her face behind a Horus mask.'

Karnac snorted with indignation. 'Peshedu should have kept her on a tighter rein. She deserves to be buried out in the Red Lands. Yes, Nebamum?'

His manservant, who had been standing patiently beside him, nodded. 'I advised you at the time, sir, the likes of her are not for the likes of you.'

'And the Divine One?' Amerotke changed tack.

'What about her? I rejoice when her face smiles on me.'

The reply, demanded by etiquette, slipped from Karnac's lips but his eyes were mocking. The way he slouched in the chair spoke more eloquently of his true feelings for his Pharaoh-Queen.

'Have you had . . . ?' Amerotke gazed up at the ceiling, decorated with red sunbursts and silver stars.

'Well, come on, man, say it!'

'Have you had words with the Divine One? About the Scorpion Cups?'

'I have. The cups should be returned to the families of the heroes. It's a more fitting tribute.'

'So, it has nothing to do with the legend?' Amerotke insisted. 'That, when all the cups are returned, Thebes shall be ruled by a mighty Pharaoh-Queen?'

'I don't deal with legends, Amerotke, but hard facts. The cups were awarded to the heroes by the Divine One's grandfather. It's more appropriate they should stay with them.' Karnac straightened in the chair. 'I've also tried to point out the error of—' Karnac recalled himself just in time. 'I have tried to persuade the Divine One,' he said quickly, 'that a more fitting tribute to the army, the regiment of Seth, and to the Panthers of the South in particular, should be built in Thebes.'

Aye, there you have it, Amerotke reflected: Karnac was a very brave warrior but he was also a ruthless, arrogant man. He'd resent a young woman like Hatusu. He would seek every opportunity either to embarrass her or demand more honours and triumphs in return for his support. He sat like a Pharaoh, only answering Amerotke's questions because, if he didn't, Hatusu would summon him to the House of a Million Years and insist on his compliance.

'General Peshedu is very stupid,' Amerotke declared, pushing back his chair. 'I warned him at the Oasis of Ashiwa, as I warn you now, General Karnac: the Sethian is not going to be satisfied until he has taken all your heads.'

'Then he'll have to take mine, won't he, Amerotke?'

And, getting to his feet, Karnac walked out. Nebamum smiled apologetically, bowed and followed quickly behind.

'You made an enemy there,' Valu smiled impishly.

'I don't care.' Amerotke stared at the door. 'Karnac must find it so difficult kissing Pharaoh's painted toes. If I were you, Eyes and Ears of Pharaoh, I would watch my Lord Karnac.'

The smile disappeared off Valu's face. 'Do you think he's a traitor?'

'No, he's a man who hates everyone but himself. That makes him very dangerous.'

'Do you think he could be the killer?' Valu asked.

'Of whom? Ipumer? I could say he resented such an upstart but he didn't care for the Lady Neshratta, so why should he bother?'

'But of Lord Balet and Ruah?'

'Possibly!' Amerotke beat his fist against his thigh. 'But the real question is why?'

Valu's head went down, he shuffled his feet.

'You have something to tell me?'

The prosecutor gazed sheepishly sideways. 'I bear messages from the Divine One. I doubt if this case will return to court.'

'Oh yes it will,' Amerotke retorted. 'What I have begun I will finish. If the Divine One wishes to be present, that is her right.'

'Is that your reply?'

'That's my only reply, Lord Valu. Now I think we should question Neshratta's mother, the Lady Vemsit.'

Valu, lost in thought on how he would convey Amerotke's response to Pharaoh, got to his feet and walked to the door. He had a whispered conversation with the waiting chamberlain and then took his seat beside Amerotke.

'This,' he whispered, 'is going to be strange.'

'What do you mean?'

'Wait and see,' Valu replied enigmatically. 'I tell you this, Lord Amerotke, if you and the Lady Norfret have secrets, I would keep them well hidden. It's wonderful what you learn from servants' chatter.'

The door opened and Lady Vemsit swept in. She hardly greeted them but flounced down in the chair. A plump, jowly woman, her face covered in paint, jewels dazzled round her neck and her fingers were heavy with rings. She wore a bright brocaded shawl over her white robe but the gown she wore was diaphanous, open at the front, revealing swelling breasts which she kept dabbing at with a small sachet of perfume. She was all a-fluster and kept moving as if to make herself comfortable, tapping her silver sandals on the floor, impatient to leave.

'I . . . I really don't know what you want,' she blustered, her black eyes moving from Amerotke to Valu. 'Really, I should only be questioned in the presence of my husband. I wish he would return. He has enough troubles but he always has to do what he wants.'

'Does that include the night Ipumer came to this house and was killed?' Amerotke demanded.

Vemsit's body went slack. She gaped at Amerotke. 'What has that to do with it? He only came near this house. He wasn't allowed in.'

'Do you have much control over the Lady Neshratta?' Amerotke insisted.

'None whatsoever.' Vemsit's lips pursed in annoyance. 'Stubborn of heart and stubborn of will,' she wailed. 'She'll be the death of us.'

'And the night Ipumer died? Lord Peshedu?'

'Lord . . .' Vemsit's eyes fell away. 'My husband was

absent on business. He never returned until after dawn. He often does that.'

'And you, my lady, were in your bedchamber?'

Vemsit's head came up. She looked frightened, like a timid cat cowering in the chair.

'Did you leave your bedchamber at any time during that night?' Amerotke insisted.

'Are you implying that I met Ipumer?'

'It's possible,' Valu jibed. 'Ipumer had a silver tongue. He may have had a weakness for,' he smiled, 'beautiful but mature women.'

Vemsit simpered back. Amerotke sensed the prosecutor knew a great deal about this woman.

'Answer the Lord Amerotke's question,' Valu purred. 'Did you leave your bedchamber? I mean, you were there by yourself?'

'I have a witness,' Vemsit whispered, refusing to look up. 'But I beg you, sirs, not to embarrass me.'

'And who is this witness?'

'My maid, Ita; she is my handmaid,' Vemsit continued hurriedly. 'My Lord Peshedu is often away. I become frightened . . .'

Amerotke kept his face impassive. Vemsit's reply was telling enough. He'd often heard of such practices amongst the wealthy ladies of Thebes. Norfret had touched upon the delicious scandal which bubbled beneath the veneer of polite society.

Vemsit sat, shoulders bowed. 'Please!' she whispered. 'I'll take whatever oath you want and so will Ita. We were together all night. It's hard,' she sobbed. 'The Lord

Peshedu is a difficult man. My daughters live in their own world. I become lonely, frightened.'

Amerotke stretched forward and grasped her podgy hand. In his heart he knew this woman was telling the truth. He could not imagine her slipping through the darkness, out into some shadowy grove to make love to the likes of Ipumer. A woman who'd had enough of the world of men.

'My lady,' he urged, 'do not distress yourself. What you have told us will not be repeated in any court, nor will any record be kept of it. You are concerned about your husband?'

Vemsit glanced up. Her tears had turned the kohl into dark black streaks down her painted cheeks.

'He will return soon enough,' Amerotke comforted, 'and he needs to see you at your best. Now, I would like to see your younger daughter, Kheay.'

'She's an innocent,' Vemsit wailed.

'I know. But we do need to question her.'

Vemsit blew out her cheeks and sighed. Like a sleep-walker she rose and left the room.

'I told you,' Valu whispered. 'The chatter of servants can be more precious than pearls! You believe her, don't you, Amerotke?'

'May the Gods protect her! I think she is a woman hiding from her family.'

Amerotke paused as the door opened and Kheay slipped through. She was different from both the mother and her sister, a slim gentle girl, her hair bound up in a filet behind her head. She had large expressive eyes and a sweet face. The way she walked and sat reminded Amerotke of a gentle doe. She showed no fear but gazed round-eyed at both of the officials. She was dressed simply in a gown, a gold bracelet on her wrist, no rings on her fingers.

'Your name is Kheay?' Amerotke asked.

'Yes, my lord.'

'And how old are you?'

'Fourteen summers, my lord.'

'Do you love your mother?'

A slight smile.

'And the Lord Peshedu?'

The smile faded.

'And your sister Neshratta?'

She smiled dazzlingly. Amerotke had his answer.

'Neshratta's very brave,' she whispered. 'She always protects me from Father. She shares her jewellery and always listens to me. She's not as stubborn as she appears. She has been hurt.' Kheay bit her lip as if she had said too much.

'Hurt?' Amerotke demanded.

'Oh, nothing, just in matters of the heart.'

'Did she love Ipumer?'

'No. She thought he was interesting. I think she was more keen to upset Father.'

The answer came so coolly Amerotke laughed. 'And did she go out to meet Ipumer in the city?'

'Sometimes when we were shopping.'

'And at night?'

'Sometimes, but then she stopped. She said Ipumer

bored her, that he was fast becoming a nuisance. Sometimes she seemed troubled.'

'Troubled?'

'I don't know why. She tired of Ipumer and resented his
threats.'

'Did you ever meet Ipumer?' Valu demanded.

'Sometimes, when Neshratta and I went to the city.
We'd meet in one of the small wine shops, well away from
the public view.'

'And what did they talk about?'

'Oh, I didn't listen. They would sit in the garden beneath
the trees. I would pretend to go and look at the fishes or
the flowers. He'd leave, Neshratta and I would continue
our shopping.'

'And the night Ipumer visited here?' Valu demanded.
'Your sister is accused of poisoning him.'

'She couldn't have done that.' Kheay's face assumed the
same stubborn expression as Neshratta's. 'I had nightmares about the large red bat and a Crocodile Man coming
out of the marsh into our garden. I woke screaming.
Father was gone and Mother – well . . .' She shrugged
prettily. 'So I went along to Neshratta's bedroom. The
maid was outside, sleeping on a couch. I opened the door
and went in.'

'What time was this?'

'Oh, my lords, it was not yet midnight. My sister is kind.
I climbed into bed. We lay and talked for a while. I slept
lightly. I was aware of the maid opening the door every
so often to see that all was well.'

'And your sister never left that bedroom?'

'My lord, how could she? I slept lightly because of a stomach ailment.'

Valu clutched his own belly as if the very thought of such a complaint reminded him of his.

'That's all I know.' She gazed soulfully at them. 'My lords, I cannot tell you what I do not know myself.'

Amerotke glanced at Valu, who shook his head.

'Did your sister ever talk about Ipumer? Do you know anything about the scribe?'

Again the vigorous shake of the head.

'Very well.'

Amerotke dismissed her. For a while he and the prosecutor sat in silence.

'The Divine One is correct,' Valu murmured. 'The Lady Neshratta may be much suspected but little can be proved. There is no evidence to convict her of Ipumer's murder, though for the rest of her life people will think she did it.'

Amerotke sat and stared out at the garden. Baffled, mystified, he got to his feet and walked to the door. He asked the chamberlain to send Shufoy along.

'What are you going to do?' Valu called.

'I am going down to the Hall of Archives and the House of War.' Amerotke scratched his forehead. 'I want to discover anything I can about the Panthers of the South and Ipumer. We've questioned enough. We are like dogs chasing our tails. Nothing comes of nothing. Ah, Shufoy!'

The dwarf came lumbering into the room and glared at Amerotke.

'I have been waiting a long time. They haven't even offered me anything to drink or eat.'

'And you look as if you have been starving,' Amerotke teased. 'I have a task for you. I want you to go down to the Scavenger's house, the one in the Perfume Quarter.'

'Why?'

'Stay still and I'll tell you. The houses of Intef the physician and Felima were deliberately burnt to the ground. Therefore the murderer is trying to hide something by destroying them. I want you to see if the Scavenger found anything. You carry my seal?'

Shufoy nodded. 'Anything in particular, Master?'

'You will know when you discover it. I also want you to go to my lord prosecutor's office, the House of the Eyes and Ears of Pharaoh,' Amerotke added sardonically. 'Once again I would like you to go through Ipumer's possessions, list them, see if there is anything untoward.'

'Much good it will do, but . . .' the prosecutor got to his feet, clutching his stomach, 'Nature calls, my Lord Amerotke. I must ease the cramps. I am, as always, the humble servant of my own innards.'

The prosecutor waddled out, waving his hand.

'I saw something strange,' Shufoy whispered after the prosecutor closed the door behind him. 'I was in the entrance hall and the Lady Neshratta passed by me quickly. She looked as if she had been crying but I wasn't sure.'

'The Lady Neshratta,' Amerotke confided, 'is the key to all this mystery. I am sure of it. Shufoy, on your way. If you meet the lord prosecutor ask him if he remembers anything suspicious about the widow Felima or Intef the physician.'

Shufoy left. Amerotke stared round the chamber. So much wealth, so much ease, yet so much misery. He idly wondered where Peshedu was. He recalled those paintings he had seen in the Red Chapel at the Temple of Seth and hoped one didn't contain details of yet another murder. He went out into the passageway.

'Is my lord judge leaving?' the chamberlain asked.

'My lord judge will soon be leaving,' Amerotke smiled. 'First, I would like to visit the Lady Neshratta's bed-chamber.'

The man drew his brows together.

'I want to inspect it,' Amerotke declared.

The fellow led Amerotke deeper into the house and up what he called the Panther Staircase. Amerotke could see why it had been called this. The wall was covered in hunting scenes depicting an officer from the regiment of Seth, bravely confronting the most ferocious-looking panthers. The gallery above was of polished wood. Amerotke realised this was one wing of the house; Lady Neshratta's bedroom was further along. A simple reed bed stood outside. The chamberlain opened the door. The bedchamber was handsome, spacious and airy, with an immense four-poster bed set in the centre, elegant tables, stools and cabinets around the walls. The bed itself was hidden behind a mesh of white linen hangings to provide coolness as well as keep away the insects and flies. There were armchairs and footstools, tables and wooden stands for washing, jugs and bowls. A large ostrich-plumed fan perched in the corner.

Amerotke noticed how the Panther motif or the insignia of the Seth regiment seemed to be everywhere. No wonder Neshratta objected so much!

He left the chamberlain standing in the doorway and went round the bed. There were two large windows in the far wall. One was shuttered with gaily coloured panels, the other had a wooden lattice-work frame carefully eased in. Amerotke grasped this and noticed how smoothly it pulled away. He ignored the chamberlain's gasp and put the frame on the floor beside him and stared out. On his left he saw two large studs of wrought bronze embedded in the wall. That was where Neshratta had placed the rope ladder which she probably kept in a large trunk underneath her bed. The drop was about the span of two men into a small walled garden with bushes around. Amerotke studied the path across the lawn to a small postern gate built into the curtain wall. Satisfied, the judge put the lattice-work frame back and rejoined the chamberlain. He noticed that, as he walked, the wooden floorboards creaked.

He left the house as mystified as he'd come and, for a while, he just stood in the shadow of the gateway. Ipumer had definitely come here the night he had died. He had gone along to that gate and met someone. But who? Neshratta had certainly not left. Amerotke was convinced, on that matter at least, she was telling the truth, but that was only part of it.

He leant against the wooden gateway and watched the fishing smacks in mid-river on the Nile. Amerotke wondered if he would ever discover the truth. Unless they solved the murder of Ipumer, everything else would remain shrouded in shadows. He looked up at the sky, shading his eyes against the sun. He would love to go home, enjoy the fullness of his garden, perhaps teach the boys how to fish. Then he recalled the House of Death, the souls of those mangled corpses demanding justice, a justice that must not wait much longer.

Amerotke sat cross-legged on cushions in the Temple of Ma'at and leant back against the refreshingly cool wall. He had taken his sandals off, and purified himself by washing his hands and feet and cleansing his lips from the holy water stoup. Amerotke could hear the faint sounds of the temple servants as they finished for the day and prepared for the evening sacrifice. The Hall of Two Truths was deserted, except for servants, changing the flowers in the vases and buckets.

Amerotke looked up at the cedar-wood beams edged with silver and gold paint and glanced once more at the wall painting of Ma'at. He sighed: his visit to the Hall of Archives had been fruitless. Of course, the scribes remembered Ipumer but could tell him nothing new: an industrious young man who had few faults and was always conscientious. The chief scribe was more concerned about young Hepel, who had disappeared from work and had not been seen at his lodgings nor around the city.

Amerotke was convinced Hepel was dead. The Sethian had removed anyone who might pose a danger, who might prove some connection between himself and Ipumer. Hepel, Lamna, Felima, Intef – they had all been killed to silence their mouths and remove any evidence. One thing Amerotke had discovered: according to the *Book of Records*, Ipumer had experienced a deep interest in the regiment of Seth and the Panthers of the South. He'd taken out their records which he'd signed for. Ipumer claimed he had always been fascinated with their history but, as the months passed, his interest in them abruptly declined. Apart from that, nothing remarkable.

Amerotke started at the knock on the door.

'Come in!'

Shufoy and Prenhoe, looking rather tired and woebegone, slipped through. They immediately knelt, purified themselves with dabs of holy water, took off their sandals and leant against the door.

'A waste of time, Master.'

Prenhoe emptied the contents of his wallet on to the floor beside him.

'First, Ipumer's possessions.' He picked up a ring and tossed it to Amerotke, who caught it: two snakes writhing, a small diamond in the centre.

'That's probably Neshratta's,' Amerotke declared. 'She was wearing a similar one today. She must have given it to Ipumer as a love token. Anything else?'

Shufoy slipped something across the shiny floor. Amerotke picked it up. It looked like a brooch damaged by fire.

'The Scavenger discovered that at Felima's house.'

Amerotke held it up against the light.

'It's two gazelles,' Shufoy explained. 'Isn't that the seal of Lord Peshedu? The same emblem hangs on the house gates.'

'Again, probably from Ipumer.'

Amerotke put it down. Shufoy came over with scraps of papyrus.

'Nothing at Intef's but these are Felima's. She kept a lot of powders and potions. Lord Valu thinks she sold aphrodisiacs.'

Amerotke examined the fire-stained scraps, no more than lists of substances. He put these down on the floor.

'Why was the widow woman killed?' he asked.

'I also went to the Street of Oil Lamps,' Shufoy chattered on. 'I asked that merchant, could the Horus mask wearer have been a woman? He said it was possible but he was certain it was a man.'

'So, why should the Lady Neshratta lie?'

'The merchant said the person always came at night or in the shadows. It was more the way he walked and talked. The merchant can't recall much but he was sure the Horus mask wearer was a man.'

'True, true,' Amerotke murmured. 'But Neshratta is quick-witted and probably a born mimic. It makes sense that she and Ipumer must have had a place to meet. But, there again, she and Ipumer often went to wine shops. I can't make—'

Another knock on the door. Asural thrust it open, almost sending Prenhoe flying. The chief of temple police apologised but stood, legs apart, helmet cradled in the crook of his arm.

'You were right!' he shouted. 'They should have been more careful. The river scavengers have brought in the remains of General Peshedu and his servant.'

'What?' Amerotke clambered to his feet. He tightened the sash round his robe. 'You are sure of this?'

'They could tell by what was left of him: bracelets and an anklet he wore.'

Amerotke sat back down on the cushions.

'They saw his boat drifting,' Asural explained. 'Its hunting nets and baskets were full. A quiver of arrows was found but no bow. The paddle was also missing. They searched amongst the papyrus groves, attracted there by the crocodiles feasting on something. What was left of Peshedu and his servant was dragged out and taken to the House of Death. A fisherman distinctly remembers seeing them down near the old Temple of Bes. I haven't viewed the corpse myself but they say both men were killed by arrows.'

Amerotke put his face in his hands. Who could it be? he wondered. True, he had no knowledge of the whereabouts of Heti and Thuro but that could soon be established. Karnac? Perhaps. And Nebamum? He'd certainly not left Thebes.

'How easy would it have been,' Prenhoe asked, 'to learn where General Peshedu was fishing?'

'Well known,' Asural declared. 'He always visited the same stretch of river. Lord Karnac claims he sent a messenger to warn him of Ruah's murder but he couldn't be found. Apparently Peshedu liked to take a break from hunting—'

'Yes,' Amerotke interrupted, 'and, of course, he would pull into a bank beneath the shade of an overhanging tree. No wonder he couldn't be found. So, Peshedu is dead. I wonder what will happen now at the House of the Golden Gazelle? Listen,' he got back on his feet, 'I must stay here and think for a while. Shufoy and Prenhoe, you had best visit General Karnac. See if he has discovered anything.'

'Lord Senenmut has been looking for you,' Asural declared.

'Well, he'll have to keep looking, won't he?' Amerotke shooed them to the door. 'See if you can discover the whereabouts of our other heroes. Discover if any of them left Thebes.'

Shufoy and Prenhoe grabbed their sandals. Shufoy looked daggers at his master.

'I am tired.'

'Soon you'll sleep,' Amerotke reassured him. 'But, in the meantime, we must plot.'

He gently ushered them through the door and listened to them leaving. The temple was now quiet. Amerotke closed the door. He returned to his seat, stared at the shrine and reflected on these grisly murders.

Amerotke recalled the technique once taught him by an old priest: to sit and reflect, let his soul choose that which was important. Amerotke did so. Images came and went. Out in the Red Lands, trudging behind the Panthers of the South; the empty gaping tomb; the black-robed Sand Wanderers closing in. The Street of Oil Lamps and that masked Horus figure. These images came and went. Karnac, stone-faced and hard-eyed, and then Neshratta, full of life and courage, with her sharp answers and keen wit. And Kheay, her doe-like sister. Both girls showed great hurt but what was the source? Ipumer? Certainly not! Something else, but what? Amerotke recalled the bed outside Neshratta's room. The maid was very faithful, diligent, but why sleep there? Did Neshratta also suffer from nightmares? And why this sudden change of mood? Shufoy claimed Neshratta had been crying but when she had left Amerotke she was composed enough. The judge lay down on the cushions, making himself comfortable, staring at the lights. He glanced up. The window high in the wall was now darkened, the sun had set.

'I made a mistake,' Amerotke whispered.

Ipumer had trapped them all. They had concentrated on Ipumer's death and on the events since then but, if Neshratta was the key to all this, then what had happened before? What had fanned the hatred against her father? Was she the Sethian, the killer? He would have to go back but whom would he ask? He closed his eyes and drifted into sleep. When Shufoy returned they would take a different direction and go back into Neshratta's sombre, dismal past.

SETH: assassin of Osiris, father of Horus.

CHAPTER 11

The Sethian stood in the fluttering light of the Tomb of Heroes in the Necropolis: a large, cavernous chamber, dug deep into the rock high above the City of the Dead. The keeper of the tombs had allowed him in through the Mastaba, the small temple house which fronted the sepulchre proper. The Sethian smiled behind the golden Horus mask and why not? He bore the cartouche or seal of the Seth regiment with a snarling panther in the centre; his anklets and rings bore similar insignia. As for the mask? Well, this was the City of the Dead, night had fallen and the place of tombs had a life of its own. The keeper had thought he had come to pay his respects. The Sethian sat on one of the gaily caparisoned stools. Respect? How could he pay respect to men who had carried out such an abominable crime? Why should they be allowed to live the life of demi-gods then be transported here as if they were the beloved of Amun-Ra? He coughed to clear the dust from his throat and stared around the tomb: a veritable treasure house with its gleaming coffers and caskets, the sarcophagi bearing the mummified remains of his comrades, the vividly decorated Canopic jars and all the treasures heaped around: statuettes, precious stones, chairs and tables of the finest wood. A gold and silver statue of a reclining cat gleamed in the torchlight. The air was sweet from the open jars of ointment and the perfume-drenched ostrich plumes placed along the walls, covered with paintings extolling the deeds of these god-like warriors.

The Sethian got to his feet and walked deeper into the tomb. If life had been sweet, he eventually would have been laid here along with the rest. His hand caressed the gilt-edged corner of a sarcophagus. This was Amunak: small and lithe, with the cunning of a fox and the courage of a lion. He and the rest were safe. He bore no grudge against these.

He walked across the tomb and stood before the sarcophagus of Kamun, a beautiful piece of carpentry, a gold-edged casket covered with precious stones. Kamun was a different matter. Like Ruah, Peshedu and Balet, he did not deserve to travel into the West. He should pay for his crimes. The Sethian took out his dagger and, finding the slit, broke the seals and pushed back the lid. A gust of perfume wafted up. The Sethian stared down at the mummy wrapped in its linen bands, a blue and gold silver mask laid over the face. The Sethian removed this and tossed it into the darkness. Picking up the wineskin he'd brought, he poured in the blood purchased in a flesher's yard. It gushed out, seeping through the exquisite linen until the corpse seemed to be floating on a lake of blood. Its stench stifled the fragrance of the embalmers: the beeswax, cassia, cinnamon, cedar oil, henna and juniper. The Sethian stepped back to admire his handiwork.

'What are you doing?'

The Sethian whirled round. The keeper of the tomb was coming forward. He had been drinking, and staggered slightly, his wig askew, his fat face full of concern. He clutched the wine cup to his chest.

'What is this? What are you doing?'

'I am paying my respects.'

The Sethian walked across. The keeper of the tomb looked round.

'But you've opened the casket?'

He saw the blood brimming at the lid, he dropped the cup and made to turn but the Sethian was too quick. In one stride he was across: one swift brutal thrust with his dagger. The keeper of the tomb sagged, the Sethian put a hand across his mouth, driving the dagger deeper as he watched the light of life fade in the man's eyes. The keeper crumpled, choking quietly on his own blood. The Sethian laid him gently on the floor. He withdrew the dagger, wiped it quickly on the man's robes and got to his feet. He stared around at his handiwork. Kamun's remains were polluted, as was the entire tomb. He took off the mask and wiped the sweat from his face. He went to the door, slipped through and, padding silently, made his way into the gathering night.

Keeping to the shadows, he moved quickly down the streets of the Necropolis, now and again standing aside as a funeral cortège made its way up towards the tombs. He passed the great statue of Osiris and reached the quayside. He clambered aboard one of the ferries and stared across at the lights glowing in the city of Thebes. He was satisfied he had done good work but the night was not yet finished. Amerotke! He would have preferred to let the judge stumble around; let him draw his own ridiculous conclusions. But, like the rest of his companions, he had underestimated that royal bitch's judge. Amerotke was tenacious, skilful and cunning. He would have to be silenced. According to reports, the judge had returned to his chambers at the Temple of Ma'at and, if rumour was correct, he would stay there for the greater part of the evening.

The Sethian half-listened to the chatter of the other passengers returning to the city after a day's trading in the Necropolis. How was it to be done? The boat ferry nosed its way in towards the bank. The Sethian caught the light of the makeshift markets set up along the quayside: a range of booths and stalls which sold everything from jewellery to pets. The Sethian recalled some of the exploits of the Panthers of the South. One in particular caught his imagination. He smiled. Yes, that's how Pharaoh's judge would die!

Amerotke woke: his muscles ached. He felt slightly cold so he rose to his feet, opened a coffer and took out a thick embroidered mantle which he placed across his shoulders. Some of the oil lamps had gone out but the cresset torches still burnt brightly. He went to the far corner where two scented braziers glowed and crackled. He spread his hands and listened to the sounds of the temple. Once he was warm, Amerotke took a sip of wine and ate some of the bread and fruit a temple handmaid had brought in.

He opened the door, went down the small passage and stood at the entrance to the Hall of Two Truths. All was silent: shifting shadows with the occasional lamp flickering bravely against the darkness. Amerotke always found it strange to come into his court at night. He could vaguely make out his own judgment chair, the table, the long row of pillars with cushions where the Director of his Cabinet and the scribes would sit – so quiet now yet often the scenes of violent emotion, allegation and counterallegation, judgment, sometimes even death.

Satisfied, Amerotke returned to his chamber. He closed the door and squatted on the cushions where, once again, he concentrated on what Neshratta and Kheay had told him. He rued his mistake and cursed his own foolishness. Peshedu and his family, Karnac, Nebamum and the rest were strangers but, like a typical judge, Amerotke had concentrated on different strands and forgotten what he had been taught in the School of Life.

'What you see, Amerotke, in court,' his teacher had instructed, 'is sometimes only the flower. True justice in pursuit of the truth, you must grasp the stem and pull out the root.'

Amerotke conceded he had failed to do this. Peshedu's daughter was the root of all that was happening. Now he would have to wait until Shufoy and Prenhoe returned. No matter how late the hour, or the mourning taking place in Peshedu's household, the questioning would have to continue. Amerotke picked up the items which Shufoy had brought: the twisted but still recognisable golden gazelles and the scraps of parchment. He studied the list of powders which the Scavengers had taken from Felima's household and read their names aloud.

'Mandrake.'

He knew little about the secrets of medicine and wondered what Felima would want with disgusting ingredients such as lizard's blood, the teeth of swine, the juice of stinking fat. Amerotke had learnt from Shufoy the different remedies sold by the charlatans and Scorpion Men of Thebes. Some of the items he recognised, such as the fat of the woodpecker and the powder from ground bones. The more he concentrated the more he realised that Felima had sold more than aphrodisiacs. One he recognised: the use of figs mixed with the milk of a woman who has borne a boy – an ancient remedy given to a woman who might be pregnant. If she vomited she would bear a child, if not, she was barren. Or another where the patient was told to make two holes in the ground, throw barley into one and wheat into the other, then pour into both the water of a pregnant woman and cover them with earth. If the wheat sprouted before the barley, it would be a boy, but if the barley came first, it would be a girl.

Amerotke placed the scraps down on the ground. No wonder Valu was suspicious: these potions accounted for Felima's wealth. Had she set herself up as a wise woman? To sell aphrodisiacs but also to help the barren conceive? And what if she was involved in something more nefarious? Witchcraft? Amerotke's mind teemed. He was about to return to this when he heard a sound in the temple. Shufoy and Prenhoe must be returning. Amerotke gathered the pieces together. However, there was no footfall, no shouted greeting. Amerotke was certain he had heard that sound. Perhaps a priest or a temple maiden? A shiver of fear caressed his back. He relaxed as he heard a knock on the door.

'Come in!'

The door swung open. Amerotke was aware of a basket being thrust through. It happened so quickly he couldn't react. The basket was tipped and writhing vipers fell on the floor, squirming and twisting. The door was shut abruptly. Amerotke crouched in terror. It had happened in only a few seconds. The door opening, the tipping basket, now these deadly, venomous snakes writhing on the floor. Amerotke stayed still. These could be bought at any marketplace, their flesh and skins being used for various purposes. He also realised the snakes had been roused, deliberately agitated. A good two dozen, perhaps more, writhed there. Different varieties, they coiled and slithered, hissing angrily, confused and agitated. Amerotke knew their attention would be attracted by heat or sudden movement. He breathed a sigh of relief as this mass of coiling, writhing venom moved towards the braziers, drawn by their heat. Of course! The marble temple floor would be ice-cold to them. Amerotke felt a pain of cramp in his legs. It was a nightmare. Here he was in his temple chamber, yet, only a few yards away, a coiling mass of venomous poison. He dare not breathe. He studied the thin, dark line of the snakes' bodies, the broad snouts, the flickering tongues, heads slightly raised. He had been trained on how to deal with these – never to interfere or to attract their attention.

The snakes began to separate. Being of different types one attacked another and drew apart, hissing. Amerotke thanked Ma'at for the braziers. Just as the snakes were drawn by the heat of campfires or the warmth of some animal, now he was being saved by a mass of gleaming charcoal as well as the smell of soups and bread from the nearby baskets. The snakes, moving sideways, slithered along the chapel floor. Amerotke closed his eyes. Some had remained near the door. At last, however, his patience was rewarded. The gap between the snakes and the door grew, an ever widening passage. Amerotke moved. Quietly, picking up two of the cushions to protect his hands, he moved slowly on all fours towards the door.

He was safe. He tossed the cushions in the direction of the snakes, leapt to his feet, grasped the handle, opened the door and threw himself out, pulling the door quickly closed behind him. He ran into the hall, picking up other cushions, whatever else he could find. He raced back and placed these to block the gap between the bottom of the door and the floor. He was sweat-soaked, his heart beating as if he had run a long, arduous race. Amerotke sat in one of the window seats, crossing his arms, trying to stop the trembling in his body. His legs felt like lead. Pain throbbed at the back of his head. For a while he thought he was going to be sick. He felt like running, leaving this temple, but he hadn't the strength nor could he leave with that chamber full of its writhing, hissing venom.

At last he managed to control the panic seething within him. Every so often he would check the bottom of the door. He almost cried out with relief when he heard the sound of voices – Shufoy and Prenhoe, as usual, arguing noisily about one of the scribe's dreams. He watched them come striding up the corridor.

'My Lord Amerotke!'

Shufoy dropped his new parasol and ran towards his master. He crouched and peered up. Amerotke's face, even in the poor light, looked pale, haggard, drawn. Prenhoe went towards the chapel door.

'Don't!' Amerotke shouted.

In hasty, abrupt sentences he told them exactly what had happened. Shufoy fairly danced with rage.

'I've told you before! I've told you before!' he exclaimed. 'The Lady Norfret has!'

'The Lady Norfret must not be told of this!'

'I've told you before,' Shufoy continued. 'Doors have bolts; they are meant to be drawn.' Shufoy shook his fist at the door. 'I'll give them snakes!'

Prenhoe, however, was more level-headed. He hurried off to rouse servants and guards. These soon arrived bearing torches, baskets and long poles with nets on the end. Some of the guards had donned their boots and covered their legs with tightly fastened leather guards. The chapel door was opened. In a jumble of torchlight, shouts, curses and exclamations, the chapel was cleared, the death-bearing vipers swept up into baskets. By the time they had finished Amerotke felt more composed. Shufoy also quietened down, sharing his unasked-for wisdom on how to deal with vipers.

'He must have known you were here,' the little man murmured. 'It's a nasty schoolboy trick: this time more deadly. You did well, Master. Many another person would have screamed, tried to flee. The vipers would have struck time and again.'

'I was too frightened,' Amerotke smiled. 'And I thank Ma'at for those braziers. If it hadn't been for the bowls of burning charcoal . . .'

'You must be close to the truth,' Shufoy declared.

'I think I am,' Amerotke nodded. 'I am beginning to understand why Intef and Felima had to die but I am still clutching at straws. You went to see General Karnac?'

'Oh yes. They've heard about Peshedu. Karnac is turning his mansion into a fortress. He even has the Vulture squadron on the road outside.' Shufoy referred to a crack chariot unit. 'Every gate, window and doorway is guarded. Heti and Thuro are doing the same.'

'Yet the killer's one of them,' Amerotke laughed drily. 'I am sure he is, but proving it is another matter.'

'The temple's cleared!' Prenhoe declared, ushering out the last servants and thanking the guard. 'I wonder where Asural is. Do you know, Master,' he chattered on, 'last night I had a dream about a snake, nine yards long, with enormous jaws and—'

'Shut up!' Amerotke and Shufoy chorused.

'Master,' Shufoy got to his feet. He looked quickly into the chapel and came back, 'you said that the Sethian must be one of the Panthers of the South but they were all in Thebes when Peshedu was killed. It would be easy to find out who cannot explain his movements tonight.'

Amerotke made a face. 'Perhaps, perhaps not, but the killer himself must have thought of that. No, I think I'll go hunting in a different direction.'

'It's late!' Prenhoe wailed.

'It's never too late!' Amerotke got to his feet. He still felt shaken but determined to settle this matter. 'The Sethian is striking right and left. It's only a matter of time before he realises one person he has forgotten.'

'Who?' Shufoy asked. 'Kheay?'

'More importantly,' Amerotke gripped Shufoy's shoulder, 'Neshratta's maidservant. You are to go to General Peshedu's house now. Take two of the temple guards with you.' Amerotke raised a hand. 'Of course, offer my condolences and commiserations. Ignore all objections. Show them the cartouche you carry, arrest the maidservant and bring her here.'

Shufoy and Prenhoe made to object.

'No, no, do it now.' Amerotke almost pushed them out of the corridor. 'I'll be safe. I'll go to the kitchens and find something to eat and drink. I'll stay there until you return.'

Shufoy and Prenhoe left but only after Amerotke gave assurances that he would not remain alone.

Amerotke walked out of the Hall of Two Truths into the perfume-filled, moon-bathed gardens. The temple had been aroused by the commotion. Guards stood about, servants clustered gossiping. Even some of the priests had been roused from their wine-laden slumbers, eager to find out what had happened. The temple kitchens lay just beyond the Pool of Purity. A sleepy-eyed cook sprang to attention when Amerotke entered the large, stone-paved room. One look at the judge's grim face and the cook was only too eager to serve him: bread just fresh from the ovens, dried meat on a bed of lettuce and a jug of beer. Amerotke sat just within the doorway. He ate and drank slowly. Every assassin, he thought, makes a mistake. He quietly prayed that the maidservant, who had been so obdurate in her defence of Neshratta, was the loose thread he'd been searching for.

He was disturbed by Asural, who had been in the city where he'd heard about the commotion. He burst into the kitchen like a war god. Amerotke calmed him down and told him to wait until Shufoy and Prenhoe returned. They did within the hour. The maidservant, shivering with fear, was held fast by two guards.

Amerotke led the party across to a small chamber used by the chapel priests to meet their clients. Everyone else was told to wait outside. Amerotke gently ushered the young woman to a high-backed chair and crouched before her. He grasped her cold hand and tried to reassure her.

'I have told the truth!' the girl wailed.

'What is your name?' Amerotke demanded gently.

'My name is Sato. I have told you the truth so many times! Why am I arrested in the dead of night? The household is already grieving.'

'No, I don't want to talk to you about Ipumer.' Amerotke squeezed her fingers. 'I don't want Lord Valu here to interrogate you. I want to take you back in time, a year or more before Ipumer ever met your mistress.' He felt the girl relax. 'You are very close to the Lady Neshratta, aren't you?'

'Oh, yes I am.'

'And she suffers from nightmares?'

'Yes, how did—'

'How long has she suffered from these?'

'Oh, about two years . . .'

'Something happened, didn't it?' Amerotke insisted. 'About a year before Ipumer appeared, something dreadful happened to your mistress?'

Sato's agitation grew.

'You must tell the truth,' Amerotke insisted. 'Before Ipumer, did the Lady Neshratta have a lover?'

Sato shook her head.

You are lying, Amerotke thought. You are hiding something.

Sato saw the suspicion in Amerotke's eyes. 'I only became close to my mistress,' she explained, 'after the nightmares began.'

'But what happened?' Amerotke leant forward. 'If you don't tell me the truth, there might be even more hideous murders. You and your mistress are not safe.'

Sato stared down at the floor.

'I know very little about this. There are rumours of a terrible quarrel between General Peshedu and his daughter.'

'How long ago was this?'

'It was during the Season of the Planting, about two

years ago. Screams, shouts, vases being thrown, stools, chairs kicked over. I don't know the true details. One night my mistress was taken from her bed.'

'Taken?'

'A gardener who worked in the house – he's now left – he thought the Lady Neshratta had been drugged. She was taken in a palanquin by her father and the others. She was brought back just before dawn.'

Amerotke sighed. At last! 'And you knew nothing of what happened?'

Amerotke felt as if he could shake this girl. Suspicions, sown by what Shufoy had collected from the Scavengers, were now developing into a certainty. Something hideous had happened to the Lady Neshratta. She was the root of all this evil, unwilling accomplice though she may be.

'I don't know what happened,' Sato repeated. 'My mistress never told me but I think she was hurt. Her soul, her Ka seems to have diminished.'

'I know what happened to your mistress.' Amerotke held her gaze. 'Which is why tonight you must lodge here in the temple. I have work to do. Perhaps we will speak again.'

He called in Asural and told him to put the young maid under house arrest. Then he sent a messenger to inform his wife that he would be staying in the city. Shufoy was ordered to make up a makeshift bed in the chamber and to fetch a roll of papyrus and a casket of styli and ink.

'Shouldn't you sleep?' Shufoy protested.

'In time,' Amerotke smiled. 'Now, you and Prenhoe are to take messages to the House of a Million Years. The Divine One will want to know. The same goes for Lord

Senenmut and the Eyes and Ears of Pharaoh. Tell my servants to prepare the Hall of Two Truths.'

'Why?' Shufoy demanded.

'Because Pharaoh's judgment is going to be given.'

Amerotke dismissed them and arranged for more oil lamps to be lit. Shufoy returned with a roll of papyrus and styli from the temple stores. Prenhoe brought the transcript of the trial. Amerotke made himself comfortable and unrolled the papyrus. He closed his eyes and said a short prayer to Ma'at to guide him to the truth. He sketched six columns and wrote down the names: Neshratta, Kheay, Karnac, Thuro, Heti, Nebamum.

Amerotke sat. He thought of that figure with the Horus mask, slipping up the Street of Oil Lamps. Ipumer running home. Lamna, Intef and Felima being brutally murdered. Those pictures in the Red Chapel! Amerotke smiled grimly. Hadn't he seen one where spies from the regiment of Seth had murdered a Hyksos nobleman by sending him a viper in a casket?

'Well, I am Pharaoh's viper,' Amerotke whispered, 'and I shall strike deep and fast.'

He began to put down everything he had learnt, all his suspicions. At one time he became frustrated and replaced the papyrus parchment with another. All the time he worked, developing his theory as he would in court, he began to see the subtle mind of the murderer and quietly marvelled at the Sethian's intense malice. Amerotke now knew the reason but he had no real proof, except for Neshratta. Yes, she and her younger sister!

* * *

Dawn had broken above Thebes, the resurgent sun shimmering in the gold-plated tops of the obelisks, pouring through the doors and windows of the temples. It roused the heralds and the trumpeters so the priests could worship the glory of Amun-Ra and, more importantly, greet their Pharaoh, who had decided to process in majesty through her city.

It was the ninth hour yet the sun was hot, beating down on the marines, their bodies gleaming with sweat, as they pulled at the long oars of the splendid royal barge, *The Glory of Amun-Ra*, which cut through the waters of the Nile. The Divine One, Pharaoh Hatusu, the Imperial Pharaoh-Queen, the Incarnation of the Golden Hawk, the Beloved of Ra, the Sister of Osiris, the Defender of her Peoples and the Shatterer of their enemies, had left the House of Adoration. She had decided to show her face and smile on the people by sailing in glorious triumph along the Nile to the Great Mooring Place near the Temple of Isis. Along the banks marched battalions of élite foot soldiers from the regiment of Seth. Beyond, chariot squadrons bearing the Eagle insignia guarded their flanks. The hot air vibrated with the sound of music and the applause of the crowds. The most delicious perfumes were wafted across by the great ostrich plumes which almost shrouded the Divine One's presence. Hatusu sat on a gold-plated throne in the centre of the barge, her face set in a look of divine serenity.

Since before dawn the Keepers of the Perfumes, the Holder of the Royal Slippers and the Chamberlain of the Imperial Wardrobe had helped her wash, oil and perfume her beautiful light copper body. Dark shades of green had been rubbed into her eyelids, black kohl rings enhanced her glittering gaze and protected her eyes from wind-borne sands. Her lips were carmine-painted, a luxurious, perfume-drenched wig had been placed on her head, its strands plaited with tiny jewels. It was bound to her head by a gold encrusted filet on which the Uraeus, that spitting cobra which defended Pharaoh's presence, lunged in ferocious display. A gorget containing the most precious gems circled her throat, in the centre, a blue sapphire carved in the shape of the eye of Horus. Hatusu wore exquisite linen robes, edged with gold, and the royal coat of nenes, clasped by a silver chain, hung round her shoulders. Her feet were sheathed in closed sandals of costly fabric and embroidered with silver thread. In her hands she carried the crook and flail, the symbols of Pharaoh's power.

Hatusu sat rigid. She always made sure the throne was well cushioned on both the seats and the back because, as she giggled to Senenmut before they left, she sometimes felt so stiff she felt she could never get up. The time for such giggling and personal teasing was over. Crowds had flocked out to the city to look upon her, God's own worthy, the Incarnation of the Divine Will. Hatusu turned her face slightly and smiled. The roars of the crowd grew. Hatusu looked away, eyes fixed on the jutting prow of the barge, carved in the shape of a ferocious dragon. It was good for the people to see her and she had prepared this Imperial going forth in great detail. The barque was the finest of the royal fleet, its hull overlaid with gold, the masts silver-shod and decorated with flying red and white pennants. Between these was a small naos so that Pharaoh could commune with her father, Amun-Ra. The people must not forget this day.

Hatusu smiled in satisfaction. Amerotke knew his place in the scheme of things. It was not for him to pass judgment on the Panthers of the South. Oh no, Pharaoh would grace his court with her presence. Amerotke may question, but the final decision and judgment would be hers. Hatusu gripped the crook and flail more tightly. How she had looked forward to this!

The messenger from Amerotke had arrived in the early hours bearing a specially sealed scroll which Hatusu had quickly studied. She had been so happy she had roused the Lord Senenmut and filled goblets of wine, toasted him and, for a short while, danced naked before him. Hatusu glanced quickly to her left where her Grand Vizier stood, one hand slightly resting on the back of the imperial throne – Senenmut, her Grand Vizier and lover, wearing all the jewels and paraphernalia of office. He would be present when judgment was delivered.

Hatusu bit back her smile. She did not like General Karnac: the arrogance of those eyes, that slight chilling smile round his lips which always told her that he tolerated, but did not accept her. Well, today it would be different! Today he would know her justice. He would kneel and kiss her sandalled feet and recognise her power. Why? Hatusu's head slightly tilted back and she stared up at the sky. Because she was stronger, faster. Because she was born to rule and bask in divine favour!

'My lady,' Senenmut whispered, 'look to the right.'

Hatusu sighed and did so. Her every move would be watched. She must bestow her smile on all those who waited. The crowds on the near bank roared their applause, almost drowning the hymns of the priests and priestesses, the braying of the musicians, the temple hesets shaking the sistra.

Hatusu looked straight ahead as the barge changed direction, preparing to slide into the quayside. The gold-topped obelisks and the pink-coloured temple colonnades of her city welcomed her. Hatusu moved slightly, raising her head as an officer on the imperial barge rapped out an order. The waiting quayside was fast approaching, the oars came up and the barge slid into its imperial berth. Liveried servants sprang aboard, bearing long poles which they slipped through the sockets on either side of the throne. These were then garlanded with flowers. On either side the ostrich-plume holders gathered, holding them up to shade the Divine One's face from the sun. Senenmut checked that everything was well. An order was issued. Hatusu, seated on her royal throne, was gently lifted up. The bearers walking slowly, carefully, down the ramp on to the quayside. Hatusu kept her face impassive but, as she'd confessed to Senenmut as they'd lain entwined in their great four-poster bed, this was the moment she always dreaded.

'Can you imagine,' Hatusu had shrieked with laughter, 'the Divine One being plunged into the Nile?'

Hatusu felt like giggling now. Instead she bit her lip and stared round. Units from the regiment of Seth were ready with their long lances, red headdresses and huge oblong shields. She also glimpsed the Panthers of the South. She did not turn her face towards them. They would have to wait for that. The cortège moved off, a host of priests going before it, sending great clouds of incense up from their swinging censers whilst the temple maidens strewed flower petals, drenched in perfume, before the royal throne. On either side marched her bodyguard; behind, the choirs of different temples chanted the divine psalm.

> 'How wonderful are you, Hatusu.
> Egypt's great glory!
> Eye of the God,
> You have deigned to show your face to us!
> Our hearts melt like wax.
> Our bodies sing with pleasure.
> We have drunk of your smile,
> Heaven's sweet wine . . .'

The palanquin made its way slowly up the Avenue of Sphinxes. As she passed, the crowd fell quiet and prostrated themselves. Now and again Hatusu turned and smiled. At last the Temple of Ma'at came into sight. They went through the soaring pylons, across the sun-drenched, flower-covered concourse and stopped at the foot of the steps. On the top of these Amerotke knelt waiting on a cushion. He wore the pectoral, rings and anklets of office. The judge lifted his head as the waiting trumpeters gave shrill blasts, the sign that the Divine One had arrived.

You look tired, Hatusu thought. She grinned and winked at the judge. The palanquin was set down. Courtiers and chamberlains helped her to alight. Little girls came and strewed the steps with rose petals, sanctifying the stones where Pharaoh would tread. Hatusu was aware of the heat but, according to the ritual, climbed slowly. When she reached the top, she stood before Amerotke, who quickly kissed her sandalled feet. Hatusu stretched out her hand, a sign of great friendship.

'Stand up, my lord.'

Amerotke did so. Hatusu, aware that no one else could see her, quickly blew a kiss and allowed the judge to lead her through the colonnaded entrance and into her court, the Hall of Two Truths. No spectators had been allowed. Only the Director of Amerotke's Cabinet, Prenhoe and Shufoy sat on the cushions where usually the scribes would kneel and record the proceedings of the court. All three prostrated themselves as Hatusu took the Chair of Judgment. Amerotke pushed the silver-covered footstool under her feet.

'I would love some wine,' Hatusu breathed, 'but only after this.'

'You shouldn't be speaking,' Senenmut whispered, coming up to stand behind the chair.

'I am Pharaoh!' Hatusu snorted. 'I will do what I want!'

Amerotke knelt on the cushion before the imperial footstool, his back to Pharaoh. He glanced quickly to his left. Shufoy and Prenhoe looked half asleep. The Director of his Cabinet, pompous as usual, was preparing his writing tray. In the small porticoed transept on his right gathered

Karnac, Thuro, Heti, Nebamum and, some distance away from these, Neshratta, holding her younger sister's hand. The doors to the hall were closed by Asural, who took up guard, arms crossed. No one else had been allowed in.

'Pharaoh has spoken!' Senenmut proclaimed. 'Her justice will be known! The court is in session!'

Amerotke lifted his hands and intoned the short ritual prayer to Ma'at. Once he had finished, he glanced to his right.

'All those who have been summoned to hear the word of Pharaoh may approach!'

Prenhoe and Shufoy jumped up and brought six cushions, which they arranged in a semicircle in front of Hatusu.

Karnac and his companions came and knelt; Neshratta and Kheay also took up their positions. They made their ritual obeisance, foreheads touching the cold shiny floor. Hatusu deliberately kept them waiting before Senenmut proclaimed that they may look upon the Divine One's face.

'My lady,' Karnac protested, ignoring the hiss of disapproval from the Director of the Cabinet. 'Divine One,' Karnac remembered himself, 'why are we summoned here?'

Hatusu did not reply. The silence lengthened. Senenmut coughed quietly.

'You are summoned here,' Amerotke declared, taking his cue, 'because the Divine One wishes to hear the truth and, before long, the truth will be known. You have been searched for weapons.' He glanced at the Panthers of the South, then the two young women. 'You must not move either to the right or to the left until the Divine One has spoken. Lady Neshratta, did you kill the scribe Ipumer?'

'I did not.'

The young woman had definitely been crying. He caught the quick glance between her and her secret lover.

'Yes, you did, and no, you didn't.' Amerotke replied. He toyed with the ring on his finger. 'The night Ipumer visited the House of the Golden Gazelle, you did not leave your bedchamber. But your sister Kheay did.'

'No, no!' The young girl's hands flailed out, her eyes rounded in terror. She would have jumped to her feet but her sister grasped her wrists.

'Ipumer was a silver-tongued rascal,' Amerotke continued. 'He paid court to the Lady Neshratta but, in his assignations with her, he also flirted with you, Kheay. Now your sister grew tired of his attentions and Ipumer became threatening. He declared he would commit suicide. The Lady Neshratta laughed. He said he would proclaim their love affair to all the city and Neshratta mocked. He threatened to reveal other secrets and the Lady Neshratta would ask him what he was talking about.'

'And what was he talking about?' Karnac demanded.

Amerotke ignored him.

'You, Kheay, must have been flattered by this young scribe. Your father is dead and my heart goes out to you but, I suspect, there was little real love between General Peshedu and his two daughters. Neshratta cultivated Ipumer for dalliance but also to revenge herself. You did likewise.'

The two women knelt close together, hands on their thighs, eyes fixed on Amerotke.

'Neshratta was an accomplice to this. She didn't really care until Ipumer began to hint at other matters.'

'What other matters?' Neshratta whispered, head down.

'I will come to that in a moment. However, you decided, my lady, that Ipumer had to die. You bought poison and, on the afternoon before Ipumer arrived, you and your sister put your heads together. You knew your father would be absent that night, so you made your preparations. To the side of the House of the Golden Gazelle lies a small glade carefully protected by bushes, trees and shrubs. You or Kheay, just before nightfall, placed drink and food there in preparation for Ipumer's visit. However, you had to be careful. Kheay pretends to have a nightmare and comes along to your bedchamber, well protected by your maid, Sato. You allow her into your bed. The maid, if she peers in, can, through the gauze protecting sheets, see you and would naturally conclude your sister lay on the other side. She did most of the night but, at the appointed hour, Kheay rose quietly and quickly left. The wooden latticed frame was removed. She climbed down the rope ladder and into the garden. You, Neshratta, quickly put the lattice-work frame back and returned to your bed. If your servant heard anything she would open the door and see you sleeping. Meanwhile, Kheay slipped across the garden and out through the postern gate. She meets Ipumer at a secluded spot. She has food and fruit ready. The young scribe is flattered by such attention. I cannot say what happened except that the wine cup given to him contained a deadly venom. There would be murmurs, kisses, dalliance and Ipumer, satisfied, decided to return to his lodgings. He is full of himself and boasts to a soldier of what he has done. But, as he approaches Lamna's house, the poison he has drunk begins to take effect. He has felt these symptoms before. I suspect he had been poisoned at other meetings but, the amount had been too small or, because of his delicate stomach, both wine and poison were vomited out.'

Amerotke paused at the hammering on the door.

'Open the door!' Senenmut proclaimed.

Asural obeyed. Valu, the prosecutor, almost stumbled through. Even from where he sat, Amerotke could see how the fat man was flustered, not knowing whether to clutch his stomach or mop his brow. Amerotke glanced at him. Valu should have been here at the beginning. Valu came forward and prostrated himself, face down on the floor, hands outstretched.

'Divine One, my humblest apologies.'

'You were summoned,' Senenmut declared, 'to bask in the Divine One's face and favour.'

'I had other business,' Valu wailed. 'Hideous blasphemy, Divine One. I have found the remains of Meretseger!'

SETH: opponent of Isis, mother of Horus.

CHAPTER 12

For a while all was commotion. Karnac jumped to his feet before remembering himself. Even Thuro and Heti were whispering like children whilst the two young women were relieved to be free of Amerotke's questioning. Valu was given permission to rise and Shufoy brought a cushion. The Divine One, noticing her prosecutor's distress, ordered some wine to be served and gave him time to collect his thoughts. Valu knelt on the cushions on Amerotke's right, still facing Pharaoh, muttering his thanks whilst sipping at the copper beaker Prenhoe had brought. Amerotke could see that the Chief Prosecutor had prepared himself well but, whatever had happened had caused consternation. Valu's face was shaved and oiled; even from where he knelt, Amerotke could smell the fragrant perfume he must have dabbed all over his body. Yet his hands looked rather soiled, the hem of his robe wet.

'Well, my lord prosecutor?' Hatusu smiled at this sharp-minded official who probed the secrets of the city. She had a soft spot for this fat, busy little man, whose loyalty to her was unquestionable and whose support during the first year of her reign had been invaluable. 'My Lord Valu,' Hatusu's voice was soft, 'I noticed your absence when I arrived. You are never far from my mind. I realise it was some pressing business, so you had best explain.'

'Divine One,' Valu put the beaker on the floor and joined his hands, 'I rose early to prepare to come here when a courier arrived from the Necropolis. The Tomb of the Immortals, the Heroes,' he gestured towards the Panthers of the South, 'was visited last night by a mysterious figure wearing a Horus mask. The tomb has been polluted.' He continued, ignoring the horrified gasps. 'The keeper murdered, knifed to the heart!'

'What happened?' Karnac shouted.

'Silence!' Senenmut bellowed, his voice harsh and cutting. 'This is a warning, Karnac. Any further interruption will not be tolerated!'

'Divine One, I went out to the tomb,' Valu continued. 'The sarcophagi of four of the other heroes had not been disturbed but General Kamun's had been filled with blood.'

He paused. Amerotke watched Karnac. He knelt rigid as a statue, fists by his side, eyes blazing. Heti and Thuro put their faces in their hands, quietly muttering prayers at this heinous desecration.

'The keeper's blood also covered the floor,' Valu declared. 'The tomb will have to be cleaned, purified and blessed again. I have notified General Kamun's relatives. I then made careful enquiries. As you know, Divine One, my

Eyes and Ears are constantly busy in the Necropolis.' Valu elliptically referred to his legion of spies which swarmed like ants everywhere. 'Now, whoever was allowed into the tomb,' he continued, his voice more composed, 'must have been someone in authority who carried the cartouche or insignia of the regiment of Seth. Apparently the desecrator has visited the Necropolis before. One of my spies recognised him leaving the city and climbing up to the rocky outcrop above the city. Such a figure has not been seen on the road to the Valley of the Kings so he must have gone the other way. A guide took me up, just after dawn, into a small ravine honeycombed with caves – about thirteen or fourteen in all. In one of them I found what I believe is Meretseger's skeleton.'

'How do you know it's hers?' Hatusu asked.

'Two items. One was a curse, a prayer of vindication to her demon spirit.'

'And the other?'

'Decayed, rotting.' Valu clutched his stomach. 'What remained, I believe, of General Balet's eyes.'

'And the witch's bones?' Hatusu asked.

'They have been placed in a casket awaiting your bidding.'

'My bidding you shall soon know,' Hatusu retorted. 'Do you hear what my Eyes and Ears have said, Lord Karnac? Only a member of the regiment of Seth could gain entry to that tomb!' Pharaoh's voice was brittle with anger. 'Only a member of your Panthers, your companions, knew where Meretseger was buried!'

'I hear you, my lady. My heart is distraught.'

'I shall return to this matter,' Hatusu threatened. 'But, my Lord Valu, you may now turn. Your colleague Amerotke is, I believe, leading us to the truth.'

Valu made an obeisance and turned. He caught Amerotke's eyes and smiled.

'Lady Neshratta,' Amerotke continued, 'we were talking about the night Ipumer was killed by a poison administered by your sister.' He raised a hand at Valu's gasp. 'On that particular night enough poison had been given the scribe to kill him once and for all. By the time he reached the quarter of the Perfume-Makers, the poison was probably having its effect. He may have called at Physician Intef's but that sly, cunning man would have little to do with him. Ipumer continued back to his lodgings where he later died. Once he'd gone, Kheay here,' Amerotke held the younger sister's frightened gaze, 'left the House of the Golden Gazelle by the postern gate and retrieved the cups, platters, plates, whatever had been used for their midnight revelry. These would have been hidden away in a bush. Kheay climbs the rope ladder, gently tiptoes across the room and slides into bed. The floorboard of your sister's chamber may creak under sandalled feet, but a young girl on tiptoe . . . ?' Amerotke shrugged. 'Whilst the latticed window frame slides in and out as smoothly as a knife from its sheath. Your elder sister would have helped you come and go. As I have said, for I have visited Lady Neshratta's bedroom, if the maid opened the door, she would only see the side of the bed on which Neshratta lay. She would presume that you stayed with her. You made two journeys,' Amerotke insisted. 'First to meet the flatterer. Secondly, to remove the cup and platters. You even dabbed on ointment and wore a thick perfumed wig to disguise any smell of the grove where you met Ipumer.'

Kheay's lower lip quivered.

Valu raised a hand. 'I have news, my Lord Amerotke, on the scribe Ipumer. He came from the city of Avaris. He was known by that name, a junior scribe in the House of Life at the Temple of Nait. Little is known of his origins, though he did boast that he was of Hyksos descent. However, very few people knew him, even fewer cared. He left Avaris abruptly, claiming he had preferment here in Thebes.'

'Did you know this?' Amerotke asked Neshratta.

She shook her head.

'What did you know about him?'

Neshratta opened her mouth but then closed it and glanced away.

'I think you knew more than you ever told us,' Amerotke declared.

She muttered something under her breath.

'What was that?'

Neshratta's head came up, a defiant look in her eyes. 'My advocate, Meretel, is not here.'

'Well said,' Amerotke smiled. 'But he is your advocate, not your sister's. Kheay administered the poison. It is your sister who committed murder and it is your sister who will feel the full brunt of Pharaoh's justice. Do you know the sentence for a poisoner? Do you want Kheay – what, only fourteen summers old? – to be buried in the hot sands of the Red Lands?'

Neshratta was breathing quickly, bosom rising and falling as if she had run a great distance. Beads of sweat appeared under her wig. Her sister looked as if she was in a trance, large dark eyes in a pale face.

'Are you going to let your sister die?'

'What is it you want?'

'Do you deny my story?'

Amerotke fought to keep his voice steady. If Neshratta held out, if she decided to risk everything to protect her secret lover, all of Amerotke's scanty evidence, and the theory it supported, would collapse like a house of straw beneath a savage wind.

'Shall I help you?' he asked. 'You have a secret lover, my Lady Neshratta. Or you had one. He loved you and you loved him. Such an intense passion conceived a child.'

Neshratta's shoulders began to shake. She kept staring at a point above Amerotke's head.

'You were going to be betrothed to General Karnac, weren't you? But then your courses stopped and your father found out. General Peshedu was furious, so were his companions. Am I not correct, Lord Heti? Lord Thuro? Lord Karnac?'

The three Panthers of the South were now openly discomfited. Karnac's lip curled but Amerotke chose Heti as the weakest. He sat back on his heels, shoulders hunched, refusing to meet Amerotke's gaze.

'Forced abortion is a terrible crime,' the judge continued, 'but for a daughter of one of the Panthers of the South to become pregnant, to refuse to name her secret lover to her father . . . Were you drugged, Lady Neshratta?

346

I suspect you were, taken from your bed and carried through the night by these brave men to the house of the widow Felima. She was Intef's collaborator. Openly she sold aphrodisiacs, love potions. Secretly she was an abortionist who received powders and potions from Intef. She acted on his behalf and on his guidance. After all, a physician found guilty of a forced abortion could face a death just as hideous as the one facing your sister. The deed was done at night; drugged, you were brought back to your father's house. You hated him before this happened, now your hate spilt over into vengeance. My lady, answer me this. Did you have an abortion?'

'You have no proof!' Neshratta countered, swallowing hard. 'Nor do you have any proof that my sister met Ipumer out in the dark!'

'Oh, but I do.'

Amerotke undid the small wallet on the floor beside him and gently took out the scraps of parchment, the burnt seal and the ring Shufoy had found amongst Ipumer's possessions.

'Is that your evidence?' Neshratta's voice jibed.

'Yes it is.' Amerotke tapped the parchment. 'These are the powders Felima used to purge your body. This,' he picked up the half-burnt seal, 'is, I believe, your father's. He would have to pay a woman like Felima. She would demand some guarantee that she would not be prosecuted. After all, your father was a most powerful man. He probably paid her in precious stones, or a deben of silver and gold. He would have also given a letter of favour with his seal attached. But this –' Amerotke picked up the ring –

'have you noticed it? Two coiled silver snakes with a gem in the centre? Do you have a ring like this?'

Neshratta stretched out her hand, fingers splayed.

'Of course I do!'

'It was specially fashioned, just for you? General Peshedu doesn't buy trinkets from the market but orders hand-crafted rings and bracelets for the women of his house-hold. He bought one for you and one for your sister. This is Kheay's.' Amerotke slid it along the floor towards her. 'Try it on, Neshratta.'

Neshratta looked as if she was going to refuse.

'Do as my lord orders!' Senenmut shouted.

Hands slightly shaking, Neshratta tried to force it on her ring finger but it was too small.

'It won't fit,' Amerotke declared. 'Give it to your sister.'

Kheay, who still seemed as if she was in a trance, quickly obeyed and the ring slipped on snugly. She lifted her hand and stared at it.

'Why should Ipumer have your sister's ring?' Amerotke questioned. 'My Lady Neshratta, do not lie. I can send my servants out to the gold- and silversmiths of the city. One of them will recognise his handiwork and come to this court to take a great oath: that the rings were specially made for the two daughters of General Peshedu.'

Kheay put her face in her hands and began to sob.

'I do not know the true relationship between Ipumer and your sister,' Amerotke observed. 'But I do know that Ipumer was greedy and vainglorious. He probably gave Kheay a pledge and demanded one in return. That's the only explanation.'

Neshratta licked her dry lips. She glanced quickly at the Panthers of the South. 'I . . .' she stammered, 'I . . .'

'Tell him!' Kheay took her hands away from her face. 'Neshratta, can't you see he knows all?'

'Shut up!' Neshratta shouted back.

She tried to grip her sister's wrist but Kheay fought her off.

'I didn't know all this!' Kheay gazed terrified at Amerotke. 'I never knew about the abortion. I know my sister was sick for a while, confined to her chamber and that Father was very angry. I suspected she had a lover before she met Ipumer. He would come to the house at night—'

Again Neshratta tried to seize her arm but Kheay fought her off.

'Lady Neshratta,' Amerotke interrupted, 'restrain yourself or I'll have your wrists bound.'

'My sister, Kheay, tells the truth.' Neshratta had made her choice. 'Ipumer was handsome, silver-tongued. I enjoyed baiting my father, but I soon grew tired of Ipumer. When we used to meet, Ipumer would protest and try to make me jealous by chattering to Kheay.'

'And on the night he died?' Amerotke insisted.

'I did leave the bedchamber,' Kheay declared. 'But I never knew about the poison.'

Amerotke gestured. 'Come forward, girl!'

Kheay, almost pleased to be away from her sister, rose, brought the cushion and knelt before Amerotke.

'Ipumer flattered you, didn't he?'

She nodded.

'You have always lived in your sister's shadow?'

Again the girl nodded.

'And when she tired of him?'

'I was flattered,' Kheay whispered, her eyes full of tears. 'I begged my sister to help. She said I could do what I wanted.'

'Of course she would,' Amerotke reassured her. 'She hated her father so much she would do anything for revenge and that included using you.'

Amerotke turned away to cough and, as he did so, glanced quickly at the person he suspected to be the Sethian. He knelt, hands before him, head slightly down. No, you won't intervene, Amerotke thought. You are probably wondering how much I know.

'Right.' Amerotke gently touched Kheay's face with his fingers. 'You are an innocent child. You have nothing to fear from me as long as you tell the truth. Ipumer used to come down to your house at night. Sometimes you'd leave by your own chamber but that could arouse suspicion so you pretended to have a nightmare. Of course, your elder sister would help. Once it was dark, just before you retired to bed, Neshratta would take out to your meeting place with Ipumer a tray with cups and food for your secret tryst with him. What you didn't know is that the cup Ipumer would drink from was smeared with a poisoned venom—'

'But, my lord,' Valu interrupted, 'how would Lady Neshratta know that her sister wouldn't drink the wrong cup?'

'I don't know.' Amerotke's eyes never left Kheay. 'But you do.'

'I . . .' Kheay nodded. 'I cannot drink wine,' she murmured. 'Ever since my courses began, the physicians have told me that my humours react violently.' She caught her breath. 'Only one cup was taken out.'

'So, your sister knew you were safe? I am sure that your family physician would confirm what you have said—'

'But weren't you suspicious?' Valu interrupted. 'After these midnight revels Ipumer must have told you about the violent cramps in his stomach.'

'Oh yes, he would,' Amerotke agreed. 'But remember, my lord prosecutor, they would share the same food whilst Ipumer brought his own wineskin. That's why he never suspected. I am correct, child?' Amerotke wanted to keep Kheay calm.

'You are right, my lord,' she whispered. 'I would meet Ipumer at night. Neshratta would leave out, in our secret hiding place, bread and fruit wrapped in a linen cloth and a special drinking goblet she had bought for this purpose. So, if anything went wrong, Father wouldn't notice. Ipumer always brought his own wine.'

'Like lovers do,' Amerotke agreed. 'You supplied the food, he brought his own wine. He was probably wary of your sister and father, the thought of poison may have crossed his mind. He would look at the cup but there was nothing untoward, pour the wine and drink it. He would feel symptoms the following day. When you met again you would say you had suffered nothing. And why should he suspect? You ate the food that he did, didn't you?'

Kheay nodded.

The cup would be laced with poison but not enough to

kill him. That's why he wasn't killed earlier. Physicians will tell us that some poisons build up slowly. It was only a matter of time before he took a fatal dose. Of course, on that particular night your sister would have been more liberal with the dosage.'

'Wouldn't Ipumer have examined the cup?' Valu demanded.

'In the darkness?' Amerotke replied. 'The venom bore no taste nor odour, and Ipumer did have a delicate stomach. Tell me, Kheay,' Amerotke grasped her hand, 'what did Ipumer tell you about your sister and himself?'

'He said he once loved her, but he didn't care,' her lower lip trembled, 'now he had found me.'

'Did he buy poison?' Amerotke asked.

'Oh yes, he said it was to frighten my sister. He threatened to commit suicide. He also took opiates to calm both his humours and his stomach.'

'And what else did he say about himself?'

'Oh, he boasted a lot about how he was of noble blood.'

'And? Come on, child,' Amerotke chided.

'Ipumer said he was of Hyksos blood and had powerful friends in Thebes, that he knew a great deal about my sister.'

'And you told Lady Neshratta all this?'

Kheay nodded. 'Sometimes Ipumer frightened me.'

'Naturally he would,' Amerotke agreed. 'And he would frighten your sister even more. In fact, Ipumer signed his own death warrant. Ipumer and Neshratta had a great deal in common: not only their involvement, but the person who brought Ipumer to Thebes was the same who made the Lady Neshratta pregnant. She had to defend him, just as she tried to against me, by pretending to be the mysterious stranger who wore the Horus mask in the Street of Oil Lamps.'

The Hall of Two Truths fell silent. Even Karnac knelt open-mouthed.

'Ipumer had to die,' Amerotke continued, 'for many reasons. The principal one was to protect Neshratta's great love.' Amerotke gestured. 'Child, you may return.'

Kheay withdrew and Amerotke turned to face General Karnac.

'My lord, you are a hero of Thebes, the leader of the Panthers of the South. You have kept this band of heroes together, haven't you?'

Karnac stared bleakly back.

'And when your wife died you saw it as only appropriate that you marry the daughter of one of your companions? You are a proud man, General Karnac. Flirtation and wooing come hard to you. You must have been furious to discover the woman you had chosen was already bearing another's child. Did you think of invoking the old laws which, in these cases, merit the death penalty?'

'I did. It was my right!' Karnac spat the words out. 'I was betrothed, or nearly so, to the Lady Neshratta. If her pregnancy had become common knowledge I would have been made a cuckold, a laughing-stock throughout the city!' Fury seethed in this arrogant man. 'Yet I felt sorry for Peshedu. He was my war companion. I could have invoked the blood feud.'

'Not in my kingdom, under my rule!' Hatusu broke in quietly though her voice sounded clear round the hall.

Karnac remembered himself and bowed towards the throne.

'I decided to exercise mercy. I had acted in good faith. Why should I be portrayed as a laughing-stock?'

'But the betrothal wasn't common knowledge?' Senenmut demanded.

'It was nearly so when the woman's pregnancy was discovered.'

'My name is Neshratta, Lady Neshratta!'

Amerotke held his hand up for silence.

'Peshedu was mortified,' Karnac continued, ignoring the outburst. 'He too was shamed. He examined the law.' Karnac pointed to the books and scrolls on the table before the judgment chair. 'I can demand blood, and blood I want!'

'The death of an unborn child?' Amerotke asked. 'So, you persuaded Peshedu to drug and bundle off his own daughter? You had her taken to Felima, who did the deed?'

Karnac gazed soullessly back. His two companions, Thuro and Heti, looked nervous. Nebamum had his head down.

'Your rage, my Lord Karnac, must have been something to wonder at.'

'It was not as great as the Lord Peshedu's.'

'And Ipumer?' Amerotke asked. 'When he began to court your former betrothed, you must have objected?' Amerotke waited for a reply. 'Surely,' he persisted when none came, 'Peshedu came to you for help, advice? You must have gone to the House of War and tried to discover what you could do about this upstart?'

'His records had disappeared, there was no trace.' Karnac beat his fists against his thigh. 'I heard a rumour that General Kamun had been responsible for his appointment. But he had died shortly afterwards.'

'Didn't you consider killing Ipumer?' Amerotke queried. 'After all, you are a man of war, a soldier with a heightened sense of your own worth and that of your companions. Peshedu must have demanded vengeance, some sort of retribution?' Amerotke paused. 'Do you know something, General Karnac? I think you gave Peshedu good advice. What a way to rid himself of a troublesome daughter! Let her marry some poor upstart. Let her drink the dregs of bitterness and poverty: that's why Ipumer was safe.' Amerotke looked at Neshratta. 'Oh, I am sure your father protested, my lady, but not too much. He was acting on General Karnac's orders. He really thought that you might become betrothed to Ipumer and, once you were out of his house and off his hands, he could wash those self-same hands of you. You would be someone else's concern. After all, he had another daughter. In his eyes, you were always a nuisance.'

Neshratta opened her mouth. 'My lord . . .' She shook her head. 'My lord,' she whispered, 'I feel faint. I beg you, a cup of wine.'

Amerotke nodded at Shufoy, who went to the small alcove, poured a silver-chased cup and brought it back; Neshratta grasped it and sipped.

'I tell the truth, Lord Karnac?' Amerotke continued.

'That's why you never interfered with Ipumer. You could have challenged him had him beaten, killed, even dismissed from his post. Lady Neshratta, however, has nimble wits. She soon realised her father didn't really care so she tired of Ipumer. Only when the scribe became dangerous and threatening did she decide to act. My Lords Heti and Thuro, you were party to all this, as were Balet and Ruah: that's the only explanation. In previous times, Ipumer wouldn't have lasted a month but a deadly game was being played out. Now, my Lord Karnac, let's go back to happier days. You are of the old school, aren't you? You are a man not used to dalliance and flirtation. The betrothal negotiations for Peshedu's eldest daughter would have been formal, businesslike. You could not act the young man in love but, to press your suit, you turned to the one person who advises you, acts for you and helps you: your faithful shadow, the manservant Nebamum.'

'I . . .'

For the first time since they had met Amerotke found Karnac speechless.

'Tell me, my Lord Karnac, did you and Peshedu swear great oaths that, if you ever found the man responsible for Neshratta's illicit conception, he would die?'

Karnac nodded.

'Did you ever think, in your wildest nightmares, that the man responsible was your faithful Nebamum?'

Karnac gazed back. Nebamum, however, had now lifted his head. If anything, his face looked younger, the care lines smoothed out. He did not appear ruffled but stared coolly across at Amerotke.

'My Lord Karnac, there will be no violence here.'

Amerotke held the gaze of the man he knew to be the Sethian. 'You are the assassin, are you not?'

Nebamum's smile widened.

'You pretend to be what you are not,' Amerotke continued. 'Don't you realise, General Karnac, what a viper you have nursed close to your bosom?'

'I don't believe this,' Heti whispered. 'Nebamum is one of us.'

'Nebamum *was* one of you,' Amerotke countered.

He gestured with his hands for Nebamum to come forward. The manservant looked as if he was going to refuse but then clambered to his feet. He still wore the leather leggings but, as he approached to kneel before Amerotke, the judge noticed his clumsy gait had disappeared. He knelt on the cushions, his eyes searching Amerotke's face.

'As you can see, I survived your attack,' Amerotke began gently. 'The vipers in my chamber?'

'What is this?' Karnac interrupted.

'You forget,' Amerotke continued, 'snakes cannot abide the cold. They are always attracted by the heat. The dishes of charcoal, the brazier?'

Nebamum nodded as if in agreement.

'And the same for the other attack. Yes?' Amerotke paused. 'You are well known over Thebes, Nebamum, fetching and carrying for your master, scurrying around. Did you hire an assassin to loose some arrows above your head so as to confuse me?' Amerotke paused. 'You never left me that morning, so how could you hire an assassin?'

Nebamum smirked.

'But, of course, Lord Karnac had already instructed you to tell me all about the Seth regiment. Dressed in that Horus mask, you hired the assassin, told him to follow Amerotke and Nebamum, the manservant of Karnac, to loose a few arrows to frighten them both. Although the same assassin did more deadly work on General Peshedu, didn't he? You are a very rich man, Nebamum. You probably have more gold and silver than I have, after years of faithful service to your master. The assassin's real quarry was General Peshedu. On a lonely place along the Nile they killed him and his boatman. A fitting death, yes, for the man who arranged the abortion of your child, the humiliation and degradation of the woman you loved. Peshedu, like the rest, was robbed of an honourable life and a dignified death. No corpse for the embalmers; no easy journey for his Ka through the Underworld.' Amerotke gazed at Nebamum. 'So easy to arrange,' he murmured. 'Thebes has its own Guild of Assassins and you have enough wealth to hire the best with no questions asked. What does it matter who does the deed, as long as murder is committed and you are safe?'

'What is this?' Karnac whispered. All arrogance had drained from his face. He looked confused, helpless, a middle-aged man whose world was collapsing all around him.

'Why, my Lord Karnac, this is Nebamum, your manservant, in many ways your blood brother. A man raised in your household, the stripling who was with you the night you entered the Hyksos camp and took Meretseger's head. A man who, when the rest of you were rewarded and glorified,' Amerotke stared at Nebamum's face and felt a pang of compassion, 'wanted nothing more than to faithfully serve you for the rest of his life.'

'And I did,' Nebamum broke in quietly.

'All great hates,' Amerotke agreed, 'have their origins in great love. You were Lord Karnac's shadow, his man-servant, his counsellor. You asked for nothing but to bask in his glory. You were content with that. Lord Karnac is a hero,' Amerotke continued. 'In many ways he is a hard man with a heart of stone. Yet, I think, he would have given you anything you asked.'

Nebamum agreed, just a shift in his eyes.

Amerotke wondered what had happened. Nebamum was so poised and calm. Had his mind been turned by grief, anger, hate? He seemed to be almost enjoying what Amerotke was saying, as if he recognised that both his master and the remaining Panthers of the South were being publicly disgraced. I am, Amerotke reflected, part of your plot.

'You have one regret, haven't you?' Amerotke whispered. 'That you did not live to kill them all?'

'Yes, my lord judge. The snakes . . .' He shrugged. 'I needed time. I knew, after your visit to Lady Neshratta, how the noose was tightening.'

'Of course you did,' Amerotke agreed.

'My lord,' Hatusu broke in, 'I wish you to speak louder. What is this business about snakes?'

'When I visited the Lady Neshratta,' Amerotke declared, head turning to speak over his shoulder, 'she tried to protect Nebamum. She claimed to be the person who hired the room in the Street of Oil Lamps and wore a Horus mask to disguise her face. That was a lie. The merchant who hired the room was certain the person was a man. Before I left Lady Neshratta, my manservant Shufoy noticed how she had been crying, seemed upset. General Karnac, you visited the House of the Golden Gazelle at the same time?'

'That's right,' the general whispered.

'And Nebamum asked to be excused for a while?'

'Yes, he said he wished to see General Peshedu's wife, to reassure her.'

'I don't think he did. Instead, he had a swift, secret meeting with his beloved Neshratta. She informed him what she had told me. You, Nebamum, were furious when you discovered her lie about the Horus mask-wearer in the Street of Oil Lamps – a terrible mistake because it links her with the person who brought Ipumer into Thebes in the first place. She became upset and you tried to kill me.'

Amerotke was distracted as Neshratta picked up the wine cup and drank from it greedily.

'Do you still love her?' Amerotke asked.

'With all my heart, my lord judge. As you said,' Nebamum's face creased into a smile, 'great loves can give birth to great hates. You were my nemesis. It was a race between you and me. I am sorry.' His voice faltered.

'Did you order her to kill Ipumer?'

Nebamum raised his eyebrows. 'He was supposed to be my sword, the weapon to strike at Peshedu and the rest.'

His face became hard, his eyes gleamed. 'They took the one person I truly loved. They took away my child. I had asked nothing of them. I had not been given medals and honours. I didn't want them. All I wanted was her.'

Amerotke chilled at how tense and silent the hall had become.

'I love her now. I shall always love her.'

'And I love you.'

Neshratta knelt up, the wine cup in her hands. Nebamum turned to face her squarely. Amerotke was entranced by the deep passion in Neshratta's eyes. She gulped again from the wine cup.

'I love you all the day time,' she continued, quoting a well known love poem.

> 'I loved you through the dark,
> Through all the long hours of the night.
> I wasted away alone.
> I lay and turned and thought of you.
> What magic was in that voice of yours?
> To bring such singing delight to my flesh?
> I beseeched the darkness.'

'Where am I gone, loving one?'

Nebamum continued the poem.

> 'Why gone from her, whose love can pace me,
> Step by step to your desire.'

Amerotke didn't interfere. Neshratta still held the cup

tightly between her hands. He half suspected what she had done; for her it was the best way out.

Both lovers now chanted the poem together.

'No loving voice replies.
How much we are alone.'

Amerotke looked over his shoulder. Hatusu sat transfixed. Was that a look of compassion? He heard a sound. Neshratta had placed the empty wine cup on the floor and was leaning forward, hands gripping her stomach. She stretched out. Amerotke did not intervene as Nebamum went towards her and gripped her hand. Neshratta was already dying, head down, coughing and spluttering. As if from a distance, Amerotke heard Kheay's screams, the exclamations of others, Asural's hurried footsteps, but it was too late. Neshratta's body was now jerking as she lay in the arms of her lover. Amerotke closed his eyes and prayed the Gods would understand. When he looked again, Nebamum still grasped Neshratta as if trying to control the spasmodic jerking of her body. He pressed his cheek against her head, muttering endearments. No one interfered. Neshratta gave a loud sigh and lay still.

SETH: placed before the Tribunal of the
Gods, tightly bound in a wooden collar.

CHAPTER 13

For a while confusion reigned. Senenmut called for the guards to remove Neshratta's corpse. The young woman lay tightly in Nebamum's arms. Amerotke felt for the blood beat in her neck. It was gone. She lay as if asleep, eyes half closed, lips open. Only the pallor of her skin, the strange purple marks appearing high on her cheeks showed the manner of her death. He felt the sleeve of the young woman's robe and found the very small jar, the type used to hold exotic perfume, still lying there, its stopper in.

'She must have prepared for this.'

Senenmut had left Hatusu sitting on her throne, watching intently. Amerotke was wary of Nebamum. For a while a short struggle ensued as they tried to free the young woman from his grasp. Nebamum held on, eyes glaring fiercely.

'Let her go,' Amerotke whispered. 'She did what she wanted. She knew and prepared for it.'

Nebamum's face was tragic. He didn't cry but he had the stricken look of a man who realises that he has drunk deep of life and everything he's tasted is turning to dust in his mouth. Neshratta was released. A make-shift stretcher was made and her corpse removed. Kheay, who had crumpled to the floor, sobbing uncontrollably, was helped up. Amerotke ordered her to be taken to an adjoining chamber to be kept securely, but comfortably, until the matter was finished.

The only time Nebamum became violent was when Asural searched him roughly for weapons or poison but he could find none. From the hallway outside rose the babble of excited voices. The others just sat shocked, unable to comprehend what was happening.

The doors were closed. Nebamum sat back on his heels, staring up at a point on the wall behind Amerotke. He brushed away a bead of sweat running down his face. A man possessed, Amerotke thought.

'She should have been searched.' Karnac had now found his voice.

Nebamum turned slightly, a look of hatred in his eyes. 'I always thought it would end like this.' Nebamum's voice was harsh. 'It was bound to end in tragedy and tears. Pride, my Lord Karnac, is a hideous flower.' He gestured at Karnac's companions. 'You caused this, you and the other brave Panthers of the South. Instead of letting life have its course, you had to defend your glory, your status, your power!'

The words came out in a malevolent hiss. Nebamum still knelt close by Amerotke but the judge felt no fear.

He was convinced Nebamum meant him no ill. Neshratta
was dead. Nebamum was determined to have his say.

Amerotke glanced round the court. Shufoy, Prenhoe, the
Director of Cabinet and Asural had retaken their usual
positions. The cushions on which Neshratta and Kheay
had knelt had been removed. Only a faint stain on the floor
showed there had been any mishap. Yet the atmosphere
had changed. Hatusu, Senenmut, even Amerotke did not
control this court. All eyes were on Nebamum.

'You loved her, didn't you?' Amerotke began softly.

'I loved her, my lord judge. I always did, from the first
moment I saw her. I am Lord Karnac's servant. I once
loved him.' His voice grew firmer. 'I too am a Panther
of the South. I am also a member of the Seth regiment.
I was there when Meretseger was killed. I was the only
one to receive a grievous wound.'

'But it healed, didn't it?' Amerotke asked. 'Until two
years ago when you pretended it had got worse. When
you plotted your revenge, you and Neshratta. Who would
suspect the humble, shambling Nebamum?'

The manservant smiled to himself as if Amerotke had
said something funny.

'I used to go down to her house,' Nebamum was almost
talking to himself, 'the House of the Golden Gazelle,
bearing messages from Lord Karnac, small gifts. Lord
Peshedu was never there. He was more interested in
his temple girl, his heset, the one he spent most of his
time with. His wife, the Lady Vemsit –' again the smile
– 'she had her own interests. No, as you say, my lord
judge, no one suspected Nebamum. We began to talk,

our hands touched. Neshratta was always poking fun at the Panthers of the South and her father's pompous ways. What began as a weak flame was soon fanned into a roaring fire. We began to meet secretly in the city or at night outside her house. Nobody discovered us. A year before Ipumer arrived in Thebes Neshratta told me she was pregnant.'

'Why didn't you tell me?' Karnac shouted.

Nebamum pulled a face. 'What use would it have done, my lord? Remember your rage when you found out? You threatened the most hideous punishment on the Lady Neshratta and whoever was responsible.'

'You thought you'd wait, didn't you?' Amerotke demanded. 'If Neshratta had run the whole course of her pregnancy, no one in Thebes would have offered for her hand.'

Nebamum was nodding vigorously.

'You'd probably wait for twelve months,' Amerotke continued, 'then ask for her in marriage?'

'Yes, my lord, we planned that. After a while Lord Karnac would forget: he cares for very little. The same is true of Lord Peshedu. But,' Nebamum's voice turned mocking, 'they met as they always did to drink and boast. Their sense of grievance and hurt flourished like some rotten weed in the Nile mud. If you remember, my Lord Karnac,' Nebamum turned his head, 'I was present. I did advise tolerance, caution, some compassion: only then did I realise I was too late.'

'Yes you did,' Heti spoke up. 'Some of us might have listened.'

'Never!' Nebamum spat over his shoulder. 'Lord Amerotke

is correct, I can see it in his eyes. You are killers, born and bred. Your honour was slighted, reparation had to be made. And what did poor Nebamum know about such matters? I, who had asked nothing from you, wasn't even consulted.' Nebamum glanced at Amerotke. 'I could have warned Neshratta until I realised the hideous truth: I hadn't seen Neshratta for days. I was present when they discussed it, but only then did I realise they were talking not of what they would do, but had done! By then it was too late!'

'When they bundled Neshratta out of the house, you weren't there, were you?' Amerotke asked. 'Nor were you present when, drugged and bound, she was taken along to the house of the abortionist Felima?'

Amerotke turned to the Eyes and Ears of Pharaoh, who sat fascinated by what was happening.

'A terrible crime, my lord?'

'Hideous,' Valu agreed. 'Only those consenting to it could be part of it.'

'That in itself turned your soul, didn't it, Nebamum? You, who had been part of everything on this matter, had been excluded?'

'Two days after it happened,' Nebamum replied, 'I visited the Lady Neshratta. She was quite ill, secretly attended by that creature Intef. She had lost our child. She quietly confided to me that the damage done inside would mean she would never bear another. I swore, my hand on her head, the most terrible vengeance.' He glanced insolently at Hatusu. 'I did consider appealing to you, Divine One, but you may recall I was present when they met you.' He held out his hand, fingers curled. 'They held you as tightly as they held your brother and your father. The great Panthers of the South – who would dare take them to task? Now Neshratta's so-called sin had been discovered and her betrothal to Karnac was at an end, I had to be more prudent. I met Neshratta at night. I told her that I would plot the downfall of all of them. Her soul had died with our child and she agreed.'

'You went back to the Red Chapel?' Amerotke demanded. 'You looked at that myriad of paintings on the wall depicting the great exploits of the Panthers? You started with the first, the root cause of all their glory, the execution of Meretseger?'

'I decided to strike at the heart,' Nebamum agreed. 'When we plundered the Hyksos camp I found some of the medallions belonging to the witch. I also discovered records about her family in Avaris. I kept them all as keepsakes. I never imagined how useful they would become. When I did, I took it as a sign of how the God Seth approved of all I planned. I sent the medallions to each of our brave warriors, including Kamun. Neshratta said they had all been present when she had been taken down to that witch woman Felima.'

'And Ipumer?'

'Oh, that was easy. According to the records, Meretseger had been the mistress of a Hyksos captain and given birth to a child. In fact two. I never discovered the younger son but I did Ipumer. I hired that room in the Street of Oil Lamps, bought the Horus mask, a robe and cloak and found I could move easily along the streets of the

Necropolis. My master never really missed me. He used faithful Nebamum to go thither and hither, busy about the city. I pretended the wound in my leg had flared up again. I bought the sandals and the leather leggings. Above all, I found Ipumer.'

'You are a man of considerable wealth?'

'Of course. My master is generous to his horses, dogs and to his servant. I used that wealth to bring Ipumer to Thebes. I went to see old Kamun, a man of weak spirit and even weaker mind. I took him into my confidence. I swore him to secrecy. Would he do me a great favour? Kamun, of course, rose like a fish to the bait. Arrogant as the rest, he was only too pleased to exercise patronage, to do something for poor Nebamum.'

'And Ipumer was impressed?'

'Oh yes. I brought him to Thebes. I met him in the Street of Oil Lamps and told him about his preferment. I also informed him how I wished to use him against the Panthers of the South, the very men who had killed his mother.'

'And Felima and Intef? You discovered their secret trade in abortions?'

'Well, of course I did.' Nebamum scratched his neck, dabbing at the pool of sweat. 'I visited Felima. In one hand I held gold, in the other my sword. I went disguised, late at night. I told her how I knew all about her secret practices; I threatened how, if she did not comply, information would be laid before Lord Valu, the Eyes and Ears of Pharaoh. She was a creature of the night, frightened and greedy. I told her a young man would visit her. She would pamper him, and that posed no difficulty: Felima was as lecherous as a she-goat on heat and Ipumer was a personable young man. I made no reference to Intef but ordered Felima to arrange lodgings for Ipumer with the widow Lamna. Intef I instructed to act as his physician. She was threatened and she was bribed. She did not know what I planned. Ipumer found her agreeable and very co-operative.'

'Why didn't you strike yourself?' Valu interrupted. 'You did eventually.'

'I wished to stay in the shadows, my lord. Let Ipumer take the blame.'

'He must have objected?'

'At first he did but, by then, he was also trapped, at least for a while. I told him how the authorities would not be pleased to have a descendant of Meretseger and a Hyksos prince working in the House of War. He could easily be depicted as a spy for the enemies of Egypt. By then, of course, he had committed his first act. He called on General Kamun and helped him to the Far Horizon with poisoned wine. As General Karnac's faithful lieutenant, I visited the House of War and, when the opportunity presented itself, removed all traces of Ipumer's appointment from the archives. Ipumer became fully co-operative and compliant.'

'And the Lady Neshratta?' Amerotke asked.

'By then she knew what I was doing and, to be truthful, revelled in it. Ipumer, however, was not the man I thought. He had little desire for vengeance or for blood. At one of our secret meetings I told him how Lord Peshedu's downfall and disgrace was his next task after Kamun. He was to flirt with Peshedu's daughter. I would arrange for them to meet at one of the regimental festivals.'

'And Neshratta agreed with this? To lie with a man she didn't know?'

'You don't know the Lady Neshratta.' Nebamum paused. 'You really don't. She never gave in to Ipumer, whatever his boasts, but played him like a cat does a mouse.'

'I recall her letters in court, the love poetry she sent to Ipumer. In truth, Neshratta was really writing to you?' Amerotke asked.

Nebamum smiled in agreement.

'So, Neshratta became the talk of Thebes?'

'Peshedu was furious but so was Ipumer,' Nebamum retorted. 'So I told him to turn his attentions to the heset girl so beloved of Peshedu. Ipumer was most agreeable.'

'What went wrong?' Amerotke demanded. 'Or shall I tell you? Ipumer tired of Neshratta's games. He seduced the heset girl but, being frustrated by the Lady Neshratta, turned to the younger sister. You murdered the heset girl, didn't you?'

Nebamum pulled a face. 'Ipumer was a mistake. Oh, the ladies liked him. He seduced General Peshedu's concubine but was angry at Neshratta. He claimed she was mocking him and said he would have his revenge. I told him to stay well away from Kheay. Neshratta herself was very concerned.'

'But Ipumer grew petulant, threatening?'

'Yes, he said he might seek out Lord Karnac and make a full confession. He claimed that he didn't know the wine was poisoned and so was not responsible for Kamun's death. His intentions towards the Lady Neshratta had always been honourable and he only acted on my orders.'

'But he didn't know who you were?'

'My lord,' Nebamum scoffed. He now sat relaxed, so full of hatred he seemed unaware of where he was or who was watching and listening, 'If Ipumer had carried out his threat, it would only have been a matter of time. Ipumer also hinted that Neshratta was my accomplice, how we were both making a fool of him.'

'Why the heset girl?' Amerotke asked. 'Why did you kill her? Was it because Ipumer had been boasting to her?'

'Yes he had. I met her in a willow grove down near the Nile. I had no choice but to kill her. I hit her with a club, bound her hands and feet and threw her into the Nile. I made it look as if she was the victim of a Hyksos sacrifice.'

'Did you know she was pregnant?' Amerotke asked. 'She was carrying someone's child?'

Only then did Nebamum's face show any concern or grief. 'I didn't know,' he muttered. 'It was Ipumer's fault. Neshratta and I agreed we had made a bad choice. She too was concerned about her sister. We had to act quickly. I told her to buy the poison. At first it had little effect: the cup was smeared but . . .'

'Eventually it worked,' Amerotke declared. 'And now Ipumer was gone. Peshedu was neatly trapped. He had lost his concubine but could not protest whilst his daughter had besmirched his name. Peshedu might act the outraged father but he would not have really objected if Ipumer had asked for his daughter's hand. That must have enraged you further? That he was prepared to give Neshratta to this upstart scribe just to be rid of her, whilst your love for Neshratta had been cruelly interfered with and hindered?'

'Peshedu was a callous man,' Nebamum explained. 'Ipumer had to die. I made two mistakes: bringing him from Avaris and not killing him earlier.'

'Didn't you consider,' Valu interrupted, 'asking for Neshratta's hand? Running away?'

'Tell these arrogant peacocks the truth!' Nebamum jibed. 'Ask them to replace Neshratta's child, cure her so she could bear others! We wanted revenge!'

'So you took matters into your own hands?' Amerotke asked.

'Oh yes. I knew the history of the regiment of Seth. I would kill them all in ways described in their history. Balet was the first. I entered the Red Chapel. Balet was immersed in his dreams of glory. I knew the routine of the chapel priest. He would make sure the Lord Balet needed nothing and retire to his chamber to drink wine and play with his pretty wife.'

'But why didn't General Balet hear you come?' Valu demanded. 'The chapel was left in disarray.'

'I knew something others didn't,' Nebamum smiled. 'General Balet was slightly deaf. I'd studied him closely: the way he turned his head slightly, the narrowing of his eyes as he listened to someone. I crept up behind him and struck him with the war club. He staggered, I caught his body. He was dead before I lowered him to the ground.'

'And mutilation?' Valu asked.

'He had mutilated my Neshratta. He had slain my child. I thought that his Ka would also find it difficult in its journey to the Far Horizon. I know a little about medicine. I took his eyes, cut his hands. I upset pieces of furniture to make it look as if there had been a struggle. Afterwards, I left as quickly and as quietly as I'd arrived.'

'Balet's death was a reflection of what happened to Meretseger?'

'Yes, my lord judge.'

'And the lack of noise would only deepen the mystery?'

Again Nebamum agreed.

'And,' Amerotke concluded, 'who would suspect Nebamum, with his wounded leg and shuffling gait? You are probably the sprightliest of them all. The attack, or the pretended attack, on you? That was arranged?'

Nebamum just smiled.

'I am sure,' Amerotke continued, 'if I went down to the quayside, amongst those who live in the twilight of Pharaoh's law, if bribed or interrogated, some might confess to seeing a Horus-masked visitor in its shabby drinking shops. When did you remove Meretseger's corpse?'

'Oh, some months earlier.' Nebamum wiped his lips on the back of his hand. 'It was easy enough. A journey out into the Red Lands with a chariot and a casket. The Oasis of Ashiwa is lonely; I returned by night. I found the cave, the rocky outcrop above the Necropolis. I placed it there. It was only a matter of time before someone, my lord, like you or Lord Valu, would rise to the bait. The Panthers of the South are superstitious. Sooner or later one of them would wonder if Meretseger had returned from the desert.'

'We could have all been killed out there,' Amerotke declared, 'the day the Sand Wanderers attacked us. You enticed them with gold and silver, information being passed about how a group of Theban nobles could be caught out in the Red Lands, just beyond the Oasis of Ashiwa. Rich pickings, eh? The Sand Wanderers would be bribed, the lure of more wealth dangled before their greedy eyes: precious possessions, heavy ransoms from Pharaoh?'

'You too could have been killed.' Valu interrupted. 'You were there.'

'He didn't care,' Amerotke answered, 'did you, Nebamum? Death, capture and humiliation were not as important as revenge. Or did you know that these killers – you described them as born-and-bred slayers – would fight them off? Did you just want to see them frightened? Whatever the outcome, you must have been pleased.'

Nebamum breathed in deeply. 'I wanted them to experience fear,' he whispered. 'As you say, my lord, I don't really care about them, about you or myself.'

'And General Ruah?'

'He was such a fool. I rose early and left the house. It was only a short distance. I swam across that lake and was waiting for him. I killed him with one blow and burnt his corpse. The rest of the servants reached the island, I'd deliberately dressed in Ruah's colours. They ran around like a gaggle of geese. I pretended to be one of them and left unchallenged. I hope Ruah staggers through the Underworld.'

'And General Peshedu?'

'I was growing concerned. You were hunting me and were not far behind. I hired two men from the Devourers.' Nebamum referred to a group of assassins in Thebes. 'I hired them so as to confuse you as to my whereabouts. Peshedu was a pig and stupid with it. I had to make sure he died, his body desecrated. After that,' Nebamum rocked backwards and forwards, 'Neshratta made a terrible mistake, pretending to be me in the Street of Oil Lamps. I would have loved to have struck at my master. I needed time. I hurried across to the Necropolis, desecrated Kamun's tomb and came back to settle with you.'

'What did you hope for?' Amerotke demanded.

'That I would kill them all. That's why I hired Ipumer. I wanted vengeance and justice but, at first, I wanted to escape unscathed. One day, I thought, Neshratta and I, perhaps we'd find some peace.'

'But you would have been suspected,' Valu declared.

'Me, Lord Valu? Poor, shambling Nebamum?'

'You would have arranged an attack,' Amerotke speculated 'when you would be wounded but would escape unscathed. Are you satisfied with what you have done?'

'I am pleased, my lord judge.'

'Why did you kill Lamna, Intef and Felima? And Ipumer's colleague Hepel?'

'You know that,' Nebamum mocked. 'I found the true measure of Ipumer. Hyksos prince!' he sneered. 'He was soft and vicious, only interested in the sweet thighs of a woman. I couldn't trust him. I wondered if his tongue had wagged. And Felima and Intef? Well, they deserved to die; Hepel and Lamna also, because of what they might have heard. I killed for justice, my lord judge, and to protect myself.'

'You are as great a slayer as any here.'

'Am I?' Nebamum gestured towards the imperial throne. 'Have you served in the war, Lord Amerotke? Go to the Red Chapel, study the paintings.'

'I have.'

'In Pharaoh's name the Seth regiment stormed cities and towns. They put entire tribes to the sword – men, women and children, even their animals. I have seen battlefields ankle-deep in blood, the corpses of children thrown down wells, women raped and crucified. Lord Karnac and the rest come swaggering back to receive medals and honours and to be praised before the Gods. What's the difference, my Lord Amerotke? They killed, I killed.'

'Are you frightened of death?' Senenmut demanded. 'Because you shall suffer a hideous sentence.'

'I am dead already, my Lord Vizier. My child has gone, Neshratta has gone. I wish to hurry after her.'

Amerotke studied the manservant. He had a certain icy calm, like a soldier pleased at a task well done.

'Why didn't you?' Karnac demanded. 'Why didn't you ask? Why did you—'

'Oh, shut up!' Nebamum shouted over his shoulder. 'The great Lord Karnac dispensing his favours . . . !'

'Then listen to me!' Hatusu's voice rang clear through the hall. 'Nebamum, servant of Karnac, by your own admission you have confessed to a litany of hideous crimes. Your acts are heinous, a stench in the nostrils of the Gods. You will be taken out to the Red Lands by a squadron of the Ibis regiment. You will be bound hand and foot and buried alive! Pharaoh has spoken!'

'Oh, has Pharaoh spoken?' Nebamum sneered.

Amerotke raised his hand for Asural to come forward and gag him.

'Leave him!' Hatusu ordered. 'Let him have his say!'

Amerotke glanced quickly over his shoulder at the Pharaoh-Queen. She was leaning forward, smiling slightly. You are a cunning vixen, Amerotke thought.

'What is it?' she asked.

'I am not the only guilty person here. Karnac and the rest killed my child. They are the source of my heinous crimes.'

'And they will answer for it!' Senenmut retorted quickly.

'Will they?' Nebamum pointed. 'Or will Karnac once again remind the She-Pharaoh and her stonemason, how powerful the Panthers of the South are? What great influence they exercise in the regiment and the army? Will this matter be swept away into the shadowy corners?'

The Director of Cabinet gasped at the insult.

'Divine One!' Karnac shouted. 'I protest!'

'The Divine One has heard enough!' Hatusu coolly replied and rose to her feet.

Valu and Amerotke hastily turned and prostrated themselves. Even Nebamum followed suit. Foreheads touched the ground as Hatusu, the Imperial Pharaoh-Queen, left the throne of judgment to return to her House of a Million Years.

Later that day, as the sun began to set, its dying rays

spilling over the horizon, to turn the rocky outcrops of the Red Lands into a myriad of dazzling colours, the execution party prepared for sentence to be carried out. The chariot squadron of the Ibis regiment formed a circle. The horses faced out over the desert, the beautiful bay mounts stamping their feet and snorting, tossing their black plumed heads as if they were aware of what was happening behind them.

The charioteers stood holding their horses' head collars, staring at the small group of men in the centre of the circle: Amerotke, General Karnac – and Nebamum, who stood, hands and feet bound, dressed only in a loincloth. The chief executioner was also present, dressed in black leather with two assistants, all wearing the Jackal mask of Anubis. It was a grisly, chilling scene.

Amerotke stood rigidly. He felt so tired, the backs of his legs ached, whilst he had bruised his thigh during the jolting ride. The hot wind had died. Amerotke avoided Nebamum's gaze and stared out over the desert. A vulture, its feathery wings spread full, glided on the breeze above them. Where men of war went, rich pickings would always be had. The chief executioner leant on the ceremonial axe and watched his two sweaty assistants dig deep, preparing the grave. Amerotke glanced at Karnac: he looked as if he had aged years in the few hours since Pharaoh had passed judgment.

'May I have some wine?' Nebamum's voice was firm and strong.

'It is not allowed.' The chief executioner growled from behind his mask.

Amerotke walked over to his chariot and brought back a wineskin.

'It's not allowed,' the executioner repeated. His two assistants stopped, only too willing to have a respite from their labours.

'I will answer to Pharaoh,' Amerotke declared. He held the wine to Nebamum's lips.

'Is there an opiate?' Nebamum whispered.

Amerotke shook his head. He felt sorry: the prisoner was guilty of heinous crimes but he was a man driven along the road to murder by the arrogance and selfishness of others. Nebamum smiled slightly. Amerotke poured the wine into his mouth. Nebamum spluttered and coughed. Amerotke gave him another swig. The chief executioner was now restless. As he moved, the black and gold bracelets he wore rattled and clinked. Nebamum sank to his knees and stared down into the pit. The executioners were already preparing the planks of wood to slide down the sides.

'He will be placed there!' the executioner rasped. 'The sand will be poured in and be covered by rocks!'

'For sweet Ma'at's sake!' Amerotke whispered, glaring at the man. 'Can't you have mercy?'

The executioner stood back, shaking his head at the way the ritual was being breached. Karnac was now staring at Amerotke, a pleading look in his eyes. Amerotke nodded his agreement: Nebamum's death would be hideous. It had been known for some men to survive hours, even days. Sometimes the wild animals, the savage hyaena packs, discovered where the victim lay and came to dig him out. Karnac went to kneel by Nebamum and, using his hands, forced him to look at him.

'I am sorry . . .'

Nebamum brought his head back and spat in Karnac's face. The general acted quickly. Even before Amerotke or the executioner intervened, he drew a dagger from beneath his robe, placed his hand behind Nebamum's neck and drove the point deep, a blow straight to the heart. Nebamum coughed and spluttered but didn't struggle. Karnac held his eyes as he drove the dagger deeper. The executioner tried to intervene but Amerotke told him to stay. Nebamum's mouth opened, already coughing on his blood. Amerotke was sure his eyes smiled. He tried to form the words 'Thank you'. Karnac let go of him. Nebamum fell forward on his face, his body jerked a little and lay still.

The horses, smelling the blood, whinnied and neighed, soothed only by the reassuring voices of their drivers. The commanding officer came hurrying up. The executioner had taken off his mask and thrown it on the sand, walking up and down, hands on his hips, disgusted by what had happened.

'Pharaoh's sentence was most clear,' the officer declared. 'You saw him, didn't you, my Lord Amerotke?'

'He spat in my face,' Karnac whispered. 'I struck before I thought.'

Amerotke agreed. 'He added insult to injury,' the judge replied. 'It was unreasonable provocation. My Lord Karnac asked for his forgiveness. I would have done the same.'

Amerotke glimpsed the gratitude in Karnac's eyes: whatever he might say, the general had planned such a blow from the start. Assassin or not, Nebamum had been his brother, his servant, his war companion. Amerotke would have done the same in similar circumstances.

Amerotke asserted himself. 'The deed is done!'

The executioner tipped Nebamum's body into the grave and hurriedly covered it with sand. Karnac helped them to place the rocks on top. By the time they had finished, night was falling. Amerotke said a swift prayer. They walked back to the chariots, leaving the grave of Nebamum, a pathetic mound of stones under the desert night sky.

In the House of a Million Years, near the Great Mooring Place on the Nile, Pharaoh Hatusu swam naked in the Pool of Purity. On the marble bench beside it, Senenmut sat cradling a goblet of white wine. He watched his 'Goddess', as he called her, turn and twist like some golden fish in the clear, blue-tinted water.

'You are pleased, my Queen?'

Hatusu smiled and swam towards him. He hastily put the wine down and helped her out of the pool, wrapping her golden-tinted body in a white gauze robe.

'You'll catch a chill one day,' he murmured.

'With you beside me, my lord?' Hatusu sat on the marble bench and picked up Senenmut's goblet and drank from it. 'You asked me if am pleased, my lord stonemason. I am very pleased. Pharaoh's justice has been done and seen to be done. The malefactors have been punished.'

'Did you feel pity for the Lady Neshratta?'

Hatusu drank greedily from the goblet. 'If I had been her, I would have done the same.'

'And General Karnac?'

'Out of evil comes some good,' Hatusu murmured. She gripped the goblet tightly. 'I wager a deben of gold, my burly stonemason, that when Amerotke returns from the Red Lands, he will tell me Nebamum was killed before he was ever buried alive.'

'How?'

'First, Amerotke has a heart softer than you think. Secondly, Lord Karnac knows he is finished. Whatever his crimes, he will not let Nebamum suffer more than he has to.'

'There is a third reason as well, isn't there?'

Hatusu laughed. 'I passed a secret message to Amerotke: before Nebamum was placed in the tomb, Karnac would be allowed to show him mercy.'

Hatusu gazed at the painting on the far wall, depicting her great victory against the Mitanni.

'I must reward my Lord Amerotke.'

'And Karnac?'

'Oh, I'll make him kiss my sandalled foot. I will make him proclaim to the army how I am a true warrior queen. I'll take his solemn oath that he and his companions will offer their unstinted support for whatever I say and whatever I do.'

'And?'

'I'll demand that they give to the Red Chapel the remaining Scorpion Cups. Later on, perhaps in the Season of the Inundation, Karnac will offer the tray and the cups as a fitting gift, a gesture of loyalty and support to the Divine One, their Pharaoh-Queen!'

AUTHOR'S NOTE

This novel reflects the political scene in 1478 BC after Hatusu swept to power. Her husband died in mysterious circumstances and she only emerged as ruler after a bitter power struggle. In this she was assisted by the wily Senenmut, who had come from nothing to share power with her. His tomb is still extant, now known as Number 353, and it even contains a sketch portrait of Hatusu's favourite minister. There is no doubt that Hatusu and Senenmut were lovers. Indeed, we have ancient graffiti which describes, in a very graphic way, their intimate personal relationship.

Hatusu was a strong ruler. She is often depicted in wall paintings as a warrior and we know from inscriptions that she led troops into battle.

Ancient Egyptian history produced a number of resolute and astute female rulers, Nefertiti and Cleopatra to name but two. Hatusu can be reckoned as the first. Her reign was long and glorious but, on her death, her successor, with the connivance of the priests, had both her name and cartouche obliterated from many of the religious monuments of Egypt.

The power and glory of the Ancient Egyptian army is faithfully recorded in this novel. Promotion not only depended on knowledge of strategy and administration but personal bravery, exemplified in hand-to-hand combat or some other daring deed. Egyptian officers loudly boasted of their exploits and were decorated by their Pharaoh with what is the equivalent of our medals: silver, gold brooches, carved in the shape of bees, panthers or other animals. The army had also to be placated. Later on in Egyptian history, the 'heretic' Pharaoh Akhenaton lost the favour of the army. The consequent coup which deposed him was led by the generals, who no longer trusted or had confidence in him.

Hatusu would have been more wary, making sure she both conrolled and flattered the powerful corps of Egyptian army officers.

In most matters I have tried to be faithful to this exciting, brilliant and intriguing civilisation. The fascination of Ancient Egypt is understandable: it is exotic and mysterious. This civilisation existed over three and a half thousand years ago, yet there are times, as you read their letters and poems, when you feel a deep kinship with them as they speak to you across the centuries.

Paul Doherty

Headline hopes you have enjoyed THE SLAYERS OF SETH, and invites you to sample THE HANGMAN'S HYMN, Paul Doherty's new novel in The Canterbury Tales of murder and mystery, out now in Headline hardback.

PROLOGUE

The pilgrims had found their road again. The rain had stopped, the mist had lifted. The morning sky was as blue as Our Lady's veil and the white wisps of cloud, mere fragments, grew smaller as the sun rose strong and hot, drying up the mud and baking the country trackways. On either side of the pilgrims stretched the sloping green fields of Kent: a veritable paradise, no wonder the pilgrims were in good fettle.

'By Satan's cock!' mine host growled. 'We'll have fair travelling today and a few good tales to boot!'

The prioress stroked the little lap dog nestling in her lap. She ignored mine host and, leaning down, whispered to her handsome, olive-skinned priest leading her gentle-eyed palfrey to walk a little faster. Mine host saw the movement and he hung back, his lip curling.

'Heaven's tits!' he breathed to the bright-eyed, cheery-faced Geoffrey Chaucer from the Customs House. 'But she's a fine one, isn't she sir, with her lovelocks peeping under her coif and that medal which proclaims love conquers all! Where's the poverty of Christ in her, eh? With her soft, woollen robes, cushioned saddle and embroidered harness . . . ?'

'In God's eyes we are all sinners,' Geoffrey quipped back.

'Aye, but He doesn't expect us to be arrogant or stupid with it,' mine host retorted. He spurred his horse on and stopped by the miller who, drunk already, was swaying in the saddle farting and belching, his great tangle of bagpipes thrust under his arm. 'Steady now,' mine host soothed, fearful of this giant of a man with fists like hams. 'It's just past noon and you're already sottish!'

'Pish off!' the miller retorted and, putting his lips to the mouthpiece, blew a long, wailing blast on his bagpipes; this startled the crows in a nearby copse and they rose, protesting raucously.

Mine host pulled a face and rode on, making his way past the different pilgrims. The little friar, hot and lecherous as a sparrow, winking lewdly at the wife of Bath, whose broad hips filled her embroidered saddle. The good wife's skirt rode high, allowing all to see the red-gartered hose beneath: her broad-brimmed hat was slightly askew, her face wet with perspiration. She gave a gap-toothed smile and winked as she caught mine host's eye. The tavern master travelled on, holding his reins loosely as he studied the different pilgrims. He was quietly amused at how they seemed to know each other yet, if the truth be known, he too knew a few, albeit secretly, a matter for pursed lips and whispers in the shadows!

There was the man of law, dark-eyed and close-faced. Didn't he know my lady prioress in a former life? Then the franklin, with his costly belt and purse, who always kept an eye on the summoner, that fat, lecherous, pus-filled scandal-monger: a gallows bird if ever there was one. And the pardoner, that strange-looking creature with his white, pasty face and dyed flaxen hair? Mine host was certain that his appearance was a disguise and the screeching voice a mere ploy to hide his true nature. And the quiet ones? Those who kept out of harm's way and always stayed in the background? The cook with that open ulcer on his shin which looked like one of his own blancmanges turned sour? Didn't he know the poor priest and parson who'd told them that ghostly tale the night before about the watchers and dark deeds in a lonely, haunted church in Kent? Indeed, there were even more sinister matters! Mine host tightened his lips as he approached the head of the column. The monk, a powerfully built man with a polished face and balding pate, fleshy lips and protruding eyes, always rode behind the knight, those dark empty eyes glaring hatefully ahead of him. Now and again the knight, Sir Godfrey, would turn and stare at the monk as if he knew his true nature. To the left and right of the knight rode his squire and his yeoman: they, too, resented the monk's presence and were ever-watchful.

Mine host took a piece of dried bacon from his pouch and bit at the salty meat. The knight had told them a fearful tale, about the strigoi, blood-drinkers in the King's own city of Oxford. How Sir Godfrey had taken a solemn oath to hunt them all down and kill them. Was the monk, with his full red lips, one of these blood-drinkers? A demon from hell? The monk abruptly turned in his saddle; he caught mine host's stare and sketched a blessing in his direction. The taverner glanced away. He shouldn't think thoughts like that. After all, the monk was a man of the Church but, there again, so many priests, friars and monks had fallen away from their true vocations.

Mine host urged his horse on. He always liked to ride in front, except when they confronted danger. He secretly saw himself as leader of the pilgrims though, if matters came to push, he would always concede to the wisdom and fighting abilities of Sir Godfrey.

'Ah, good taverner!'

Sir Godfrey grasped his reins in one hand and, with the other, wiped the perspiration from his sunburned face. He moved in the saddle in a creak of leather and clink of chain, the sounds of a fighting man.

'It's good, is it not, mine host, to be travelling the Pilgrims' Way to Canterbury, to pray before the blessed bones of St Thomas à Becket?'

'God be thanked, Sir Godfrey,' the taverner replied. 'But shall we have another story?'

'Aye, and a song,' the golden-haired squire piped up, his blue eyes and smooth face bright with excitement at the journey.

Sir Godfrey turned in his saddle. 'My lord monk has a good voice, deep and merry.'

The monk grimaced, his eyes fixed on Sir Godfrey.

'Come on, Sir monk, be a merry fellow!'

The monk shrugged. 'My name is Hubert, Sir Godfrey, and my throat is dry.'

Mine host passed across his wineskin. The monk took this in one easy movement and squirted a stream of red juice into his cavernous mouth. He handed the wineskin back, gently burped and launched into a sweet, triumphant song of praise about some young woman who had caught the eye of a painter in a mansion near the Ile du Pont in Paris. He sang in Norman French; many knew that language but the monk's voice was so lusty and carrying they let him sing alone, enjoying the sound on this pleasant spring day. After he had finished they all cheered and clapped. They then stopped for a while at a well to quench their thirst and eat the dried meats and fruits they had packed away.

They continued their journey late into the afternoon listening to a story told by the squire. The sun lost its warmth as it began to set, turning the blue sky a fiery red. Some of the pilgrims became impatient. They were saddle-sore, weary and hoped that, for tonight at least, they would shelter at some cheery tavern or well-stocked priory. The countryside was now cut by hedgerows which rose like prickly walls on either side. These cast long shadows and some of the pilgrims recalled the stories they had been told about assassins, blood-drinkers and ghosts.

They rounded a bend. Sir Godfrey had already stopped. The others clustered behind him or fanned out across the lane, trying hard to keep their horses away from the shallow ditches on either side. They had arrived at a crossroads where the trackway climbed before splitting and going a variety of ways. However, it wasn't that they were lost or confused. The pilgrims just stared in horror at the scene before them.

A huge, three-branched gallows stretched up against the night sky. Beneath this stood a cart, its great dray horses hobbled, a youth grasping their bridles. On the cart stood three felons, hands bound; a group of bailiffs were busy fastening the nooses around their necks. On a horse near the cart, wearing the royal arms and carrying a white wand of office, sat a tipstaff of the court of assizes. He was dressed in dark murrey with a feathered cap on his head. A young, pointed-faced man, he was issuing orders. The felons, dressed in a motley collection of rags, their faces almost hidden by straggly hair, moustaches and beards, were protesting and shouting but the bailiffs held them fast. Around the cart stood royal archers, long bows slung across their backs; each carried a drawn sword. The pilgrims had been so engrossed in their own affairs, while the crossroads had been so well hidden by the hedgerows and trees, that it took some time for them to recover from their shock at this unexpected sight. The execution party, however, continued as if unaware of the pilgrims thronging only a few yards away. Indeed, mine host thought they might be seeing the ghosts from some dreadful execution which had been carried out many years ago. However, the tipstaff turned, holding up the white wand.

'Proceed no further!' he cried. 'In the name of the King!'

Sir Godfrey, his hand held up in the sign of peace, pushed his horse forward.

'My name is Sir Godfrey Evesden, knight banneret. I, and these gentle pilgrims, are on our way to Canterbury to pray before Becket's blessed bones.'

On the cart all movement stilled; the bailiffs and their victims now stared at the pilgrims. The tipstaff had doffed his hat as a courtesy to the knight.

'Sir Godfrey, I know your name. Mine is Luke Tiverton: chief tipstaff to the lords of assize now moving across Kent, dispensing the King's justice.'

Sir Godfrey nodded. 'Then, sir, why hang these men in such a desolate spot?'

'They are brought here because they carried out their horrible robberies, rapes, murders and other violations of the King's peace along these lonely lanes. They were caught red-handed by the sheriff. The assize lords have ruled that they are to hang on the nearest gallows to the place of their crimes!'

'Have they been shriven?' The poor priest nudged his sorry-looking nag to the front of the pilgrims.

'Aye, Father, we have but, if you want to do it again!' one of the felons shouted.

'Both God's justice and the King's have been done,' the tipstaff replied. He gestured towards the setting sun. 'My lords of assize have ruled that they must hang before dark and so hang they will. Sir Godfrey, you know the law. If no witnesses are present that is good. But . . .'

'Now,' Sir Godfrey added wearily, 'because we have arrived, we are those witnesses.'

'Sir Godfrey, you know the law.' The tipstaff stood up in his stirrups and stared over the pilgrims' heads. His eyes caught the prioress and the bold, beaming face of the wife of Bath. 'However, I see you have ladies of quality among you. They and any others, including members of the body spiritual, may turn away.'

Some of the pilgrims did so. Mine host suddenly remembered there was something at the back of his cavalcade he wished to see. The prioress had already dismounted. She stood with her back to the gallows scene. Her priest had his hand across her shoulder though mine host caught the man of law hurrying to assist her.

'I couldn't give a bugger!' the wife of Bath shouted. 'I've seen men hang and I'll see them hang again.'

She pushed her grey palfrey to the front where the squire, at his father's insistence, had turned away. However, the summoner, the monk and others craned their necks to get a good view. The evening breeze carried the tipstaff's voice as he read out the verdict of the court and many of the pilgrims chilled as the list of 'horrible' crimes were proclaimed: murder, sodomy, rape, breaking into churches, blasphemy, sacrilege, desertion from the royal levies, poaching. The long litany seemed endless. The felons on the cart, however, just stood staring impassively. The tipstaff's voice became a gabble. He finished, thrust the parchment back into his pouch and made a slicing movement with his hand.

'Let the King's justice be done!'

The bailiffs jumped out of the cart. The horses were unhobbled. One of the archers struck their hindquarters with a leather strap. The horses moved, pulling the cart away, leaving the felons to dance, jerking on the ends of the ropes like landed fish. They turned and twirled, kicking and spluttering as the nooses tightened.

The Rose Demon

Paul Doherty

In Paradise, in the glades of Eden, Eve was tempted twice: first by Lucifer. Then by Rosifer, who offered her a rose plucked from Heaven.

Matthias Fitzosbert is the illegitimate son of the parish priest of the village of Sutton Courteny in Gloucestershire. His struggle with Rosifer, the fallen angel, the spirit he loves yet hates, strives to placate but ultimately flees from, is played out against the vivid panorama of medieval life: the fall of Constantinople; the last throes of the Wars of the Roses; the terror of witchcraft; the loneliness of the Scottish marches; the battle-fields of Spain; and finally the lush jungles of the Caribbean, where the Rose Demon and Matthias meet for a final, dramatic confrontation.

'A master storyteller' *Time Out*

0 7472 5441 9

headline

madabout**books**.com

. . . the
Hodder Headline
site
for readers
and book lovers

madabout**books**.com

Now you can buy any of these other bestselling books by **Paul Doherty** from your bookshop or *direct from his publisher*.

FREE P&P AND UK DELIVERY
(Overseas and Ireland £3.50 per book)

The Field of Blood	£6.99
The Treason of the Ghosts	£5.99
The Anubis Slayings	£5.99
The Relic Murders	£6.99
The Grail Murders	£6.99
The White Rose Murders	£6.99
The Gallows Murders	£6.99
A Brood of Vipers	£5.99
The Poisoned Chalice	£5.99
The Horus Killings	£5.99
The Demon Archer	£5.99
The Mask of Ra	£6.99
The Devil's Domain	£6.99

TO ORDER SIMPLY CALL THIS NUMBER

01235 400 414

or e-mail <u>orders@bookpoint.co.uk</u>

Prices and availability subject to change without notice.